HEREAFTER 1

THE HEREAFTER SERIES

EINA MAI

ISBN: 978-1-968484-07-1

Cover & interior art by: *Chaosringen*

Editor: *Lauren Humphries-Brooks*

First Edition: July 2025

Published by: Emaho Publishing LLC

www.einamai.com

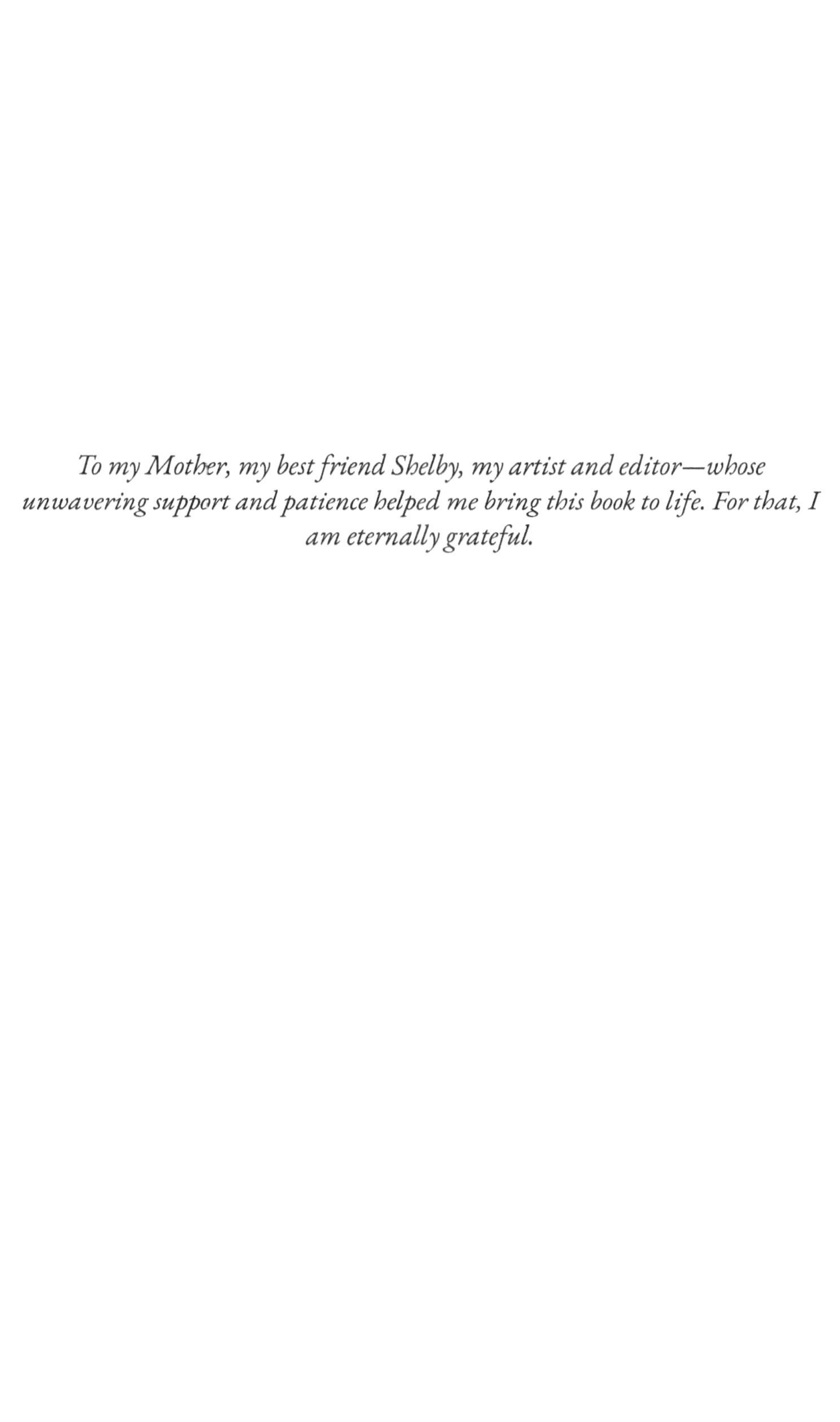

To my Mother, my best friend Shelby, my artist and editor—whose unwavering support and patience helped me bring this book to life. For that, I am eternally grateful.

CONTENTS

PROLOGUE

That day was the hottest day of July. The temperature reached an abysmal 105 degrees Fahrenheit, making it the second-hottest day recorded in New York since 1936. Even with the air conditioners constantly running, the heat still drove almost every citizen in the city to operate at a slower pace than usual. The exception was the ER workers of a small hospital in a hamlet seventy-four miles from the city. They were rushing a blood-soaked stretcher across the hallway.

"Make room, please! A serious case's coming through!" a middle-aged nurse cried at the dawdling staff.

"No ID. Caucasian male. Appears to be in his early twenties. Has three gunshot wounds in the upper chest. One has punctured the left lung. Prepare for surgery now!" said the doctor, running beside her. "Liz, apply pressure to his chest! Try to keep him awake!"

"Stay with us, honey. You can do it. Don't panic," Nurse Liz told the young patient in a soothing voice. Fear shone in her eyes. "Don't give up. You're so young and have a long life ahead of you. We'll contact your family. You'll be alright—"

The patient coughed out blood; his already pale face was now the grayish color of a corpse. His chest rose and fell raggedly. But soon, the pain became too unbearable as he gave up, eyes staring blankly at the hospital ceiling as life drifted away from him.

"Mama."

It was a hot and sunny afternoon; at 3:33 PM EDT, a young, nameless patient passed away in a small ER room.

There were no family or friends with him in his last moment.

He died with his eyes open. Blood seeped into the green irises, marring them. Like stained glass, his eyes were beautiful, cold, and dead.

The end was but a beginning.

CHAPTER 1

ALIVE AGAIN...SORT OF

A loud scream reverberates throughout a small, dirty alley. The sound comes from a figure lying half-face down in a puddle of mud. His body twitches and convulses as if it were being hit by lightning. The sudden noise and frantic movements make the rats gnawing on the figure's flesh scurry away.

"Ah...Ah...Ah," the figure gasps for air and turns away from the murky water. His face is badly bruised and covered with black mud. But all the dirt and grime only make those green eyes stand out further.

In fact, his eyes are probably the only source of lively color amid this smelly, filthy, and ashen place.

The figure lies motionless with arms and legs spread wide; his breathing is loud and heavy.

"I'm...alive," the figure pants. Sheer joy and gratitude are evident on his face.

But the happiness quickly fades.

Why the hell am I here? Did that hospital just throw me out into a puddle? What the fuc—

No need for further introduction: this is the patient who just died a couple of paragraphs ago. Somehow, he is no longer 'dead' and now finds himself in a shabby, dingy ditch in God-knows-where. Confusion, despair, and anger fill his chest as he gawks at his surroundings. That is when he notices the odd architecture of this place, which doesn't resemble any New York alley he knows.

"Where...?" His green eyes scan the place.

It takes several minutes for the patient to come to the dreadful conclusion that he's definitely not in New York. In fact, he doubts if he is still in America. It doesn't look like he's back in Russia or Kazakhstan, either.

He's not even sure if he's on Earth anymore.

"T-This is a nightmare." The patient screws his eyes shut, trembling lips mumbling over and over. "This is not real."

As he repeats those sentences like a mantra, the revolting smell of the alley begins to disagree with him. Reality slaps him when one of the hungry rats returns to finish its meal and suddenly dashes out of its hiding place. The rat jumps toward the patient with mean eyes and jagged teeth.

Before his brain can even process it, the patient's hand has already sprung forward as he smacks the crap out of that angry rat, sending it flying back to the hole it came from.

His brute action scares the rest of the rats. They make high, squeaking noises and no longer dare to attack him. The patient is so frightened by his own abnormally quick, precise reflex that he jumps to his feet and scampers out of the rundown alley.

"Help! Please help me!" the patient screams as he runs. The alley is long and filled with obstacles that cause him to trip and fall several times, but they can't slow him down.

After a while, he finally sees the exit and speeds up. The patient is so fast that he doesn't notice a pedestrian. Thus, they collide with each other, and both end up sprawling and groaning on the ground.

"I'm so sorry—" The patient is interrupted by a hard slap to his face.

"What do you think you're doing, you little mutt?!" screeches a voice as the assaulter gets up. This man then uses all his force to kick the patient harshly and mercilessly in the chest.

Everything happens so fast that the patient doesn't even have time to open his eyes. All he can do is curl up and cover his head with his arms to minimize the damage.

"That's enough, let's go," says a flat, male voice after the patient receives the twelfth kick. "You can gut it the next time you see it."

"He ruined my damn clothes!" the attacker growls as he delivers one last kick at the crouching patient. "Don't let me see your face again, you filthy beggar, or it will be your funeral!"

* * *

THE PATIENT GROANS as he slowly sits up. *Beggar, he said? Asshole,* the patient thinks, more furious about those men's insults than the threat of gutting. The gossiping from other curious bystanders brings the patient's attention back to reality as he finds himself lying in a pile of garbage.

"Fantastic!" he huffs, cursing in his head as he gets up and looks at himself for the first time. He's horrified to see the only thing he has on his body is a dirty, tattered, oversized tunic—with no underwear, let alone a pair of shoes.

Maybe those assholes weren't wrong when they called him a beggar. The sad excuse for an outfit he's wearing is even more torn than the five-year-old kitchen rag his nana refused to throw away.

The patient's mouth twitches as he absorbs the situation. He glances around and sees everyone dressed in Victorian-esque clothing.

Their outfits are dull, shabby, and a monochromatic gray shade, the same color as the buildings surrounding them. Talk about the pot calling the kettle black. Their clothes are only a bit...nicer than his.

The patient lets out a deep sigh and moves to the sidewalk, away from the attention. Keeping his head low, he begins to blend into the crowd. As he walks, he studies the area. But the more he sees, the grimmer his expression becomes.

The buildings here look like a deranged mashup of fictional medieval and steampunk architectural styles in grisly post-apocalyptic movies. The houses' structures are wonky and look like they can collapse any minute. The scenery might be appealing if not for the gagging, disgusting smell that permeates every corner of the town.

As much as the patient doesn't want to admit it, based on all the observations he has gathered so far, there are only three possible explanations for this monstrosity:

Number one: He died and has been revived as a beggar in this dystopian world.

Number two: He died and is in Hell.

Number three: He was injected with triple shots of pure crack.

Regardless, it seems that the easy, sensible solution would be to head to a cliff and do a free-fall...which he is probably not going to commit to at the moment. Even though his life is a bit effed up now, that approach is just a tad too extreme.

Plus, he doesn't want to be reincarnated as a toad.

A series of faint, strange noises interrupt the patient's thoughts and make him stop in his tracks. He looks around and feels the sounds come from underneath him. As his curiosity rises, the patient cautiously steps away from his spot and crouches to examine it. As soon as both his knees touch the ground, the surface crumbles. The patient can only yell a loud 'Fuc—' as he falls into the underground.

Surprisingly, he lands on a soft bed and suffers no significant physical damage other than feeling lightheaded and a few grazes from the falling debris.

Looks like I am not really God's redheaded stepson after all. The patient takes in a shuddering breath, beyond grateful that he has survived. However, the sense of relief shatters when the patient sits up and takes a good look at the place he just toppled on.

There are dozens of people in sheer, skimpy underwear or in their birthday suits, gawking at him: men, women, old, young, good-looking, homely, fat, thin. They all stand in a room with red lighting. There are all sorts of chains, ropes, whips, canes, gags of all kinds, and gazillions of kinky objects scattered all over the floors and walls.

The patient thinks he just crashed into a brothel.

The patient opens his mouth, but the door slams open before he can speak. A middle-aged, overweight woman in a bright, cheap-looking red gown enters the room with two burly men behind her.

Her eyes dart up to the large hole in the ceiling and then back to the patient. She shouts in a high-pitched voice that resembles the sound of a rusty metal door: "What the hell have you done to my establishment?!"

The woman's menacing demeanor and petrifying voice spook the patient. His mouth operates faster than his brain as he stammers, "I-I'll pay for all the damage!"

The woman gawks at him, then guffaws. "Pay me? You?" she sneers. "You wretch, even if you serve fifty clients every day for the next five years, that wouldn't be enough to fix my ceiling! Who the hell do you think you are? The Emperor? You better have an owner to pay for all of this goddamn damage, or I swear, I'll have them skin you alive, you filthy, wretched runt!"

The patient is stunned by the tirade from the brothel madam for a few seconds before he snaps back. "Lady, don't take it out on me, cuz I ain't gonna pay you jack. I'm just a passerby. That damn road collapsed on its own. If you have a problem, go sue the government. But I bet you can't. That's why you chose to run this shady bordello underground like some sneaky rat!"

It's not like he crashed a non-profit, secret school for underprivileged children. Sorry, not sorry, really.

The madam is now flushing red from neck to head. Her eyes narrow into two lines. She points a shaking finger at the patient. "Beat...beat this filthy runt to death for me! Now!"

The two burly men behind her stride forward and lash their thick, wooden canes at the patient.

The moment the patient sees the weapons in those men's hands, a fiery sensation flares up in his chest. The sudden, intense heat is so great that it feels like every fiber of his skin is being burned alive. Everything surrounding him begins to blur, and time seems to slow down.

Just like in that alleyway when he swatted that rat, before his brain can even think, his body has already slid off the bed.

The patient isn't sure what he's doing, but the next thing he knows, he's standing behind the two guards. His fingers curl tightly inward like an eagle's claw, gripping around both men's napes.

In a split second, the patient has a strong intuition that he could injure these two men very severely.

Stop. Stop now.

Those words flash through his mind, like a plea for his body to cease the attack before blood spills.

"Bran?! What the hell are you doing down there?!" a shrill, terror-struck voice rings out from above, stunning everybody in the room and successfully diverting the patient's attention.

A furious middle-aged woman leans against the edge of the pit. Surrounding her is a group of gossipy crowds.

"You lying, cheating, shameless, irresponsible, good-for-nothing old fart! Is this your business trip? Screwing those bony harlots while leaving your wife to tend your children?" the wife yells.

"I-I can explain if you would just calm—" the old man she's addressing down below rushes to put on his clothes.

"Damn you to hell! Damn all of you! I'll cut your prick off and burn this place to the ground!" The wife finishes her sentence by throwing a rock down at her cheating husband, but hits another male customer instead.

The underground brothel quickly becomes chaotic, with people fleeing, crying, and cursing. The patient only waits for this moment when everyone is distracted by the commotion, and he slips into the frantic crowd and runs away.

* * *

THE PATIENT LOSES count of how many stairs he has climbed, how many rooms he has barged into, and how many fences he has flown over...until he finally finds the exit to the outside. After he escapes, he continues running far from that brothel as fast as possible without looking back. Though he can still hear screaming and smashing sounds of people fighting. There is a riot behind him.

He only stops when he finds shelter in a small, empty alley. His legs immediately give out as he plops chest-first to the ground.

Heavy, shuddering breaths echo throughout the gloomy passage. Nobody can hear it, and even if they do, they wouldn't care, for he's just a filthy beggar, worthless scum.

After his breathing has stabilized, the patient balls up his fists and pushes himself up from the ground. He is covered with filth and new injuries from the earlier assault and tearing through the brothel, on top of the old wounds on his body. His tunic is so ripped it looks like he's been mauled by a large animal.

After sitting still for a little longer, the patient tilts his head to the sky and cries, "What have I done to deserve this? This is so unfair!" the patient whimpers, his body shaking with anger. "I was a good person! God, why did you do this to me?!"

This new world is dreadful. The town is poor, dirty, and stinky. The people here are nasty, cruel, and deranged. There seems to be no law here. It feels like there are creatures lurking in every corner and could jump out at any moment to feast on the living. The weather is thick and foggy. Everything here looks like it was dumped by a big bucket of sad gray paint.

"I'm better off dead," the patient growls, pointing at the sky. "Why bring me back just to torment me like this? God, can you be any crueler?!"

It sure feels good to let things out.

Half a minute later, dark clouds gather, and heavy rain pours down on the small alley. Just as if it were God's answer to his question.

The alleyway floods quickly, and floating trash leisurely swims past him. The patient looks at the sky. "Forgive me. I was just...joking."

At least it isn't a hail.

* * *

IF THERE'S anything to know about the patient, he considers himself an optimistic person, minus the occasional whine. When the downpour starts, he takes advantage of the weather and has a natural shower. As he looks at his body for the first time, he is relieved to find no bullet holes or deformities. As far as he can tell, his new body looks very similar to the old one, except that it's scrawny and covered in bruises. But he doesn't feel any pain, so it's probably a good sign.

The patient also finds a small branding mark on his left inner forearm. He can't tell what it is as it resembles a worm or a stretched number three.

After the patient feels satisfied that he is clean, he starts searching for a space with a roof to shelter from the stormy weather. After further exploring the alley, he finds a tight corner between two rundown huts with a small, conjoined roof sticking out from the top. The patient is as happy as if he had just found a gold mine. He immediately squeezes himself into the spot.

The corner can shelter him from the rain just fine when he sits with his legs pulled up to his chest, except the roof isn't wide enough to cover his feet, so he has no choice but to leave them out in the rain. For further barricade, the patient takes off his rag and hangs it like a curtain between the two huts, making a little curtain for himself.

As the patient is now sitting curled up and naked in his very un-cozy nook, looking out at the rain through the holes from his ripped tunic, he finally has the quiet time to think things over.

From afar, the setup would have scared the living daylights out of anyone. Quiet alley, pouring rain, dark and eerie corner, ripped, bloodstained curtain, and a pair of protruding pale feet. And that's precisely his intention. He wants to make his nook as creepy as possible. He doesn't want anyone or anything to disturb him right now.

If any more crazy shit happens, he will surely lose it.

With each passing moment, the rain becomes heavier. The chilly wind howls like a weeping widow. The patient is buried in thought. Soon, fatigue takes over him, and without realizing it, he drifts into a fitful sleep.

* * *

"Gigi, stop licking me," the patient groans, turning his head from the sloppy, wet tongue. "Five more minutes. I'm tired."

Three minutes later, the sloppy tongue licks him again. This time, it is on the side of his waist, running over the soft flesh and tickling the patient into broken giggles.

"Gigi, sit down." The patient becomes annoyed as he fumbles and pushes his dog away. "I swear you are—"

Since when has Gigi gotten so...big?

And why is she breathing so loud? She's a freaking Samoyed!

Sweat builds up all over his body. The patient takes a deep breath, summons all his courage, and opens his eyes.

CHAPTER 2

INTO THE WOODS

The creature's almond-shaped eyes are large and piercing blue. They're so abnormally bright that they glow in the dark. Thick, shaggy, dark gray fur covers its face and humanoid body. It has upright ears and a broad snout. Its long, mauve tongue greedily circles and licks the smooth skin of the patient's left side, treating the flesh like the most delicious, prized cut. Its eyes remain locked on its prey's—sharp and threatening, a warning not to try anything stupid.

It is already nighttime, for the late afternoon rain has long stopped. The roads are all dried up. The heavy clouds have given way for the full blood moon to shine and cast its ominous scarlet rays down to the gray, grungy town that has sunk to rest.

There is no streetlight, and none of the houses are lit; everyone has already gone to bed. Or perhaps they just don't want to see what's roaming the streets at night.

The patient is frozen with terror, unable to close his mouth or even to breathe aloud. All he can do is watch the giant, hairy creature give him the most enthusiastic licking that will make him never look at dogs the same way again.

He has never felt so violated, so appalled in his life. To make matters worse, he's fully naked, and this creature seems to be a male, making the situation even more frightening.

When the creature moves its furry, clawed hands onto the patient's pulled-up knees and tries to pry his legs open, his last nerve officially snaps.

There is a lone, rickety wall that is fifty feet away from the patient's nook. Several seconds later after the creature has made this bold move, that wall receives a hairy wrecking ball that puts a permanent retirement to its existence.

A hair-raising roar pierces through the still air and causes the ground to tremble. The creature rises from the rubble. Its chest moves up and down with every raging breath. Its eyes glower with murderous intent toward the human in the alley. Letting out another ear-splitting howl, the creature gets on all four and launches at its fleeing prey.

As for the patient, the moment he successfully sent the creature flying, he grabbed his ragged curtain tunic and dashed lickety-split out of the alley.

The good thing is that the patient used to play many high-endurance sports in his last life, so he knows how to utilize his energy well. He doesn't bother screaming for help. Instead, he focuses all of his strength on his legs and his breathing while his brain maps out an escape route and watches out for any obstacles on the road.

The patient turns to check if the monster is still after him and finds it still is, with no less ambition than before. The longer the chase gets, the more pissed the creature becomes. By the light of the hazy red moon, the patient can finally have a clear view of the beast: it's about seven feet tall, has long fangs, a hunched back, and wolf's features.

The patient can't help but roll his eyes as he runs. Of course, a werewolf would appear to make his already wretched life even more miserable. Blood moon, creepy town, foggy night, all the right conditions for the supernatural to show up and hunt down the unfortunate souls with nowhere to go.

The patient spots something scattering on the ground. When he gets close to it, what he sees makes his blood run cold.

In the center of the road lies the crown of a split head beside a mound of crudely torn body parts: arms, legs, and a dismembered torso. One eye in the head is intact, popped open, while the other dangles on the other half of the face. The patient can still see the look of terror on that face. Pieces of the white brain and coils of organs splatter on an oozing puddle of blood. As the patient runs, he finds the remaining body parts: a lower jaw, pieces of a gnawed tongue, a pulled-out, half-eaten spinal cord, and...bloody, dissected pieces of male genitals.

Thanks to the many horror flicks he's seen, the patient is able to stomach the gore by repeatedly telling himself to think of them as movie props...until he sees the raw, explicit display of 'stick' and 'stones' lying torn to pieces in a bloody pool, squashed and mutilated. Instantly, all the recklessness flushes out of his body like it has been swept by a tornado, leaving only a cell of a scared and helpless man.

Extreme fear has different effects on each individual. Some would trip and fall, while others would freeze. Some would wet themself, and some would pass out. In the patient's case, extreme fear only makes him run even faster. He has thought it through. He would rather run and drop dead from exhaustion than get caught and mauled.

After an absurdly long and anticlimactic chase that doesn't really get anywhere for either party, the werewolf is the first to give up.

The creature pants for breath and glares at the still-running human, angry veins forming on its face and arms. It stamps its foot on the ground, then looks up to the blood moon and gives a deafening, earth-shaking howl. This time, it finally gets the patient as he trips and falls under the pressure of the trembling ground.

The patient grunts as he feels a sharp pain drill into the tender part of his thigh. A small scrap of metal has cut his inner thigh, dangerously close to his manhood.

The patient bites back a scream as he pulls out the shard and dabs away the blood with his rag. He glances around, stunned to find the werewolf is no longer behind him.

"Crap!" The patient hastily gets up and scans his surroundings. He can't find the werewolf anywhere, but it knows exactly where he is, and that puts him at a serious disadvantage.

The patient puts on his rag, as he's been naked the whole time, then continues running while looking out for the creature. After passing a few roads, his ears pick up a faint flapping noise coming from above. He turns to the sky.

"What the…?" The patient is flabbergasted.

About one block away, the werewolf that has been hunting him is hovering in the air thirty feet from the ground. Behind it is a pair of large, blood-soaked bat wings waving in a steady rhythm.

It looks like those wings just sprang out of its body. That would explain the blood and flesh chunks on the membranes.

The patient turns back and runs like a deer on fire.

And the chase continues. After passing about ten blocks, a loud melody suddenly comes up from out of nowhere and startles him. With a heavy breath, the patient fearfully glances around.

Half a block away and up in the sky, the big, bad, flying werewolf is now playing a golden trumpet—intently, with great concentration.

"What the fu—" The sheer ridiculousness of the sight makes him turn back to check on the monster more often than before. Then, he decides to take a break since the werewolf is no longer chasing him.

The menacing werewolf's cheeks are puffy from blowing the horn. Its almond-shaped eyes are round. Its furry chest heaves at every musical note. The patient can see it's really trying to give a good performance; even its demeanor is that of a maestro. But the melody is godawful. Every note is like a punch to his ears.

The flying werewolf keeps its eyes fixed on the patient as it plays. After about half a minute, it stops and stares at the young human in confusion. Then, it goes back to playing the golden trumpet again. But the tune sounds rushed this time.

After regaining enough strength, the patient turns around and flees. The creature continues to blow the trumpet for a little longer before it rage-quits and lets out a roar, and then it goes back to chasing the patient again.

Give me a freaking break. Please.

The patient doesn't understand what's so appealing about him. Does he even have enough meat to sate the creature? His new body is literally a stick. But this werewolf is so persistent. And the chase has been going on for close to an hour. Damn it! Nearly one hour running on foot! He is frustrated and angry, and apparently, so is the musical werewolf, as it's been throwing howling fits.

Was it because I didn't clap at the performance? the patient wonders.

The houses are getting thinner, and the landscape is dotted with abundant trees. About ten minutes later, they finally reach the edge of the town.

The patient frowns at the view of the woods ahead of him. He doesn't want to run into a forest at night when the blood moon is high. God knows what evils are in there. But then he can't turn back either. Nobody would be gracious enough to open their door and let him in. And he can't keep running back and forth with this creature all night. The town's too open, and there's no place to hide.

God, why are you doing this to me? Do you really hate me so much that you have to make me die twice on the same day?

As he's torn by the two dead-end decisions, a thick, husky voice speaks up. *"Come back. Come back to me."*

It comes from the flying werewolf.

It speaks.

Holy shi—

"I will not hurt you. I only want to look at you. If you turn around, I'll hold you in my arms and cherish every inch of your flesh."

Well, the forest it is!

The patient speeds toward the woods. He can still hear the creature screaming for him to return.

* * *

THE WEREWOLF DOESN'T GO after him as he enters the woods. The patient thinks either there is a magical barrier or something in this forest that really scares it. The fact that he is here right now disturbs him to no end. But he has taken a leap in the dark, and now all he can do is stay on high alert all the time, hoping to survive till tomorrow.

Beneath the crimson moon, the dark woods look as though they're covered in a red veil. The patient keeps scurrying on the moonlit trail until he can no longer move. His knees give out, and his body falls to the golden leafy ground.

The night wind slips through the dry leaves, making rattling noises. The most prominent sounds are the dreary hoots of the owls and the patient's harsh breathing.

The patient is exhausted. He is gasping for air like a drowned fish yearning for water. He can taste the metallic tang in his dry throat. His entire body aches from the running. He lies there, unmoving, with his eyes closed. After a short while, when his breathing stabilizes, he attempts to hoist himself up, but an acute shooting pain immediately hits him in his crotch. It is so painful that it makes him moan out loud.

Every movement hurts. It feels like there are hundreds of needles pricking into his manhood. The patient carefully lifts his rag, and what he sees scares him to death. His genitals are swollen and badly bruised. The skin around the sack chafes and throbs with a deep red color. There are scratches on his penis caused by friction from running commando for too long.

"Oh...ah..." With a shallow breath, the patient slowly tears the hem of his tunic. The fabric comes off easily since it has been so old and ripped. The patient lies down on his back, lifts his tunic, spreads his legs, and with a deep breath, pushes his lower body up to slide the torn fabric underneath his back-side. He takes a moment to think of how to make a new jockstrap for himself. But his brain is too tired and muddled to be innovative, so he ends up wrapping the cloth randomly around his manhood.

The patient remains on the ground for a good while before he tries to stand up again. The pain has subsided and is not as unbearable as earlier. He pulls up his tunic to see his new underwear; it looks like a bad adult diaper made with toilet paper.

As long as the fabric can support his genitals, who cares about the design?

The patient stretches his arms and back, feeling the sore muscles twitch at every movement. He then looks at the surrounding area. He is in the middle of a lonely forest trail with both sides flanked by tall, bushy trees. There are no turns, so he has no choice but to move ahead.

After about half an hour of walking aimlessly on the dark trail, his stomach begins to rumble. The patient looks around, hoping to find fruit trees, but has no luck. He sighs, rubs his sunken belly, and then walks for another thirty minutes until he reaches a fork.

The patient looks at the two pathways in front of him. Both are equally pitch-black and creepy. He frowns and comes closer to the center of the two trails. There, he spots something hidden inside the clumps of bushes. With great caution, he moves the foliage with his hands and finds a wooden arrow road signpost.

The patient is over the moon with his discovery. He quickly drags the sign out of the shrubs and puts it back on the ground. But his short-lived happiness is gone when he finally sees what is on the sign under the illuminated moonlight. The right arrow has carvings of a stack of human skulls piled on top of each other; there are carvings of flowers in between each head. The left arrow has carvings of a sun followed by a wholly separated human skeleton set up in a symmetrical line: a left foot, left leg bone, the left thigh bone, half left of the pelvic bone, half left of the torso, left arm, left hand, then the human skull in the middle. The rest is the repeat order of the bones on the right, and the end of the line is the carving of a half-moon.

Very fudging helpful. Thanks a fudging lot, signs. The patient balls his fists and swallows the urge to kick down the signpost he just put up. After calming down, he inspects both arrows and decides to go with the right one because it looks less disturbing than the left and also has flowers in it. So how bad can it be? It can't be that awful compared to the left trail, right? Right?!

"Right!" The patient makes his decision. He takes in several deep breaths and does a little stretching. Then, confidently, he takes the first step onto the right trail. But suddenly, a cold chill creeps up his back and makes him shudder. He immediately turns around and finds nothing behind him.

The patient stalls for a moment; then, he continues on his way. But after a few steps, he feels something brush over his nape. He turns around again and can't hold back a scream.

There is a row of about a dozen people wearing bloody, off-white rags, sluggishly hovering in an even line. Each holds a dimly lit candle in their right hand and a blood-soaked pink flower in the other. They have no fingernails, as it looks like they were pulled out by force. In the center of the flower are a pair of gouged-out eyes that still look fresh, with the nerves attached to them. But that's not all. They are all walking without their heads!

And the fact that they are walking under the red moonlight makes this scenario ten times more horrifying.

The sight before him terrifies the patient more than the musical were-wolf, by miles. He stumbles to the ground but immediately drags himself back up and runs back to the fork. But he can't reach it, as the trail seems to get longer the further he runs. There's a rustling sound on his right. A headless ghost emerges from the tall bushes and blocks his path.

The patient's heart almost drops when he sees the ghost holding out its bloody, no-fingernails hands to him. Without slowing down, he launches a kick right at the ghost's crotch and knocks it over; flower and candle fly to each side of the trail.

After his success against the beheaded ghost, the pathway seems to return to normal. After about one or two minutes, the patient finally reaches the forest fork.

The patient breathes like a person with asthma. His ragged tunic is drenched with sweat. He looks at the signpost. The right path is obviously a no-no, leaving him with the left one. However, the patient doesn't want to go with the left trail because the sign for this trail looks absolutely unsettling. What's with the separated human skeletons all lined up sinisterly like that? That just looks sick and evil. It probably will be even worse than the right path.

And he can't just choose another path either, since the hedges surrounding the trails are too tall and dense to break through them by hand. The patient tries to poke at them and finds it's impossible to make another way for himself without a machete and a flashlight.

The patient sighs and turns to the single trail that led him here; an old crone already stands behind him. The unannounced appearance of this woman makes him shriek in a very unmanly voice as he staggers backward.

"Oh dear, I'm sorry if I scared you. Are you alright, young man?" The woman speaks in a sweet, grandma voice. Her neatly combed white hair peeks out from beneath an off-white scarf. She wears an old, ankle-length, black floral dress with a worn-out, ash-colored cardigan. She is skinny and haggard. There is a small wart on the tip of her long, hooked nose. She looks ancient, maybe around eighty or ninety years old. Despite the gentle tone, there is a look of malevolence in her cloudy brown eyes. She carries a straw basket covered with an off-white cloth on her right arm.

The patient takes one look at her, and he's already cussing in English and Russian in his head. Anyone with half a brain can see this old crone is a witch!

While the patient is considering how to escape, the witch speaks again. "You look awfully lost out here at this hour." She looks at him up and down and then smiles. "And you look like you are in need of a hot bath and a hot, hearty meal as well. Why don't you come with me? My house is not that far from here."

"No, thank you. Please excuse me." The patient puts on a straight face and walks past her. But her scabrous hand grabs his hand, and the crone pulls him back to face her.

"Now, now, child. You can't leave like that." The witch shakes her head, her voice still sweet. "Why don't you try one of my freshly baked scones before you go?" She lifts the white cloth off her straw basket. Inside it, there are many types of bread and colorful pastries. They all smell so tantalizingly good that they make his starving stomach growl even louder.

"No. I'm good. Thank you, but no thank you."

"You won't be able to make it back out looking like this. This forest is dangerous. There are many evils out there just waiting for a cute young man like you to wander in. Who knows what those creatures will do to you? It's not uncommon for youngsters to get lost in here and have their flesh stripped off from their bones, just like a deboned chicken. Heeh heeh heeh!" Her grip on his hand tightens.

"Let go of me!" The patient uses all his strength to pull his hand back.

"YOU WILL GO WITH ME!" the witch yells, and tries to grab his other hand.

The patient raises his fist, but his mind goes blank before he can push her away. His body feels as if it weighs nothing. He sees the witch laugh menacingly as she swings out her wrinkled hand and grabs his hair. Then everything sinks into darkness.

CHAPTER 3

THE MAN UNDER THE MOONLIGHT

The patient wakes up to a killing headache and aching pain all over. He blinks a few times, trying to open his eyes, but his eyelids are too heavy. He attempts to move his body but fails as well. This place reeks of rotten meat, dead animals, feces, and strong, pungent herbs mixed together. It makes him want to vomit. Suddenly, a shooting pain flares across his back and causes him to yell. But the noise comes out muffled.

"Mmm! Mmm!" The patient panics and struggles even harder and feels more pain pouring down his bare back.

"Stop moving, you little mutt!" shouts an old woman's voice, and another stroke lands on his skin.

The patient grits his teeth and forces his eyes open. He sees the old crone swing a whip at him. He isn't fast enough to dodge it and receives another lash on his back.

"Ah, you're awake," the witch sneers, then whips him again. "How dare you avoid my whip, runt?! When I beat you, you'll stay put and take it. Understand?"

The patient puffs in shock and anger as he glares at the witch. He is lying on a dark gray wooden floor, completely naked. His hands and feet are tightly bound from behind by a thick rope. His mouth is gagged with a cloth.

The witch sees the hateful look in his eyes and swings her whip again, each time harder than before. She cackles when he winces in pain but cannot do anything about it.

At around twenty strokes, the witch stops to breathe. The look of satisfaction gleams on her face as she looks down at the young man lying trembling by her feet. She hunches down to grab a fistful of the patient's brown hair and hoists him to sit. Her face leans in so close to his. He almost faints from the stink that comes from her wrinkled brown lips.

"Listen carefully, you little rascal! I've deboned many like you before. In fact, I just did that two hours ago. Why don't you see it yourself?" The witch yanks his head toward the kitchen. In the center is a large, black cauldron cooking on a stone hearth. That's where the revolting smell comes from.

On her wooden kitchen counter, there sits a pile of bloody human bones that still have some flesh stuck to them. Next to the bones is a sharp, blood-stained knife that seems to be the tool used to carve off the human flesh. Blood is still dripping from the counter to the floor.

If it weren't for the gag, the patient would throw up. He averts his eyes, but instead, he sees a pile of decapitated heads in the right corner of the kitchen. He can't help but shudder in front of the witch.

The old witch jeers at his blanched face. "You should thank your lucky stars that I got you after the Sacred Hour. Oh boy, only if I were to meet you just two hours ago, you would have made a beautiful, extra delicious main course for my ritual. Shame! Such a great shame!"

Still holding the patient's hair, she drags him across the main room, where an iron ring is mounted to the ceiling. The witch weaves a rope through the ring's opening and ties it around the patient's bare chest. The patient writhes against her grasp and receives a hard slap. But she doesn't stop there as she grabs her whip and flogs him again and again until his entire body is trembling uncontrollably, and he is no longer struggling.

"Stop yapping. You're starting to piss me off." The witch whips him one last time. "I've been tolerating a lot from you because you're a real pretty boy. But if you continue to be a dumb mutt, you're gonna join the group in the kitchen."

The witch continues to spew more threats, but the patient doesn't really listen to her. He's trying to calm himself down and think of ways to escape this evil crone. He discreetly scans his surroundings for weapons and exits. This place is just a small wooden hut with only one main door locked from the inside. The patient is then hung by a rope to the ceiling; his bound feet graze the floor. This position especially strains his body, and if he doesn't find a way to break off from the rope, he doubts he will have enough strength to defend himself against the witch.

What should I do? How to escape? Think. Think!

His head is spinning, trying to devise ways to get out of here alive and in one piece. But his view is limited, as he can't see behind his back.

"Tch, you're too thin. No meat at all!" the witch comments as she circles him. The patient shudders when she suddenly slaps his bare butt. "This will not do!"

Yes, I already know that, you psycho hag! Since I'm unsuitable to cook, can you let me go and find an alternative? An actual pig this time, maybe?

The witch goes to the kitchen and returns with a bowl of food in her hand. She removes his gag. The patient is dismayed when he sees the cloth gag is actually the underwear he DIYed earlier tonight. *Nasty old hag!*

"Eat," the witch scoops a spoonful of the mud-colored soup and brings it to his mouth. The patient shakes his head furiously.

"You little brat, I spent eighteen hours making this soup!"

Eighteen hours? Not only is this crazy hag evil and murderous, but she also can't cook for shit. That soup looks like a pile of vomit. Then, the patient spots a mounted skeleton deer head with sharp antlers on the wall, just ten feet behind the witch.

"Ma'am, I'm so hungry. Please give me some food. I haven't had anything in my stomach for days." The patient speaks in a defeated voice, looking extremely pitiful.

"Then eat the soup!" the witch snaps.

"Can I have the bread you offered me earlier?" he asks. "Please?"

"What bread?"

"Ma'am, the bread in the straw basket you showed me earlier."

"Huh?" the old witch looks confused; then she seems to remember what he's been talking about. A wicked smile forms on her face as she puts the soup bowl on the table and goes to the kitchen. She returns with the bread straw basket she carried in the forest. She brings the basket close to the patient's face and takes off the white cloth cover. "You want to eat *this?*"

The patient screams when he sees what's in the basket. There's no bread or pastries but a punch of human eyes, tongues, and severed fingers drenched in blood.

"Hey, no puking on my floor." The witch grabs his pale cheeks. "Oh dear, you look scared to death. Alright, I won't tease you anymore. It's not like I'm gonna cut you open today. We missed the grand occasion. Next time, I guess, so there's no need to be terrified."

Oh wow, very effing reassuring. Thanks!

"Open your mouth." The witch holds up a spoon of soup to him. "Ahh—"

"What's in it? Please don't force me to eat humans."

The witch snorts and gives him stink eyes, "Don't flatter yourself! You're not eating my meat supply. There are only vegetables in it."

Who the hell stews vegetables for eighteen hours?!

But then...he really doesn't have a choice now, does he? If he refuses the food, who knows what this crazy hag is gonna do to him? So, the patient takes in a big breath and swallows the soup.

It tastes like crap.

After eating a couple of spoonfuls, the patient tells the witch he's full and...thanks her for the meal. He tries to be on her non-psycho side, but when she hears him say thank you, she gives him a slap.

"Ouch!" Crap! Was it because he didn't look sincere enough when he said thank you? He thinks his voice sounded pretty genuine.

"You cheeky brat!" The witch raises her hand again.

"Please don't hit me. I'm sorry. It hurts. A lot."

Probably because of his "pretty" face, cited by the witch (not by him since he hasn't even had the chance to see what he looks like in this new life), she doesn't deliver the second slap.

"Thank you, ma'am," he says.

The old witch crosses her arms and looks at him up and down. Then she asks, "How old are you?"

"I'm twenty-two, ma'a— Ouch!"

The witch slaps him again. "Who do you think you're lying to, runt?"

Holy crap! She knows! He's actually twenty-three. Well, he was twenty-three in his past life.

"You can't be older than seventeen."

"Wait, what?!"

"Shut up and answer my goddamn question!"

"I'm seventeen," he says unthinkingly. He can't believe he is this young in this new life. It sure feels good to be reborn young again.

"Too old!" The witch looks disappointed. She walks behind him and presses his butt cheeks apart.

"What are you doing?!" the patient yelps, and he receives a brutal smack across his bare butt.

"Stand still, or I'm going to stick a knife up your ass," the witch snaps. She takes her time to spread, touch, and examine him.

The patient screams when the witch mercilessly pricks a sharp needle onto the tip of his manhood, which earns him three hard slaps. She collects his blood and drops it in a glass test tube with green liquid inside. The substance turns transparent when it touches the patient's blood.

"Alrighty, you're still a virgin. That's very good! If you already got your ass screwed, you would be in the pot now. So, feel lucky you ain't a tramp. Heeheehee!" the witch cackles, patting his cheek.

"What are you going to do to me?"

"Initially, I wanted to make a stew of you. And to be honest, I still want to cook you. Right now. But given your pretty face is just too expensive to be on a plate, I will sell you."

No. Hell no!

"Tomorrow," the witch adds and then squeezes his mouth open. "Ah, wonderful! Teeth are all straight!"

"Ma'am, can you please untie me? These ropes really hurt me."

The witch snorts and shoots a look of ridicule at him.

"I can't feel my arms or my legs. How can I walk or stand tomorrow?" he pleads. "This position is really painful. Can you at least untie my feet so I can stand up straight?"

The witch appears to consider his words. It makes sense to have him look not too worn out at the market tomorrow. Suppose she keeps him tied up all night in his current position. In that case, he won't be able to stand up straight in the morning, and she might lose a considerable amount of money for selling less presentable goods.

"Do you know how animals are prepared before cooking?" The witch crosses her arms and taps her foot on the wooden floor. "They get their throat slit open and have their blood drained off."

The patient's face turns white. The witch continues. "It's a crucial step for butchering any animal. If it's a male, you have to castrate it first. Then you slit its throat and drain its blood. After that, you start to chop off its feet, hands, arms, and legs. Take out the eyes, tongue, nose, and ears. Then you gut it. You have to ensure it is still alive while you do all that, though. Fear makes the meat more tender and delicious."

The patient hisses when the witch grabs his hair and pulls him close to her face. "Just so you know, the spot you're standing on is where I usually prepare my 'animals' before I turn them into a stew. So, if you try anything stupid, you know what's going to happen to you, right?"

"Y-Yes...ma'am." The patient nods fearfully.

"That's a good boy." The witch lets go of his hair and lowers the rope so that the patient doesn't have to stand on tiptoe anymore. "Pretty and docile. That's how you survive in this world," she sneers, patting his cheek hard.

"Thank you...ma'am."

"Now, where did I put those damn shackles?" The old witch mumbles and wheels around. But the moment she turns her back to him, the patient has already swung his body backward as far as the ceiling rope allows him to gather the maximum momentum. Then he charges at the witch at full speed and lands a powerful kick on her back, causing her to slide over to the wall where the deer's head is mounted.

The dear's head decoration is not hanging high. The old witch slams right into the sharp, skeletal antlers. They go through her chest and kill her on the spot.

* * *

AFTER SLAYING THE EVIL WITCH, the patient has to do involuntary exercise. He draws both his feet off the ground and keeps on swinging his body in the air back and forth, hard, like a ball on a string. About thirty minutes later, his efforts finally pay off as the old wooden ceiling where the ring hook is attached gives in and collapses.

After the patient gets down, he hops into the kitchen and burns the rope off his wrists. When he's free of all the restraints, he peeks at the cauldron on the hearth and sees many human body parts boiling inside it. The gruesome sight sends cold chills down his spine and makes him nauseous. He would be in this pot if he failed to kill the witch. Upon searching the kitchen, he discovers his ragged tunic inside a wooden trash barrel. He wearily picks up the rag and checks if there's any human part on it and is relieved to find only regular trash.

The patient quickly puts on his tunic and explores the hut. He discovers it's situated on a large branch of an oak tree. He can climb down to the ground if he's careful enough. While in the room, the patient avoids looking at the witch's corpse as he passes it. Even though the old witch was evil and slaughtered many people, the patient still feels extremely guilty and uncomfortable about the fact that he killed her. This is the first time he ended someone's life, and while the action was somewhat justifiable for his own survival. He isn't proud of it. Killing is bad.

As the patient is about to open the door to leave; a sharp, burning pain similar to the one he experienced at the brothel in the afternoon suddenly flares up in his chest. The patient can clearly sense a powerful surge of murderous energy from behind him. In less than a second, his body already moves several feet away from the door. Just a second later, a butcher knife lashes down at the same spot he just stood, but it misses him and sticks into the wooden door instead.

The old witch turns her head to look at him. Her hair is no longer white, but fully black now. Her face looks demonic and more terrifying than before. "I WILL SHRED YOU INTO PIECES!" she screams and pulls the knife out of the door, then launches at him again.

If this had happened an hour ago, the patient would have pooped in his pants at how petrifying the witch looked. But he isn't afraid anymore.

Because he has just confirmed that he indeed has a superpower. He dodges the witch's attacks while trying to look for a weapon to retaliate. He's sure that he can trounce her again; she still has the antlers pierced through her chest while she tries to kill him.

She is already at a disadvantage.

But he is too confident and doesn't see a small stool behind him. Thus, he trips and knocks himself to the ground.

The witch takes advantage of his fall and swings the butcher knife down at him. Even though the patient sees stars from the fall, he still manages to dodge the blade. He kicks the witch at her waist, knocking her to the floor.

Somehow, his superpower doesn't seem to work anymore, and the patient has to use his own fighting ability—of which he has none.

He quickly gets up to his feet and kicks the knife from her hand. He tries to reach for the blade, but she grabs his foot and causes him to trip. Then she jumps on top of him and starts to strangle him. But he pulls her hair, and she has to let go of him. And thus, a heated fistfight begins.

During the fight, the patient is the one with the upper hand because he's young, and she's old and severely injured. As the battle proceeds close to the main door, the patient spots a wooden broom in the corner. Without thinking, he grabs the broom and beats the evil witch with it.

After several strokes, he realizes he's been swatting her with the brush instead of the handle. *Silly me,* he thinks and turns the broom to hit the witch with the correct side.

"Oh, no. Please stop! I can't take this anymore!" the old witch pleads.

The patient doesn't stop. He hits her even harder. *Did you ever stop when you butchered those people whose heads are in your kitchen?*

"I'm an old woman. I can't take this abuse. I'll give you gold if you stop!"

He rolls his eyes. He raided her house while she was presumably dead, and she doesn't have squat.

"Dear Devils, can't you just think about the nice things I did for you? I've never treated anyone as well as I did you. I even fed you soup—"

The witch can't finish her sentence because he swats her extra hard with the broom.

After beating the witch for a while, the broom suddenly vibrates and sparks out tiny stars. The patient stops to examine it, but the broom begins to jump up and down on its own. A few seconds later, it flies out of the witch's house, bringing the patient along.

* * *

IT IS STILL NIGHT OUTSIDE, and the moon has finally put back on its silvery gown. As the red veil is lifted, the forest appears less ominous than before. The animal kingdom is enjoying its peaceful rest when an earsplitting scream tears through the cold air and wakes every forest inhabitant from their sleep.

"Slow down, you dumbass broom!" yells a young male voice.

"Aah-oooooooh," howl many wolves, responding to the sound.

"Hoooo hoooo hoooo," say the owls.

"Uh...Crap." The patient covers his mouth. He feels like he's about to throw up.

He's been riding on the broomstick for nearly half an hour, and it isn't a pleasant flight. The magical broom has been flying in the pattern of a washing machine cycle and irregular zigzags.

His tormented flight eventually comes to an end when the stupid broom launches straight into the mighty trunk of an old Sierra redwood. The broom is instantly destroyed, and its rider free-falls. Luckily, the distance isn't too high from the ground, and the patient is quick-witted and grabs any branches he can during his fall. He lands on a grassy field and miraculously survives.

The patient lies in the verdant meadow. He's so beat up that he never wants to open his eyes again. Call him a loser for all he cares, but right now, he just wants to die and get everything over with. He wants to quit this hellhole world. He's so tired of running. His body is so exhausted and in pain that it feels like someone is slowly clipping his skin with a pair of scissors.

"Mama," he mumbles before slipping into unconsciousness.

* * *

ABOUT THIRTY MINUTES LATER, the shrill howling of wolves wakes the patient. After half an hour of undisturbed rest, his mood finally improves. His ears also stop buzzing as he can hear the gentle burbles of a stream somewhere extremely near to him. With joy, he sits up and sees a glistering stream only twenty feet away. But when he tries to stand up, he realizes both of his ankles are dislocated due to the fall. He won't be able to walk.

The patient cusses and flops back to the ground. After several sessions of sulking, he finally crawls with his arms toward the stream. It is a difficult journey. By the time he reaches his destination, his forearms and hands are bruised and his ragged tunic is covered with dirt.

He examines the stream and takes a couple of sniffs to make sure nothing is unusual. Then, he greedily drinks the water like a dying man lost in the desert. He lets out a soft moan when the cold liquid flows down to his painfully parched throat.

He is splashing the water on his face when the burning pain shoots into his chest again. This time, it hurts so much that he has to clutch his chest tightly and pant for air. His ears ring, and sweat beads upon his skin. As the patient thinks he might experience a heart attack, something strange catches his attention. He doesn't fathom what it is at first, but after carefully looking at the water, he realizes there is a reflection of someone in the stream.

The patient gasps and jolts backward. On the other side of the stream stands a tall figure of a man, hidden in the black shadow. The man doesn't move or speak. He just stands still and stares at the patient.

The patient knows he is truly done this time. He can't run or fight because he has no weapon to defend himself. And even if they get into a fight, he doubts he can win against this well-built dude—supposed this guy was a human, which is unlikely since what kind of daredevil human goes into the woods at this hour?

No sane human would, except for man-hunters and their unfortunate prey.

The mysterious man steps forward, and the loud ringing in the patient's ears intensifies. The burning pain in his chest is also radiating throughout his body. The patient can't see the face of the man approaching him as he is overtaken by darkness.

CHAPTER 4

RAVENLOCKS AND THE FAIRYTALE COTTAGE

The patient wakes up to the lively chirping sound of birds and the sweet scent of flowers. Upon opening his eyes, he finds himself lying in a clean, white bed in an unfamiliar bedroom. The room is of decent size, with a mahogany wooden floor, white walls, and nice furniture. There is a large vase of red roses on the nightstand beside his bed. Each blossom is vibrant and so perfect that he can't help but lean in closer to sniff. Just as he has imagined, the fragrance is sweeter and much more intense than the regular roses from his old Earth.

Wait, this is not the time for this. The thought dashes through the patient's mind, and his face becomes tense again. He stays put for a couple of seconds to sort his thoughts out. Next, he lifts the blanket and is relieved to see his legs are still attached to his body. He doesn't feel pain anywhere, so that's a good thing. Then he realizes he is wearing white, oversized pajamas instead of his tattered rag. A few disturbing notions pass through his head, but he shrugs them off. So what if someone changed his clothes for him when he was unconscious? Big deal! He's not a girl, so what does he have to lose?

He feels good, alive and kicking, and totally not afraid of—The bedroom doorknob turns, and the patient freezes in the spot. His face blanches in anticipation of the person behind the door.

At last, the door opens, revealing a tall, drop-dead gorgeous young man with fair skin and black hair like a prince from a fairytale. He wears a white button-up shirt and a pair of neatly pressed khaki trousers.

The patient can tell the young man didn't expect to see him awake by the initial dispirited look on his face. However, when their eyes meet, the patient can see the rapid transition from bleak to elation on the young man's expression as he sprints toward his bedside. The patient's heart leaps as he almost punches the guy in the face out of fear and self-defense, but the young man drops to his knees next to the bed and cries out, "You're awake!"

Before the patient can say anything, the young man grabs both of his hands and plants a kiss on them. Then he rests his forehead on those hands and starts to ramble. "You were sleeping for so long without moving. I was so scared that you would never wake up again. Thank all the Holy Tathagatas, that was not the case, and you finally opened your eyes. You can't imagine how terrified I was when I saw you lying motionless in bed. I'm so, SO grateful. I could gladly give away half of my life or my core to express my utmost gratitude for all the Holy Tathagatas that have finally heeded my prayers and returned you to me again!"

"I—" The patient opens his mouth, but the young man's incessant monologue cuts him off. He repeats how ecstatic he is that the patient is awake, specifically thanking every deity out there, from major Gods to minor

Gods to the holy spirits of every substance that ever existed in this world. Then he tells the patient the confusing story of his woeful life from a random middle part with zero backstory.

The patient's head throbs. He is close to passing out the second time from trying to follow and understand this extremely unintelligible rambling. The young man suddenly asks, "How are you feeling now?!"

"I'm...fine...Thanks to...you?"

"I-I'm too overwhelmed to speak!" the young man cries and the patient's eyebrows rise. But before the patient can say anything, the young man speaks again, "There are no words that can possibly describe how happy and grateful I am right now! Whenever I gaze upon your wondrous face, my heart flutters with indescribable feelings. How is that possible?!"

The patient blinks, then unconsciously touches his chest and finds it still flat as a board. For a moment, he thought he had died again and reincarnated as a beautiful woman. Thank God, it isn't the case.

"Look, I—" the patient begins, but he is interrupted again. This time, the young man starts to singing praises to him.

The patient is so very confused. While he's grateful he isn't in a dirty dungeon or inside a beast's belly, he doesn't expect a scenario like this. Yesterday, he was in an unrated horror movie, and today, he is in a sappy soap opera...? What kind of Twilight Zone episode is this? Is he still in the same universe from the previous day? Or is he in heaven right now? Or is all of this some sort of grand evil scheme? Something like a nice country house with white walls in a magical forest, but the basement underneath is filled with bloody corpses and gruesome torture devices?

The patient regards the high-strung young man before him with great suspicion. However, the more he hears the young man blather about harmless things, the more his guard lowers, as this dude seems...genuine and doesn't look like he is organizing a malicious scheme...

A couple of minutes pass, the young man finally finishes his incredibly lengthy word salad monologue, and the patient realizes it's his turn to talk, but he can't string any words together!

"Uh...um...I..." the patient splutters.

The young man still beams at him, his grin so wide and bright, like a happy sunflower of summer.

"Who are you, man?"

It was a simple question. But the moment it slips out of his mouth, the patient regrets asking it. The young man's face changes from a happy spring to a dreaded winter. He now has a similar expression to a devoted wife hearing her husband declare he wants a divorce: pure shock, betrayal, and heartbreak.

"Hello?" The patient waves at the stunned man.

The young man snaps out of his shock. "W-What do you mean? Y-You don't remember me? You don't recognize me? Not even a little?"

The patient shakes his head. He can spiritually hear a cracking sound from the poor guy's psyche. The young man no longer kneels straight but sits slumped on the floor. His face is so pale and breathless that he looks like he's about to pass out.

"D-Do you want to lie down? I-I'll give you the bed," the patient stammers, genuinely concerned. He doesn't notice there is another bed opposite his, partly because of the enormous rose vase blocking his view.

"Master! H-How could you not remember me?! I-I'm your Cyril! Please remember me!" (*Pronounced **Sigh-ral**, not See-reel or—ugh—cereal.*)

The patient looks at Cyril with pity. Whatever annoyance he has had earlier for Cyril's babbling vanishes. The poor guy is so desperate, but the patient really doesn't know him. He feels tempted to tell Cyril the truth that he isn't from this world, but he isn't ready for Cyril's reaction or to be kicked out yet. At least not before he gets to eat something first.

"It's a nice name you have. It suits you so well!" The patient tries to lighten up Cyril's spirit, though he truly means it. Now that he has the chance to regard Cyril up close, he finally understands what the term out-of-this-world perfect mean. What an ethereally gorgeous man Cyril is! Heck! Even though the patient is a straight guy, he starts tingling upon gazing at this angelic face. Cyril's thick, lustrous raven hair is akin to silk, his skin as fair as a pearl, and his big, tender eyes bluer than the morning ocean. Even when he dresses in a simple shirt, it can't hide the defined outline of his sculpted muscles. If angels grace the Earth, this must be how they would look.

"Master, you gave me that name. I was picked on and ridiculed for being a nameless orphan. Then you chose the noblest name for me despite many objections and told me Cyril was a befitting name for me and not the other way around."

This dude really won't let him get a meal before kicking him out.

The patient takes a long, hard, and deep breath and then speaks to Cyril in a soft but serious voice. "Cyril, I am not your master. I'm nobody's master. I might look like someone you knew, but I'm not him. And I don't want to take advantage of you or trick you by pretending to be someone I am not."

The patient expects a sobbing fit, but Cyril takes his words better than he has thought, albeit his face still looks like he is going to faint any minute.

The patient pauses to make sure he can catch Cyril if he drops. When Cyril doesn't drop, the patient continues. "You were the man in the forest last night, right? Thank you for getting me out of that place. You can't imagine what happened to me in the forest. You really saved my life. I'm so sorry for disappointing you. If there's anything I can do for you, anything at all, please let me know, and I'll do it!"

The patient means it. To repay Cyril's kindness, he can go as far as to fire walk for him—if Cyril ever requests him to.

Cyril says nothing but stares at him like a beaten, lost puppy, devastated and speechless. He makes the patient feel like the biggest piece of crap.

The patient turns away, as he can't bear to look at Cyril's forlorn face. He wonders what's inside Cyril's head right now. It is properly overwhelmed with grief and disappointment.

"Well, thank you again. I'm sorry...for everything." The patient prays so hard for God not to smite him for unintentionally crushing his savior's noble heart of glass. "I'll take my leave now."

"Where are you going?" Cyril grabs the patient's hand when he sees him try to get off the bed.

"I-I don't know," the patient answers honestly.

"Then why do you want to leave?" Cyril's blue eyes slightly narrow in confusion.

"Because I'm not the person you're looking for, so I can't stay here," the patient replies, a little impatient. It is obvious to him, so he doesn't understand why Cyril doesn't get it.

Cyril's eyebrow rises as he listens. Then he releases his grip from the patient's hand and straightens his posture. "I apologize for being so rude and imposing on you. You're right. It's incredibly selfish and inconsiderate of me to keep asking you to remember me despite everything that happened. I beg you'll pardon my impetuousness."

"It's alright. You don't have to apologize," the patient says. He has a hunch Cyril still doesn't get it. And his feeling is confirmed to be true when Cyril gives him a charming smile.

"You've always been so understanding to me, master."

"Oh my God, I am NOT your master! Why don't you get it? Please stop calling me master. I hate that word. It's disturbing and demeaning as hell. Every human being is born equal!"

"Please don't get mad, maste—eh. It's kind of disrespectful for me to address you by your name. You really don't mind if I'm on a first-name basis with you?"

"You don't even know my name," the patient says, frustrated.

"Of course I know your name." Cyril is adamant.

"What's my name, then?"

"Your name is Ilya," Cyril responds firmly with no hesitation.

Well...the quickest way to shut Rumpelstiltskin up is to say his name right. The room instantly falls into silence as the table has turned.

"M-Master?" Cyril waves at the flabbergasted patient.

"Yes? What?"

"Are you alright?" Cyril looks worried. "Master...Ilya?"

"...Call me Eli," the patient Eli requests. There's a pause before he continues. "H-How do you know my name?" (*Pronounced* **Eh-lee**, *not Ee-lie.*)

How the hell does Cyril know his real name? Even his friends from his past life didn't know about his Russian birth name, Ilya. They only knew him by his American name "Elijah," or "Eli," if they were his close friends.

"I told you I know you." Cyril smiles, though it's no longer cheery but laced with sadness. "You may not remember me, but I can never forget you."

"Ever," Cyril emphasizes. It's only now that Eli notices red rings under both Cyril's eyes, like he has been crying.

* * *

ELI SITS DAZED IN BED. On the outside, he appears calm and serene, like a proud tuberose standing tall in the summer breeze. But inside his head, there is a thunderstorm of bewildered thoughts and numerous question marks flying in every direction. Their conversation came to a stop when his stomach embarrassingly rumbled like an alarm clock. The good-hearted lad then profusely apologized to him and left to get him food.

What a nice guy, Eli thinks.

The bedroom door swings open, and Cyril comes in with a wooden bed tray loaded with food. Eli thinks the kitchen is probably next door to the bedroom or something because Cyril left for about ten seconds max. The cheerful young man approaches Eli and puts the tray on his bed. There is a bowl of stew, a loaf of bread, a plate of colorful chopped salad, fried eggs in brown sauce, a plate of pink pastries, fruits, and tea.

"Wow." Eli stares at the mini buffet before him and then at Cyril, who urges him to eat.

Eli takes the first bite and exclaims. "This is SO good!"

"Really? Please eat more, mas—Eli!" Cyril pulls a chair to sit next to Eli's bed. "I still have a lot of food down in the kitchen."

"Did you make all of this?" Eli asks him. Cyril smiles at him. Eli is extremely impressed and thinks a perfect human does exist after all.

After Eli is stuffed, he wants to clean up after himself, but Cyril beseeches him to stay in bed and insists on taking care of the dishes. Eli tells the good lad he can't just sit around and do nothing. Cyril looks at him with wide-eyed. "What are you saying, Eli? Don't you know both of your legs are broken?"

What the fudge? "They are?" Eli blinks.

Cyril puts the tray on a table next to a bay window and pulls off the blanket. Eli rolls up the hems of his pajama pants and sees long strips of white bandage densely wrapped from his ankles to below his knees.

"I didn't notice because I don't feel any pain," Eli says.

"You're sure they don't hurt you at all?" Cyril looks deeply concerned.

"No, here. Let me show you," Eli flicks at his left leg. "AHHHHHHH!"

"Ah, that's normal then." Cyril lets out a sigh of relief.

* * *

"I'm going to be disabled now, aren't I?" Eli's morose whimper is so low that it is barely audible.

"No, you'll recover in a week!" Cyril says with absolute confidence.

"Are you sure? Are you a doctor?"

"No, but this type of injury isn't severe enough to damage your legs permanently," Cyril reassures Eli while holding the showerhead over Eli's hair and assisting him to take a bath. "Don't you worry, mas—Eli. Should you ever sustain any serious injury, I'll give away my core if it's the price to get you well and healthy."

"What do you mean 'core'? What does core mean?" Eli asks.

"My life."

"Please, don't ever do that," Eli says in a serious voice.

Cyril says nothing but grins at him.

* * *

After Eli is done with the bath, Cyril leaves the bathroom momentarily to give Eli some privacy. He returns to get Eli after he finishes towel-drying himself and putting on a new set of pajamas in the bathtub. Eli pretends not to be bothered from being picked up and carried around princess-style by a man, as he tells himself it's a nice and necessary gesture of help from Cyril the Angel. And there's nothing gay about it.

When Cyrus walks past the bathroom mirror, Eli turns his head to peek at his reflection. Cyril sees it and steps back, holding Eli in front of the mirror so Eli can get a better look at himself.

"Thank you," Eli mutters.

"My pleasure," Cyril responds with a soft smile.

Eli has been excited to see his new face since the old witch told him he looked pretty. But now, as he is looking at the mirror, the reflection of this new face can't be any more familiar. It's exactly the same as his old face from his past life, with an addition of a few purple bruises and grazes here and there.

Well, wait…it's actually the same face Eli had when he was sixteen or seventeen. So he is about six years younger in this life! That's not too bad, he thinks.

"I'm done. Thanks a lot, Cyril," Eli says and immediately feels embarrassed. He only knows Cyril for like…less than four hours, and he's already dependent on him. That's really bad.

"You always look so strikingly beautiful," Cyril whispers.

"Excuse me?"

Cyril repeats, and Eli, despite his great effort not to hoot at his angel-like savior's cheesy choice of words, slips out a dry "heh." "You're joking, right?"

"No. What do you mean, mas—Eli?" Cyril sounds genuinely astounded.

While Eli doesn't think his appearance would hurt people's eyes, he's definitely sure his look will be nowhere near the "strikingly beautiful" term. If anything, those two words fit Cyril best.

"Never mind." Eli shakes his head.

Cyril looks at him. "In my eyes, you will always be the most gorgeous person in the world. And despite what you're thinking, I'm not being biased because you are my master, Eli. Anyone who met you before all agreed with me. In fact, back then, you were always the center of attention whenever you graced a room."

"Cyril, you…are so nice." Eli smiles crookedly. He has a really hard time believing Cyril's words. Still, at the same time, he is truly moved by Cyril's tremendous effort to compliment his worn-out, wet mouse of an appearance.

* * *

THE BATHROOM and bedroom are upstairs, next to each other. Before Eli took his bath, Cyril had to unwrap the bandages on both his legs, so now, when they get back to the bedroom, Cyril has to help him put them back on again.

Cyril sits Eli down on a soft, cushioned bench by the bay window. Then, he kneels to apply new bandages to Eli's legs. This time, Eli is wearing a new set of cream-colored summer pajamas with short sleeves and short pants to make it easier for Cyril to tend him.

Eli's legs are purple and badly swollen. It must be the adrenaline kicking in that he felt no pain after falling from the witch's broom. As Eli thinks about all the crazy things that happened to him yesterday, he can't help but shudder at the thought of his fate if Cyril hadn't shown up and taken him here. Eli doubts he will still be alive now.

"I'm sorry. Did I hurt you?" Cyril notices Eli shivering.

"No, no. You didn't. I just…"

"Yes?"

"I just want to thank you again," Eli says. "Thank you for saving me last night, Cyril. If it wasn't for you, I would probably be dead now. With my legs like this."

Cyril's expression turns grim as he listens to Eli. He lets out a long sigh and holds Eli's hands. "I'm so sorry, Eli. I'm sorry I got to you too late. I don't dare imagine what kind of horrible things happened to you. You will never know how much I despised myself when I saw your injuries after bringing you home. If only I paid attention, I would have gotten to you right when you woke up. You wouldn't have to go through all of those horrors."

"What?" Eli doesn't understand Cyril's apology or what he is saying. How is it Cyril's fault? The way Cyril put it makes it sound like he could have prevented all the crazy things before they happened to Eli. But then that's impossible because a normal person can't predict the future, unless Cyril is the incarnation of God.

"But I assure you, Eli, that I will make…I will seek justice for you," Cyril says, his quivering voice hard and solemn. "Those who laid their hands on you will be condemned for their hideous crimes. All of them."

It's probably the first time Eli hears Cyril speak in such a stern and authoritative voice that sends a chill down his spine, and he involuntarily nods his head like a kid acknowledging an adult's words.

Eli doesn't know what kind of face he makes, but it makes Cyril break into a chuckle. "Well, let the past be gone, and from now on, we'll only focus on making the fullest and happiest memories together, yeah?" Cyril says in the most cheery and inspiring tone.

"Yeah!" Eli responds without thinking. But a second later, after he finally processed the whole meaning of Cyril's words, he balks. "Wait, what?"

What does "making happy memories together" mean exactly?

Cyril then asks if Eli wants to take a tour of the house with him. Eli says yes because he is desperate to occupy his thoughts with something else besides analyzing everything Cyril has said. There is a shipload of red flags in almost every sentence, and if Eli dives deep into every word, he's afraid he might jump out of the window and flee out of fear for his virgin butt.

With keen eagerness and joy, Cyril scoops Eli up into his arms. He even thoughtfully wraps Eli in a knitted throw blanket before carrying him princess-style out of the bedroom.

Cyril is very thorough and informative during the tour. He takes Eli to every room in the house, even the half bathroom downstairs. This place has no basement, so Eli's fear of a bloody underground torture room is crossed out. During the tour, Eli also doesn't spot any questionable items (like bloody butcher knives, voodoo dolls, human body parts, kinky items, S.O.S notes, etc.) that would shatter Cyril's angel-like status. Thus, his trust and liking for Cyril are one notch higher.

The tour ends after thirty-five minutes. Now, one must be wondering how big of an estate this place is since it took about a quarter the time of a full tour of Buckingham Palace. Nope! This house is a small, one-bed, one-and-a-half-bath country home. The furniture is lovely but not gilded with gold or jewelry. So basically, this tour should only last ten minutes max instead of thirty-five. Consequently, after the tour finishes, Eli's liking for Cyril is half a notch lower than before.

"So, what do you think about our house?" Cyril asks enthusiastically, still carrying Eli firm in his arms.

"Mega dope," Eli mutters, trying to keep his eyelids open.

"Huh? What does 'mega dope' mean, mast—Eli?"

"It means da best house tour ever! So thorough, educational, and inspiring. Cyril, you are so good with words; you would make an excellent tour guide or a fantastic museum label writer."

Ah, fudge! Why did I say that? I'm such a prick! Fortunately, his blatant sarcasm completely flies over Cyril's head as the gorgeous lad blushes and is genuinely happy at that "compliment."

"Now, let me show you the garden!"

"There're more?!" Eli exclaims, appalled.

Cyril shows him the backyard first, and to Eli's surprise, the garden is absolutely amazing. It looks like a classic landscape oil painting by old-school artists. Plush, green grass covers the entire garden, stretching into the endlessness of the faraway forest. It's bordered by verdant boxwood hedges speckled with tiny purple flowers. Large bushes of white roses spiral along the two white oak posts of the patio. There are shrubs of various pastel flowers brimming from every edge of the yard. A grove of three beeches peacefully flanks the left of the house, and their cascading branches drift down to screen the white porch from the dull heat of the summer's sun.

This time, Eli is excited for Cyril to give him a good description of all the flowers in the garden. But Cyril only says, "This is the backyard," then walks inside.

"Wait, that's it?" Eli looks at Cyril, surprised and disappointed. This dude spent at least ten minutes listing every mundane thing in each room, yet he has no comments about this world-class garden?!

"You want to stay outside?" Cyril turns his heel back to the yard.

"I thought you would say something *more.*"

Cyril stares at the garden with deep, musing eyes, then says, "There are white and yellow flowers on the green grass, three trees. Ah, no, five trees. Green leafy fence."

* * *

CYRIL CARRIES Eli to the front porch. If the backyard were an oil canvas, the front yard would be straight out of a fairytale. Exuberant bushes of red and white roses climb the posts and railing of the deck and remind Eli of the fairytale "Snow White and Rose Red." Eli is admiring the view of the enchanted garden when Cyril suddenly strides down the porch and heads out of the garden.

"W-Where are you going, man?" Eli asks, startled.

Cyril holds him five feet away from the front gate and says, "I want to show you how our house looks from the outside! And here it is!"

"Ah, gotcha!" Eli views the house. "Oh, my!"

What a beautiful house Cyril has! A true fairytale cottage with white walls and green gable roofs nestles in an enchanted forest. Eli's heart flutters with child-like joy just from looking at the adorable house and its dreamy scenery.

They spend a couple of minutes outside before heading back to the house. But when Cyril is about to approach the main door, Eli stops him.

"Hey, hold on. Let me walk by myself through the door."

"Huh? Why? Your legs are—"

"Yes, I know both my legs are wrecked. But I'm not ready to have you carry me over the threshold yet, man! We know each other for, like, what? Less than six hours," Eli says.

"What is a threshold?"

"Oh, it's a doorsill."

"Doorsill?"

"It's a piece of wood usually at the bottom of a door," Eli explains, pointing at the white threshold of the main door.

"Ah, I always learn new things whenever I'm with you, maste—Eli!" Cyril grins. "Threshold. Doorsill. Mega dope."

"You're welcome." Eli cracks up, then frowns. "And please forget about the last word."

"Every word you say is engraved deep in my heart," Cyril states firmly.

"Man, you're so dramatic."

"But it's true!" Cyril remarks, looking very sincere.

"Alright, I believe you." Eli chuckles and gives Cyril a friendly pat on his firm chest.

"I have a question, though. Why can't I carry you over the threshold?"

"Because...Cyril, let's just forget all of this, okay? Let's go inside."

"Do you want me to help you walk in?"

"No, too complicated. Let's just go in the same way we went out."

"As you wish, maste—Eli!" Cyril chirps.

While busy talking, they didn't notice a small, sneaky green toad chilling by the flower bucket next to the door. When Cyril walks toward the entrance, he steps on the little "gift" the toad left on his white wooden porch —a pile of slimy saliva. As a result, he skids and trips over the threshold, falling face-first to the floor alongside Eli.

"Ahhhhh!" Eli screams as both his fractured knees smash onto the hardwood floor.

"Oh, no, no, no! Eli!" Cyril picks up himself and rushes toward Eli. But the toad's saliva is still on his shoes, and thus, he slips the second time and falls on top of Eli, smashing Eli's left cheek against the floor.

During his second fall, Cyril also hit the console table by the stairs, causing the glass vase to wobble.

Luckily, Cyril manages to catch the vase before it drops on Eli's head. However, he grabs it upside down, and thus, Eli receives all the water and flowers on his newly washed hair and face.

And that concludes the tour of Cyril's little fairytale cottage in the woods...

CHAPTER 5

A DAY IN FAIRYTALE TOWN

"Hmm." The old doctor gazes at Eli's battered face sympathetically, then turns and gives Cyril a confrontational glance. "Well, sir, as dreadful as it is that our great nation still allows the detestable, shameful practice of involuntary servitude, I do believe that there is a strictly observed law called 'protection for the laborers,' signed and executed by His Majesty, Emperor Haemon the Magnificent. Now, that law specifies that there will be grave penalties for employers that inflict *any* physical reprimand on their employees. Such employers will be subjected to a large fine or even given a life sentence and have their assets forfeited if the victim of the abuse is a minor—which is the case that we have here. Should I inform the social and justice services?"

"Oh no, no, no, you have misunderstood, doctor." Cyril waves his hands, his face blanched at the accusation. "I-I was not...I mean, it wasn't I—"

"Doctor, he wasn't the one that beat me up. Others did," Eli says briefly and glances at the panicking Cyril. *Dude, it wasn't you, so what are you fretting about?*

"Holy Tathagatas! Do you know the names of these people?" the kind doctor asks Eli.

"No sir, they bagged me. I escaped, and he found me."

The old doctor seems convinced and keeps shifting his gaze between Cyril and Eli.

"Doctor, this young man here is my precious young master whom I hold nothing but the utmost respect for. I would never dare to hurt him nor harm a single hair on his head," Cyril tells the doctor in a sincere voice.

"The bruise on his left face suggests otherwise," the doctor says as he examines Eli's cheek. "These are new wounds accumulated in less than the past twenty-four hours, and it looks like someone roughly slammed him into a hard surface." The old doctor raises an eyebrow at Cyril.

"Oh, that's my fault. It was an accident. I threw my master inside the house and crushed him," Cyril explains. The old doctor and two female nurses behind him gasp.

Just shoot me! "Dropped. Not 'threw,'" Eli corrects Cyril. "Doctor, yesterday we were outside on the porch, and he slipped on something while carrying me. I fell out of his arms onto the wood floor. He tried to pick me up but tripped again. It was an honest accident."

The medical staff seems to be at a loss for words upon listening to Eli's explanation as they all give Cyril complicated looks. The old doctor fakes a cough to break the awkward atmosphere. "Well...please be more careful next time." Then he turns to Eli. "Would you like me to assign a live-in nurse to stay with you until you fully recover?"

Cyril looks heartbroken when he hears the doctor's proposal but doesn't dare to object. His large, pretty blue eyes cast down like a sad, little puppy being reprimanded by his owner.

Eli sees the face Cyril makes and feels uncomfortable, as if someone were pricking him with a needle over and over. He smiles at the doctor and speaks in a composed manner. "Thank you for your thoughtful offer, doctor. But Cyril is great, and he has been taking care of me for as long as I can remember. And I was the one who distracted and caused him to trip." He turns to Cyril. "Right?"

"Yes, master! I mean, Eli!" Cyril replies, his face brightening up with joy and gratitude. Eli pretends not to see Cyril's hardcore fan-boy heart eyes and nervously chugs down the glass of water the nurses gave him earlier.

The two young nurses glance at Cyril and Eli, then cover their mouths with their clipboards and whisper something to each other, giggling.

"Ahem!" the old doctor coughs. "Very well then, this is for our patient's record. How old are you, child?"

At the same time, Cyril says, "Sixteen," while Eli answers, "Seventeen."

The doctor raises his eyebrow at them.

In unison, Cyril says, "Seventeen," while Eli replies, "Sixteen."

When the doctor is about to throw his pen at them, Cyril explains. "My master is sixteen now, but he will be seventeen next month."

"Yeah, what he said." Eli nods emphatically.

The old doctor regards them with skeptical eyes before turning to Cyril. "And you, guardian of the minor, how old are you, sir?"

"Uh..." Cyril pauses for a disturbingly long time for a simple question.

Dude! Eli has to nudge his elbow at Cyril's toned belly for Cyril to sputter out, "I'm twenty-four! Ah, sorry, it's just that sometimes I forget my age..." Cyril laughs awkwardly.

"Alright, please follow the nurses to get your master's prescription." The old doctor gives Cyril wary glances while scribbling down the script. "Come back in three days for the blood work result. He cannot have seafood because it will interfere with the drugs, and he might develop a rash. And for your master's sake, please be careful when you help him move around the house."

The doctor then regards Cyril thoughtfully and says, "Young man, if you want, I can also prescribe some medicines that will help your...uh, condition. You seem to have symptoms of manic-depressive illness."

"I do? What kind of illness is that?" Cyril asks, confused.

Eli tugs at Cyril's sleeve and makes a cuckoo sign, twirling his index finger near his ear.

"I'm not crazy! I just...have a lot of things on my mind," Cyril says defensively.

* * *

ELI MAKES a small pop while eating the translucent red strawberry-flavored tootsie pop the nurse gave him. Cyril gazes at him fondly. "If you like, I'll get you more candies after lunch. Which flavor do you like best?"

"Hmm?" Eli muses without releasing the candy from his mouth. "Hmm...No, thanks. It's fine. I don't have a sweet tooth," he replies, eagerly nomming the lollypop.

Cyril looks unconvinced.

"I have low blood sugar in the morning. That's why I'm eating this."

"Ah, I see." Cyril gives Eli a nod, yet his lips curl into a wide, mirthful grin.

"What's with that smile? You don't believe me?"

"Ah, of course not, Eli. How could I ever doubt your word?" Cyril replies with an innocent face.

"I'm telling you, man, I might look like a sixteen-year-old, but I'm not sixteen. I...have the soul of a grownup."

"Oh? So how old is your soul now, may I ask?" Cyril presses his lips together, holding back the laughter in his throat.

"Twenty-three," Eli calmly responds with a cool look on his baby face.

"Alright, twenty-three then." Cyril desperately struggles to suppress the laugh and ends up wheezing. "Ah, we're at the restaurant. Please drop us off here," he tells the coachmen.

Cyril gets out of the carriage first and then carries Eli in his arms. The restaurant is a quaint, one-story, redbrick house with green-painted wooden double casement windows and doors. At the entrance, two large shrubs of white and pink roses climb all over the brick wall to the green clay roof. Just like Cyril's house, the restaurant and all the buildings in town are fairytale-esque. There is a wooden sign on the rooftop that has carvings of three bears and some strange swirls.

"I can't believe the clinic ran out of wheelchairs," Eli grumbles.

"Ah, yes. That was quite unfortunate. But worry not, master—I mean, Eli! I'll be your crutch as long as you need me to, and I swear I will never make the same mistake as yesterday. I will never let go of you even if I plunge into the pit of Hell!"

"What?!" Eli shudders as he listens.

"Wait, that doesn't sound right. I meant the only time I will ever let go of you is if I were to ever fall into the pit of Hell. I want you to live the longest and fullest life!" Cyril corrects himself, and Eli feels as if his IQ has dropped a point.

"So if you were to fall off a cliff or into a river, you'd still drag me with you?"

Cyril blinks and appears to seriously contemplate an answer. Eli gives him a couple of light pats on his broad chest. "I'm just messing with you. Thank you, Cyril. You're officially the coolest, bestest person I've ever met in my life." Eli smiles sweetly at the handsome lad, whose face now blushes like a ripe strawberry.

A distracted man is striding toward them in the other direction. Eli is busy talking with Cyril and notices it is too late, so he yells, "Watch out!"

Within a blink of an eye, Cyril evades the inevitable collision with a perfectly even and lithe semicircle turn. His movement is precise, swift, and yet so very impossibly balanced and light that Eli doesn't feel dizzy or even a tremor in Cyril's arms. He only realizes Cyril moved after he completed that impeccable spinning.

The distracted man only reacts to Eli's "watch out" after he passes them.

"What?! How?" Eli looks at the hurried man, still pacing long steps behind them, and then to Cyril.

"I told you," Cyril tilts his head to the left to block the glaring sunlight from Eli's face, "I will never let you fall from my arms again."

* * *

"HI THERE! How are you doing, sirs? I hope you're doing excellently well! Welcome to Three Bears Diner! We open every day of the week from 7:00 AM to 11:00 PM. And please rest assured that our establishment does not overwork our staff, dutifully abiding by His Majesty, Emperor Haemon the Magnificent's edict, the 'Fair Labor Act.' There are two different shifts with different employees in a day except for the owner's daughter, which is me, and I work from 7:00 in the morning to 11:00 near midnight. And—"

"Good Heavens! Just get table five. They've been hooting for a refill in the last five minutes!" A middle-aged man who seems to be the diner's owner kicks his daughter to the side. "Sorry about that. She can be a little high-strung when meeting new customers. Welcome to Three Bears Diner! We open every day of the week from 7:00 AM to 11:00 PM. Would you like to sit indoors or on the patio?"

Eli is the first to successfully snap himself out of the girl's super bubblegum welcome. He then elbows Cyril out of his daze.

"I-Indoors, please," Cyril responds and follows the owner.

After they sit at the booth and the owner has left, Eli tells Cyril. "Hey, you and that girl can make a cute couple!"

"Please don't tease me, Eli," Cyril sighs.

"She's very pretty." Eli looks at the girl. She's three tables away from them and is chatting with the customers. The owner's daughter is a petite blonde with large blue eyes and a bubbly personality. Her hair is done into double buns. She wears a cute, brown-bear-ears headband with red ribbons. Her red, knee-length, frilly Victorian-style dress has a fluffy skirt and a white apron.

Cyril tilts his head to look at the cute blonde, then turns back to Eli and shrugs. "She's alright. Nothing special."

Eli rolls his eyes and sips the water, but he ends up choking on it when Cyril says, "You're so much more beautiful."

Eli is about to retort, and the cheery girl comes to their table and talks to them in the merriest voice. "Hi, sorry about earlier. My dad is a little curt sometimes. My name is Winnie! I'll be your waitress today. Have you decided on what to get yet? Our specials today are...well, all the things on the menu. Our cooks are very good! Heeheehee! Ooh, your eye color is so pretty!" Winnie leans over to look at Eli.

"Oh, thank you! You have beautiful eyes, too!" Eli blushes at the compliment and at the glimpse of Winnie's impressive bosom. In his two lives, he only knows two Winnie bears: the first one is fat and yellow, and this second one is a win-win in every way. Just when Eli is about to flirt with Winnie the Boo, Cyril pokes him with the menu.

"Let's see," Eli happily opens the menu, but after reading the first line, his expression turns from merry to dreary. "What...what language is this?"

Cyril and Winnie stare at him. Cyril quickly orders some food. When Winnie leaves, he asks Eli. "You don't recognize this language?"

Eli shakes his head. Cyril says. "It's Elgarian."

"El...what?" Eli stammers.

Cyril repeats.

"I am not speaking Elgarian right now," Eli cries. "I'm speaking English, and so are you!"

Unless the English language in this world is called "Elgarian," Eli doesn't believe he's been conversing in Elgarian the entire time. The words are English in his ears!

"It's alright, Eli. That's not a big deal." Cyril squeezes Eli's hand to comfort him.

Eli says nothing but hyperventilates in response.

"Hey, hey, breathe now," Cyril gets up and comes to sit next to Eli so he can pat Eli's back.

"I'm crippled and illiterate," Eli whimpers.

"You're not crippled, Eli. And in my eyes, you will always be a wise and refined person." Cyril speaks in a tender voice.

Eli is crushed, but Cyril's implausibly cheesy compliment cracks him up.

"See, isn't it better to just laugh it off?" Cyril grins with him.

"You're real smooth, you know that? You must be very popular with chicks—eh, women."

"Eh? No, I don't think so. It's quite the opposite, actually." Cyril purses his lips. "I'm not really interested in women."

"Why not..." Eli's voice trails off, unable to finish his question.

Fudge!

"Whoosh! This weather sucks! It's so hot in here!" Eli changes the subject as he fans himself with the menu frantically.

"Y-Yeah, the heat is intense today." Cyril's face flushes red as he nervously guzzles the glass of ice water before him. "Oh, shoot, this is your glass. I'm sorry, Eli!"

"It's fine! It's fine! I'm not thirsty anymore! You can have all of it."

"No, no. Take my glass. I haven't touched it yet," Cyril hurriedly switches his glass to Eli's.

"Your order's here! Ooh, you changed your seat!" Winnie comments.

"Ah, uh, I-I'm returning to my seat, excuse me!" Cyril clumsily goes back to his bench.

Winnie puts down their orders while carefully glancing at both of them. Before she leaves, she gives them the sweetest smile and says, "Enjoy your lunch! You guys are so cute together!"

* * *

AFTER LUNCH, Cyril carries Eli in his arms, and they stroll the downtown streets. It's afternoon, and the sun is scorching. Cyril buys Eli a straw bowler hat since Eli has been squinting his eyes in the sunlight. A few bystanders look at them curiously but eventually move on when they see Eli's bandaged legs.

After some time, Eli asks Cyril if he is tired of carrying him around for so long. Cyril replies, "Absolutely not! You're as light as—"

"Not feather, please," Eli frowns. There is only so much gross cheesiness that he can tolerate.

"...A camellia petal."

Fudge.

* * *

CYRIL TAKES Eli to a pricey-looking tailor shop to get new clothes. Upon his arrival at the store, Cyril announces to the owner he wants every style of the most expensive clothing sets they carry. But Eli elbows him hard in his ripped chest. "Dude, what midlife crisis are you having?! We live in a cottage, not a mansion. We are freaking peasants! Why are you spending like a big-shot? Are you out of your mind?!"

"But Eli—" Cyril wants to refute, but Eli cuts him off.

"No, you have to save that money!" Eli tells Cyril in a firm voice. He turns to the thrilled shop owner. "Please excuse my friend, ma'am. I will only need three of your most affordable sets of clothing."

"Three sets? You're going to re-wear them during the week?" Cyril scrunches his face in disgust. "That's awful hygiene, Eli!"

"Excuse me?" Eli lifts an eyebrow at the ravenhead.

* * *

THEY VISIT a candy shop before going home. At first, Eli nags Cyril that he doesn't like candies or anything sweet. But then Cyril swirls the vodka-infused chocolate at Eli, and he instantly shuts up. However, when they check out, the candy shop clerk refuses to sell them the wine-filled chocolate because Eli is underage.

"No, miss, I'm actually twenty-three," Eli desperately tries to explain. "I just have a baby face. That's not a sin, is it?"

"Young master, our nation prohibits underage drinking. The penalty for the perpetrator is three thousand gold coins," the cashier says. "And the accompanied adult that buys alcohol for the minor will be subjected to jail time and be revoked the right to look after that minor," the cashier shoots Cyril a questionable glance.

"I'm sorry, Eli, but we'll *NOT* be getting this candy," Cyril firmly shakes his head, and Eli gasps in horror. "Nobody will look after you if I were in jail. So NO."

"What is the legal age to drink then?" Eli asks the cashier, still not giving up just yet.

"Twenty years old, sir." The cashier smiles apologetically. When she sees his fully bandaged legs, she gives him an orange-flavored tootsie pop for free. "Get well soon!"

* * *

THEY GET HOME AROUND 4:00 PM. Cyril does get Eli a big bag of ten different kinds of chocolate-covered fruits to make up for the liquor-filled chocolate that Eli won't be able to buy for the next three years (since he's turning seventeen next month).

The first thing Cyril does is give Eli a bubble bath. Eli is annoyed when Cyril puts a winking floaty yellow wooden duck toy, a promotional gift from the candy shop, in his bathtub, so he pesters Cyril and tells the ravenhead not to treat him like a kid.

"But Eli...you are a kid."

"Man, I'm telling you for the last time. I'm twenty-three!" Eli says, irritated. "If anything, I'm actually only a year younger than you."

"Soul age doesn't count, little kit." Cyril boldly flicks the tip of Eli's nose, leaving soap bubbles on it.

* * *

CYRIL PUTS the freshly bathed Eli down on the bay window sofa in the bedroom and changes new bandages for him. Then he gives Eli the chocolate-covered fruit before leaving to take a shower. Eli leans over to open the window and view the beautiful backyard while munching the candy.

Life is full of surprises, Eli contemplates. Who will believe the lost, dirty beggar, who wandered the street in Creepyville two days ago, is now the young master of a beautiful house in the forest? It's the most insane and probably the shortest journey of rags to riches Eli has ever seen, and he still can't believe it's happening to him. While the road to the happy ending was relatively quick and anticlimactic, Eli is grateful that God has landed him straight to his happily ever after instead of making him earn it.

I would have effed it up so badly, Eli thinks and grimaces. Then he thinks about Cyril, and a smile forms on his lips. *Oh, Cyril! Sweet Cyril! What am I going to be without thou? Probably dead meat, for sure!*

Eli giggles at his silly thought and pulls the brown shopping bags from the floor to the sofa. He opens the first bag and takes out the two brand new pairs of shoes Cyril bought for him; the first one is a pair of shiny, black leather Oxford loafers, and the other is a pair of brown calfskin ankle boots. Though the style is simple, they are both well-made and beautiful.

Eli empties the second bag from the tailor shop, and his jolly face turns black.

"Two, four, eight...sixteen! What the f—" Eli exhales angrily.

Sixteen sets of clothes! Back at the shop, Cyril agreed to only get eight sets for him, yet he secretly bought double the number behind his back!

The bedroom door handle turns, and Cyril walks in, drying his wet hair with a towel. "Eli, what have you been doing—" He stops talking when Eli holds the clothes up and looks pissed. "Let me make you some chamomile tea. I'll be right back!"

"Uh-uh. I need to talk to thee! Thee come back here right now!" Eli snaps.

Knock, knock, knock.

"I'll get the door! Be right back!" Cyril flees the scene.

Eli hears Cyril walking downstairs and opening the door. There is the noise of over two people talking and then hurried footsteps creaking on the wooden stairs. Eli jumps a little when the bedroom door springs open, and a strange woman bursts into his bedroom.

CHAPTER 6

THE WELCOME WAGON

The woman is beautiful and appears to be three to four years older than Cyril. She is tall, has a fair complexion, blonde hair, blue eyes, and wears a red and blue ankle-length dress with a frilly white apron.

The woman and Eli stare at each other, long and awkward. When Eli is close to calling Cyril for help, the woman trudges toward his seat and gives him the most heartwarming smile.

"Hello," she greets him nervously.

"Hello," Eli echoes. Cyril has gone upstairs and is now standing by the bedroom door.

"H-How are you doing?" the woman asks Eli.

"I'm good...How about you?" This is super weird. What the fudge is happening? Eli glances at Cyril, but Cyril just gives him the constipated "I have no idea" look.

"I'm good too! Better than good!"

"My name is Ilya," Eli introduces himself.

"Oh! I'm sorry. I'm so rude! My name is Mariposa. I'm your neighbor. My house is just a five minute walk from yours," Mariposa says.

"Oh, you're my neighbor!" Good God! He thought she was his mother in this world! "Very nice to meet you. Mariposa means butterfly, right? What a beautiful name you have!"

"Oh, yes. Thank you. You're so...sweet and kind. Please call me Marie."

Eli is about to respond to Mariposa, and another person rushes into the room. This time, it is a tall and handsome gentleman who seems to be of Indian descent. He's holding a huge straw basket of baked goods.

He and Eli exchange a long, awkward stare. Then he approaches Eli and says, "Hello."

"Hello?" Eli blinks in confusion.

"H-How are you doing, young master?" the Indian gentleman with a kind face asks.

"I'm doing great. How about you, sir? My name is Ilya."

"Pardon my rudeness, young master. M-My name is Haidar." Haidar pushes the baked goods basket to Eli's hands. "This is for you! Please accept it!"

Eli looks at the jumbo-sized basket filled with all sorts of colorful pastries and sweets and sees a red and blue ribbon attached to the rim. Then he glances at the colors of Mariposa's dress—blue and red. "Are you guys—"

"Oh, I'm so sorry. I completely forgot to introduce ourselves. Young master, this man is my husband!" Mariposa grabs Haidar's arm.

"And she's my wife!" Haidar affirms. "Young master!"

"Oh, nice!" Eli smiles at the couple. "Oh, and please, call me Eli."

The couple looks at each other and then back at Eli, their faces puzzled.

"I implore you to call me Eli," Eli adds.

"As you wish, Eli," Haidar bows.

"Thank you." Eli nods politely.

The three of them talk for a bit. The couple asks Eli about his legs and how he likes the house and the town, etc. They seem to care greatly about Eli's well-being.

"Eli, please come to our house whenever you like! We live just five minutes away from you! You can visit us anytime you want. And if you need anything, please don't hesitate to come over. I...I...," Mariposa wheezes, her face flushes. "I...you...uh..."

"Marie, are you okay?" Eli asks with concern.

"No, I'm fine. I'm just..." Tears trail from Mariposa's blue eyes, and she has to turn away to dab them off. "I'm sorry. I think I have to...uh...take my medicine. My asthma is acting up again."

"Oh no." Eli turns to Marie's husband and finds that he, too, is in tears. "Haidar? What's going on? Are you alright?"

"I...please excuse us, Eli. I also...I'm also having an asthma episode right now. We'll visit you later...after we get better." Haidar stands up and bows to Eli, then drags his wife out of the bedroom. "Please get better soon, Eli! We'll see you again very shortly!"

"I'll come back to visit you!" Mariposa calls out from a distance.

* * *

ELI ASKS Cyril to carry him downstairs to see their neighbors off. After the couple leaves, Eli asks his gorgeous housemate, "Cyril, what just happened?"

"They are our neighbors," Cyril says indifferently.

"Do you know them well? Are they going to be alright? They seem... odd." Eli wonders if it's a normal thing for residents in a fairytale town to burst into their neighbor's bedroom to introduce themselves. The couple is very nice, but they're also a bit weird.

"Yes, I do know them. They are nice folks. And I think they'll be fine after they...take their meds."

When Cyril is on the fifth step of the stairs, three knocks ring at the front door.

"Someone's at the door," Eli tells Cyril.

Cyril narrows his eyes, debating whether to take Eli upstairs first or bring him downstairs. Eli tells him to do the latter and not keep the person outside waiting.

Cyril has to walk back to the main foyer and put Eli down on a bay window seat near the front entrance. When he opens the door, the person outside pushes past Cyril and enters the house. It turns out to be a very cute little boy, around eight or nine years old. He has dark hair, pale skin, and hazel eyes. The boy looks around the house, and when he sees Eli, halts for a couple of seconds and then takes a deep breath before striding toward Eli.

"Hello there." Eli gives the boy a friendly smile.

The boy blinks and looks at Eli up and down; his eyes stop on Eli's bandaged legs. He just stares at them without saying anything.

"Hi?" Eli waves at the kid.

"Hello. How are your legs? Do you feel better? Are they still hurting you?" the little boy asks.

"Oh, they're not hurting me at all. Thank you for asking." Eli is a little surprised at how oddly articulate this kid is. "My name is Ilya, but I would like to be called Eli. What's your name?"

"My name is Gallahan." The boy gives Eli a formal bow. "And I'm ecstatic to hear that your injury doesn't bother you."

"Very nice to meet you, Gallahan. Do you live near here?"

"Likewise, Eli." Gallahan bows to Eli again. "And yes, I do. I'm your neighbor. My house is five minute walk away from yours."

"You live with Mariposa and Haidar?"

"Yes, I do. They are...my mom and dad."

Eli is slightly puzzled because Gallahan doesn't seem to resemble either Mariposa or Haidar.

"I'm adopted," Gallahan says as if he has guessed what Eli is puzzled about.

"Oh, that's nice." Eli smiles awkwardly. "Well, thank you for coming over. Your parents are very lovely! Do you want some chocolates?"

Gallahan politely declines and says he doesn't like sweets. Then he excuses himself, runs back outside, and returns with a gift box with a red ribbon on top. "This is for you. Please accept it."

"Oh, thank you so much!" Eli is pleasantly surprised at the boy's sweet gesture. Gallahan gives Eli a look of anticipation; his eyes keep switching between the gift and Eli.

"Oh, you want me to open it?"

The kid eagerly nods.

"Alright! Ah, I'm so excited!" Eli unwraps the gift. It turns out to be a thick book with teal clothbound, gold embossed title and border. Eli flips a couple of pages and can't understand a word since it's in Elgarian.

"I hope you like it. It's a very rare book. It took me a long time to find it." Gallahan smiles shyly, scratching his head.

"I-I love it. What an amazing gift. Aren't you sweet? Thank you so, so much!"

The two of them chat for a bit. Like his parents, Gallahan is highly interested in Eli's health and overall well-being. After a while, Eli notices the boy's voice becoming shaky and his face reddening.

"Gallahan, what's wrong? Are you alright?"

"I'm fine. Don't worry about me," Gallahan waves his hand to signal he is alright. But his small shoulders are trembling.

"No, you're not. Come here." Eli pats the cushion next to where he sits. Gallahan has been keeping his distance the entire time.

When Gallahan sits down beside him, Eli asks him in a soft voice. "What's wrong, buddy? Are you hurt? Where are you hurting?"

Gallahan shakes his head and answers in a thick voice. "No...I'm sorry. I'm being rude...just...I..." His hazel eyes glisten with tears.

"Oh no, why are you crying?" Eli doesn't know what to do. What's going on here? Why is everyone crying when they see him? He quickly looks at Cyril, who is just standing by the door with his arms crossed, looking irritated.

"C-Can I visit you often? Please?" Gallahan gives him a puppy look.

"Of course you can. Any time—" Eli forgets this is Cyril's house, so he turns to the ravenhead to ask for permission.

"This is your house, Eli." Cyril smiles softly at him.

"You can visit me any time you like!" Eli wipes away Gallahan's tears. The boy's face immediately brightens up.

"Hey, kid, time to go home. Your parents are waiting." Cyril impatiently knocks on the door.

Gallahan glares at Cyril, then turns back to Eli. "Please get well, Eli. I'll visit you again very soon. And you can come visit me whenever you want, no matter day or night! If you need anything, *anything at all,* please let me know, and I'll make sure I'll get them for you, no matter what."

"Oh, w-why thank you!" Eli chuckles. Children are his weakness. He asks Gallahan if he wants a hug, and the boy is thrilled. They hug for a long time.

"Alright, that's enough. Go home so we can have dinner." Cyril ushers the boy out.

After Gallahan leaves, Eli lets out a big exhale and tells Cyril, "God bless them! That's the friendliest and nicest family I've ever met!"

"Yeah. They sure are," Cyril mumbles dryly.

* * *

Cyril sits Eli down on a sofa in the living room, and three knocks echo at the front door. This time, Cyril completely ignores the knocks as he pretends not to hear them.

"Cyril," Eli tugs Cyril's sleeve and glances at the main door's direction.

"Ignore them, Eli. I'm pretty sure it's just peddler," Cyril says.

"What kind of peddler peddlees at this hour?" Eli looks at the walnut mantle clock on the fireplace. "It's 7:00 PM."

"Exactly! Very sketchy characters indeed, so just ignore them."

The person knocks repeatedly, as if they won't leave until someone answers the door. Cyril eventually has to go greet the visitor. Eli hears noisy exchanges in the main hall and heavy footsteps thumping on the hardwood floor. His heart lurches when a tall, muscular man in well-worn but formal navy pirate attire bursts into the living room.

"Cyril," Eli calls aloud for help as the fearsome pirate marches toward him.

The pirate is a very attractive man, around twenty-eight or twenty-nine. He has dark brown hair, ocean-blue eyes, and subtle stubble. But he doesn't have an eye patch or a hooked hand to complete the pirate cliché, though.

Captain Seven-Seas stands before Eli and gives him a long, hard, and creepy stare without saying a word. Then, he suddenly crouches to the floor on one knee, causing Eli to jump in his seat. Because he's so tall, his eyes are on the same level as Eli's.

"Hello." The pirate salutes Eli, his voice deep and husky.

"Ahoy? I mean, hello!"

"How are you doing...young master?"

"Superb. How about you?"

"Mighty good."

"Oh, wonderful!" Eli smiles. Captain Seven-Seas returns a grin. Then no one says anything, and the room falls into awkward silence. Eli glances at Cyril and sees the ravenhead rubbing his temples exasperatedly.

"M-My name is Ilya." Eli brings out his hand for a handshake.

Captain Seven-Seas takes Eli's hand, but instead of shaking it, he kisses and rests his head on it.

What the fuc—

Captain Seven-Seas suddenly stands up again and takes off his feathered tricorn. Then he gives Eli a full bow, a gesture that Eli only saw in period movies in his past life.

"My name is Wolfgang. I'm very honored to make your acquaintance, young master!" Pirate Wolfgang says in a charming voice. Then he excuses himself to go to the main foyer and returns with a gift box with a blue ribbon on top. "Please accept this humble gift. I've traveled through many exotic lands in order to obtain it."

"Oh no, that's too precious—"

"Please, young master, I implore you to take the gift!" Captain Seven-Seas is on his knees again.

"Okay, okay. Please, sir, stand up! I'll accept your gift!"

"Please don't be so formal, young master. Call me Wolfgang."

"Alright, thank you for the gift, Wolfgang. And please call me Eli," Eli tells Wolfgang.

Wolfgang raises an eyebrow at him, acting as if he misheard what Eli just said.

"I insist on being called Eli. And Wolfgang, please, sit down." Eli shows Wolfgang the armchair beside his sofa.

After Wolfgang sits down, the pirate glances at the gift and then Eli. His blue eyes glint with excitement and anticipation. Eli gives the handsome pirate a knowing nod and unwraps the gift. It's another very expensive-looking book with plum clothbound and gold-gilded trims.

"How...exquisite! What splendid craftsmanship!" Eli flips the pages. They are all in Elgarian, so he doesn't understand jack. "Thank you for your thoughtful gift, Wolfgang."

"I'm beyond happy, young ma—Eli." Wolfgang gives him another deep bow.

They talk for a while, and Eli learns that Wolfgang is his neighbor.

"I live just a five minute walk from you," Wolfgang says.

"You share the house with Haidar and Mariposa?"

"Oh no, young mas—Eli, their house is five minutes from yours in the South. My place is five minutes away in the West," Wolfgang responds.

"Oh, I see."

"Excuse me, can you come back later? It's past dinnertime, and my young master needs to take his medicine," Cyril chimes in, his voice flat and irritated.

Wolfgang turns a deaf ear to Cyril. He wishes Eli a fast recovery and invites him to come to his house whenever he wants or needs anything. Basically, he says the same thing as Haidar, Mariposa, and Gallahan. About ten minutes later, Wolfgang bids Eli adieu. He doesn't even nod at Cyril when he skirts past the ravenhead.

* * *

CYRIL CLOSES the door with a bang and returns to the living room. Eli speaks up first when he sees Cyril walk in. "Man, our neighbors are super interesting! I can't believe you neighbor with a pirate!"

"Wolfgang is not a pirate. He just likes to dress up as one," Cyril sighs, shaking his head.

"You're kidding!"

"Not at all. The man is a little eccentric." the ravenhead makes the cuckoo sign.

Eli only chuckles. His dear housemate should be the last person in the line to make the nutcase gesture, as "Snow White" himself also belongs to the wacky group—doctor certified.

"Are you hungry yet? Do you want to have dinner now?" Cyril sits down next to Eli.

Eli looks at the clock. It's almost 8:00 PM. "It's late. Let's eat. I'll help you prepare the food."

"Thank you, Eli, but there's no need. It's already cooked, so I will just preheat it," Cyril smiles softly at him. "Let me get you upstairs so you can rest, and then I will bring your dinner up when it's done."

"Oh, it's fine. Let me keep your company in the kitchen while you heat up the food."

"Well, if that's your wish, then I shall obey," Cyril gets up and bends his knee, giving Eli a bow similar to Wolfgang's.

Am I the only normal person around here? Eli wonders.

* * *

Dinner has the same dishes as yesterday: portobello mushroom steak, pan-fried potatoes, salad, bread, and creamy mushroom soup. In the middle of the meal, Eli says to Cyril. "Hey, Cyril. Can I ask you something?"

"Of course, Eli. You can ask me anything," Cyril puts down the fork. "If you need something, please don't hesitate to let me know. I will do whatever it takes to give you whatever you want!"

"Dude, calm down. I just want to ask you a few questions. Actually, I only want to ask you one question."

"Sure! What is it?" Cyril beams.

"As you can see, I have no memories of you or myself. You said you have known me for a long time, so I wonder if you can tell me the story of my life?"

Cyril pauses. About thirty seconds later, he mutters, "Uh, what do you want to know?"

"Anything that you can tell me about myself before I...uh, 'lost' my memory."

"Umm. How far back do you want to know?"

"From the beginning, if possible," Eli says and regards Cyril warily. He doesn't like how jittery and hesitant Cyril is. When someone reacts like that to a simple question, it means the answer will not be pleasant. "Please?" Eli adds.

Cyril zones out for a long time, but Eli still patiently waits for him to talk without rushing or pressuring him. When the ravenhead realizes he can't stay quiet any longer, he slowly speaks up in an unconfident voice. "It's a really long and complicated story, and it would take a long time to tell if you want to know everything since the beginning."

"Well, then, can you give me a short version?"

"It's too long and too complicated to...summarize," Cyril stutters.

"Dude, I'm seventeen years old! How long and complicated can my life story be?!" Eli snaps, losing his patience.

"Please don't be mad, master—Eli."

"I'm not mad! But you are beating around the bush here! Why can't you tell me? Or was it something that I did? Did I do something so horrible you couldn't tell me?" Eli is terrified. "Or...or did I commit it a crime? Did I murder someone? That's why we have to hide in the woods?"

"No, Eli, you did no such things. And we aren't hiding in the woods. We just went to town today." Cyril's blue eyes darken. "You were a just and honorable person."

"Were?" Eli raises an eyebrow.

"Before you were...kidnapped, I meant," Cyril elaborates.

"Kidnapped?!" Eli exclaims, stunned by the information. "I was kidnapped! How?"

"You know, kidnappings happen a lot around here," Cyril says. "It's quite common, unfortunately."

"So, how did it happen?" Now that he thinks about it, being kidnapped would somewhat explain why he was in that dingy alley in Creepyville in the first place.

"I made a mistake. I didn't pay attention, and someone took you from me." Cyril's face is hard and grim as he speaks. "Not a single day goes by that I haven't stopped thinking about you. I could never forgive myself for making that grave mistake. I thought I lost you forever."

"Cyril..." Eli is at a loss for words for a moment. He doesn't expect Cyril to react so emotionally. Cyril's eyes are now red and brimming with tears.

"D-Don't cry."

"Cry?" Cyril mumbles, surprised. He brings his hand to his face and finds a single tear roll down on the pale cheek. "Oh...it's indeed a tear."

"Are you alright?" Eli asks timidly.

"Ah, I'm fine. Don't worry about me, Eli." Cyril waves his hand and puts back on his cheery face.

Eli watches Cyril pensively; then he reaches for Cyril's hand. "Cyril, it wasn't your fault."

"What?" Cyril freezes.

"Cyril, don't beat yourself up for something you couldn't prevent." Eli gives Cyril's hand a light squeeze. "You aren't God."

Cyril blinks. His gorgeous face fills with surprise and complex emotions. Then, like a little kid, he clumsily nods in agreement with Eli. "You are...right mas—Eli."

"So, when did I go missing?"

"Huh? Uh...a long time ago," Cyril responds vaguely.

"Can you be a little more specific, please?" Eli takes his hand back and throws the ravenhead an irked glance. "A long time is how long? Three months? Six months? A year?"

"Um...t-three years."

"Three years?!" Eli cries. "What?!"

Cyril just gives him a solemn nod and murmurs, "Each year felt like a century to me. I was losing my sanity."

The kitchen falls into stark silence. Nobody utters a word; they just stare at each other with conflicting emotions. Eli breaks off the gaze, then grabs his water glass and drinks it. This conversation is making his throat dry for all the different reasons.

"Well, you found me. And I'm here now, alive, and not missing a limb. So, there is a good ending to the story, after all."

"Yes, you're right." Cyril sighs and drinks his water. "Except that you don't remember me at all."

"Cyril, I—"

"But that's fine. The most important thing is that you're here with me right now, and it isn't a hallucination made by my desperate mind. You can't imagine how happy and grateful I am right now, Eli," Cyril smiles fondly; his exquisite blue eyes sparkle with contentment and affection. "I'm so grateful we got the second chance to be together again."

Eli gives Cyril a contemplative stare. After a long and carefully thought-out moment, Eli decides to be blunt. "Cyril, were we together before I lost my memory?"

"Yeah, we were very close and always together," Cyril answers innocently.

"No, no. I'm not talking about 'together' that way. I meant 'together-together.' Do you understand?" Eli taps his two index fingers together to make a gesture of a couple kissing.

"Huh?" Cyril is dumbfounded, then he shakes his head. "No, I don't understand your question, Eli."

You're killing me, Cyril! How can a twenty-four-year-old person be this dense?! "What I'm trying to ask is: did we sleep together before I was kidnapped?"

Cyril appears to be thinking. "As you can see, there are two beds upstairs, so..."

Eli holds his breath and swallows down the gigantic urge to say mean things or tell Cyril he's a fudging idiot—which he is.

"Well, Cyril, I see that reading in between the lines isn't your forte. Even though there was literally no metaphor, and the point couldn't be any clearer. I hope you'll excuse my bluntness then."

Cyril only blinks and gives Eli a clueless nod.

"Did we have sex before I lost my memory?" Eli pronounces each word loud and clear.

Cyril's pretty lips hang open, and his right hand lets go of the glass, causing the water to spill all over the table and drip down to the floor.

"Is that a yes or no?" Eli inquires.

"W-What are you..." Cyril wheezes. His gorgeous face overflows with shock and incredulity. "Master! What are you saying?!"

"What the—are you serious?! Have sex means—"

"No, no, no. Please, master, stop! I understand what you meant. I just can't believe I would ever hear you talk about such things!"

"Okay, so that's a no, right? We never do the deed, yes?" Eli lifts an eyebrow.

"Of course not! Master, I would never, ever dare to think about it, much less commit such a heinous act! I can never ever disrespect you like that!"

"Oh, alright." Eli exhales in relief. "Thanks. That's all I wanted to know."

"Master!" Cyril suddenly raises his voice and startles Eli. "D-Did someone d-defile you when you were...kidnapped? Did you finally remember what happened?"

"No. I don't remember anything," Eli recollects, scratching his hair. "I don't think anyone has touched me that way. An evil witch didn't butcher me because...I'm a virgin, according to her. She did a magic test on me. My blood turned a vial of green substance transparent."

Cyril looks appalled as he listens to Eli. His gorgeous face then turns white with pure anger. Eli has to speak up to distract his housemate, who is close to losing his last bolt. "Hey, man, I'm fine. Calm down. I'm not missing any body parts."

"Though, all thanks to you, if you hadn't showed up that night, I'd definitely be in the pot." Eli fails to hold back a shudder as he recalls the cannibalistic witch's kitchen, the piles of decapitated heads in the corner and the boiling pot filled with bloody human flesh.

Eli glances at the ravenhead and spots a cold, dark expression on his face, not at all the simple and merry Cyril that Eli has known.

* * *

"Good night, Eli." Cyril smiles affectionately as he tucks Eli into bed. It's cold in the evening, so Cyril pulls the blanket all the way to Eli's neck and only leaves his face sticking out. "I wish you the sweetest and merriest dreams, and no nightmares shall disturb your rest."

Eli just shoots his housemate a disturbed side-eye. He probably was wrong about Cyril after all. Maybe Cyril doesn't want to "do" him but be his dad instead. What else could explain this high-key daddy complex this dude has?

"What is it?" Cyril asks softly. "You're not sleepy yet?"

"Uh...don't know, man," Eli responds indifferently.

"Do you want me to read you a story?" Cyril picks up the book Wolfgang gifted Eli.

"No, man. I'm not a kid!" Eli nags. "And also, your storytelling skill sucks! We spent two hours talking about the past, and it didn't get anywhere.

I still haven't learned jack about myself, except I was kidnapped for three years, and we're not fudge buddies."

"Eli!" Cyril exclaims. "Y-You should not—urg!"

Eli still gives Cyril a challenging look, not at all repentant for all the mean things he said.

Cyril bites his lips and crosses his arms. But he doesn't return Eli's rebellious gaze with a stern gaze or even scold him. After a few seconds, the ravenhead surrenders and speaks to Eli in a compliant tone. "You are right. I'm sorry for disappointing you with my inefficient communication skills. I know it's frustrating, but...what can I say? I'm not very good with words. Especially when I'm with you, all the words just escape my mind."

"Are you sure we're not fudge buddies?" Eli frowns because that sounds super gay, especially the last part.

"Eli! Stop saying that word!" Cyril gives him a disapproving look.

"Well, friends with benefits then," Eli says.

"Y-You!" Cyril stares at him. When Eli thinks the ravenhead will reprimand him for sure, Cyril caves. "Alright, go to sleep. You need a lot of energy because we'll have a picnic tomorrow. There's this beautiful park just an hour away from our house, and the scenery is very nice. I'm sure you'll love it."

"Huh?" Eli can't believe in his ears. He only gawks at his housemate. "What?"

Cyril reiterates, and Eli pulls his blanket down. "Cyril, do you realize you're rewarding my bad behavior with a picnic?"

"Eli, I'm not rewarding you. I planned to take you out tomorrow earlier today. I want you to get some fresh air, and a change of scenery will be good for your health." Cyril chuckles, "Aw, Eli, are you expecting something else?"

"You're not mad at me for being awful to you?"

"No. Never," Cyril answers firmly, his blue eyes gazing tenderly at Eli. "No matter what you say or do. I will not get mad at you. Even if you did awful things, I would not judge you. I would be your accomplice. I will always stand by you."

Now it's Eli's turn to become flustered. He pulls the blanket over his nose to hide his blushing cheeks, leaving only two green eyes visible. "Why would you do that? Who in their right mind would go through the troubles to stand by a terrible person?"

"Ah, that's a difficult question, Eli. Why do the sun, the moon, and the stars rise in the East and set in the West? Why do you mean the world to me, Eli? I don't have an answer to that, for, like you said, I'm not a God. And according to that old doctor in town, I'm not really in the right mind, either."

"Cyril, are you positive we aren't friends with benefits?" Eli asks, genuinely this time.

"I see what you're trying to do here. If you wanted me to be a model guardian, you could have just asked. After all, I do have a legal responsibility to you, Eli." Cyril raises an eyebrow, his long fingers tapping on the mattress.

"Wait, you really are my legal guardian?"

"Uh-huh."

"I thought you made that up at the clinic."

"Uh-uh." Cyril shakes his head. "Why would I make that up? Pretending to be a minor's legal guardian is called kidnapping. That's a serious offense."

"Oh. So what?" Eli is deliberately being a brat. He doesn't believe he can't get a rise out of Cyril. He wants to prove to the ravenhead that no one can stand a terrible person, no matter how infatuated they are. "T-The old doctor says it's a serious crime to physically reprimand a minor in this country per the Emperor Ha...uh, whatever his name is...order. You can't punish me."

Cyril bursts into a deep laugh.

"Oh, Eli," Cyril chuckles, shaking his head. "I have not and will never punish you. No matter what you say or do. Oh no, did I just let that slip out? What should I do? Ay, I can't believe I just said that. I literally just gave you the full leverage over me, in case you haven't realized that already. Tch, tch."

"You!" Eli is mad. Not only does he fail to prove Cyril wrong, but Cyril also gets the last laugh.

"Ay, but then there's one thing I can do, Eli. As your legal guardian, I do have a say in what is good for your well-being. You know, blame the law, and it seems like overindulging in all the sweets during the day has made you very hyper at bedtime. That's not good, so I'm afraid I'll have to take back all the ten different types of fruit chocolates I got for you today, as well as all the pastries Mariposa gave you.”

“W-Wait, hold on,” Eli stammers, but Cyril shushes him.

“They aren’t good for you. And you have been keen on saying you don’t have a sweet tooth. Well, from now on, you will not have any sweets during the day. I know, I know. You have low blood sugar in the morning, but you will have to get used to it; it’s for your own good. I’d rather you sleep soundly at night and give you nutritious food during the day to combat the low blood sugar thing.”

“Whatever,” Eli says in the coolest voice he can muster. Then he turns to the wall and closes his eyes, pretending to sleep. He can hear his legal guardian giggle at him.

“Good night, Eli.” Cyril strokes Eli’s brown hair.

About ten minutes later, Eli asks. “Why are you still sitting here?”

“I’m waiting for you to sleep,” Cyril answers in a sweet, dulcet voice.

“Go to sleep.”

“Not before you are asleep first.”

“Why are you being so nice to me? What if I’m not your master? You know, two people who share the same face but aren’t blood-related isn’t unheard of. What if you got the wrong person, and your real master is still out there, alone and scared?”

“Here we go again,” Cyril sighs.

“I’m being serious with you.” Eli says, turning around to face his gorgeous housemate. “What if I’m not the person you’re looking for? What if I’m never going to remember you?”

“Oh, Eli. How are you so sure that you’re not my master?” Cyril asks him. “You think I can’t recognize my master when I see him in front of me?”

“Of course I’m sure because I know I am not! I didn’t know you until yesterday,” Eli argues. “You’re a good person, and you saved my life. I-I don’t want to take advantage of you.”

“Oh, Eli.” Cyril lets out a deep sigh. “Eli, let me ask you this. Why are you so sure that whatever memory you have now is real?”

Eli blinks but can’t retort. Cyril continues. “I’ve never doubted that you are my master. And after tonight's conversation, I'm sure I got the right person."

"W-What does that mean?"

"Like you said, there can be two people not biologically related yet share the same face. However, there can never be two people who share the same face plus the same exact birthmarks, voice, personality, and bearing. You both have the same frown when you're displeased, the same scowl when you're angry, the same rare shade of green eyes, and share identical birthmarks behind your nape, left earlobe, and right sole. And those are just a few examples. How do you explain that? Coincidence?"

That's a little creepy. Eli feels goosebumps forming on his skin and quietly pulls the blanket up to his neck again. Cyril sees it. He takes the knitted blanket at the end of Eli's bed and lays it on top of Eli's cotton blanket.

If this isn't proof of Cyril's daddy complex, Eli doesn't know what is.

"Is it warmer now?" Cyril purrs.

Eli nods. "Thanks...Dad."

Cyril's brow rises at Eli's latest sass, but then his lips curve into a quirky smile. "Just so you know, Eli: a legal guardian may not physically reprimand a minor, but parents and adopted parents can. So..."

Eli suddenly feels cold. His body sinks deeper into the mattress.

Cyril's blue eyes watch Eli's every move in the dark, and he certainly catches that slight shudder Eli made. He pats Eli's brown hair. "I'm just teasing you. I can't be your father. Heaven would smite me. So don't you worry about it. And I promise you I will never ever hurt you, Eli. You're the most important person in my life. And I—"

"Dude, go to sleep so I can sleep!" Eli snaps, rolling his eyes.

"Ohh. S-Sorry—"

"Also, please stop telling me all of these cheesy things when we aren't even together. It's very confusing to me, and you're even weirder than that dude who pretends to be a pirate!" Eli says.

Cyril gasps. "Y-You."

"I am what?" Eli scowls.

"Hah! This attitude right now is exactly the same as how you always acted before you...lost your memory, and yet you keep telling me you don't remember me! Now I really doubt if you ever lost your memory at all or you are just trying to punish me by pretending not to know me!" Cyril crosses his arms. "And also, what does 'cheesy' mean in this case?"

"What the—?! Okay, okay! One last time, I'd never met you until yesterday! And say, if I'm really your master because anything can be possible in this weird-ass world, then you're out of luck because I don't remember you! Also, what do you mean by the same attitude before I lost my memory?! You actually let a thirteen, fourteen-year-old kid talk to you this way with no consequences?! Dude! You're a terrible guardian! And what does cheesy mean? Cheesy is when you tell me, 'Oh, Eli, you meant the world to me. You're my life and my soul, my everything, my moon and my stars.' And when I asked you about our relationship, you told me we didn't bang! Oh, what does bang mean? Bang means fudge! If we have never banged, why would you say something like that? Do you know what that's called? It's called leading people on, and it's a bad thing! It's a good thing I'm a guy. If I were a naïve girl and listened to what you said, I would have fallen for you and gotten knocked up. Then you would be like, 'Oh, but I never think about you that way because you're my mistress.' Then the girl would be stuck with the baby, no husband, and would be miserable, yada yada."

Cyril stupidly gapes at the fuming boy. He raises his hands, trying to express himself, but no words come out. He is too stunned to speak, yet his trembling hands keep swirling in the air.

"What are you doing?" Eli stares at his guardian.

"You." Cyril looks down at Eli. "You."

"Uh-huh? I what?"

"Hah! Nice try." Cyril grins. "No matter what you say or do, I will never get mad at you."

Eli is truly speechless this time.

"Alright, my moon and stars, time for you to sleep, or you won't be able to stay awake for the picnic tomorrow." Cyril tucks the dumbstruck Eli into bed. "Eli, you really do mean the world to me, and you are indeed my life, my soul, and my everything. Thank you for that final confirmation; you are my master, the person I have been hopelessly searching for so long. Sweet dreams, Ilya," Cyril coos in Eli's ear.

CHAPTER 7

PICNIC AND SNAKES

The next morning, Eli wakes up from a nightmare so vivid and disturbing it has him in tears. Luckily, Cyril is already awake and finds Eli sobbing in his sleep.

"Eli, wake up. It's just a dream. It's not real," the ravenhead whispers in a warm and lulling voice as he holds Eli's shoulders to steady him from his sporadic jerks.

Even after Eli is fully awake, he's still trembling uncontrollably. His green eyes are wild with terror, and his thin chest heaves with every shallow breath.

"Hey, look at me. It's just a nightmare. You're safe. I'll not let anyone hurt you, Eli." Cyril brings both of Eli's trembling hands to his lips and lays small kisses on them. "Don't be scared. You're safe, Eli."

Eli is too petrified to object to the kisses or to pull back his hands. He just sits dazed against the headboard while trying to steady his breathing.

"S-Someone...No...a-a lot of people...tried to kill me," Eli whimpers.

"It was a nightmare, Eli." Cyril caresses Eli's cheek. "It's not real."

"B-But I could feel the pain. It felt so real. I-I..." Eli chokes. "I-I can't see their faces. They all blurred out. But t-this person had...had a long knife...a long, silver knife and he...he shoved it straight into my chest, where my heart was...A-And, he kept on stabbing me...over and over again."

"What?" Cyril's face turns ashen. The hand cupping Eli's cheek falls to the mattress.

"He was trying to rip my heart out. B-But, instead of a mercy kill, he avoided stabbing at my heart. H-He kept on grinding the knife deep into my chest. A-And I...I didn't die. I couldn't die. I-I couldn't do anything, but... but watch him kill me slowly...painfully...and repeatedly. A-And there were... There was a lot of blood...dripping from a table in front of where I stood..." Eli retches.

Cyril quickly carries Eli to the bathroom so he can puke into the toilet.

All the while, the ravenhead gently pats Eli's back and whispers sweet, reassuring words in his ear. Cyril is extremely patient and waits for Eli to stop throwing up completely before carrying him back to their bedroom.

Cyril puts Eli on his bed instead, as Eli's mattress has dampened with sweat. He swiftly changes Eli's pajamas and wraps the blanket around him.

When Eli still shows signs that he won't stop panicking anytime soon, Cyril gets into bed with him and holds Eli tight in his arms.

It takes over thirty minutes for Eli to fully recover from the intense panic attack. He slowly breaks off the hug. "Thank you. I'm fine now."

They were so close that Eli could hear Cyril's heartbeat. He can still feel the warmth from his legal guardian's firm chest...

Is it him, or has his relationship with Cyril been progressed at an abnormally accelerated rate?

No.

No.

No.

I'm not gay. This is just a very strong...bromance. Cyril is his...his legal guardian. Cyril obviously adores him like a little brother. Yeah, it's brotherhood—a *pure* and beautiful brotherhood.

"Urg, my head hurts." Eli rubs his temples.

"Let me get you some hot honey lemon tea," Cyril suggests and hops off the bed.

Eli pulls Cyril's arm back. "No, no. That won't help. Do you have something stronger? Like a pint of vodka would be awesome."

"Excuse me?" Cyril's face distorts.

Eli repeats himself, and Cyril denies a direct request from him for the first time. "No. You can't have vodka, Eli."

"You can give me a few slices of bread to go with the vodka. You know vodka is...actually a vegetarian drink. It's made from vegetables. So, in a sense, it's vegetable, and it's very healthy for the gut."

Cyril glances at the wall clock, then turns back to the little horror in the bed. "It's 6:30 in the morning, Eli."

"Okay, two shots, then." Eli puts up two shaking fingers.

Cyril inhales sharply.

"Fine, one shot." Eli gives his guardian doe eyes. "Please. Just give me one shot, and you'll be the best guardian that ever lived."

Cyril sits down on the bed and squeezes Eli's hand. "I don't drink, so I have no alcohol in the house, Eli."

* * *

"Wow," Eli utters, impressed by the view before him.

Under the mid-morning sun, the lake gleams with various gold and emerald shades that gradate throughout its glassy surface. The white, dainty lily pads floating on top of the shimmery water are like fine pearls embroidered on a silk veil, accentuating the lake's beauty. Numerous wildflower bushes of bright, cheerful colors trim the bank and evenly spread out on the misty jade grass. Thickets of soft green and yellow willow, beech, pine, and almond blossom trees line the edge of the lake and stretch out to the lush mounds and silent hills afar. The scenery is so dreamy and enchanting that it looks like a landscape painting instead of real life.

"It's beautiful, isn't it?" Cyril beams, carrying Eli in his arms.

"It's like a fairytale." Eli gapes and lolls his head around to view the landscape. "It's super lit, man!"

"What?! Where's the fire?!" Cyril panics and looks around for fire.

"Oh, no. There's no fire. Sorry, lit means cool." Eli grins, embarrassed. "Super lit means super cool."

"You're cold? I bring a blanket with me. Let me get it!" Cyril puts Eli down on the green grass.

Eli facepalms himself for his inept hipsterness and explains to Cyril that lit and cool means great, excellent, and exciting. As he expects, Cyril looks baffled yet quite amused after being enlightened with the 21st-century slang.

"You've never ceased to amaze me, mast—Eli. Even after you lost your memory and the ability to read and write, you're still a remarkable wordsmith! At my age, I can still learn a lot from you!" Cyril fawns, hands clasped together, and blue eyes sparkling with adoration and genuine admiration.

If it wasn't for the absolute sincerity in those puppy blue eyes, Eli would be positive that Cyril was mocking him. But he can see Cyril actually means what he says, and that makes Eli facepalm himself even harder.

"Cyril, please...don't take every word I said seriously. And please don't take after my phraseology, or you'll become unpopular real quick among your peers and the folks in town," Eli tells Cyril with a sour face.

"No way," Cyril disagrees while laying a red gingham cotton picnic blanket on the grass. "I learned everything from you. The man I am today is all thanks to your relentless guidance and exceptional teaching."

"Oh, really? I'm glad. Can you remind me how old we were when we first met?"

"You picked me up when I was six," Cyril answers, taking the food out of the straw picnic basket. Two seconds later, he turns to Eli, who's narrowing his eyes at him.

"Teen." Cyril flashes a charming grin. "I was sixteen when we met. Sandwich?"

"So I was around nine then." Eli takes a bite of the sandwich; it's egg and avocado. "Holy sh—avocado?! There's avocado in this period?!"

"Oh yes, it's a quite popular fruit in this country. We use it in salads, main dishes, breakfast, lunch, and dinner. There's this avocado ranch not very far from—"

"Okay, good to know. Let's get back to the previous topic, shall we?" Eli gives Cyril a half smile.

"A-Alright." Cyril stops yammering. His beautiful face falls like a scared little pup in front of his owner after breaking something.

Despite his best efforts, Eli is still somewhat affected by Cyril's extremely cute, sad puppy face, and the fact that he is an ex-dog owner doesn't help.

However, after several long seconds of consideration, Eli decides not to let Cyril give him the runaround like last evening. He adjusts his sitting posture and puts on a straight face. "You said we met when I was nine and you were sixteen, correct?"

Cyril nods.

"And you said the nine-year-old me taught you how to read and write?"

"Yes, that's right."

"Listen to yourself. Can you hear how ridiculous you sound?"

"No. Not at all," Cyril answers. "You did take me in, gave me my name, and taught me everything I know today."

"A nine-year-old kid did all of that?"

"The nine-year-old you," Cyril corrects him. "And yes, you did all of that."

Eli takes another bite of the sandwich. After he finishes chewing and swallows the bit, he looks up at the ravenhead. "Cyril, do you think I'm an idiot?"

"I would never dare to think that!" Cyril's face blanches.

Eli says nothing but shoots him a brooding gaze—while taking another bite of the avocado sandwich; it's a really good sandwich, and the chef is also really good-looking. Too bad he is a fudging terrible liar.

"Well, the truth is..." Cyril falters.

"Uh-huh. The truth is what?"

"You were a prodigy. You were extremely well-read and had a vast knowledge of many subjects. That was the reason why you were able to teach me many things despite your young age."

"What?" Eli puts down the sandwich. Incredulity and imminent ire fall over his soft baby face.

"B-Before you throw that sandwich at me, please let me tell you everything first." Cyril gulps. When he sees Eli go back to eating, albeit still eyeing him suspiciously, Cyril begins to tell Eli the story of their past.

According to Cyril, Eli came from an unknown but influential family from a small region. Cyril doesn't know much about Eli's parents because Eli didn't tell him anything about them. Eli was raised by his relatives. From a young age, Eli was deemed an exceptionally intelligent and beautiful young master. One day, Eli was out in town and saw the sixteen-year-old Cyril struggle on the street, being cruelly beaten up by others. Eli pitied the unfortunate teen and asked if he wanted to come home with Eli. The teen said yes, and they began living together at Eli's relatives' estate. Eli gave the older boy the name Cyril, which meant nobility, and taught him how to read and write. They became very close to each other. Four years later, on Eli's thirteen birthday, Eli and his relatives got into a heated disagreement; Cyril didn't know the reason for the conflict. Eli decided to move out and brought Cyril with him. Because Eli was still a minor, he made Cyril his guardian to legalize the process.

They moved to another land, settled in this town, built the storybook cottage in the forest, and lived a very happy and trouble-free life together. But just a year later, one afternoon, Cyril was busy and didn't pay attention to the fourteen-year-old Eli, who was reading in the front yard. When Cyril came outside to get him, Eli was gone. Cyril went mad looking for him and even returned to Eli's relatives' estate, as he thought the relatives had something to do with Eli's disappearance. But he was dismayed to learn that the estate had been burned to the ground, and everyone who lived there had perished. Despite hitting a dead end, Cyril still didn't give up. He searched for Eli for years until four nights ago, when Cyril finally found his beloved young master in the Forbidden Forest and brought him home. Though Eli has lost all of his memories and doesn't remember him, Cyril believes that one day—

"Wait, wait, hold on," Eli raises a hand to stop Cyril. "What do you mean four nights ago? It's three nights: that night in the forest, then the next day, when we first talked to each other, and then yesterday we went to town. That's three days. When is the fourth?"

"Oh, you actually slept for an entire day when I brought you home that night in the forest. You woke up the day after," Cyril explains.

"What?! And you only tell me this now?!"

"Please, don't be mad." Cyril strokes Eli's back and gives him a glass of honey milk. "I forgot to tell you that because I was so happy that you were back with me. I could hardly think of anything else."

Eli's face softens, though those green eyes still glint with a slight temper as he slowly sips the milk and watches the ravenhead.

Cyril does the same. He returns his precious young master's stare with adoring eyes. Then he can't hold back himself and pulls Eli into a tight hug. "I'm so, SO happy that you're right here in front of me. Oh, Eli! I'm so happy I can die!"

"Dude, calm down." Eli grimaces but doesn't push Cyril away. He even pats the ravenhead's back. "You're literally my only family here. Who's gonna teach me anything about this world if you die? So stop saying that."

"Y-You're right!" Cyril's laugh is boisterous and full of joy. "Don't you worry, Eli! I'm a very strong and healthy man, and I'm sure we'll live a very long and happy life together!"

"I hope so, too," Eli mutters. He hopes this new life will be a little longer than the previous and that he will die of old age in a soft bed rather than three bullets in the chest.

* * *

DESPITE THE DECLARATION the night before, Cyril brings a lot of sweets to the picnic and lets Eli eat as much as he likes. He clearly doesn't mind all the mean things Eli told him the night before. Cyril's nurturing and leniency toward Eli touch him, and he apologizes to the ravenhead for his unacceptable behavior from last night. But to Eli's surprise, Cyril is downright shocked when he listens to Eli's apology. When Eli asks him why he reacts that way, Cyril reveals Eli has never apologized to him before—ever.

"What?" Eli raises his brow. "Never?"

Cyril nods.

"That's awful! Why would you tolerate that?"

"Well, you were mostly right about everything. And you are my master. I wouldn't dare to displease you in any way."

"But you are the guardian! You have to teach the kid what's right and wrong!"

"No, Eli. You taught me what's right and wrong," Cyril stutters. "T-There were times that I tried to...Uh, discuss with you about a second opinion, but you...well, I was lucky that you only gave me a good lecture every time."

"I-I can't believe this." Eli gawks at Cyril with wide, incredulous eyes.

"But most of the time, you were very kind and lenient to me," Cyril adds.

"Cyril, you can't let a little kid treat you like a doormat! You need to knock some sense into him and assert your authority!"

"Knock some sense?"

"Meaning you smack his ass until he listens to you," Eli says, and Cyril gasps in fear. "Oh, common, stop being soft. Kids need to be disciplined to grow and learn to respect others. I do not condone physical punishment, but sometimes, a good, old-fashioned spanking is necessary to teach an unruly brat to behave and respect their elders."

Cyril only stares at Eli. A good minute later, the ravenhead slowly nods and mumbles, "I see."

Eli nods with him. But when he sees the strange gleam in Cyril's eyes, he snaps. "Dude! Don't you even dare think about smacking me! If you do, you have another thing coming!"

"Y-Yes." Cyril jumps a little. "O-Of course not, mas—Eli."

Cyril gives his young master a timid smile, then after some thinking, he asks, "But then, what's the point of telling me to...assert my authority...to you?"

"Who says you can assert your guardian authority to me?" Eli crosses his arms. "I'm not that little brat who mistreated you back then."

"Why are you referring to yourself in third person, maste—Eli?" Cyril scratches his head. "And also, that little bra—that you and the...old you back then are the same person...so—"

"No, no. Not the same. Cyril, I don't have any memory about my old self, you, or this world I live in, so you can't count me as the same person back then. And based on your story and actions, you seemed absolutely fine, letting that 'old me' treat you awfully. That's not right, Cyril!"

"Right." Cyril dumbly nods.

"Cyril, my man, I promise you those days are long over, and you'll never be disrespected like that ever again." Eli pats his handsome guardian on the shoulder.

Cyril gawks at Eli, recalling their "conversation" before bed last night. He gives Eli a dry laugh. "Very lit. Anything you say...Eli."

"Hey, Cyril. Are you sure that is all? The story of my life?" Eli asks with his eyes closed and the straw hat Cyril bought him yesterday over his face.

"Yes, that's all, Eli," Cyril answers calmly, blue eyes gazing at the blue sky. They are basking in the sun next to each other on the picnic blanket.

"Did you leave any part out?"

"No, I did not. Unless you want me to go into details like what subjects you taught me or what you did when you were mad at me."

"No, that's okay. I've already felt guilty enough for being a little turd to you, even though it wasn't really me but my ex-counterpart," Eli mumbles in a flat voice.

"What does 'turd' mean?" Cyril's brows furrow.

"A gigantic piece of dung."

"Oh no, please don't say that!" Cyril gasps. "You have always been an absolute angel to me!"

"Stop brown-nosing, dude. From now on, you're welcome to cuss at me whenever I'm a jerk to you," Eli says. "And trust me, I know I can be extremely obnoxious at times. I know myself well."

"Oh no, I wouldn't dare do that." Cyril shudders.

Eli sighs, then continues. "The reason I asked if there's more to the story is because I believe I have a superpower, Cyril."

Cyril's eyebrows rise.

"The day I met you, earlier that day, I almost crushed two escorts at a brothel and successfully escaped from a werewolf that tried to make advances on me...or he was just trying to eat me. Hard to tell."

"WHAT?!" Cyril shrieks, bolting up from the picnic blanket.

"Jesus, my ears!" Eli flinches, and the straw hat falls off from his face. He turns to Cyril and sees his guardian gawking at him with blue eyes filled with terror and wrath.

"Dude, calm thy tits." Eli sits up and puts his straw hat on Cyril's head. "I'm fine."

"What does 'tits' mean?"

"You don't need to learn that word. It's for your own good."

"What were you doing at a brothel, Eli? D-Did someone take you there?

Did they f-force you to...to...” Cyril can't finish the question and has to halt to breathe.

“I'm fine, Cyril.” Eli gives his guardian's hand a light squeeze. “I accidentally stumbled into an underground brothel. I didn't engage in any underage prostitution.”

Cyril says nothing, but his jaw clenches, and those blue eyes visibly darken. All the warmth and cheeriness are withdrawn from his face faster than a receding tide.

Eli is not a fan of serious, moody Cyril, as he is almost a different person to the silly, smiley Cyril that Eli has gotten used to.

“I'm fine, Cyril. Really.” Eli gives his guardian a slight pat in the chest.

Cyril catches Eli's hand. His long fingers gently caress the soft flesh of Eli's palm. Then he returns the straw hat to Eli's head and speaks in a tender voice. “Eli, I've wanted to ask you about what happened to you before I found you that night. But I didn't do it because I was afraid I would put you in a bad mood by forcing you to recall unpleasant memories. I did plan to ask you about it after we get home later today. But now that I've learned about how atrocious and serious the circumstances were, I just can't wait for the right time anymore. Eli, I beseech you to please tell me everything that happened to you that day, anything that you can remember, the names of the people you met, those who hurt you, how they hurt you, and what they look like. Please don't leave out any details, no matter how small or seemingly insignificant they seem. I swear to you I will make—I will bring those that did you wrong to justice!”

“O-Okay,” Eli nods and begins to tell his guardian about his epic-fail journey when he was resurrected into this strange world.

When Eli tells Cyril the part of the musical werewolf, the ravenhead suddenly leans his entire body so close to Eli that their noses almost touch. Eli falls back to the picnic blanket. “W-What are you doing?!”

“Shh,” Cyril shushes while on top of him, though he makes sure their bodies don't touch each other. Then he springs his left hand to grab something on the grass above Eli's head.

Eli lets out a frightened gasp when he sees a big-ass green snake with long fangs wrapping around Cyril's toned arm and hissing menacingly at the ravenhead. Cyril then turns and casually throws the snake toward the woods, away from their picnic spot.

Cyril's movement is exceptionally swift, clean, and effortless. Eli gawks as the snake hisses one last time before disappearing into the blue sky.

Eli glances at the snake pitcher and sees him wiping his left hand with a linen cloth. Cyril then turns to him and offers him his right hand.

"Would you like to get up?" The ravenhead flashes Eli a charming smile.

Eli takes his hand, gets up, and sits stumped before he stutters, "What the hell was that?"

"Don't mind it, Eli. Just a little snake. Please continue. You were talking about the werewolf playing the clarinet."

"Cyril, you just pitched a snake like a baseball! D-Did it bite you?" Eli grabs Cyril's hands to check for any injury.

"Are you worried about me?" Cyril chuckles, gazing softly at Eli.

"Of course I am," Eli sighs in relief when he sees no bite marks on Cyril's hands. After hearing the answer, Cyril pulls him into another bear hug. "G-Get off me!"

"You're so adorable, Eli. Thank you for worrying about me!" Cyril gives him heart-eyes. "Aww, Eli. My sweet, precious Eli! What do you like, Eli? I'll give you anything you want!"

"Thanks. You already bought me everything I need," Eli says.

"Just remember, Eli, if there's anything that you want, let me know, and I'll give it to you! No matter what!"

"Thanks, man." Eli nods. "Actually, a bottle of vodka would be awesome!"

Cyril's face drops. "Anything except alcohol, Eli. Do you want me to be thrown in jail and you to become an orphan?"

"Pretend I never asked that." Eli coolly sips the lemon tea from a teacup.

Cyril ruffles the Eli's brown hair. "Alright, please continue the story. We were at the part where the werewolf pulled out a golden clarinet."

* * *

"And that's everything," Eli concludes the tale of his peculiar adventures. "Crazy, isn't it?"

Cyril doesn't respond. He just sits there with a stone-cold, gloomy face. The air surrounding them is uncomfortably thick with negative energy.

"Hello?" Eli waves at his guardian.

Cyril unexpectedly pulls Eli to his chest and wraps his arms around Eli's thin body. Though his embrace is strong, Eli can feel the tremors and the racing heartbeats in the ravenhead's firm chest.

"Holy Tathagatas, Eli! I can't believe how many times I could have lost you again just in one night. I'm so, so sorry, Eli! Please forgive me for coming to you so late!" Cyril weeps.

...Here we go again.

* * *

It takes Cyril a long time to calm down, much longer than Eli expected. Cyril has had multiple meltdowns and cried his eyes out. He blames himself and apologizes to Eli again and again. His sobbing is so intense that the passersby throw Eli contemptuous glances, thinking Eli is bullying Cyril.

Being a concerned housemate, Eli lifts his caregiver's spirit by telling him to get a grip. "Dude, you're such a drama queen! I, the victim, didn't even cry about it, so what the heck are you blubbering about?! You drop this embarrassing act right now. Sit up straight and talk to me like a normal person!"

"B-But—"

"No but! Let go of me! Why the hell are you clinging to me like a desperate chick begging for the boyfriend to return?" Eli fumes.

It takes a little more time for Cyril to fully revert to his usual non-hysterical self. The ravenhead adjusts his sitting posture and apologizes for acting like a hot mess.

"Eli...were you afraid when you...were chased by those creatures?" Cyril sniffs, holding Eli's hands in his.

"No," Eli responds right away, but a couple of seconds later, he mutters, "Actually, I was."

Cyril's face once again fills with pain.

"But you got me out of there. Now I have you and somewhere that I belong to. I'm not afraid anymore." Eli looks Cyril in the eyes. "I hope I will never be chased by monsters again in this life."

"Eli, as long as I'm alive, I promise you will never be in the same horrendous situations or hardships ever again," Cyril promises, then gently kisses those smaller hands in his palms.

"Thank you...Cyril." Eli decides to look past the kiss. He wonders if it makes him an easy person in this world since he has been hand-kissed a lot recently, and by two dudes: Mister Snow White, and his dashing pirate-wannabe neighbor.

"I swear to you, I will kill that werewolf that dared to lay its claws on you."

"Sure." Eli nods unthinkingly. But shortly after his brain has grasped what Cyril just told him, he looks at his guardian in horror. "What the fu—Absolutely not! What the hell are you saying?!"

Cyril firmly repeats it, but Eli interrupts him before he can finish.

"Dude! You're not going after that werewolf, or the witch, or any person I mentioned in my story!"

"They hurt you," Cyril says in a solemn voice. "They have to pay."

Eli takes a deep breath and opens his mouth. The words that come out are less than pleasant, even though no profanity is used. Eli gives his housemate a long harangue, which ends with a threat of leaving home and never returning if Cyril goes out to avenge his "honor."

Instantly, the fearsome, bloodthirsty wolf poofs back into a scared little pup and jumps to Eli's lap, begging him not to leave.

"No, Eli, please don't ever do that! I would truly die if I were to ever lose you again this time," Cyril pleads, clinging to Eli like a koala in a burned-down forest with only a tree left.

"Only if you promise not to go after that werewolf!" Eli tries to push his guardian away but fails to do so as Cyril's grip is super-strong. "Or any of the shady-ass individuals in my story, or I'll leave the house with a bottle of vodka and never come back, join a gang, go to a casino, and watch a strip show at a brothel in Creepyville!"

That was an incredibly tactless and stupid threat, even for his airhead guardian. Only a true idiot would be intimidated by it. However, Eli has perhaps given Snow White's intelligence too much credit. To Eli's utter disbelief, Cyril takes his obvious empty threat seriously and makes an expression that mirrors the painting "The Scream."

"Noooo, Eli. Nooooo," Cyril cries, both hands clasped on his cheeks. "Not the gang! Not the casino! Nooooo! How can you say such things?!"

Dude, you've got to be kidding me! You actually bought it?! Eli facepalms but still keeps a smug look on the outside and declares, "If you don't listen to me, I'll do all of that. Try me!"

"Alright! I promise I'll not go after those wretches myself. In return, you have to promise me that you'll never do such awful things like that!" Cyril agrees.

"Okay, I won't if you keep your promise," Eli answers, nose in the air.

Poor Cyril looks traumatized, and yet he can only helplessly stare at his rebellious young master. He doesn't dare to reprimand or upset him. The ravenhead then swipes off the rolling sweat on his forehead with his arm. He gulps down a bottle of water offhandedly instead of drinking from a glass like usual, showing how shocked he is still after listening to Eli's outrageous threat. A moment later, he mutters, almost to himself, "I can't believe you are just as wild as I was as in my youth. I would never have guessed it."

"What do you mean?" Eli asks, eating a mini strawberry tart.

"It means I adore you more and more each day, Eli." Cyril gives Eli a playful flick on his nose. "I adore you so much I want to give you the world!"

THEY SPEND the afternoon eating delicious snacks, breathing fresh air, and enjoying the dreamy landscape. Sometimes later, in the midafternoon, Cyril gives Eli a piggyback ride for a stroll in the park.

Turns out, this place is an enormous arboretum with many greenhouses that preserve various exotic plants from around the world. They visit every botanical exhibition available in the summer season. Eli is highly impressed and astounded by the meticulous details and work in everything he sees. His initial subjective impression regarding this world as primitive has shattered, and his eagerness to properly learn about the land he lives in grows. He asks his guardian questions about the nation and its ruler.

"What is the name of this country we live in?"

"It's called Aspenia, Eli," Cyril smiles.

"Aspen like the tree?" Eli wonders.

"There is a tree called Aspen?"

"Yeah, that tree over there is an Aspen tree," Eli points in the tree's direction.

"Oh, I didn't know that. Thank you for teaching me, maste—Eli!"

"No problem! Can you remind me about the name of the ruler again?" Eli requests, "He's called Ha-something."

"Haemon. That's his name," Cyril answers.

"Mmm, what an interesting name! I wonder what its meaning is?" Eli ponders.

"It means bloody in Elgarian."

"Oh." Eli gulps. Awkward. "Hold on, we're from Aspenia, but the language we speak is called Elgarian and not Aspenish or Aspenese?"

Cyril laughs so hard that his large shoulders shake. Eli figures he probably just asked a really stupid question.

"Oh, my precious Eli, you really don't remember anything, do you?" Cyril turns to look at Eli on his back. His blue eyes are soft and full of affection.

Eli candidly shakes his head.

Cyril goes on to give Eli a brief history of Aspenia. This country was discovered by a group of Elgarians thousands of years ago. It was originally a colony of Elga but gradually gained its independence. Back then, Aspenia was divided into twelve realms until Emperor Haemon successfully united the lands and turned them into one nation called Aspenia.

"That's so impressive!" Eli exclaims. "What is your opinion about our Emperor, Cyril? Is he a good king? Do you like him? Despite the bloody name, people seem to have a favorable view of him from what I've seen when we were in town yesterday."

"Ooh! I'm not really keen on politics, Eli. But if you want my opinion, I think he's alright. And the nation seems to do well under his reign compared to the chaotic state it was years ago. Right now, there are many ongoing wars around the world. Yet Aspenia is one of a few nations that is enjoying a long, peaceful period. I guess that's why people hold the Emperor in high regard," Cyril says, then giving Eli a soft but amused smile. "You seem to be interested in the Emperor. Would you like to meet him someday?"

"Um...I think I'll pass, thank you. And I'm not interested in the Emperor but the world that we live in. You see, I have absolutely no knowledge or any ideas about this land or its culture, and I would hate to be oblivious on top of being an illiterate and useless bum that I already am." Eli sighs.

"Eh? No! Don't say that, Eli. You're not useless at all!"

"Cyril, you're piggybacking a crippled man that can't read or write. If that's not a definition of useless, then I don't know what is anymore."

"You are sixteen, Eli. And you were...kidnapped for...three years! And you lost all of your memory, so I believe you deserve a pass this time," Cyril opines.

"You're right, I keep forgetting I'm only seventeen—"

"Sixteen," Cyril corrects him.

"Cyril, when's my birthday here?"

"It's on Saturday the twenty-eighth, the last day of July."

"How is that the last day of July?" Eli asks.

Cyril stops walking and turns around to stare at Eli like he were a talking donkey.

"Hello? I got amnesia," Eli taps Cyril's shoulder.

Cyril grins and apologizes. Then he explains that the people here use a calendar with 13 months and 28 days each. The first day of the month is always on Sunday, and the last day is on Saturday. The day after December 28 is New Year's Day. In the leap year, there are two New Year's Days. Today is the 20th of Vairo, the month between June and July.

"Oh...I see," Eli mumbles and then converts his birthday of August 12 to the new calendar. After a few seconds, he gets the July 28 result. "Dang! We actually share the same birthday! That's creepy!" Eli tightens his arms around his guardian's neck.

"Who are 'we'? You and...?" Cyril asks, baffled.

"And your master. My younger counterpart in this world," Eli mutters. "This is confusing, man."

"I'm not sure why you keep separating yourself into two different entities. I wonder if that's part of a normal adolescent phase."

"When's your birthday, Cyril?" Eli asks.

"Um, I'm afraid I might scare you with the answer."

"Why would I be scared of the answer, dude?"

"Alright, my birthday is on the same day as yours. The last day of July." Cyril chuckles

"Eh? Really?! Cool!" Eli exclaims, intrigued but not creeped out.

"You're cold? Let me take out the blanket—"

"No, cool here means nice, man. And keep that blanket in the bag! It's super-hot right now!"

"Oh, alright!" Cyril laughs. "Eli, you're not bothered that we share the same birthday?"

"Why would I be bothered?"

"But then you're concerned that you and your previous—I mean younger self share the same birthday?" Cyril asks.

"It's difficult to explain, man." Eli sighs. "Cyril, you would hate me if I'm really not your master, wouldn't you?"

"Didn't we go through this last night?" Cyril responds with a lifted brow.

"But w-what if I'm never going to remember our past? What if I'll never return to be the same person who you once grew to like and care for? Would you resent me for it?"

Cyril halts and tilts his head to look at Eli. His eyes are so blue and beautiful that it makes Eli fluster. Cyril's lips move, and the words that come out are as tender as the expression on his gorgeous face. "Then can we get to know each other again, Eli?"

Eli doesn't know how to respond to that question, and his face involuntarily recoils behind his guardian's broad shoulder, just like a little turtle hiding in his shell.

"I really like you, Eli, both back then and even more now. Will you allow me to get to know you properly once again?" Cyril beams. His smile is as bright and lovely as the sunflower of summer.

A gusty wind passes by and whisks up the fallen yellow petals on the cobblestone path into the air, creating a brief flower rain. The sun is less harsh than it was an hour ago, and its rays coruscate on the flitting petals, making them twinkle like golden fairy dust. The blooming cassia flowers are undoubtedly beautiful, yet they will never be as striking as the smile Cyril is giving Eli right now.

Eli's heart begins to thump. It takes him a while to utter a clumsy response, "Dude, stop hitting on a minor. Do you want to go to jail or something?"

"H-Hit on? I-I would never dare raise a hand at you, Eli!"

"Dude, no! Hit on means flirt. Are you for real?" Eli huffs.

"Oh...ohhhhhh!" Cyril flushes red; the sweet sunflower has now turned into a hibiscus; he hurriedly splutters. "S-Sorry, Eli. I-I—"

"Okay, Okay, Cyril, calm down, my man," Eli steadies Cyril's head so he can look straight and watches for the path ahead. "I got you, man. Of course, we're going to get to know each other. Heck, haven't we been doing that all day today? The only steps left are to braid each other's hair and paint our toenails. Dude, I'll be honest with you. I have never warmed up to *anyone* as fast as I am to you. Our relationship progresses faster than the Juno spacecraft, man! In fact, I think we need to slow down a little bit."

"Huh? What? Who's Juno? What is a spacecraft? What?" Cyril's head turns around to Eli for an explanation.

"Keep your eyes on the road, please," Eli instructs as they enter the rainforest building.

"Don't worry, Eli. I promise not to let you fall off my arms again! I'll hold you tight no matter what!"

"Heh, you better, man. If you drop me— Holy sh—is that an anaconda?!" Eli gasps and turns Cyril's head to the right.

Before them is a large glass cage with intricate wrought iron trim. Inside is a mid-size jungle and a *huge* anaconda that idly lounges on a metal pole, ogling at them with its half-opened amber eyes.

Eli looks at the size of the snake and swallows hard. He nudges his guardian's shoulders. "Hey, Cyril, I think we should visit other buildings."

"Are you afraid of snakes, Eli?" Cyril sounds very amused, and it hurts Eli's manly pride.

"Well, this is not a snake, dude! It's a giant anaconda! That's like six times the average size of a regular anaconda...Shoot! It's close to a hundred and twenty feet long! Uh-uh, get out of here right now, man. I'm not spending another second in this place. You should already know by now that I'm jinxed, and you don't want to take any risk!" Eli frantically shakes Cyril's shoulders.

"What is an anaconda? This snake, you mean?" Cyril doesn't share Eli's fear.

"Yes, Cyril, anaconda is the name for a type of large snake. And this one here is the biggest anaconda I've ever seen! Can we go now? Oh, and don't forget that you slung a snake earlier this morning! This anaconda might detect the scent of its kin on your body. This is too risky, man. Let's go!" Eli urges Cyril, inspecting the anaconda behind the glass cage.

"Alright, my young master, your wish is my command." Cyril chuckles. "Oh, and don't worry, Eli. This snake is not that big. I've seen worse. And the glass is enchanted, so it won't break easily. Even if it broke, I will protect you, Eli." Cyril turns and gives Eli a wink.

"Huh? Hold on, enchanted? You've seen worse? What?" Eli is swamped with unexpected information.

"Yeah, the glass is enchanted. You couldn't crack it even if you used an iron ax on it!" Cyril explains.

"Wow, this is so cool, Cyril!" Eli gapes at the glass cage. "Then can we stay for a little bit? I want to take a look at the anaconda."

"Of course, Eliiiiiiii—" Cyril's voice drags, and Eli suddenly sees his surroundings fly forward at an ultra-rapid speed. Then his view abruptly winds to a sharp forty-five-degree angle backward, his green eyes face the ceiling, his back slams to the ground, and his legs around Cyril's waist point up to the sky.

CHAPTER 8

FELONY UPON FELONY

Eli isn't sure what Cyril stepped on that caused him to slip and start the entire chain of disasters.

As Cyril skids across the floor and slams face-first into the glass cage holding the giant anaconda, Eli's already fractured knees smash against the unbreakable glass. When Cyril falls backward to the ground with Eli on his back, Eli's head hits the floor, giving him a slight concussion with a very sore back. Then, a nanosecond later, Cyril's head slams straight into Eli's face and breaks his nose. And final-effing-ly, Cyril's entire muscular body smashes on top of Eli's skinny frame, squishing him flat on the hard ground.

That is when a paradox happens. Cyril, a six-foot-three man, doesn't look like he weighs too much, despite his ripped physique. Yet when this clumsy mother-trucker falls on top of Eli, in that brief moment, Eli really thinks this is the end for him. His heart momentarily stops as if an elephant were sitting on top of him.

Snow White ends up dislocating both of Eli's shoulders, bruising his chest and back, and unintentionally breaking his knees and nose.

"OH NOOOO! NOOO! ELI! Eli, are you alright?!" Snow White shrieks as he hastily tries to get up to check on Eli.

Eli is too hurt to respond or move, as he lies in a very unattractive pose. He lets out an agonizing cry when Cyril touches his disjointed shoulders.

"I-It's alright! I'll fix you," Cyril rambles, utterly frightened. "Oh, Eli! I'm so sorry! Your nose! Your shoulders! I'm sorry. Please forgive me! Uh?" Cyril balks when he sees blood droplets dribble on Eli's face. Cyril touches his nose and discovers it is also broken.

Cyril awkwardly cleans off the blood on his young master's dazed face with a handkerchief. Then he gently clutches Eli's left shoulder. "Please bear with me. It'll be over in a few seconds!"

"W-What are you doing?" Eli murmurs, immobilized with pain.

"I'm going to put your shoulders back in place. Please stay still!" Cyril declares, and Eli's eyes widen in terror.

"NO! Absolutely not! Get your hands— AHHHHHH!" Eli howls.

Cyril soothes him. "Now I'll fix your right shoulder, and that'll be it, alright? Very fast and painless! I promise!"

"W-Wait! Hold on, you—AHHHHHH! You fud—" Eli huffs, his fingers curled up and hackles rising. He will strangle Cyril if both his arms aren't killing him. "Y-You lit—little—"

"See! Your shoulders are back to normal now! Oh, I know it's painful. I'm so sorry, Eli." Cyril gives Eli an encouraging hug.

"Cyril, you—oh!" Eli's swear gets stuck in his throat when the sight behind Cyril catches his attention. "O-Oh shit!"

"I'm so, so sorry. You can yell at me all you want, but after we get you to the doctor first, alright?" Cyril scoops Eli up from the ground.

"B-Behind you!" Eli cries. Cyril turns around, and both jump when they see a large crack forming on the enchanted, "unbreakable" glass into which Cyril slammed his face.

"Y-You told me the glass was enchanted!" Eli berates, fretfully watching every movement of the giant anaconda behind the glass cage.

"I-It is enchanted and unbreakable...B-But don't worry, Eli, it's just a slight crack—" Just before Cyril finishes his optimistic statement, the crack starts to disperse rapidly. "Oh, shoot!"

"Oh my God! The giant anaconda is going to get out! Crap! Crap! Crap!" Eli panics. "Go! Go now!"

Cyril runs to the exit with Eli in his arms. But then he stops and returns to the cage, putting Eli on the ground.

"W-What are you doing?!" Eli squeals. "Dude, we have to run and call for help!"

"I got this!" Cyril announces with a reassuring smile. Then he turns around and holds his hands up to the glass cage.

An enormous, roaring blaze in the form of a red phoenix soars from Cyril's palms to the cracked surface, creating a wall of flame. The scene is so epic that it makes Cyril look like a God unleashing his power.

Eli is mad-impressed for three seconds. But after that, he realizes how stupid Cyril's action is. "Cyril, what the hell are you doing? Please don't tell me you're trying to mend the crack with fire!"

If you do, you're an effing idiot! Eli thinks and prays he is wrong.

But to Eli's dismay, Cyril turns to him and says, "Isn't fire used to make glass?"

"You're freaking kidding me, right?! Stop shooting fire at the glass, or it will explo—"

The glass cage bursts into thousands of pieces that rain down onto the ground. Cyril immediately dashes to Eli's side and shields him from the broken shards. Then they hear a shrill hiss from behind. They turn around and are horrified to find the flame has spread into the little jungle inside the cage, and the giant anaconda is on fire.

"Crap!" Eli screams as the burning snake throws itself everywhere in an attempt to put out the fire. But that only makes the flame spread to the entire building.

"I have to help that snake!" Cyril cries.

"Yes—wait, no! Not you! You'll kill that snake and both of us!" Eli snaps and pulls Cyril's shoulder.

Luckily, a group of people who appear to be the vivarium supervisors comes to their rescue. Two of them check on Eli while the rest approach Cyril, who briefly explains what happened. Like Cyril, the vivarium supervisors also have magical powers. Still, none of them possesses hydrokinesis. Thus, they end up having to put out the fire in the uncool, mortal way: throwing buckets of water to extinguish the flame.

An hour later, Cyril and the supervisor group successfully defeat the blaze and save the day. Luckily, no one has perished from the incident, including the giant anaconda, unconscious and burned, as it is carted out in an extra-long stretcher carried by a group of brawny men. Eli's stretcher follows after the snake's.

Needless to say, their picnic ends in a total disaster. Despite being injured and pissed, Eli grabs Cyril's hand when he is lying on the stretcher. "Cyril, are you going to be in trouble? I can testify for you."

"T-Trouble? What are you saying, Eli?" Cyril looks surprised.

"Cyril, are you aware that you just literally committed arson, vandalism, and animal cruelty?" Eli croaks with difficulty.

Cyril pauses, then shrugs and flashes Eli a toothy grin. "Don't worry about me, Eli. I will be fine!"

"You better! I will deal with you when we're home!" Eli snaps and shoots his guardian a glare.

"Y-Yes, maste—Eli!" Cyril jumps.

"FYI, I'll join a gang if you're in jail," Eli reminds him with a mean scowl, and poor Cyril looks terrified.

* * *

ELI LOOKS at his reflection in a hand mirror. He can barely recognize himself. He looks as if he just had plastic surgery or is a model from a child abuse poster. His entire head and nose are wrapped in white bandages; his cheeks and lips are bruised and swollen due to being smacked by Cyril's iron head—unintentionally. Who would believe all of these injuries were accumulated from a picnic trip instead of a fistfight? Heck! He wasn't even this beat up when he faced a flying werewolf, a witch, a mob, and a group of headless ghosts a few days ago!

So much for having a caretaker! Eli thinks furiously and puts the hand mirror on his bedside table.

It's the morning after the picnic incident. Eli was admitted to a medical clinic in the arboretum and wasn't released until late last night. On the way home, Eli dozed off in the carriage beside Cyril. It's now 9:30 AM. Eli awakes in bed, and Cyril is nowhere to be seen.

"Cyril!" Eli calls for his guardian, his voice hoarse.

Eli moves his bandaged legs to the floor to see if he can walk at all. He gets an instant answer when a deep, excruciating pain flares from his kneecaps and spreads to his entire body. His face turns white as he lets out a painful whimper.

The bedroom door opens, and Cyril walks in. He panics upon seeing Eli's pained face and rushes to pick him up and put him back to bed. "Eli, what are you doing?!"

"Where were you?" Eli frowns, sore and annoyed.

"I was downstairs talking to—" A loud gasp interrupts Cyril. Eli looks toward the bedroom door and finds Haidar and Mariposa standing there. Their faces fill with shock and horror.

"Maste—Eli! What happened to you?!" Mariposa approaches his bed with Haidar.

"Who did this to you?!" Haidar asks, his face concerned and angry.

The surprised appearance of the neighbors baffles Eli. He's about to answer them, and two more people come to the room: Gallahan and pirate-wannabe Wolfgang. Like Haidar and Mariposa, Eli's mummy face knocks Gallahan and Wolfgang's socks off as both gape at him, furious and appalled.

"Who dare did this to you?!" Gallahan growls as he and Wolfgang stride toward Eli's bed.

"Young master, please tell me the name of this fiend who dared lay his hands on you. I'll make sure he pays a steep price for his atrocious crime!" Wolfgang grits his teeth.

While it's super weird to have all of his neighbors meet up in his bedroom again this early in the morning, it's good to know there's a supportive squad behind his back, and their concerns warm his heart. Eli gives his neighbors a crooked smile. "Good morning, everyone. The culprit you're all looking for is here," Eli mercilessly points at Cyril.

The gang simultaneously turns to Cyril and shoots him scalding glares. Eli enjoys the brief, mean satisfaction of seeing Cyril fidget under fire as revenge for yesterday's incident. But when he catches Cyril biting his lips and hanging his head with guilt, Eli's stomach twists uncomfortably. As his clumsy guardian splutters for a coherent explanation, Eli decides to speak for him. "It was an accident. He didn't mean to hurt me."

Eli tells everyone what happened yesterday. After the story ends, Eli is ticked off again at how ridiculous and stupid his guardian handled the situation as he glowers at Cyril.

"I'm sorry, maste—Eli," Cyril apologizes in a low voice. His large puppy eyes droop down, sad and repentant. "You can punish me in any way you please. I won't say a word."

"What the—I will not punish you. Are you nuts?"

"What does 'nuts' mean?" everyone in the room asks at the same time.

"Crazy," Eli says simply.

"Ohh!"

"Well, he is indeed a bit unstable. If you want, I'll gladly be your guardian, maste—Eli." Wolfgang flashes Eli a charming smile.

"You can stay at my place. We have a lot of spare bedrooms," Mariposa suggests. Haidar and Gallahan nod with her.

"You can have your own room," Gallahan comments.

"Hey, nobody is stealing my master. I can't believe all of you are indecent enough to persuade him into leaving me right in front of me, you shameless master-stealing bandits!" Puppy Cyril turns into an aggressive wolf and snarls at his neighbors.

Eli and the neighbors all gasp. "Who did you call a bandit, you clodhopper?!" Gallahan snaps.

"Get outside, and we shall fight until only one man's left standing!" Wolfgang rages.

"You are the youngest one in here, Cyril!" Mariposa says in a very disapproving tone.

Haidar says nothing but rubs his forehead exasperatedly.

Eli doesn't know what the heck is happening, but it looks interesting, so he won't interfere. He is also a bit curious about who might win the fight, as Wolfgang looks even more burly than his guardian. Eli tugs Cyril's sleeve as he's about to retort at the fuming Wolfgang. "Hey Cyril, can you please get me some food first before you spar with our neighbor?"

"Yes, of course! I'm so sorry, I forgot about your meal." Cyril sweeps Eli into his arms and carries him downstairs, yet still not forget to talk smack at his neighbors. "After my master takes his nap, I'll gladly go one-on-one with all of you. But I suggest you should all come at me at the same time to save me the trouble of defeating each of you individually!"

The gang becomes obstreperous at Cyril's cocky statement, and Eli starts to get a headache from the bickering. "Guys! Please, calm down! Why are you all fighting? Don't you think it's too early for a brawl at this hour?"

"Sorry, master," the group apologizes.

"And you, what are you thinking, challenging our neighbors to a fist-fight?" Eli flicks Cyril's bandaged nose, making him wince. "Haven't you committed enough felonies yesterday? Now, you want to add battery to the list? Are you really that desperate to find a boyfriend in jail?"

Cyril scrunches his nose in disgust at the mention of an inmate boyfriend.

* * *

During breakfast, Eli learns that Haidar is a lawyer. After Eli finishes his meal, he sits in the living room with Cyril and their neighbors.

"Haidar, as you've learned the story, would my guardian stand a chance to avoid the possible prosecution?" Eli hands Haidar a cup of tea.

"Ah, thank you, young master—Eli." Haidar takes the teacup with both hands. "Well, for your inquiry, I will have to go on a trip to that place to assess the damage. I still haven't imagined how badly the vivarium was destroyed."

"Quite badly, I'm afraid." Eli takes a shuddering sip of tea and tells Haidar the details of the damage. He gulps when Haidar removes his eyeglasses to shoot an incredulous glance at Cyril. Mariposa, Gallahan, and Wolfgang also do the same thing.

"I'll be fine, Eli." Cyril throws his arm around Eli's shoulder. "Don't worry, I'll not go to jail."

"Heh, isn't that the Peridot Arboretum? One of Emperor Haemon's favorite gardens?" Gallahan comments after taking a sip of tea. "There are twelve major arboretums in Aspenia, and each is considered the nation's pride. There is a grand parade in two months at that place. I guess it'll be canceled now since you've destroyed one of the core conservatories. A very costly mistake you did, *neighbor.*"

"Gallahan." Mariposa sighs.

"T-The Emperor's favorite?!" Eli's back runs cold with sweat. He completely forgets that this nation is an absolute monarchy, and the Emperor has complete power over someone's life. "W-What should we do?"

"The Emperor is a very reasonable person. He won't punish anyone over a blunder they didn't deliberately mean to do." Cyril pats Eli's hair.

"He's right, Eli. Your guardian will not be subjected to any punishment," Mariposa tells him; Wolfgang and Gallahan all nod in agreement.

While Eli is relieved about everyone's positive inputs, he's pretty discombobulated about the idea that Cyril can get off scot-free after severely damaging a significant building of a national garden. When he poses his query, everybody gets tongue-tied momentarily before Haidar replies, "Oh no, Eli. Cyril won't get a free pass for his misdemeanor at the vivarium. We're just talking about the high possibility that he won't face jail time or serious punishment, but he will surely be prosecuted. I suspect a subpoena will be sent to your residence in a few days."

Now, this comment is realistic enough for him to start brooding about! Eli squeezes his bandaged temples. Though he is deeply immersed in serious thoughts, his mummy-wrapped head and scrawny body inadvertently make him appear rather humorous in everyone's eyes.

"I'll be fine, Eli," Cyril giggles, side-hugging Eli. "You're so adorable, worrying about me. Thank you."

"Cyril, this is not a laughing matter," Eli mumbles in distress.

"He'll be fine, Eli," Gallahan reassures him, and so do his parents.

"My beautiful Eli." Captain Seven-Seas suddenly appears in front of Eli and sits on one knee. "Please don't be troubled by those disheartening thoughts. I assure you I'll not let anyone jail this unworthy galoot even though he very much deserves it for damaging a momentous site and accidentally hurting you and an innocent snake. For your ease of mind, I'll make sure no one touches a single hair on your guardian's head and would even break him out of jail if it comes down to it, for he still owes me a duel for honor as well. So please, precious Eli, keep the smile on your face, for I can't bear to see you so sad like now!"

Silence falls over the living room as everyone throws indifferent gazes at the dashing Wolfgang. While Eli is ultra-moved by Wolfgang's attempt at cheering him, he thinks it's a good thing that his entire face is wrapped in bandages, which somewhat restricts his facial muscles from moving at will. Otherwise, he would have burst into an ungracious laughing fit at Captain Seven-Seas' speech.

"T-Thank you, Wolfgang," Eli beams, trying to choke back his laugh. "Please sit." He points at an empty armchair.

"I'll pretend I have not heard anything about jailbreaking." Haidar raises a brow.

"What duel that I owe you?" Cyril inquires, clueless.

"You insulted me an hour ago. You called me a bandit," Wolfgang reminds him, crossing his arms.

"Ohh, that," Cyril exclaims. "Well, all of you did openly try to steal my master! So you all deserve that label, and no one can sway me to take that back!" Cyril disses all his neighbors, causing another uproar.

Eli only rolls his eyes at the ridiculous dustup unfolding before him. He thinks it's a blessing that there are no cars in this world yet, since everyone in this room clearly has serious anger issues. It would be a nightmare if each has a vehicle and operates it in heavy traffic.

"Cyril, take back what you said and apologize to everyone, please." Eli sighs, his head throbbing from the argument.

Half a minute later, Cyril sputters, "I...apologize for...losing my head..."

It is a forced apology, but it does settle the disagreement, and everyone is happy in the end, except for Cyril.

* * *

"You're positive you won't go to jail, right?" Eli asks his guardian when he's in the bathtub.

"Eli, I promise you I'll be fine." Cyril gives Eli a sweet smile, rubbing the soap sponge on his small back. "I swear to you, you won't have to face any hardships ever again! So don't you worry, Eli! I'll always be with you until you're bored with me and order me to leave!"

What a mushy comment from Snow White! Eli thinks and purses his lips into a pout. He wants to scratch his back, but his shoulders are still too hurt to permit the action. Cyril has to help him find the itchy spot and scratch it for him.

"Down. Down. Even more. To the left, please. Yes. Down a tiny bit more. Ah, yeah, that's the spot!" Eli instructs his guardian and lets out a soft moan when the itch has been relieved.

Goddamnit! This is such a disgrace! Eli hopes he will never be in a scenario where he needs someone to help him bathe and scratch his back at age sixteen instead of eighty-five. This is all Cyril's fault! Eli shoots his guardian a melting glare.

"S-Sorry, mast—Eli! Did I hurt you?" Cyril fidgets upon catching the extra mean scowl.

"Yeah, you did! Look at my head!" Eli points at his mummy face and starts to give Cyril a long nag.

"I'm sorry." Cyril puts his head down repentantly. "Though, I think you still look really cute regardless of the bandages. Hehehehe, you'll make an adorable mummy for Halloween!"

"Say that again, you—Wait, there's Halloween in this world?" Eli is taken aback by this new information.

"Yeah! It's on October 13, 14, and 15!"

"Mmm. Is there a Christmas here?"

"What is Christmas?" Cyril asks.

"Do you guys celebrate any winter holidays?" Eli specifies.

"Yes, we celebrate Winter Solstice in the last two weeks of December!" Cyril answers.

"Ah, okay. Well, they're pretty much the same thing."

"Huh?"

"Nothing, Snow White," Eli says snootily. "Oh, and don't you dare mention mummies again!"

Cyril grins silly at his fuming little mummy.

* * *

CYRIL HAS to cancel the trip to the museum the next day, as Eli isn't confident about going out with him unless it's necessary, like a visit to the doctor's office. They end up having a barbeque in their backyard instead.

"Please, Cyril, I beg you to be careful and don't burn down the house," Eli pleads. "And please, don't drop me. I'll be a vegetable this time if I take another fall."

"I'm so sorry I've worried you this much, Eli!" Cyril laments, his face fills with agony. "I promise you I'll be extra careful, and even if I fall again, I'll make sure to let you sit on me instead of the ground!"

"What the fudge kind of analogy is that, you klutzy weirdo!" Eli elbows his guardian hard in his chest. "If you drop me one more time, I'll look for a new legal guardian!"

Cyril puts Eli on a laid-out white linen blanket on the green grass and gives him a bag of fruit chocolates. "Please don't eat all of them in one go. Your tummy will hurt," Cyril tells him and puts the straw hat on Eli's head.

"I'm not a kid," Eli says petulantly.

Cyril just smiles softly at him and pats his head. "I'll prepare the charcoal!"

Eli lounges around while waiting for Cyril to grill the food. It's a real bummer that he's illiterate in this world and can't read anything. It's such a tremendous disadvantage, and Eli has been bothered about it since that day at the Three Bears Diner.

I wish I had my smartphone. Eli lies back and daydreams. He misses his Soho apartment, all of the electronic devices that gave him endless entertainment, the books he used to read when he was bored, his grandparents, and his dog, Gigi.

"Hey, Cyril, what year are we in now?"

"Hm? Um, it's Haemon 199, maste—Eli," Cyril responds.

"That's not very helpful," Eli sighs. But after a moment of thinking, he shrieks. "Wait! 199th?!"

"Y-Yeah," Cyril flinches.

"Cyril...does that mean the Emperor has ruled the nation for nearly two hundred years?!"

"Yes, I believe so," Cyril confirms as he cooks the food. Eli's mouth hangs open. "Quite a long time, isn't it?"

"Cyril, what is the life expectancy in Aspenia?"

"Um...I believe eighty-five years for regular people, nearly three hundred or more for Sages. There has not been a fixed limit for how long a grand Sage can live, but many Sages can live up to at least 250 to 330 years."

Eli's mouth drops at the information. He is indeed in Fairytale Land! "A-Are Sages people with magic and superpowers?"

"I would not say superpowers. It's more like abilities. Some Sages can control natural elements like fire, water, air, and so on."

"That's a superpower, Cyril! If a person can live over two hundred years and control fire and stuff like that, they can't be categorized as humans! They're some sort of superheroes!" Eli raves.

"Or super evil," Cyril chuckles. "You seem to be very interested in this subject."

"This world is getting cooler and cooler, man!"

"You're cold? Let me get you a blanket!" Cyril puts down the spatula.

"No, no, cool here means great, awesome."

"Ah, 'lit' you mean?"

"Yeah." Eli gives him a thumbs-up. "So, you are a Sage, right? You can control fire!"

"I am." Cyril goes back to cooking. Then he turns back to Eli and snaps his fingers. Three flame butterflies form from the fire in the BBQ pit and fly toward Eli. They then give him a little dance performance before dissolving into the air.

"That's so amazing!" Eli claps his hands, highly impressed. "Cyril, you're the coolest!"

"Why, thank you, Eli. I'm very flattered. I'm glad you enjoyed that little trick," Cyril says with a loving smile. "The food is ready!"

There are ten different types of BBQ and salad dishes. They look and smell heavenly. Despite his apparent clumsiness, Cyril is clearly a looker and a cooker. Plus, he's also a superhero who can control fire! Eli feels a strong sense of pride and admiration for Cyril like a child has for his older brother.

Eli notices none of the dishes contain meat. So, he asks Cyril if he is a vegetarian, to which the ravenhead responds yes.

"Cyril, that is so wonderful!" Eli exclaims. That explains the absence of meat in all the food Cyril has given him so far.

Eli was a strict vegetarian in his previous life, as he would get violently sick if he accidentally consumed meat. This caused him so many beatings from his dad's wife…Anyway, none of Eli's close friends, family, or exes were vegetarian. Thus, his liking for Cyril has reached the maximum level after this latest discovery.

They chat, and Cyril reveals to Eli that his counterpart in this world, young Ilya, was also a strict vegetarian and that Cyril has been embracing this healthy diet after being taken in by young Ilya.

"So, Cyril, how and when did you learn about your superpower?" Eli asks, eating a grilled chicken of the woods mushroom skewer.

"Oh my, that was a very long time ago," Cyril says. "I discovered my power when I was very young. Hmm…I discovered my power about three years before I met you!"

"You told me we met when you were sixteen and I was nine. So, about eight years ago, right?" Eli comments.

"Yeah, that's right," Cyril simpers.

"Hm, when you said a long time ago, I thought you meant like when you were a kid. So, under which circumstance did you discover your power?"

"Um, I kind of…set a place on fire by accident." Cyril scratches his head.

"Ooh, what happened then?"

"I managed to run away. I lived on the street until the day I met you. That day, I accidentally set another building on fire, and you showed up and saved the day!" Cyril gushes.

"Wait, didn't you tell me we met at a marketplace, and I saved you from street thugs?"

"Well, I accidentally burned a place…which led to me being beaten up by others…then you showed up and saved me."

"Oh." Eli nods, though he still feels a little odd at the answer. He changes the subject and asks if Cyril can remember anything about his parents. Cyril tells him he was an orphaned tramp his whole life before he met Eli.

"I'm sorry for asking."

"Oh, please don't ever apologize to me, Eli. Meeting you was the best thing that ever happened to me! Being with you like this after all these years feels like the wildest, happiest dream that I never want to wake up from. I can sacrifice all of my power if that were the price to be with you!"

Eli gives his guardian a bashful smile. Despite the extreme cheesiness in Cyril's speech, Eli can tell Cyril means what he says, and that truly moves him.

"Same here, Cyril. I'm grateful that I met you. Is there something on my face? Why are you staring—ugh! Let go of me!" Eli grumbles when Cyril pulls him into a bear hug.

"So, do I have any superpowers, Cyril?" Eli asks with great excitement. "I'm pretty sure I have one! I-I punched a werewolf with bat wings and sent it flying! Did I ever show you my superpowers? Can I influence fire or control water? Ooh, is there a school for people with special powers? Can you learn about magic?"

"Oh yes! You definitely have a wonderful and unique power that no one else has," Cyril laughs.

"What power is it?" Eli's green eyes twinkle, hands clasping together.

"Your adorableness that melts hearts and makes people wobble under your angelic charm!" Cyril swoons and squeezes Eli's chubby cheeks. "Aww, my heart always flutters whenever I'm near you!"

"What?" Eli's zeal deflates like a pricked balloon. He puts his hands on his hips. "So, do I have power or not?"

"You know, having a special ability is not a blessing. A lot of evil and bad people target Sages. It's not unusual for many Sages to keep their power a secret from everyone," Cyril says.

"It's that dangerous?" Eli blinks, and his body slightly recoils.

"I'm afraid it is indeed very dangerous, Eli. So, if one day, you ever discover your ability—well, superpower, as you like to say, you have to keep it a secret and don't tell any strangers about it."

Eli fearfully nods. "B-But you used your power yesterday in public. Aren't you afraid people will find out about it?"

"Well, I can take care of myself. Besides, my ability is quite aggressive, which makes me a hard target to take down. However, your ability, your charm, falls under the category of a 'soft' ability, but it is still considered a Sage ability. That makes you a Sage and a very vulnerable and easy target!"

"O-Okay. Hold on, you weren't joking when you said m-my superpower is…a-adorableness?"

"Yes, Eli. Your power is adorableness," Cyril confirms. "You don't like that power?"

"No! That's such a lame power!" Eli complains. "I'm not a chick. Why would I be happy about having such a useless power?"

"It's not useless." Cyril chuckles. "A lot of people wish they had that power."

"Look, man, I think you're making this up! There's no way that is a real power. I don't believe you at all!" Eli gives Cyril a side-eye.

"Oh, Eli! Why would I make up such a thing?" Cyril appeals, his blue eyes soft and loving. "It's not only me. Don't you notice how Mariposa, Haidar, Gallahan, and Wolfgang all liked you the first time they met you? They are not the easiest people to befriend!"

Cyril does have a point…Now that Cyril mentions the neighbors, Eli can't help but feel a little strange about them. But he just can't quite figure out exactly what it is at the moment.

* * *

A FEW HOURS LATER, their BBQ is cut short by an unexpected downpour. Dark, heavy clouds blot out the clear, blue sky, and rain starts to fall down on the evergreen land. The weather instantly cools down as howling wind blasts through the trees, making them sway like inebriated dancers.

Ever the devoted mother hen, Cyril picks up Eli with one hand while gathering all the picnic stuff with the other at an inexplicably fast pace before retreating inside their house.

Eli watches the falling rain through the large bay window in the bedroom, feeling bored and glum. There are no televisions or running electricity in this world yet, so they can't watch a movie. It's a shame since horror movies are perfect for weather like this. Cyril interrupts Eli's aimless daydream by putting a knitted blanket over his shoulder and handing him a cup of hot chocolate.

"Thank you, Cyril." Eli takes a sip and lets out a gleeful moan. It's simply heaven to drink sweet hot chocolate on a rainy day.

"Are you warm now?" Cyril sits down on the cushioned bench opposite Eli.

"I am, thank you." Eli snuggles in the blanket. "Ah, it's so good to have a roof over your head when it rains. It also rained this hard the first day I got here."

"What?".

"Oh, I meant it also rained the first day I woke up in the alley in Creepyville," Eli clarifies.

"Did anyone give you shelter from the rain?" After hearing Eli's negative response, his gorgeous face darkens.

"It wasn't that bad. Thanks to that rain, I was able to shower. I was literally covered in trash, man!" Eli downplays to keep Cyril from worrying.

Cyril's blue eyes are colder than the stormy wind outside.

The atmosphere in the room turns heavy, and the awkwardness slowly grows. Eli wants to say something to lighten the mood. Still, it's hard to brainstorm humor when your housemate has the expression of a serial killer, and the weather is playing emo rock outside. Thus, Eli decides to keep quiet and goes back to enjoying his hot chocolate in silence.

When Eli puts the cup on the table, something unusual catches his attention. At first, he can't make out what it is until he realizes the skin on his left inner forearm is perfectly smooth and unblemished.

"Cyril, the night that you brought me back, did you notice any scar here?" Eli shows his guardian his left inner forearm. "There used to be a small scar on here. It was squiggly and loosely resembled the number three. It looked like a branding mark. Did you see it?"

Cyril's fingers trace the soft skin of Eli's forearm. After a while, he replies, "No, I didn't see any scar on your hand, Eli. You're perfect, just as always."

"This is so creepy, Cyril! I swear there is...there was a raised scar on the back of my left forearm. I still saw it the moment I passed out in that forest when you made your entrance and almost gave me a heart attack!" Eli shivers as he recalls that memory.

"I'm sorry for scaring you back in the forest," Cyril stutters, looking a little embarrassed.

"Cyril, do you have any idea about the people that kidnapped me? I feel like that scar would have given us clues about my kidnappers."

Cyril stays quiet for a moment. Then he gets up and comes to sit next to Eli.

"Eli, don't you worry about that. You're home and safe now. I will never let anyone take you away from me again. As I promised you yesterday, I'm willing to put the painful past behind us. But that is it, Eli. From now on, if any miserable fools dare to harm you, I swear, whoever they are, I will find them, and I'll make them pay."

The dark response is absolutely unexpected. And the fact that Cyril casually says it when his blue eyes are still so tender and full of love sends a chill down Eli's back.

"Are you cold?" Cyril asks in an eerily sweet voice.

"Cyril, I know it's raining, there's nothing fun to do, and you are bored, but this is not a good time to roleplay a creep! Dude, I'm already scared shitless by the mysterious disappearance of a physical scar on my arm. I don't need you to spook me even more, alright?" Eli snaps.

"I-I'm sorry. I don't mean to scare you." Cyril poofs back into a harmless little pup.

Eli is about to retort, but the bedroom windows suddenly spring open due to the strong wind, causing all the lights to go out at the same time. Cyril immediately closes the windows, but the room is pitch black now. It's only around 6:30 in the evening, but it's raining so hard that there's barely a source of light outside.

"Cyril?"

"I'm right next to you. Don't be scared." Cyril squeezes Eli's hand.

"I'm not scared."

"You're trembling, Eli."

"It's a little drafty in the room, man."

"Ah, alright." Cyril chuckles. "Well, do you want me to hold you?"

"Dude, just light the candles, will you?"

"Well, the matches are downstairs. Let me go fetch them then." Cyril is about to get up, but Eli tugs his sleeve. "Yes?"

"Why do you have to get the matches downstairs? Don't you have the power to shoot fire at will?"

"I do. But the fire I summon is not regular. It's akin to inferno blazes, very destructive fire that isn't suitable for everyday use," Cyril explains.

"Weird flex, but okay," Eli mutters in the dark.

"Huh? Flex? What does flex mean in this case?"

"Nothing, dude.".

"Mmm, Eli, do you want to come downstairs and get the matches with me?"

"Huh? You dropped me twice in broad daylight, and now you want to carry me in the dark? Are you conspiring to kill me or something?"

"S-Sorry," Cyril responds in a low, mortified voice.

Lightning suddenly strikes a pine tree twenty feet from their house. The blow is so strong it splits the tree in half and makes Eli jump in his seat.

"There, there, I'm right here with you." Cyril lifts Eli onto his lap and pats his back to comfort him. "Don't be scared, Eli."

Cyril's body is insanely warm and cozy. His large arms and soothing voice are so comforting that Eli feels embarrassed when he realizes he unconsciously leaned closer to that broad chest instead of pulling away as he intended. Before Eli has the chance to fix his mistake, Cyril tightens his arms around Eli and gives him a big and affectionate embrace.

"Let's go downstairs and get those matches," Cyril coos, and Eli nods in agreement.

* * *

FOR SOME WEIRD-ASS REASON, Cyril doesn't even stagger walking in complete darkness, and he knows where to get the matches while still carrying Eli in both arms. That makes Eli suspicious of whether Cyril tried to kill him before or if this guy is actually Batman. They're about to go back upstairs when a string of knocks peal outside their main door.

"Neighbors?" Eli wonders.

"Can't be," Cyril mutters.

Eli doesn't know why Cyril is sure it isn't their neighbor. The temperature in the house has dropped to a freezing point that Eli can feel cold air escape from his lips every time he breathes.

"D-Don't open the door, Cyril." Eli tugs Cyril's shirt. "I have a bad feeling about this."

Cyril says nothing but stands still in the dark hallway. The rain is still raging, and the knocks have become more threatening. After a brief while, Cyril strides toward the front entrance with Eli in his arms. Suddenly, the door swings open without him touching it. Another lightning bolt strikes a tree near their cottage, briefly illuminating the dark sky and revealing a tall, black figure standing by the entryway.

Eli gasps when he sees the suspicious man pull something from his cloak. His first instinct is to grab Cyril's neck to shield him from a possible attack. But Cyril reacts even quicker as he lands a kick at the man's chest and sends him flying all the way to the front yard. The man in black crashes through their white garden gate and stays on the ground.

"Are you okay?" Eli asks his guardian.

"I'm fine, Eli. Don't be scared. I won't let anyone hurt you," Cyril reassures Eli.

"Who is that person? What did he want?" Eli squints at the man lying outside. "O-Or, could it be the kidnappers coming back for me?!"

"I don't think so, Eli."

"Well, is he someone you know?"

"No, I've never seen that person before. He's not from around here," Cyril answers, his voice sharp.

"C-Cyril, please just close the door and get inside," Eli begs. "I-I don't want us to get into trouble or you to get hurt."

"I'll be fine, little kit. Wait here for me. I'll go check on that man." Cyril laughs.

"No, no, no! Don't go out, man! What if the guy has accomplices just waiting to jump you when you go outside?"

"If that's the case, then tonight will be their last day of committing evil deeds."

"Goddamnit, Cyril! Don't you know the aggressive hunk always ends up dying the worst way in the movies?!" Eli snaps, frustrated and scared for Cyril's sake.

"I really don't understand what you're saying—"

"Just lock every damn door and window in the house and retreat upstairs," Eli instructs, but he is interrupted by a foreign yell.

"What the hell is wrong with you people?!" The man in black slowly gets up. "Ouch, my damn back!"

"State your name. Who ordered you to come here?" Cyril commands.

"The name's Willy. What do you mean who ordered me?!" the man in black barks.

"What are you doing at my house at this hour? What's your intention? Speak at once!"

"I have mail for you!"

"Who delivers letters this late at night?"

"I'm an express mailman!" Willy snaps. "I have a court summons for a Mister Cyril!"

...*Uh oh.* Eli gulps nervously.

"That would be me. But why didn't you put the mail in the mailbox?"

"Because your mailbox was destroyed by thunder! Come outside and look! Do you know I had to walk for two hours in the rain to get to your place? And then, instead of a nice welcome, you attacked me! Cyril, right? I'll remember your name and report you to the higher authority for battery! See you in court!"

CHAPTER 9

CASE I – THE BOHEMIAN SHOP OF THE
MIDSUMMER FAIR – PART 1

"You poor thing!" the old doctor exclaims at the sight of Eli's face after he unwrapped the bandages. He inspects the injuries and then turns to Cyril. "What happened to him? Don't tell me you dropped him again!"

Cyril is racked with guilt at the doctor's demand for an explanation. Eli has to cover for his guardian and tell the doctor he caused these injuries by accidentally falling out of Cyril's arms during a picnic trip.

The old doctor is not convinced. He speaks to Cyril in a stern voice and says he will notify the authorities if Eli is presented with more injuries in his next visit.

"Mister Cyril, you ought to take good care of your young master. Despite his healthy appearance, he isn't well. Are you ready to hear his blood work results?" The doctor flips a page on the report.

Eli's face is grim upon hearing the term "not well." He knows he has a strong streak of rotten luck, but this news really catches him flat-footed. Eli is about to ask the doctors for details, and Cyril suddenly squeezes him to his large chest as if Eli will grow a pair of wings and fly away.

"Please, doctor, I can't lose him again! Please save my master! I'm willing to pay any price just to have him healthy again! Money is not an issue! And if necessary, I can give him my core so he can live!" Cyril wails, tears flowing freely from his eyes while squeezing Eli in his iron grasp.

Eli is beyond embarrassed by his guardian's full-blown romance-tragedy telenovela reaction. The two young nurses behind the old doctor are giggling about them behind their clipboards. Though Eli's pissed, he puts on a soft guise and strokes Cyril's back. "Hey, hush. I'll be fine," he soothes Cyril through gritted teeth.

"You have a core? You're a Sage?" the old doctor asks with a lifted brow.

Cyril nods, bawling his eyes out. "If my master has an incurable illness, I'm willing to do a core transplant."

"Stop it, Cyril. You will *not* do that! I won't agree to it!" Eli objects.

"H-Hold on, everyone. Nobody is dying, so please calm down," the old doctor reassures them. "I just said he isn't well. It doesn't mean he has an incurable disease."

Cyril and Eli exhale in relief, but only Eli feels embarrassed for jumping to conclusions. After Cyril swipes off his tears, he instantly puts back on the most neutral look, acting as if the person who just had the overdramatic breakdown seconds ago wasn't him.

The old doctor reads the results. Though Eli doesn't have any life-threatening disease, he is not anywhere near healthy. Eli has multiple vitamin deficiencies, anemia, low blood pressure, and rat-bite fever.

"I was bitten by rats back in that alley," Eli recalls.

"According to the test, you have had this disease multiple times before," the old doctor comments. "People who repeatedly get rat-bite fever like this are usually confined in a dark place for a prolonged period of time."

Cyril's fists clench by his side. Eli pats his guardian's hand and briefly tells the doctor his kidnapping story. Everyone in the clinic is dismayed by it, and the old doctor finally drops the suspicion that Cyril has something to do with Eli's feeble health and malnourishment.

* * *

THE NURSES GIVE Eli a lot of candies when they leave, and everyone wishes him a fast recovery. As Eli comfortably sits inside the cab loaded with sweets,

Cyril surprises him with a bear hug and a second round of cheesy meltdown for their entire ride back home.

After that doctor's visit, Cyril goes on a journey of spoiling Eli rotten. It isn't like the ravenhead didn't coddle Eli before. But now, the overindulgence gag has quadrupled to the point that Cyril is giving Eli vodka-infused chocolate. He gives it to Eli despite the fact that Eli isn't of legal drinking age, and Cyril could go to jail and lose custody of Eli if anyone ever found out.

"Please don't tell anyone about this. I could get in serious trouble," Cyril tells Eli while giving him the liquor candies. "But even if you do, I will still adore you no matter what!"

Eli legit freezes at that unbelievably obsequious statement. Cyril obviously forgets Eli's advice to clean up his act and use his authority. Eli thinks Cyril is lucky that he is actually a twenty-three-year-old adult instead of a real sixteen-year-old kid. Any typical teenager would milk Cyril's leniency and generosity to the last drop. Then, those kids would grow up and become entitled douchebags. In short, Eli thinks Cyril will make a lousy father for his serious enabling tendency.

It doesn't stop there. Cyril goes on an insane spending spree and upgrades Eli's bedding to silk, buying him more expensive new clothes and shoes. Currently, Eli has fifty sets of summer outfits, six pairs of shoes, and many hats. That is more clothes than he ever owned in his previous life in the modern world of 2019.

"I'll get you *anything* you want, Eli," Cyril tells Eli for the hundredth time.

At the first dozen times, Eli would pester his guardian for his lavish spending. But then he realizes it all falls on deaf ears and eventually stops nagging his housemate and accepts the pampering. It does feel good to be spoiled and have someone genuinely care for him without asking for anything in return. Eli takes it as the universe's compensation for putting him away too early in his last life.

* * *

Two weeks have passed, and Eli wakes up this morning in an especially ecstatic mood. Today is a special day for two reasons. First, it is a national Midsummer holiday in Aspenia, and Cyril has promised to take him to the fair. Second, and most importantly, Eli's vegetable life has finally come to an end! Eli can walk again without Cyril's help!

Words can't describe how happy Eli is to be able to walk by himself. He was so sick of being spoon-fed in bed and had to ask for assistance every time he wanted to use the bathroom.

As usual, Cyril has already woken up and is probably downstairs making breakfast. Eli gleefully walks to the bathroom to wash up. He skips every three steps and even hums a jolly tune. This is perhaps the first time that Eli truly feels alive and contented with his new life. He has a house and a family, and he can walk on his own two feet! Oh, and no more mummy face!

In his previous life, it usually took Eli fifteen seconds to pick his clothes. He was always a decisive person. But today, Eli spends five minutes choosing an outfit to wear to the fair.

Looking at himself in the mirror, Eli is pleased with what he sees. He's wearing the new clothes Cyril bought for him: a white, loose-fitting cotton shirt with a wide sailor collar, a pair of structured linen knee-length shorts in camel, and a pair of brown calfskin ankle boots with white socks. Eli looks like a vintage porcelain doll with neatly combed chestnut hair donned with a straw boater hat and a healthy, unblemished complexion. While his current appearance isn't macho handsome by any means, he certainly doesn't look unattractive at all.

A strong part of Eli wishes he would be manly-handsome like Cyril. But then he's only almost seventeen now, so he has plenty of time to bulk up.

When Eli comes downstairs, he sees Cyril standing in the hallway and reading a letter. His guardian is wearing a semi-fitted, white button-up shirt with rolled sleeves that reveal his toned forearms, an ivory vest, and camel linen trousers.

For some reason, they're wearing matching outfits today.

Cyril puts away the letter to his vest upon hearing Eli's footsteps. His blue eyes sparkle with sheer joy when he sees his beloved young master. "Good morning, Eli! Oh! You look absolutely beautiful!"

"Thank you. Good morning." Eli smiles sheepishly. Eli has figured out by now that he is Cyril's number-one idol, and Cyril would think he's a ten out of ten, even if he were zapped by thunder or in a full-body cast.

Eli swaggers toward his nanny—eh, guardian—with excitement. He has been curious about their height difference for a while, but never had the proper chance to check. Eli was six-foot-tall in the modern world and around five-foot-nine or five-foot-ten when he was sixteen.

"Please stand straight up, Cyril," Eli requests, and Cyril immediately obeys.

However, when Eli stands side by side with the ravenhead, he is horrified to learn that the top of his head barely reaches Cyril's neck, which means Eli's shorter than in his previous life by at least five to six inches!

"I'm only five-foot-seven?!" Eli cries out. He has to bend his neck to look at his guardian in the eyes. "Nooooo!"

Eli's screech startles Cyril, and he immediately asks Eli what's wrong. After he learns what Eli is upset about, the ravenhead bursts into an irrepressible laugh.

"Aww, you're so cute, Eli," Cyril squeezes his young master's chubby cheeks.

"Dude, stop laughing! What's so funny about it?!" Eli grumbles and shakes off his guardian's hands.

"Ay, ay, you will grow taller. Remember, you're only sixteen! I'm pretty sure you'll be around 180cm five-foot-eleven in the future," Cyril gives him a thumbs up.

"No! That's too short! I was—I have to be 183cm, at least!" Eli disputes, but Cyril shakes his head.

"180cm, I'm telling you," Cyril grins, oddly confident. "And also, you don't look 170cm (five-foot-seven), Eli," he comments and leaves to get a measuring tape.

"Ooh, a-am I 175cm (five-foot-nine) then?" Eli stands up straight so that Cyril can record his height.

"Mmm, yep, I was right. You're not 170cm," Cyril looks at the number on the tape. "You're 162.5cm (five-foot-four)."

From this day forward, daily stretching exercise becomes Eli's top priority in life.

* * *

ELI LOOKS out the window from his cab. It's about 9:30 AM, and the weather is amazingly sunny. Every house and corner of the street is decorated with colorful banners, garlands, and fresh flower wreaths to celebrate the holiday.

Cyril doesn't decorate their house because it is already inundated with flowers from their garden. At one point, Eli even asked Cyril if he ran a florist business, and his guardian thought Eli had an active imagination, as if it was baseless of Eli to make that guess. Snow White is oblivious to the fact that his garden has more flowers than an average flower shop. If Eli were to sensitive to fragrance, he would pass out just by standing in their house, for the place is always filled with intense floral scent—even in the upstairs bathroom!

After over a week, Eli finally learns the name of the fairytale town he lives in. It is called Glade Mallow, named after a wildflower that grows throughout the neighborhood. The Midsummer Fair is held annually for three days in the next town, Hepatica, which is about thirty minutes away by carriage. When they are ten minutes away from the festival site, the paved road is packed with carriages. From the window, Eli can see the town folks clad in bright, beautiful clothes and merrily stroll to the fair. Everyone is chatting, happy, and in high festive spirit.

"I think we should walk from here. We'll get there faster; the road is jammed," Eli suggests, and the ravenhead agrees with his request.

"Please stay close to me, Eli. The fair is very crowded, and I don't want you to get lost," Cyril tells him.

"Don't worry. I already memorized the directions. I'll just walk home if I get lost!" Eli says wittily.

"Always so bright, even at a young age." Cyril smiles softly at him.

"Thanks?" Sometimes, Eli wonders if it's him or if there is a deeper meaning underneath every sentence Cyril says.

* * *

IT APPEARS that Eli might have made a mistake in his first judgment of the time period of Aspenia and this world in general. When he was in Creepyville, whose actual name is Crimson Vale, he thought he was in the medieval period circa fourteenth century due to the town's impoverished environment. But after Cyril took him home and Eli saw a flushable toilet and a bathtub with a showerhead, he figured the timeline had to be around the 1800s. But of course, to the mass population here, the current year in this world is Haemon 199.

Eli mentions timeline and technology because he has been shooting the breeze with a group of old inventors at the science tent in the last twenty minutes. And what have they been talking about? Electricity, of course!

Eli is basically begging the inventors to invent electricity, and he pitches how significant and life-changing electric power can transform their world. The old scientists are so deeply engrossed with Eli's ideas that they scribble down every word he says. Unfortunately, Eli majored in business in his last life, so physics and science aren't his strongest subjects. After he provides as much information as he knows about modern technology, the scientists are so impressed that they give him a beautiful crystal award for his contribution to science...

"I told you. You are a genius! A prodigy!" Cyril praises him with heart-eyes.

"Please, Cyril...just no."

ELI AND CYRIL take part in many festive activities together. They watch a Midsummer parade and visit many artisan tents where Cyril buys some floral-infused honey for Eli to have with tea. They join a pottery painting contest where Cyril questionably chooses the girliest sculpture of two cherubs picking flowers on a floral ground (Eli doesn't object his guardian's choice, but he does shoot Cyril a side-eye). After one and a half hours of vigorous painting, they win second place. The reward is a free set of oil paints. Then, they take a break to enjoy the festival food and drinks, which are various types of veggie BBQ skewers, potato salad, shaved ice, fruit slice candies, and honeydew juice.

After lunch, they settle in a flower crown DIY tent where Cyril makes Eli an elaborate flower crown.

"Aww, you look so adorable, like an angel!" Cyril swoons after he puts the crown on Eli's hat.

Eli sighs at how pathetically smitten his nanny—Cyril is with him. Now that Eli has a flower headband, he no longer looks so out of place at the festival since everyone from young to old wears some sort of flower. That leaves Cyril as the only person who doesn't have appropriate festival attire.

Eli picks out some flowers from his crown and puts them in Cyril's vest pocket.

"There you go!" Eli pats his guardian's shirt. "Now, we both look the part."

Cyril leans down to give Eli a loving pinch on his little nose. "Why, thank you, Eli. You're truly a little angel!"

"For the hundredth time, I'm not a kid! Stop treating me like one!"

* * *

ABOUT TWO HOURS LATER, Eli and Cyril stand in an atrociously long line to buy the assorted fruit pastries—a must-try Midsummer's delicacy of Aspenia. The wait is so long that Eli takes the bathroom break two times, and it still isn't their turn.

"What's in this fruit cake that everyone is so crazy about?" Eli asks his guardian.

"I have never had it before. This pastry seems to be an annual favorite of many." Cyril reads the fair's flier.

"Can I go look around for a bit? We must have been waiting in line for over an hour," Eli entreats, his face surly.

"Of course, Eli. But don't go too far from here, alright?" Cyril smiles and pats Eli's hat.

* * *

ELI STROLLS down the aisle of bright-colored tents lining both sides of the dirt path. These festival shops sell unique and intricate goods that Eli has never seen before. He is fascinated with a string of colorful fairy lights. According to the merchant, the lights operate by magic instead of electricity! Unfortunately, Eli doesn't have any money to buy it, so he has to move on.

After passing a few tents, a little bohemian shop by the end of the road catches Eli's attention.

It's an artisan store that sells handmade decor and all sorts of pretty trinkets. The tent is made from Paisley patchwork fabric. Many string lights of various colors hang everywhere in and outside the shop, making it stand out among the other vendors.

Eli isn't interested in shopping for cute but impractical gewgaws. Yet, something about this little shop draws him in—it's warm and has inviting energy, but the warmth feels...artificial? Anyhow, as Eli stands in front of the store, there's no shop owner or any salesperson to greet him, making it easy for him to browse the goods in peace.

Interesting design. Eli muses, glancing at an oddly shaped bowl painted a bright red color. A strong impulse urges him to pick it up, and he does just that.

Immediately, an image of a person screaming and running flashes through Eli's mind. It is a young man around Eli's age. He is utterly terrified, and his clothes are covered in dirt and blood. Someone is chasing him, yet he still pleads with that person behind him to let him go. Eli can't see the face of the attacker. The young man doesn't make it. He trips and falls, and his assailant catches up to him. He is then brutally dragged by his hair to a small shed made of patched human skin. There, he is chopped into tiny pieces by a large, rusty butcher knife.

"Are you alright, dear?" a raspy but incongruously calming voice asks Eli, jarring him from his harrowing vision.

"I-I'm fine." Eli feels as if his soul has just returned from an unintended meander to the realm of the dead. He immediately puts the bowl back down to the display table. The haunting voice of the unfortunate young man crying for his mother still rings in Eli's ears. He glances over the shop, and everything looks normal. There is no trace of blood or mutilated body parts anywhere.

"Honey, you're so pale. And you're sweating so much," the stranger says, looking worried. She's a middle-aged woman with brown hair, brown eyes, and pleasant features. Eli can tell she's the owner of this shop from her outfit and hairdo—it has the same eccentric, bohemian vibe as the colorful patchwork tent.

"You might have a sunstroke. This has been the hottest summer I've seen in a long time!" the lady comments, laughing. "It's almost as if all Hells have literally broken loose."

Eli gives her a vague smile and turns on his heel to leave. But the lady grabs his arm and gently pulls him back. She takes out a white handkerchief from her dress and dabs away the running sweat on Eli's face.

"There you go. If you go out in the sun all sweating like that, you could get sick," the lady speaks to him in a motherly voice.

"Thank you, ma'am," Eli stutters.

The lady looks at him up and down. Then she gives him a sweet smile. "You're such a beautiful young man. Your mother is a very fortunate lady. If I have a kid as gorgeous as you, I'd love him to death."

"Thank you. Excu—"

"Did you find anything that interested you? I have more exquisite stuff inside the tent if you want to take a look," the lady says, gesturing with her polished red nails toward her shop.

"Oh, I'm good. I'm just looking. I don't have any money, and I have to get back. My...dad is waiting for me."

"Well, get back to your father, then. Don't let him worry," the lady smiles, carefully folding the white handkerchief and putting it back into her dress pocket. "Happy Midsummer, love."

* * *

ELI SPRINTS like a hunted rabbit amongst the press of the fair's folks back to the pastry tent; he only slows down to breathe when he spots Cyril standing in the long line, still waiting for his turn to buy the fruitcake. As if their minds were connected by a strong link of telepathy, Cyril intuitively turns his head in Eli's direction. The ravenhead gives Eli a bright smile and waves at him, gesturing him to come closer.

"Eli, where did you go? I almost left the line to go look for you." Cyril wipes away the rivulet of sweat on Eli's face. "Are you alright? Your face is as pale as chalk."

Eli looks at the line before them. There are only five more people until their turn. Considering that Cyril has been waiting almost two hours to get this Holy Grail cake, it will be a mind-bogglingly bonkers call to abandon this post.

"I-I'm fine. It's the heat," Eli tells his guardian. "It's insanely hot today."

"It is hot," Cyril agrees, fixing Eli's hat. "I've been thinking about going on a vacation with you before your birthday. Where would you like to go? A trip to the beach or maybe a stay at a lake house?"

"Uh, do you have the money for that?" A summer vacation would be a nice getaway from this scalding weather. But Eli doesn't want Cyril to plunge into a lifestyle he can't afford and end up in debt.

"Oh, Eli, of course, I can afford it. Money is not a matter of concern in our household," Cyril declares with absolute swag.

"Alright, if you say so, boss. Just don't sell me if you end up in heavy debt."

"That will never happen!" Cyril gasps. "You're priceless, Eli. I wouldn't trade you for the world."

"You were never offered the world. How would you know you won't trade me for it?" Eli counters.

"Eli..." Cyril grips Eli's shoulders and levels his gaze so their eyes can meet. "I would die for you."

Those five words are like knives plunging into Eli's chest. For some inexplicable reason, Eli senses tears well up in his eyes. The funny thing is that while his brain regards what Cyril said as dippy nonsense, his heart does not. It feels like someone coexists within him, and that entity is immensely grieved by Cyril's foolishly selfless vow.

"...I don't believe you," Eli tries to sound indifferent and snotty to hide the emotional disarray inside him. "Also, what did I tell you about hitting on a minor, dude?"

"S-Sorry." Cyril's innocent face flushes red. "But I was telling the truth. I don't think that's considered…uh…f-flirting?" When he sees his young master crossing his arms and throwing him a grumpy look, the ravenhead quickly apologizes and bribes Eli back into a good mood with candies.

* * *

ELI MISSES the chance to tell Cyril about his gory vision. It's partly because he doesn't want to ruin the merry mood they have. Besides, that vision is probably harmless, and he's safe with Cyril by his side. Second, after getting the fruit pastries, he is distracted by all the festive activities. Eli hates to hype up things, but he must admit that those fruitcakes are truly worth the two-hour wait. They even buy extra to bring home and to gift the neighbors. When they get home at around 6:30 PM, they are welcomed by a pleasant surprise as Wolfgang, Haidar, Mariposa, and Gallahan throw them a dinner party at their cottage. Everyone gathers around, eating, drinking, and playing board games. Their neighbors only leave until late evening.

It's fair to say Eli's first Midsummer in fairytale land—Aspenia was a huge success.

After Eli finishes showering and retreats to bed, Cyril conducts the last step of his nanny routine—tucking Eli in.

"I hope you had a great day, Eli." Cyril's smile is tender.

Eli's answer is positive, and he asks if Cyril had a good day.

"Every day I'm with you is the best day of my life."

Eli's good mood drops at a catastrophic rate as he listens to that cringe-worthy answer. He taunts Cyril for his corny lingo. As always, Cyril doesn't dare to reprimand Eli's bratty behavior as he only gasps in helpless shock and then laughs it off.

"Good night, Eli."

"Good night," Eli echoes. A moment later, he adds, "Thank you, Cyril."

Cyril looks surprised.

"Thank you for getting me home." There are so many things Eli wants to say to Cyril. He wants to thank Cyril for giving him a home, taking care of him, and always putting him first before anything. But he can't say all that out loud because he sucks at confessing or saying mushy things, and he doesn't want to embarrass himself. Also, it's Midsummer, not Thanksgiving, so there's plenty of time and occasions for Eli to express his appreciation for his guardian in the future.

Cyril stares at his young master hiding under the blanket and facing the wall. Seconds go by, and the ravenhead breaks into a soft chuckle. He brings his hand to shuffle Eli's brown locks. "Thank you for being back in my life again, Eli."

* * *

ELI IS AWAKENED by a strange buzzing noise and an awful stench that isn't at all the usual floral scent infused in their house. At first, Eli tries to sleep it off, but the sound is getting irritably loud, and he can't ignore it anymore.

"Cyril, what is that smell? Why are you—" The complaint gets stuck in his mouth when Eli opens his eyes and sees large brown and bloody stains all over his bedroom's ceiling.

What the hell?! Eli immediately bolts up from his bed and scans his surroundings. His heart almost stops beating when he spots a decapitated head lying at the end of the bed.

"Cyril!" Eli grabs the head and is relieved to find it isn't his guardian's. It belongs to a stranger with dark hair.

Eli can barely recognize his bedroom. It looks extremely grungy, and everything is slathered with blood. Cyril's bed is destroyed—split in half. Eli feels his blood running cold when he sees his guardian's blanket tattered between a pile of feathers and soaked with blood that he prays isn't from Cyril.

Mama. Eli clutches his chest as he pushes himself to stand up. His feet are shaking. He has to calm himself and look for Cyril. In a critical moment like this, he knows he will die if he panics.

Mama, please guide him to safety. Eli stifles his tears and carefully listens. He hears footsteps thumping on the staircase—but they are too heavy to be

Cyril. The person outside has to be huge, and there's also a clanking sound of metal grazing along the wooden railing. Eli's heart leaps when he sees the bedroom door is wide open, and Eli rushes to lock it. But the moment the intruder hears Eli's footsteps, he sprints toward the bedroom. Eli slams the door shut before the person reaches it.

A series of shrill, jarring noises of the wooden door splintering echo throughout the house. The person outside speaks to Eli in a breathy and gravelly voice.

"Come out, come out, little rat. It's the butchering hour."

CHAPTER 10

CASE I – THE BOHEMIAN SHOP OF THE MIDSUMMER FAIR – PART 2

There are only two things on Eli's mind:

First is to find a weapon to defend himself.

And second is Cyril.

Eli's sure he can outrun the intruder. Based on the deafening creaking of the wood floor from the man's heavy plods, Eli assumes he has to be extremely overweight. Also, the intruder is using all his energy to break down this sturdy wooden door. By the time he breaks down the door and gets inside the bedroom, he should be tired, and Eli should be long gone by then.

That's the plan anyway.

Weapon, weapon, weapon. Eli searches the bedroom, rummaging through the built-in closet and looking under the beds. But he finds nothing of use.

Despite being utterly concerned for Cyril's safety, Eli mentally swears at his guardian as he puts on a black hooded cape borrowed from Cyril and slips into a pair of house shoes. *Goddamnit, Snow White! Were you afraid I was gonna commit suicide or something?! Why didn't you leave any weapon in the bedroom? I'm so gonna pluck your leg hair with freaking tweezers when I find you!*

"*I will chop you to pieces, rat,*" the intruder hacks at the door. While the door is still intact, the top edge of the knife has already come through the wooden panel.

Crap! Time's up. Eli drops the search and grabs a broken bed leg from Cyril's bed. Then he lurches toward the bay window between their beds. There are two bay windows in the room. The first one, where the cushioned benches are, faces the back garden. The second window, which Eli chooses to make his escape, faces the right side of the house.

Eli opens the windows and climbs down the rose vine. It's a relatively easy climb, and he doesn't get pricked by the roses' thorns, thanks to the house shoes. Escape 101, you need a good pair of soft shoes that make little noise when you move and dark-colored clothes. Eli is wearing white pajamas, hence the need to blend into the dark surroundings.

As Eli has successfully hopped to the ground. He hears a scream from the intruder inside the cottage.

"I WILL KILL YOU, RAT! I WILL PULL OUT YOUR TONGUE AND GOUGE OUT YOUR EYES. THEN I WILL SHOVE THOSE BACK TO YOUR THROAT AND RIP THEM FROM YOUR GUT!" The intruder laughs menacingly. His loud, hurried footsteps stomp down hard on the second floor.

Right. Like, I'm just going to stand there and let you kill me, Eli scoffs in his head, though he does have a slight wave of goosebumps imagining the intruder's macabrely descriptive threat. While the creep is spewing BS upstairs, Eli has gotten back inside the house and grabs a knife from the kitchen. He tries not to pay attention to the row of decapitated heads, severed hands, feet, and fingers scattered all over the kitchen counters and in the sink. None of the heads have raven hair, which reinforces Eli's hope that his guardian is alive and gives him the strength and encouragement he needs to escape this ghastly nightmare.

As Eli hears the rushing footsteps of the intruder on the staircase, he knows he can't escape through the front door. The stairs are in the main foyer, which is where the front door is. The only room that the main hall links to is the kitchen and breakfast room. From there, one can enter the grand dining room facing the left side of the house or the living room that has the entrance to the backyard, which is where Eli's headed.

The reason Eli keeps on nagging Cyril for his opulent spending on Eli is that they're not rich. Duh. From the description of the house layout, one might think this place is big, or at the very least, spacious, but it is not. This house is a humble, average-sized cottage. Thus, the journey from the kitchen/breakfast room to the backdoor in the living room is fifteen feet max. Within three seconds, Eli is already in front of the back entrance. When he opens the door, strings of mutilated hands, feet, and sliced organs threaded together like sausage links hit him in the face. Though Eli is able to dodge them, those revolting human-meat garlands almost give him a mini heart attack. Eli can't help but retch.

"The longer you make me chase you, the more horrible and painful your death will be, RAT!" The intruder's voice echoes in the main foyer. But instead of being intimidated by it, the gruesome threat only pisses Eli off more.

Cyril's beautiful white cottage is destroyed. Every room looks like it has been abandoned for five decades or belongs to a haunted asylum. The walls, the floors, and the fine furniture are covered in gooey blood and putrid brown stains that Eli doesn't want to identify. There are body pieces of random people all over the house and in the garden. Cyril's freaking *world-class garden!* How dare this bastard destroy Cyril's fairytale garden like this?

Screw this asshole killer! Who is he? Why is he after me? What's the freaking motive? And most importantly, where the hell is Cyril?! Eli's so mad that he has an internal debate on whether he should try to set up the traps and defend Cyril's house or run to the neighbor's house and ask for help. As he quietly stands behind the red azalea bush on the right side of the garden and peeps through the living room window, he finally sees the intruder.

It's a tall and obese man clad in an off-white, bloodstained butcher's outfit. His face is covered by a white capirote with a pointed hood like a creepy cult member, leaving only a pair of eyes visible. His calloused right hand is holding a long, probably twenty-inch butcher cleaver that drips with blood. The butcher is screaming threats while frantically searching the living room for Eli.

My nanny will burn your ass, you bastard. Eli grits his teeth. Glancing one last time in the living room, Eli is relieved that the vile butcher is still in there looking for him instead of running to the yard. As Eli's predicted, the killer isn't very bright. Without wasting another second, Eli sprints to Wolfgang's house.

Aside from Cyril, Wolfgang is Eli's only reliable ally when it comes to a physical showdown. Over the past two weeks, Cyril carried him over to Wolfgang's and Haidar's a lot for dinners and casual tea get-togethers; thus, they have quickly become good friends with each other. But Eli doesn't want to get Haidar and Mariposa involved in this repulsive mess, as they have a kid while Wolfgang has no liability.

The distance from his house to Wolfgang's is short. Eli should be there in a few minutes. Keeping his breathing steady, Eli rushes to Wolfgang's place while remaining highly alert to his surroundings.

During the run, Eli prays to all the Gods and Saints he has ever known. He prays Cyril is still alive and unharmed.

A great part of Eli prays he will find Cyril at Wolfgang's—even though such a thought is unlikely.

Cyril is alive. He has to be.

Eli can't get to his destination.

Why is it taking so long?! For some reason, Eli can't reach Wolfgang's house, no matter how fast he runs. Without stopping, Eli slows down while gripping the broken bed leg in his right hand. It is pitch-black outside, and all the streetlights are strangely out.

Eli runs for about ten more minutes and sees a faint silhouette of a house partially screened by a large, sagging oak branch from afar. With immense relief, Eli speeds up and races toward the direction of the house.

But as Eli dashes to Wolfgang's house, he spots a hazy shadow of someone sprinting toward him from ahead.

Eli nearly trips when he realizes the moving figure belongs to the murderous butcher. The vile man wields the sharp, bloodstained cleaver in the air and scuttles toward Eli at a clunky, constant speed. Eli quickly realizes the house isn't Wolfgang's—it's Cyril's house!

"I SEE YOU!" the evil butcher rasps maniacally. There is more blood on his clothes than when Eli last saw him in the living room. *"I WILL CATCH YOU, RAT. THEN I WILL MINCE YOU INTO PASTE!"*

Eli's finally terrified this time, but he doesn't freeze up. He instantly turns around and heads back in the direction he initially fled from.

The butcher is right behind Eli, reciting the nauseating mantra of gruesome human-butchering 101 he will do to Eli if he catches him. Each new threat is more violent and disgusting than the last. At one point, the vile butcher even threatens to sexually assault Eli and thrust the butler cleaver up his backside. That threat scares Eli more than anything.

Eli is running at his top speed, yet for some bizarre reasons, he can't outrun that fat butcher. Every time Eli manages to outpace his pursuer, just a short while later, the butcher spawns right behind him. The butcher has almost successfully grabbed Eli three times.

Eli starts to panic. His breathing becomes shaky and shallow. His heart pounds against his bony ribcage.

Eli was wrong.

He's going to die tonight.

After twenty minutes of petrifying chase, Eli returns to his house once again with the butcher close behind him. Eli barges through the front door and throws anything within his reach at the resilient killer to slow him down. Several flower vases, ceramic lamps, wooden cutting boards, and heavy dinnerware. But they are all useless. The butcher doesn't flinch or show any sign of pain, even though his white capirote is now soaking with blood after all the objects hit him. If anything, Eli's retaliation makes the killer's eyes gleam with sick fascination at the sight of his little prey fighting for his life.

"Cyril!" Eli screams his guardian's name as he is chased upstairs. "Where are you? Please save me! Cyril!"

"You're cornered, rat!" The butcher lashes the cleaver at Eli's head but misses him. *"I promise you that your death will be the longest and most painful than anyone I've ever killed. You wretched little MUTT!"*

The bedroom becomes a chaotic battlefield. Ruined furniture scatters all over the floor. Eli defends himself by throwing all the heavy objects he can grab at the maniac butcher. He tries to keep a distance from his attacker, for Eli knows he will instantly lose if he engages in a fistfight with him. But over time, it's become increasingly difficult for Eli to move around as the bedroom piles up with broken junk.

The butcher lashes out several times at Eli, but he manages to dodge them all. Nevertheless, the butcher manages to cut Eli twice on the right arm and the right side of his waist.

As the bloody fight advances, Eli, alas, becomes worn out and trips over a fallen chair. As a result, his head bashes into the wall, and he is stunned for a moment.

"Die!" The butcher swings the knife at Eli. Luckily, Eli snaps himself out of the concussion and throws himself to the floor just in time. The sharp blade went through his brown locks and nipped a few strands of his hair.

The cleaver temporarily jams into the wall. Eli takes that chance and plunges the sharp point of the broken bed leg at the butcher's heart, but it ends up going through his left hand. The vile butcher lets out a roaring wail as his right hand lets go of the knife on the wall.

"Mama! My hand! My hand hurts!" the butcher sobs hysterically. *"Mama, help me! This wretched rat hurt me so much!"*

The bloodstained capirote falls off to the floor due to the butcher's wild thrashing. Underneath the hood is not a human face. It resembles a lump of pasty, rotten flesh attached to a thick, flabby neck. There are crisscrossing black stitches that ooze yellow pus and brim with *squirming* maggots. They hold patches of sagging, decayed skin together. The butcher has no nose besides two tiny nostrils in the center of his face. His left eye is abnormally large and protruding, while his right is narrow and slanted downward. His mouth is deformed by a double cleft lip.

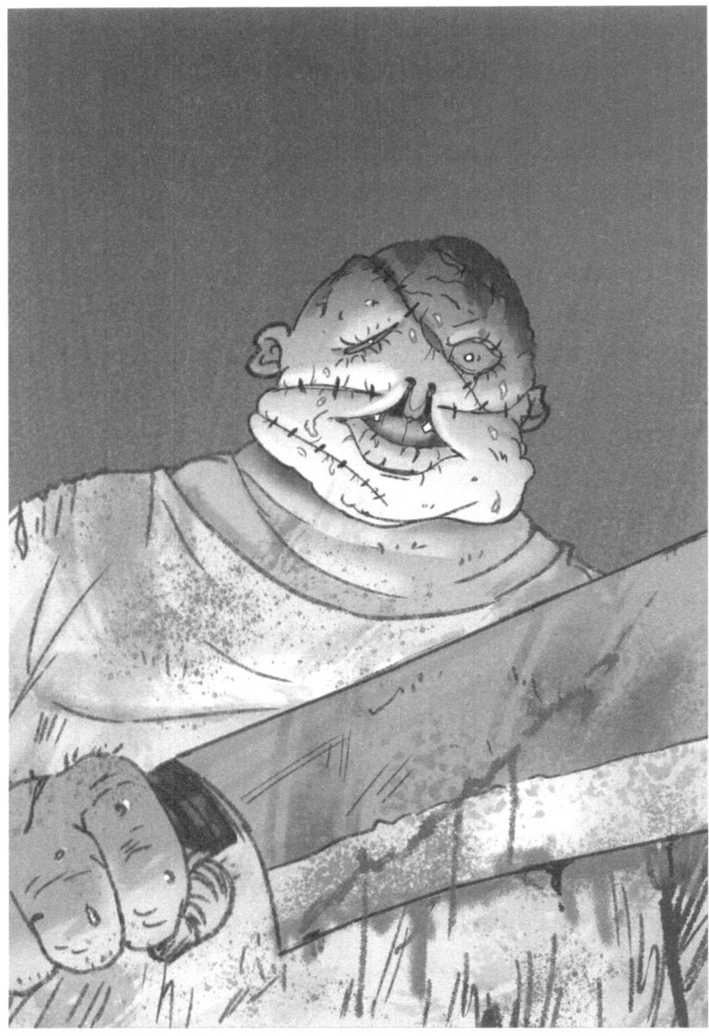

"I...will...kill...you," the butcher growls and goes ballistic. He attempts to grab Eli with his uninjured hand. But Eli acts quicker. He grabs the kitchen knife hidden deep in his black cape's pocket and repeatedly lashes at the butcher. However, the butcher lets the knife go through his left hand and punches Eli hard in the chest with his injured right hand.

Eli coughs and clutches his chest in tears. That blow is so brutally strong it leaves him breathless and his vision blurry.

The vile butcher yanks his bloody cleaver off the wall and runs toward Eli, who is cowering under Cyril's broken bed. *"Die, you rat!"*

Cyril. Eli shrews his eyes shut.

An unbelievable thing happens. The evil butcher trips on something that causes his entire heavy body to fall right at the row of broken, pointy wood slats of Cyril's destroyed bed. He is impaled from his lower belly to his neck, dying on the spot.

* * *

ELI'S CHEST heaves in an erratic rhythm as he stares at the corpse of the patched-face butcher. He glances at the butcher's feet and finds the object that caused the vile murderer to trip and save his life. It is no other than the winking yellow bathtub duck toy, the promotional gift from the candy shop, back when Cyril first took him to town.

The little duck now lies broken on the floor with its head separated from its body from the butcher's weight.

Eli crawls out of the nook of Cyril's bed to pick up the shattered toy. He cradles its remains to his chest and weeps. Cyril had to put the duck away in the desk's drawer due to Eli's nonstop complaint that he was treating him like a kid. The toy must have fallen out during the fight and ultimately saved Eli's life.

There's so much blood spilled everywhere—on the floor, walls, ceilings, and shattered furniture. His once beautiful fairytale bedroom now looks like a torture chamber from Hell.

Eli eventually stops crying and picks himself up. He stops in front of the mirror by the closet and is shocked by his reflection. The pretty, unblemished porcelain doll from earlier this morning now looks like a discarded, broken toy with blood splattered across his face and body.

What will Cyril think if he sees him right now? Would those beautiful blue eyes still look at him with adoration and gentleness?

I have to wash off the blood, Eli thinks and rushes to the bathroom. When he gets there, his heart drops when he sees a decapitated head with pale skin and raven hair sitting idly in the sink. Eli's scream echoes throughout the house as he sprints to grab the crown.

It isn't Cyril. The head belongs to a woman who bears an uncanny look to his guardian.

Pretty girl. Eli stares at the female head in his hands. He blinks slowly. The bathroom mirror is broken, and torn pieces of human flesh and fractured bone shards fill the sink's drain. It's unusable, so Eli sluggishly drags his feet to the bathroom downstairs.

Cradling the girl's head in his bloody hands, Eli treads to the upstairs corridor. He wants to give her a proper burial. A human head is quite heavy, though this girl's head is not as big as Cyril's. Back when they were at the Peridot Arboretum, when Cyril carried him on his broad back, Eli measured the size of his guardian's head with his palms and teased the ravenhead. And Cyril, as always, would only laugh it off and reward Eli's mischievousness with loving words and sweets.

Eli glances at the bedroom and stops dead in his tracks.

The butcher's corpse is gone.

Eli's face grows pallid as he rushes into the bedroom. The corpse is no longer impaled on the bed. The pool of blood still dripping on the sharp, broken slats is evidence that the body was previously there, and Eli didn't make up the whole thing. The bloody cleaver on the floor is gone, too.

CRAP! Eli swings around. There is no way that fat butcher could move without Eli noticing. There has to be magic involved in this.

Eli rushes outside of the bedroom while still holding the girl's head with his other hand. When he's about to run downstairs, he senses something coming at him. He immediately sidesteps and evades a close shave as the cleaver misses him and gets jammed into the wooden railing. The raging butcher appears from nowhere from behind Eli and punches him hard in his gut, causing him to tumble to the floor.

"I'll skin you alive!" the patched-face butcher screams as he stomps his foot down at Eli's face, but Eli rolls over and dodges it.

The butcher lets out an animalistic snarl. He wildly attacks Eli, throwing punches and kicks. After a while, he manages to corner Eli against the wall at the end of the balcony. The vile butcher hoists Eli up to his feet by his pajama shirt's collar and begins to choke him to death.

Eli struggles fiercely, but no matter what he does, he can't budge the iron grasp of the butcher. When Eli's close to passing out, his eyes catch a glimpse of a red cluster on the floor behind his attacker.

It's the head of the raven-hair girl. But it isn't a full head. During the fight, that butcher stepped his hulking foot on it, crushing half of the head into a pile of slushy mass.

The pretty girl with raven hair and pale skin.

Just like Cyril.

Eli trembles, but not from the fear that he's going to die. Instead, it's pure, burning rage. His green eyes become bloodshot. A blazing flame bursts inside his chest and radiates throughout his entire body.

The last thing Eli can remember is him grabbing the butcher's head with two hands. Then everything goes red.

* * *

"I'M SORRY," Eli mumbles to himself as he gathers the soppy, bloody chunks of flesh from the girl's head into a bag. "It's over. I avenged you. You can rest in peace now."

"My nanny also has blue eyes like you," Eli murmurs when he picks up the girl's eyeball. "But his blue eyes are different. It's a deep, ocean-blue color. A very rare shade of blue. Can you guide him back to me? I don't know what to do...I think I'm abandoned again. He said he would take care of me forever. That was just two weeks ago. Now look at me, I look like goddamn Carrie. Can you see how much of a lousy nanny he is?" Eli chuckles as he snivels.

"You probably don't know Carrie. She's not from this world. Just like me. I'm also not from this world. A bunch of stupid brats throw pig blood at Carrie as a prank." Eli takes a short break to wipe the butcher's blood off his face, but it won't scrub off.

Eli stops talking. A brief moment later, his lips twitch into a bitter smile.

Maybe Cyril finally realizes Eli's not his real master, and that Eli has been tricking him all along. That's why he left without saying goodbye.

Or maybe he found his real master and is by his side right now. Taking care of him and coddling him. Completely forgetting about the shameless imposter who took advantage of him.

Eli goes back to pick up the rest of the raven-hair girl's remains. "I guess I deserved it this time. I am a fraud. I...did tell him...I'm not his master," Eli mumbles. "He probably never wants to see my face again...I don't need him," Eli finally collects everything from the girl's head. He holds the bloody bag to his chest and starts to limp downstairs.

When Eli crosses the main foyer, the sight of the brass mirror by the front door stops him. Eli approaches it and puts the bag on the mahogany console table under the mirror.

Eli flinches at his own reflection. He looks like a demon, covered in blood from head to toe. Where's the 'adorable little angel' that Cyril saw in him?

"Who's that?" Eli croaks and turns around. His ears pick up a very faint whisper.

There's no one behind him, and yet the whisper continues.

"Who's there?" Eli walks to the kitchen. Everything looks still. Then he feels cold behind his nape. He turns around but once again finds no one standing behind him.

But Eli no longer cares at this point. He goes back to retrieve the bag with the girl's head inside. When his eyes trail up to the mirror by the foyer, he jumps at the image on the glass and drops the pouch to the floor.

That reflection shares the same face as the adult Eli in his previous life, when he passed away at twenty-three. It is staring at him with a dead look in its green eyes. Its brown hair is very choppy like it was forcibly cut by a knife. It is wearing a tattered, bloody shroud, similar to the tunic Eli wore when he was first awakened in this world. There's a large, deep wound that is fairly new in the left side of its chest.

Eli looks at the reflection of his real self in the mirror. That chest wound matches with the nightmare Eli last week. In that dream, he was chained to a wooden post and brutally executed. Someone shoved a sharp dagger into his chest over and over again.

"What are you trying to tell me?" Eli brushes his fingers on the glass. Just as he has predicted, his reflection is unmoving. It only stares at him.

"Is this how I'm going to die in this world?" Eli whispers, his voice empty. "Being stabbed to death?"

When Eli's fingers touch the bleeding gash on the chest of his reflection, the mirror cracks and explodes into hundreds of gleaming shards. Eli instinctively covers his face with his arms to shield himself from the pointed fragmented.

It's then that he spots an old, yellowing envelope embedded behind the brass frame of the mirror. On the front, only one word is written in faded black ink: *Ilya.*

Ilya. His Russian name.

This letter is for him.

Eli extends his hand to get the envelope, but he suddenly feels a strong presence of someone standing behind him. Eli spins around, determined to see this entity.

This time, the person doesn't vanish. He stands tall and looks down at Eli with veiled green eyes that resemble those that belong to a corpse.

This person before him is the Eli from the mirror. His adult self from the past life.

"What...do you want?" Eli shifts his gaze between his adult self's cold face and the bloody hole in his chest. "What do you want to tell me?!"

His older self, Ilya, says nothing, but studies him with his lifeless eyes. Eli can't tell if Ilya understands what he's saying. When Eli is about to repeat his question louder, Ilya's brows furrow. He grabs Eli's pajama collar and slams him into the wall behind him.

"What the fuc—" Eli grits his teeth.

"WAKE UP! NOW!" Ilya thunders, his hollow voice resonating throughout the house and making the ground tremble. Their surroundings crumble, and everything starts to get sucked into an endless black hole—except for Ilya, who stands firm and still at the edge of the gulf, watching Eli fall deep into the bottomless pit.

* * *

ELI SCREAMS as he jerks awake and falls off the bed to the wooden floor, dragging along the vase of pink roses from his nightstand.

"Ouch," Eli groans, clutching his head and rubbing his nose. He can feel a red bump rising on his forehead.

Eli is in a dazed heap and hears hasty footsteps echoing on the wooden stairs. His blood freezes when he sees the bedroom door is wide open. Biting back the pain, Eli scrambles to his feet and tries to shut the door, but it's too late. A tall figure rushes into the room and almost bumps into him.

"Eli? What happened?!" Cyril cries, picking up the scared-stiff Eli and carrying him back to bed. "Eli, are you hurt?!"

Cyril's concern amplifies when Eli doesn't respond to him. Eli only gapes at him, dumbfounded and terrified.

"Eli, you're bleeding!" Cyril grabs Eli's right arm.

Blood soaks the right side of Eli's pajamas, particularly around his waist. The same goes for the right arm. The gashes are fresh and clean cuts caused by a sharp knife.

So it wasn't a dream. Eli's encounter with the patched-face butcher in white did happen!

Eli takes a gander around. The bedroom is not destroyed—his and Cyril's bed, the bay window sofa, the desk, and the fine, vintage furniture... everything looks polished and orderly.

So it was just a nightmare?

Then how the hell did he get these cuts?!

What the hell is going on?!

"Let me get the bandages. I'll be right back!" Cyril announces, getting up to leave. But Eli pulls him back.

"Please...don't leave," Eli croaks, his trembling voice airy.

"But we have to treat the wound now, or else you might get an infection," Cyril reasons softly.

"NO! Don't go!" Eli cries out, clinging to Cyril's arm like a needy panda to a bamboo tree. "Please don't leave me alone. I don't want to die!"

"D-Die?! E-Eli, are you crying?"

"Dude, I'm not crying," Eli snaps as tears stream down his cheeks. "I—I..."

Years later, Eli still cringes in deep mortification whenever he recalls what he did that night—bursting into inconsolable sobs in front of Cyril. The only excuse he uses to save face is that he was barely seventeen then.

Though, in his mind, that still doesn't change the fact that Eli was never a kid when he came to this world. Though he possesses the body of a teenager, he was a twenty-three-year-old man from the start.

Of course, nobody knows about this, even Cyril. Well, Eli tried to explain it, but the ravenhead didn't seem to believe him. It's a little secret Eli keeps to himself for many years to come.

"You're safe, Eli. I won't let anything like this happen to you ever again," Cyril coos, holding the trembling Eli to his chest and gently stroking his back to calm him.

After Cyril bandaged up Eli's wounds, Eli told him everything. His gruesome vision at the fair when he first touched the oddly shaped bowl, his encounter with the bohemian lady and her peculiar shop, and the details of his nightmare. The only part he leaves out is seeing his older self and the discovery of the yellowing envelope behind the brass mirror frame by the front door downstairs.

"Eli, next time, whenever you meet any suspicious person or experience an enigmatic vision like that, you have to tell me right away. That's the only way for me to prevent the bad things from happening," Cyril requests tenderly. He has never once shown any anger or disappointment regarding Eli's poor decision to keep the vision a secret from him in the first place.

Eli nods. His hands are still shaking, no matter how hard he has tried to calm down.

"Don't be scared, my little kit. I'm here with you." Cyril holds Eli's hands. "I promise you, something like this will never happen again."

"Thanks," Eli sniffs.

"I'm sorry. I wasn't upstairs then. If I did, I would have noticed you were bleeding, and I could have woken you up or joined you in the dream."

Eli glances at the wooden clock on the wall. It's 4:45 AM right now. He woke up from that nightmare thirty-five minutes ago, and Cyril wasn't in bed then.

"Where were you, Cyril?" Eli asks. "What were you doing at four o'clock in the morning?"

"I was working. I couldn't sleep."

"What were you working on?"

"Some paperwork related to my work."

"Cyril, I have never seen you going to work ever since I lived here," Eli says. "Do you have a job?" It seems to Eli that Cyril's full-time job is being his nanny.

"I do have a job, Eli," Cyril responds.

"Well, what is it then?"

"...Wood. I work with wood."

"Huh?" Eli lifts a brow.

"I-I mean. Uh, eh. I—uh, c-carpentering. I'm a carpenter."

Eli slightly shudders when he imagines his klutzy nanny making a wooden object with a metal hammer without nailing his fingers—super unrealistic. That's why he finds Cyril's answer unconvincing.

"Cyril, you've been staying home with me for over two weeks without going to work. Aren't you afraid you'll get fired?" Eli asks.

"I own the business, Eli."

"Oh..." Eli exclaims. "Anyway, back to the main topic. What do you mean when you said you can join me in my dream?"

"Well, I'm a Sage, remember?" Cyril reminds him. "I'm positively certain the bohemian merchant hexed you at the fair. That bowl you touched must be cursed. She must have sent the butcher entity after you through astral projection. If they got you in the nightmare, you would die in the same fashion in real life."

"W-What should we do now?" Eli asks, terrified.

"You go back to sleep, Eli." Cyril strokes the Eli's cheek. "And leave everything to me."

"Are you kidding?! I can't go back to sleep! I literally just escaped from death," Eli objects.

"Do you want me to sleep with you?"

"Excuse me?!" *What the heck?!*

"I can sleep on the same bed with you if you're scared," Cyril clarifies.

"Dude, that will never happen! Don't you even think about it!" Eli snaps, making Cyril jump. "I will be a fudging cow if that ever happens!"

"A-A cow?" Cyril gapes stupidly at him.

Eli sighs. "It's not important, dude! What are we going to do about the bohemian witch?"

"I'll go to the fair and find out about her whereabouts. Then I'll make sure she will never hurt anyone ever again."

"H-How about the butcher?" Eli quivers every time he mentions the ferocious killer that he was fortunate enough to escape in one piece.

"Well, you defeated him in the dream, right? He's probably dead in real life."

"I really killed him," Eli mutters, horrified.

"It was self-defense, Eli. You also did the world a grand favor." Cyril squeezes Eli's hand. "The corpses you saw were probably his victims in real life."

Eli rubs his temple. The images of all the mutilated body parts scattered throughout Cyril's house in the dream still make him nauseous. "Okay, let me come to the fair with you today. I will show you where her tent is. What time does the fair open?"

Cyril gets up to get a leaflet from the desk drawer by the foot of his bed. "The Midsummer Fair opens from 8:30 AM to 12:00 AM. However, the vendors will have to be there earlier to set up their tents and merchandise. We can get there around 7:00 or 7:30."

"Yes, let's," Eli sighs.

* * *

Eli can't go back to sleep, so he goes to check the winking yellow duck toy in the desk's drawer and is relieved to find it still in one piece. There are also no decapitated heads in the bathroom. After taking a quick shower, he has an early breakfast with Cyril. Both then get into a cab and take off to the Midsummer Fair at 6:30 AM.

"Cyril, what are you going to do to the bohemian woman?" Eli asks when they're in the cab.

"I'll make her pay for what she did to you," Cyril responds with grim affirmation.

Eli is worried. "Can we just report her to a higher authority? I...don't want you to get hurt."

Cyril's smile is brighter than a blooming sunflower. "Thank you for worrying about me, Eli. I'll be fine. The law is on my side, for she and her accomplice are the ones who commit these horrendous, unforgivable crimes."

"Also, I have superpowers, remember?" Cyril flashes him a confident smile. A flame butterfly forms from Cyril's left palm. It flies toward Eli and gives him a little dance before dissolving into thin air.

ELI AND CYRIL arrive at the Hepatica town square, where the Midsummer Festival is held at 7:05 AM. Today is a Saturday morning, and they are the only visitors coming to the fair this early, as the event isn't open until an hour and a half later.

Eli leads his guardian through the throng of bustling merchants to where he met the bohemian woman yesterday. But she isn't here today, as the grassy land where the paisley patchwork tent was set the day before is empty now.

"Was it this area?" Cyril points at the empty land, and Eli nods.

Cyril observes the empty space. Then he steps onto the center of the ground where the tent used to sit and closes his eyes. Several moments later, Cyril opens his eyes and speaks in a grim tone. "I saw them. I saw how they died."

"What?" Eli feels goosebumps forming all over his body.

"There is a lot of dead energy lingering at this spot," Cyril states. "The victims weren't killed here, but their murderers brought their remains here and sold them as merchandise. These ghosts have become vengeful spirits."

Crap. "What are we going to do next?" Eli asks.

"Let's go talk to the festival director. He should have the list of all the vendors who participate in this event," Cyril says, approaching Eli.

"Right. Let's go." Eli blinks when Cyril holds his hand.

"Don't be scared, Eli," Cyril tells him with a smile. "Since you defeated one of the murderers, these spirits are not as vengeful anymore. I'll take care of the last one."

Eli and Cyril come to talk to the festival director about the bohemian woman. They learn she isn't from here and only visited Hepatica for this Midsummer event. At first, the director doesn't seem eager to help them, complaining that he has stuff to do. But after Cyril gives him a gold coin, he tells them where the bohemian woman currently stays.

"You should find her at the caravan motel twelve miles from here by the Fair Fork River on the outskirts of town," says the director.

Cyril thanks the man and calls the cab. When they get inside it, Cyril asks the coachman to take them back to their fairytale cottage.

"Wait, we're not going to the caravan motel?" Eli asks, stunned.

"I'll go there by myself. You should go home and rest." Cyril grins.

*　*　*

WHEN ELI RETURNS, he is surprised to see Wolfgang, Haidar, and Mariposa at the house. Apparently, Cyril asked the neighbors to come over and babysit Eli while he was gone.

"Be good, Eli. I'll be home soon!" Cyril tells him. Then he gets back into the cab and goes off.

*　*　*

"MARIE, WHERE'S GALLAHAN?" Eli asks Mariposa. It's a little strange not to see Gallahan here with his mom and dad. Among all the neighbors, the boy has always been the clingiest, to the point that he makes Cyril quite jealous.

"Oh, he's at the Summer Camp," Mariposa replies while setting the table.

"I see," Eli comments. Gallahan mentioned nothing about attending a camp yesterday during their Midsummer dinner party.

After lunch, Eli is dead tired, but he doesn't dare go to sleep. So, he asks Haidar about the process of Cyril's lawsuits regarding the accidental vandalism at the Peridot Arboretum and…the accidental assault on the mailman. He tells Haidar he hasn't seen Cyril take any action about the charges since he received the express court summons over two weeks ago.

"Ah, good news, Eli. Cyril doesn't have to go to court for these two incidents," Haidar discloses. "He only has to pay for a fine. I believe he received the fine notice yesterday."

Eli recalls he saw Cyril reading a letter yesterday morning before they came to the Midsummer Fair.

"Um, do you know how much he has to pay?" Eli asks.

"25,780 gold coins before tax. With the ten percent tax, the final number is 28,358 gold coins."

"WHAT?! 28,358?!" Wolfgang and Mariposa shriek at the same time.

"How much can you buy with one gold coin?" Eli is wide awake now.

"Food for a family of five for a month," Mariposa answers.

"A dozen bottles of fine wine," Wolfgang adds.

"I feel dizzy." Eli collapses. Wolfgang and Mariposa catch him before he drops to the floor.

* * *

CYRIL GETS home around eight o'clock in the evening. Wolfgang, Haidar, and Mariposa also leave around that time. Eli rushes to his guardian but is repelled by the strong odor coming from Cyril's body.

"Cyril, what's that smell?" Eli covers his nose.

"Oh, I'm sorry, my little kit. It's been a long day. Let me take a shower first, then we'll talk, alright?" Cyril flashes him a smile, then hurries to the bathroom upstairs.

Finally, having a moment alone, Eli listens to the sound of water from the showerhead falling on the ceramic bathtub. When he's sure Cyril's washing up, Eli walks to the console table next to the front door, where the brass mirror is hung.

Eli regards the mirror thoughtfully before lifting it up and turning it around.

He freezes upon seeing an old, yellowing envelope behind the brass frame of the mirror. He picks it up and flips it around. On the old paper is an Elgarian word written in faded black ink.

This envelope looks very similar to the one Eli saw in the nightmare, except the English word "Ilya" isn't there.

* * *

After the shower, Cyril tells Eli about his encounter with the witch while having dinner. He eats alone, as Eli has already eaten with the neighbors. According to Cyril, when he came to the caravan, he found the witch mourning for her son—the patched-face butcher that attacked Eli in the nightmare. This witch practiced a type of dark magic that could prolong her life like that of a Sage's when she feasted on the flesh and blood of young adolescents, especially pretty, virgin boys, whom her deformed son had an intense animosity towards. They would stalk their victims through the dream and kill them there, then collect the bodies in real life. Or they went after their victims in person. Together, these two murdered over fifty teenagers. The youngsters were cruelly tortured, then flayed to death. Their bones were then used for artisan crafts and sold as merchandise. And their skins were patched together into a large quilt. It was hidden between the two layers of the paisley patchwork fabric from the tent as a form of demonic ritual.

Eli's face blanches. "That's so sick."

"Eli, you have to be careful. The reason these two came after you so fiercely was because you're a Sage. If they were to kill you and consume your body, they would have inherited your longevity," Cyril states.

"B-But I didn't tell that witch I'm a Sage! How would she know?" Eli cries.

"You stand out. While it isn't a rule that every Sage is good-looking, but in general, the people who possess striking beauty, like you, carry a higher possibility of being a Sage. These evil witches rarely dare to go after older Sages. But they would kill to feast on a young and inexperienced Sage like you."

"Should I be sloppy and wear a potato shack from now on?"

"I doubt that will make any difference, my dear," Cyril laughs.

* * *

ELI STARES at his comfy bed with indescribable yearning. He is drop-dead tired but doesn't dare to sleep. Earlier, Eli claimed he would be a grazing cow if he shared the same bed with a man. So Cyril comes up with a brilliant solution to sleep near his young master while keeping Eli from being a cow: He moves their beds next to each other.

"Seriously?" Eli shoots Cyril an exhausted side-eye.

"It's the only way I can join you in your dream should you encounter a spiritual attack again," Cyril says grimly, but his eyes are oddly sparkling.

"Okay, let's go to sleep then. I'm so tired." Eli gives up and rolls into his bed.

"Good night, Eli," Cyril says cheerily, lying in his bed beside Eli's.

"Good night," Eli murmurs.

About fifteen minutes later, Eli speaks up. "Cyril, you're still up?"

"Yes, Eli. What is it?"

"What did you do to the witch?"

There is a pause. "She'll never be a threat to anyone again."

"How about the soul of the victims? The vengeful ghosts?"

"I collected all the bones in her caravan and gave each of them a proper burial. That was why it took me so long."

"I see," Eli mutters, then closes his eyes. "Good night, Cyril. Thank you for what you did," he adds in a low voice.

"You don't have to say thank you. It's my obligation to protect you, Eli," Cyril replies. "I'm the one that has to apologize to you. I failed you. I let you fend for yourself against a dangerous fiend. If something happened to you, I'm afraid I would—"

Cyril stops when he hears Eli's soft snoring. He pulls Eli's blanket higher to cover his small body. Then Cyril lies back in his own bed and stares at the ceiling in silence.

"Eli?" Cyril whispers. But there's no response. He turns to his young master and gazes at his face.

"Ilya," Cyril says softly.

Eli suddenly replies, "What?"

"Y-You're still awake?!" Cyril stammers, spooked.

"I was sleeping, but I heard you call my name." Eli looks at his guardian. "What did you want?"

"Nothing, I-I just...wanted to say your name." Cyril flushes.

"Are you crazy?"

"S-Sorry, master—Eli."

"Go to sleep." Eli closes his eyes.

"G-Good night," Cyril stutters.

Three minutes later, Eli speaks up again. "Cyril?"

"Yes! Eli!" Cyril responds immediately.

"I trust you already knew I have powerful hands that can snap bones easily, right?" Eli reminds him. "Remember what I did to that butcher's head?"

"Yes?" Cyril innocently nods.

"If you try anything when I'm sleeping, I'll crush your nuts." Eli gives his guardian a faint smile.

"M-My nuts?"

"Ah, you'll find out what they are if you try to do anything shady to me. Good night."

CHAPTER 11

OUR LITTLE SECRET SAFE HAVEN

That night, Eli has a strange dream—not a nightmare, though it is odd, nonetheless. Everything looks black and white in that dream, like an old movie.

Eli is in a dark gray, empty space with two other people. They have long waist-length hair and blurred-out faces. Eli thought they were two women at first, but when he looked carefully, their chests were flat, and their body frames were too buff to be female. Both wear elegant white outfits like the main characters in a fantasy adventure game. The light-haired man is brushing the other's long, dark hair. The blond has his hair tied into a ponytail while the brunette lets his hair hang loose.

The two are talking about something, but Eli can't understand what they are saying. The sound comes out like a long, noisy hum in his ears.

My past self's memories? Eli muses and approaches the two men in the dream. He seems to be invisible to them. Eli observes the brunette's silhouette and confirms he is a full-grown adult.

Not a memory, then.

"Hello?" Eli waves his hand at the two, but they can't see or hear him.

Eli then observes the blond. Strangely enough, this man reminds him of

Cyril. Both have very similar builds, tall and ripped. The differences are their hair length and color.

"Cyril?" Eli attempts to talk to the blond, but nothing happens.

Eli looks at the brunette again. This time, despite the blurry face, he can sense some uncanny resemblance to his old twenty-three-year-old self in the modern world.

"Ilya," Eli calls out to the brunette. But again, no response.

Eli takes a step back to observe both men before him again. The more he looks at them, the more certain he feels they are Cyril and him. And that makes no sense at all!

If this isn't a memory, perhaps it's a prediction of the future? Eli wonders. But the clothes these two wear seem dated compared to the current Victorian-esque men's fashion in this country. Are people going to rock medieval clothes in the next couple of years?

Eli eventually grows bored after a while. He mutters "bye" to them and walks away.

After some time wandering, Eli finds himself in a crowded marketplace. This time, the scenario happens in muted colors instead of black and white. Everything looks ordinary until Eli hears a commotion ahead of him. He moves forward and spots a small, shoeless, hooded person sprawling on the ground like he was pushed. Surrounding him is a group of equestrians clad in expensive clothing. They're all wearing black and have their faces partly covered by a black hood and facemask. It looks like the small, hooded person accidentally ran into these sketchy people's horses and got himself knocked to the ground.

Nobody is gonna help him up? Eli ponders. Like before, all the faces of the people in the dream are blurred out. Suddenly, something catches Eli's attention—he sees a familiar scar on the small, hooded person's left forearm.

The branding mark?! Eli hurries closer. He recognizes the skinny frame and chestnut hair underneath the shabby, tattered cloak. That person is him!

Is this when he—uh, I was kidnapped? Eli observes the hooded, faceless Eli in the dream. *What is hooded Eli doing in the marketplace? Did he manage to escape his captors? Was this scenario before I woke up in that alleyway in Creepyville?*

Eli checks hooded Eli's clothes and finds they don't match the tattered tunic he wore when he was revised in this world.

"Lift your head," the most richly dressed equestrian commands.

Eli and his dream self jump in unison, but for different reasons. For Eli, it's because of the pure astonishment to finally hear a coherent sentence instead of gibberish for the first time in this dream. However, for Dream Eli, it's probably due to the intimidation of being addressed by an aristocrat.

Dream Eli pulls down his hood and flees instead of obeying the rich man's request. Eli watches his dream self fearfully scamper away like he is being chased by a ghost or a mafia loan shark. Seeing his past self appear so lowly and helpless in front of these snobby people frustrates Eli as he glowers at the rich guy on the horse for scaring his dream self away.

"Would you like me to go after him?" another equestrian proposes. He appears to be a subordinate.

"No," the rich man answers after some consideration, then turns his horse. "Let's go."

"Yeah, bug off, you high-horse douche!" Eli boos.

After they're long gone, Eli continues on his way—moodily. After some time, he reaches a running stream in an evergreen forest. Finally, away from the faceless people, Eli takes in some fresh air and sits by a boulder near the creek, watching the spring water flow downstream.

"I want to wake up," Eli grumbles out loud, cheeks leaning on his palms.

"What do you want for breakfast?" a youthful male voice suddenly speaks up from behind Eli and scares the living daylights out of him. Before the mysterious person can utter another word, a punch meets his face and knocks him to the ground. "Ouch!"

"What the hell is wrong with you?!" Eli shrieks, grabbing the edge of the rock as he almost falls into the stream.

"I-I'm sorry." Cyril clumsily picks up himself. "I didn't mean to scare you. Are you alright?"

"Hell no! You almost gave me a heart attack! Do not sneak up behind me like that, Cyril! It's creepy as fudge!"

Cyril looks traumatized by Eli's swearing. But instead of scolding the youngster's obscene language, Cyril s coaxes his young master, promising to buy Eli new clothes and sweets and take him on vacation.

"Seriously?" Eli rolls his eyes. "We can't go on a vacation, Cyril! You have an outrageously large fine from the vandalism and assault lawsuits."

"How do you know about this?!"

"Your lawyer told me!"

Cyril's expression turns annoyed, but a few seconds later, he goes back to being cheery again. "You should not be concerned about money, Eli. 28,500 gold coins are nothing. I will take care of it."

"It's 28,358," Eli corrects.

"Ah, right. I tend to round up numbers." Cyril laughs.

Eli says nothing but shoots Cyril an exceptionally wary gaze.

"I'm a business owner, remember?" Cyril gently reminds him.

"The woodshop?"

"Yes! The woodshop. My business is doing extremely well. A couple of thousands of gold coins are a very small amount of money."

"Okay, if you say so," Eli mumbles. "Hey, Cyril. What did you tell me earlier?"

"I'm sorry?" Cyril blinks in confusion.

"You brushed my hair a while ago. What did we talk about?" Eli taps his feet impatiently.

"I-I don't know what you're saying, master—Eli." Cyril scratches his head.

Eli gives Cyril a long, cold look that has the ravenhead fidget. Then he abruptly turns away, sullenly crossing his arms and speaking in an aloof tone. "Go away. I don't want to talk to you anymore."

"W-What?! Why? What have I done?" Cyril panics.

"I thought you were my family. But turns out you're not!"

"Eli!" Cyril exclaims, horrified. "You're the most important person in my life! I adore you more than anything in the world!"

"Yeah, you keep saying that. But if you really think that way, then you would not keep so many secrets from me."

"W-What secrets are you talking about?" Cyril gasps in horror.

"Humph! Now that you asked, there is—" Eli begins, but abruptly stops.

Cyril is waiting for him to continue.

"Who are you?" Eli takes a step back.

"I'm Cyril."

"Which Cyril is this? Cyril from my dream or the real Cyril?" Eli regards the man before him cautiously.

"I don't understand what that means," Cyril falters. A moment later, he sheepishly says, "Oh...it's the latter, Eli."

"You're stalking me in my dream?!" Eli fumes. What a close call! He almost slipped out about the yellowing envelope.

Sneaky bastard!

"This is a serious breach of privacy! I want to wake up right now!" Eli rages.

"R-Right away," Cyril stutters. Their surroundings start to fall apart, taken over by blinding white light.

* * *

When Eli opens his eyes, he finds Cyril waking up at the same time on the separate bed next to his. Eli is about to bite his guardian's head off when he sees a fresh, pink bruise on Cyril's left cheek—the exact spot where Eli punched him in the dream.

"What the—?!" Eli grabs Cyril's face, and his mouth hangs wide open.

"I'm fine, Eli." Cyril beams at Eli upon catching him guiltily staring in shock at the punch mark.

"I'm so sorry," Eli stutters. His hands fall down to his side.

"No, no. It was my fault for scaring you like that. I'm sorry," Cyril squeezes Eli's hand, gesturing that everything's fine.

But everything is far from fine.

"This place is so insane," Eli mutters.

"What do you mean?"

"I feel really lost." Eli rubs his temples. "I-I don't know what to say, Cyril. I hit you in the dream, and you get hurt in real life? How is it possible?"

"Aw, Eli. I'm fine, I swear."

"That's not the point, Cyril," Eli cries out. "The point is this world is crazy, and I don't know a thing about it! And I keep having these nightmares or weird dreams almost every night that make no sense to me at all! I don't know anything! I can physically hurt people through a dream! That's freaking insane! I feel so...so...stressed out!"

Cyril patiently listens to Eli's rant. Despite the pent-up frustration, Eli doesn't mention anything about the secret envelope behind the mirror. After he finishes his rambling, the ravenhead pulls him to his chest and embraces him.

"Thank you for telling me all of this," Cyril whispers with his dulcet voice. "I understand the fear, confusion, and helplessness you are feeling, Eli. But you shouldn't feel that way. You have to understand that you're not alone. I'll always be here for you. Please lean on me," Cyril's words sound like a desperate plea.

Eli stares at Cyril with mixed emotions. He almost asks Cyril about the secret envelope, but something inside him holds him back. In the end, he only nods in agreement with his guardian.

"Also, Eli?"

"Hm?" Eli mumbles.

"It was a good punch, stronger than I expected. I'm proud of you." Cyril grins, lovingly flicking the tip of his young master's nose.

* * *

For a change of pace, Cyril takes Eli to the Three Bears Diner for breakfast. Cyril has been extra chirpy this morning, trying super hard to keep Eli in a good mood. Eli feels as if Cyril is trying to make it up to him.

"So, where do you want to go? The beach or a trip to the lake house?" Cyril asks merrily.

"Um...which one is cheaper?" Eli asks, sipping a cup of hot lemon tea.

"Eli, I told you money is not an issue in our household. Believe me, I will make sure you want for nothing!"

"Alright, Gatsby." Eli sighs. "Let's see. A trip to the lake house seems nice."

"Well, the lake house it is." Cyril grins.

"Ay, wait a second. Where is this lake house located?" Eli interjects. "Are there going to be other buildings surrounding the house, or is it a private property in an isolated area?"

Cyril tells him it's the latter, and Eli is immediately put off by the answer.

"Oh no, no, no, no, no! We're definitely not going to that lake house in the forest unless you want to be chased by a creepy axe man with me!" Eli shudders as he remembers the frightening ordeal with the patched-face butcher and his bohemian-witch mom that happened just yesterday. "Let's just stay away from forests for a while, okay?"

"Eli, I swear to you that, from now on, I'll be closely watching you anywhere you go, and I'll be nowhere over ten feet apart from you." Cyril speaks fervently, holding Eli's hands. "I'll protect you, even if I have to sacrifice my life. If needed, I can burn down the forest surrounding that lake house to ease your mind."

What—the—fudge?

"...I believe you, man," Eli responds after a long silence. Initially, he was close to making douchey remarks about Snow White's melodramatic oath. But he changed his mind when he saw the pink mark on Cyril's flawless face. "But what's the point of going on vacation if we have to gear up like we're about to enter the wolf's den? That makes no sense, man. Plus, you can't be with me all the time. That's not doable, and it's weird."

"What's so weird about that?" Cyril asks with genuine confusion.

"Because I want freedom, and you'd look like a pedo-kidnapper if you're hand in hand with me all the time!" Eli snaps, finally losing the last stretch of his patience. He really believes Cyril's common sense is inversely proportional to his beauty.

"Oh, s-sorry." Cyril flinches.

"Also, no more burning down public property! Is being a convicted criminal your life goal or something?"

"Of course not. My life goal is to live a long and happy life with you."

"Well, you can't do that if you're in jail," Eli chides.

"Oh, Eli. I will not go to jail." Cyril's blue eyes begin to sparkle as he gazes at Eli with utter affection. "I'll never leave your side, and I'll take care of you forever!"

"Cyril, honestly, you worry me sometimes with your overzealous brother complex," Eli shoots his heart-eyed guardian a concerned glance.

"What does 'overzealous brother complex' mean?" Cyril asks, finally stopping his idiotic giggling.

Eli is about to explain when the diner door springs open. A swell of cold and solemn energy sweeps through the small dining space. Eli stops talking and looks toward the diner's entrance.

The young man is around Cyril's age, about twenty-four or twenty-five. He is tall and has an incredible physique that resembles a statue of a Greek God. His skin is the same shade as the silver moon, winsomely contrasting with the lustrous raven locks and his lavish, dark navy outfit.

The diner falls into silence as almost everybody, men and women, is gaping at the new customer by the door, thoroughly captivated by his presence.

That young man is the most beautiful person Eli has ever laid his eyes on.

Yet, despite possessing such breathtaking beauty, there is not a single trace of warmth or amiability on the young man's flawless face. Especially those blue-gray, feline eyes are akin to those of a wild, ferocious lion.

Another odd thing about this young man is that he wears a full suit with black leather gloves despite the scalding summer heat.

The god-like beauty strides toward the direction of Eli and Cyril's booth. When he is about three steps away from their table, Cyril turns around for the first time and smiles at the gorgeous young man. "Oh, what a surprise to see you here!"

The gorgeous young man halts and gives Cyril an impassive gaze.

"Please, sit down with us." Cyril stands up to give the man his seat and sits next to Eli. Then he turns to Eli and says, "Master, I would like to introduce to you my long-time colleague. This is Dante. He works at the woodshop with me and is the co-founder of my business."

"What?" Eli and Dante exclaim in unison and then look at each other awkwardly.

"Dante, this is my precious young master, Ilya, who went missing for three years. I found him about three weeks ago. He suffers from amnesia."

"My condolences," Dante utters after a silence and holds out his hand to Eli. "I hope...you'll recover soon."

"Thank you very much. Nice to meet you." Eli shakes Dante's gloved hand. "Dante, are you and Cyril related?"

Dante looks taken aback at the question. "What makes you say that?"

"You and Cyril look very much like each other."

"We look completely different from each other," Cyril says.

"Different?" Eli lifts a brow and carefully regards the two men. He discards his initial assessment that Dante is the most handsome man he's ever met. It's incredibly challenging to determine who's more beautiful between Cyril and Dante. For their resemblance aside from their god-tier beauty, they both share similar heights, body builds, facial structures, hair colors, and skin tones. As for their differences, there are only two: Dante has slightly narrowed blue-gray eyes, while Cyril has big, blue eyes.

"You two look like full-on siblings to me," Eli comments after his assessment.

Dante and Cyril gawk at Eli as if he has just made the silliest statement ever.

"Interesting." Cyril smiles at Eli. "But we're definitely not related."

"Unless my father was unfaithful, which is impossible," Dante comments. His eyes are now fixed on Eli with a certain interest. "So, you don't remember anything, huh?"

Eli nods in response.

"None at all?"

"Yep," Eli replies.

"You look very young," Dante says. "Much younger than I imagined."

"Oh? How so?" Eli asks in an even tone.

"Based on what Cyril has told me about you, I always imagined you to be much older," Dante glances at Snow White. "He said you taught him everything he knows."

"That's the truth. My master is a prodigy," Cyril squeezes Eli's shoulder. "If it weren't for him, I wouldn't be here today. He's the most important person in my life."

"Please don't listen to him," Eli elbows his guardian hard in the chest. "He's exaggerating. I'm not a prodigy. Even if I was, it was all in the past."

"Mmm." Dante shifts his posture, leaning against the booth and thoughtfully regarding Eli and Cyril. "The Cyril I know is quite bad at giving compliments. It is probably the first time in a very long time that I have seen such a happy smile on his face."

"I see," Eli drawls, and shoots his guardian an impish glance.

"That's nothing new. You are the sole joy of my life." Cyril fondly flicks Eli's nose, then turns to Dante. "And you, my friend, are particularly chatty today. You, too, seem to be in a better mood that I've seen in a long time. Do you mind sharing what's made you so...sociable? I suppose you came all the way here to meet me for a reason other than painting me in a good light to my master."

"You're right. I am in a good mood today," Dante responds with a smirk. "My good friend finally reunited with his long lost, dearest master. Both of you look in excellent health, so—Cyril, isn't it the right time for you to come back to work?"

Cyril acts like he has no idea what his friend is saying.

Dante taps his gloved fingers against the table.

"You know what, my master is actually not doing well...at all! Despite what you're seeing, he…uh, he's still in a fragile state that requires my utmost attention. I need to spend a little more time with him until he fully recovers." Cyril is suddenly speaking with a lisp.

"His face's glowing." Dante gestures at Eli.

"Well, he's not. If you don't believe me, read this." Cyril gives Dante a paper from his vest pocket.

Dante takes the paper. "What is this?"

"My master's medical report," Cyril says. "You can see that he has serious complications of streptobacillosis, avitaminosis, anemia, and hypotension!"

Dante reads through the report. Eli can tell the poor lad doesn't understand jack of what's in the paper as he looks like he just attempted to finish *Moby Dick* in two hours.

"So, are these illnesses dangerous?" Dante asks.

"Good gracious, of course not! Would I be sitting here if they were?" Cyril snaps at Dante for asking such a hapless question. "However, those conditions are by no means harmless. The doctor has ordered him to be under close care until he's fully recovered."

Dante stares at Cyril and then at Eli. "Why don't you get a few servants to look after—"

Cyril's appalled gasp cuts in; he looks at his friend dead in the eye. "Dante, you knew how destroyed I was when he was kidnapped. How could you suggest I let some strangers look after him when I have only just gotten him back? He's a child—"

"Hey." Eli glares at his guardian while eating his berry pancakes.

"He's a young man," Cyril corrects himself. "But he's completely lost his memory. He doesn't know anything. He is like a little innocent snowflake. I can't trust him to be under some strangers' care. The last time I let my guard down, he was taken away from me."

Dang! Eli feels the goosebumps forming on his arms. Though Eli does not doubt that Cyril means what he said regarding Eli's safety and welfare, Cyril's excuse for the extended leave is unbelievably lame. Yet, somehow, his delivery is so heartfelt that it would make anyone feel immoral to turn down his sincere request. Dude really wants to go on this beach vacation.

Contrary to Eli's expectations, Dante is more softhearted than he appears to be—despite his stony, no-BS façade. He seems to fall for Cyril's excuse.

"Well then, how much time do you think you'll need until you can return to work?" Dante asks, sounding genuinely sympathetic.

"Oh, Dante! You're such a wonderful person! A marvelous friend! How would I survive without you?"

Dante cuts off Cyril's incessant praise. "Just give me a date."

"Great!" Cyril claps his hands together. "I predict it would take at least a year for my master to fully recover."

Dante's face turns ashy gray the moment he hears the word 'year.' His gorgeous feline eyes widen to full circles.

"Don't fret, Dante. I would not leave you to be in charge of...my shop for a year," Cyril assures his terrified friend.

Dante slowly breathes out in relief.

Cyril flashes a charming grin at Dante. "Today is July 2. So, let's round up to August. I think it's best if I come back in February next year."

The charming grin doesn't work; if anything, it's no different from adding fuel to the open fire. Dante gives Cyril a good, long lecture for his irresponsibility toward his work—which is well deserved.

"Good grief! You're being overdramatic, Dante. I have given you full power over my business. Others would kill to be in your position; it's the opportunity of a lifetime," Cyril scoffs, mildly annoyed at his friend's nagging.

"Opportunity of a lifetime? What kind of a woodshop are you guys running?" Eli asks.

"A quite successful and profitable one." Cyril smiles gently at Eli. "Are you interested in running it one day when you're all grown up?"

"Eh, thanks. But I'm good," Eli shrugs and receives affectionate pats on his head from his guardian.

"I really wish you would take your work seriously, Cyril," Dante says.

"I do take it seriously. That's why I let you, the co-owner, run the place when I'm absent. I even let you have the full benefits and absolute power when you're in charge, so I really don't understand where your disappointment comes from," Cyril remarks moodily.

"I don't need those superficial benefits, and I'm not the co-owner!" Dante snaps.

Eli is confused. "Wait, are you just employed at his woodshop?"

"No!" Dante cries out. "I was doing him a favor by looking after his... shop when he's been absent for the past two weeks!"

* * *

CYRIL PULLS Dante outside of the diner to continue their conversation in private. Long story short, Cyril manages to convince Dante to keep looking after his business for one more month. Cyril will have to return to work on the first day of September. However, Cyril is not thrilled with this negotiation; he's glum the entire time they're in the carriage home.

Eli tries to lift the ravenhead's spirit. "Hey, it's not so bad. We can still go on that beach vacation like you want, and we have plenty of time to hang out for an entire month!"

"I just want to spend more time with you," Cyril squeezes Eli's hand. "I only just got you back...after all these years. Just thinking that I must leave you at home all by yourself really kills me."

"Oh, Cyril! Stop worrying!" Eli groans. "I can look after myself! You know it!"

"Uh...no?" Cyril answers honestly.

"What do you mean 'no'? You know all about my heroic accomplishments!" Eli feels a little offended.

Cyril's eyebrows knit together.

Eli huffs, highly irritated. His overprotective nanny is obviously trying to downplay his capability. Eli reminds Cyril about his past triumphs against the brothel mob, the musical werewolf, the headless ghosts, the evil witch, and the patched-face butcher—all by himself!

"Here, look!" Eli pulls up his right sleeve and shows Cyril his bandaged arm. "I'm not a wuss!"

Cyril's brows furrow. "A wuss?"

"A weakling."

"Ah, of course, you're not a weakling, Eli. You are the bravest person I've ever known!" Cyril pulls his young master into an embrace. He looks Eli in the eyes and sighs deeply.

"I'll be fine, Cyril." Eli pats Cyril's back. "I promise from now on, I'll be careful and not get myself or you into any trouble."

Cyril then tells Eli how sweet and thoughtful he is and that he's such a little angel, but Eli can still see the apprehension weighing in Cyril's blue eyes.

* * *

WHEN THEY REACH HOME, Eli sees Gallahan sitting on the cushioned bench by the cottage's front porch, waiting for them. When Eli gets off the carriage, Gallahan runs to greet and gives him a tight hug.

"Eli! Are you alright?" Gallahan asks with great concern.

"I'm fine, buddy," Eli replies cheerfully. He notices Gallahan looks jittery. "Gallahan, is everything okay?"

"Yeah, everything's good." Gallahan checks Eli from head to toe. "How are your injuries? Did you just come back from the doctor? What did he say?"

"M-My injuries?" Eli is a little surprised that Gallahan knows about the butcher incident. Then he remembers that maybe Haidar and Mariposa told him. "They're just scratches! We actually went out for breakfast, not the doctor."

"That's good then." Gallahan exhales sharply.

Eli holds the kid's hand and takes him inside the house. While Cyril leaves to make tea, Eli sits in the living room and talks with Gallahan. Then he remembers something isn't right.

"Gallahan, I thought you went to the Summer Camp. What happened?" Eli asks.

"Hm? What camp?"

"You didn't go to a Summer Camp yesterday? Your mom said you—"

"Oh! That's not a camp," Gallahan waves his hand. "It was just a meeting with a bunch of kids. Kids my age. My classmates. From school."

"Oh, okay."

"They were so immature, so I came back early."

"Aw, I see." Eli chuckles. Gallahan is an old soul, for sure.

Gallahan is exhilarated every time Eli smiles at him. Before, he used to be timid and keep some distance from Eli. But now, he will throw himself at Eli and hug him whenever he can.

"I only want to be around you," Gallahan coos as he wraps his little arms around Eli's waist.

"Aww, I love hanging out with you too!" Eli strokes the boy's dark hair.

Gallahan stays over for lunch. Eli tells the kid about his upcoming beach vacation with Cyril, which Gallahan is not thrilled about.

"Of all the holiday destinations out there, why the beach?" Gallahan questions Cyril during teatime in the backyard.

"You don't like the beach?" Eli asks. Don't kids usually love going to the beach in the summer?

"They're alright. But I feel they're a bit noisy and crowded around this time of the year. And you are still injured."

"Oh, I see," Eli mutters.

"Eli wants to go to the beach," Cyril responds. "I'll be with him the whole time. It'll be fine."

"It better be." Gallahan gives Cyril stink eyes, which Cyril immaturely returns with an equally mean glare.

* * *

"ALL IN ELGARIAN," Eli grunts as he skims through the two-page letter for the fifth time.

Right now, it's six o'clock in the evening, and Cyril is in the shower. It's the only alone time Eli has for himself. Thus, he uses it to examine the mysterious yellowing envelope that he found hidden behind the bronze mirror yesterday.

After several careful read-throughs, Eli concludes that the composer of this letter cannot be Cyril. The paper looks decades old, definitely older than Cyril's twenty-four years.

"Mmm," Eli muses as he studies the Elgarian word on the outside of the envelope. Then an idea flashes through his head.

Eli quickly jumps off his bed and rushes to the light oak desk by the corner. He rummages through the desk drawers and looks for any papers with writing on them.

According to Cyril, he and Eli are the only residents who have ever occupied this house. So, if Eli can find anything that contains Cyril's handwriting and compares the fonts to the one in the letter, he might be able to rule out whether Cyril is the composer or not.

Part of Eli wants the correspondent to be Cyril, so he can put an end to this mystery. However, if the letter is indeed from Cyril, then Cyril has a lot of explaining to do, and Eli doesn't think he's ready to hear them. His life has been too lethally complicated to handle already.

But Eli finds nothing useful in the desk drawers. There are only blank notebooks and a few books inside. Eli does check the paper's quality in the notebooks and compares them to the letter, but they don't match.

Eli sighs and closes the desk drawers. Then he hears Cyril's footsteps on the balcony outside. Eli hurries back to his bed and hides the envelope underneath his mattress.

Cyril and Eli hang out for half an hour until Eli gets hit with a brilliant idea to get Cyril's handwriting.

"Hey Cyril, can you teach me how to write simple phrases in Elgarian?" Eli suggests. "I want to leave notes to you in the future when we don't see each other often."

"What?! What do you mean we won't see each other often in the future? Are you planning to leave here?" Cyril panics, his face pale.

"Oh, no, no, no. I'm not going anywhere." Eli waves to calm his guardian. "I just want to learn how to write basic phrases. Something like 'Hey, I made dinner for you, man, no need to cook' or 'I'm at the neighbor's, will be home around eight.' You know, stuff like that."

Cyril exhales, but then looks baffled. "But why? I will make your every meal, and please, don't go out by yourself after six in the evening. It's dangerous."

"They're just an example, dude! Are you going to teach me how to write or not?!"

"Y-Yes, of course I will. Let me get paper and pen." Poor Cyril hurries to the desk to get the stuff he needs.

When Cyril sits back on his bed next to Eli's, he scribbles down something on the paper and then shows it to Eli.

"This is one long note. What does it mean?" Eli asks, looking at the Elgarian paragraph in the notebook curiously.

Cyril shoots him a bashful grin and reads what he just wrote out loud. "'My young master Eli is the best person in the world. His beautiful face puts the silver moon to shame. His eyes are deeper than emerald. His lips are akin to budding spring roses. His intelligence is that of the Deva of Wisdom. And his compassion and patience are as vaster than the Seven Seas. Oh dearest Eli, I am the luckiest Sage on earth to have the privilege to be your humble companion and have you as my master.'"

That note has Eli dumbstruck for several long moments before he can snap himself out of the mental lapse and remember his initial objective. He examines Cyril's handwriting and finds it completely different from the one in the secret letter.

"Beautiful handwriting," Eli comments as he looks at Cyril's gorgeous cursive calligraphy, feeling somewhat relieved. Then he remembers the cheesy meaning of the note and nags the ravenhead. "Anyway, what the hell is this, dude? I asked for normal, everyday phrases, not this cringey crap!"

"Sorry, maste—Eli," Cyril hangs his head down. "I promise I'll improve my writing skills and make you proud in the future."

"That's not the—never mind!" Eli huffs. "How do you write your name and my name?"

Cyril writes down his and Eli's names in Elgarian.

"How do you write my full name 'Ilya'?"

Cyril writes the name 'Ilya,' and Eli's face turns gray. That is the same word on the mysterious envelope. So that letter is indeed addressed to him.

"Eli, what's wrong?" Cyril frets after noticing Eli's tense expression. "Are you feeling unwell?"

"N-No, I'm fine," Eli lies. "It's just that I don't recognize the language at all, and I feel so awful about it."

Cyril gives Eli a hug. "That's nothing to feel sad about, my sweet Eli. You can always relearn the language. We have a very long life ahead of us, and I'm sure you'll be a polyglot in just a few years."

Eli chuckles at his silly nanny's overly optimistic encouragement. "Thanks. That's very reassuring."

"I have no doubt about your intelligence, El.," Cyril grins. "I'm sure you'll tutor me in Elgarian's grammar soon, just like back then!"

Eli laughs and then becomes slightly disturbed by Snow White's last statement. "Hey, Cyril. Can I ask you a few questions?"

"Sure, Eli!" Cyril beams.

"In the past, did we ever grow our hair long to the waist?"

There is a pause, and then Cyril shakes his head.

"Are you sure? What was that hesitation?" Eli regards his guardian suspiciously.

"Oh, I was just trying to remember if we ever had our hair grow past our shoulders," Cyril tells Eli with puppy eyes.

"Did any of my dead relatives have long hair?"

Cyril looks stumped at the question. "Um...not that I knew of."

"Are you sure?" Eli presses. "Did I maybe have a relative with the same hair color as me who kept his hair long?"

"No."

"Did you, by any chance, dye your hair black?" Eli asks, and Cyril looks at him strangely.

"I have never dyed my hair before."

"Were we ever in a cult that required us to dress in white robes?"

"Cult?" Cyril balks, then breaks into a laugh. "No, Eli, we've never been in a cult."

"Are you positive?"

"Eli, I swear to you we have never ever joined a cult." Cyril sniffs, desperately keeping himself from cracking up. "Aw. What's with that look? Are you disappointed that we weren't in a cult?" Cyril teases when he sees Eli's face drop.

"No, of course not." Eli elbows his upbeat guardian. He feels a little discouraged that his investigation has hit another dead end.

Cyril then cheers Eli up by making a chocolate bonbon appear from a puff of purple smoke. However, this little magic trick ends up leaving confetti all over their beds.

This dummy.

"Eli, may I ask you something?" Cyril begins after Eli finishes the candy.

"Sure, what's up?"

"Can you tell me about the dream you had this morning?"

Eli feels no reason to keep the dream a secret from Cyril, so he tells him everything. After he finishes with the market dream sequence, Cyril pulls him into his arms and hugs him tight.

"I'm so sorry. Please forgive me," Cyril whimpers.

"Why are you sorry?"

"I got to you too late." Cyril's voice breaks. "It breaks my heart every time I learn about a fragment of your past."

"Cyril, are you crying?" Eli feels dampness on his shoulder.

"I'm...not," Cyril lies, still sniffling. "B-But when you...told me about... the part where you wandered in the market...I...I just..."

"Seriously." Eli rolls his eyes but still gently strokes his guardian's broad back to soothe him. Cyril keeps mumbling apologies over and over.

"Dude, calm down. The scenarios in the dream might not be real, so stop apologizing," Eli reasons with the ravenhead. "Also, I don't have any memory about my, eh, traumatized past in the last three years or whatever, so you don't have to feel sorry for me."

"You truly don't have any recollection of the time you were kidnapped?" Cyril's face is all red and teary. "Not even a little?"

Eli shakes his head. "The only memory I have is waking up in that alley in Crimson Vale. Aside from that, nada."

"...What does *'Nada'* mean here?"

"Nothing."

"...Oh." Cyril numbly nods, though his face is still upset. "In all cases, I truly think it's better that you don't remember anything from the past three years. Those memories are nothing good, and they would do more harm to you in the long run."

Eli shrugs. "What do you think about the long hair part? Do you think it holds any significance? Perhaps a future omen?"

"Um...it seems to be nothing more than a dream to me," Cyril falters, scratching his head. "As for my thoughts, I think..."

"Yes?"

"I think we would look great with long hair!" Cyril winks, flashing his pearly white teeth. His blue eyes look into the distance, possibly daydreaming about how he and Eli look with long hair.

"Cyril, it's a crime to talk about growing out our hair in this state of weather."

"Oh, you're hot?" Cyril turns to his bedside table and pours a pitcher of iced strawberry lemonade into a glass. Then he hands it to Eli. "Please drink this. It will help you cool down."

"Thank you," Eli receives the glass with both hands. While he drinks the lemonade, Cyril diligently cools Eli with a folding fan.

"Cyril, I'm freezing. You don't have to fan me," Eli lies.

"Huh? But you're sweating," Cyril points out.

"Cold sweat," Eli fibs and takes the fan from Cyril's hand. Then he starts to fan his guardian's back.

"Oh, no. You shouldn't. It's my obliga—"

"Not obligation, dude. Now, sit still." Eli fans the ravenhead with one hand and signals him to stay put with the other.

Cyril only stares at him. Then, he eventually gives up on persuading Eli and lets him do what he wants. Less than a minute later, Cyril holds Eli's hand and stops him from fanning.

"It's enough, Eli. I'm all cold now." Cyril smiles at him.

"Cyril, you're sweating," Eli dabs the sweat on the side of Cyril's face and shows it to him.

"My sweet, precious Eli, I know you mean well, but don't you worry about me. I'm a strong man, and I can take care of myself," Cyril gently takes back the fan. "And it is my obligation to look after you. You must understand that without you, I wouldn't be sitting here today and leading a good life like this."

Eli feels guilty whenever Cyril gets serious and talks about the past like this. He's not the person who saved Cyril. He's just someone who took over this body and used it as his own. That Ilya, whom Cyril once loved and cared for, is dead.

"I can take care of myself, too," Eli mumbles. He can't come clean with Cyril. He doesn't want to lose him.

"I know, Eli. I know you can," Cyril grins, petting Eli's cheek. "But we were parted for so long, Eli. All of these years, half of my soul truly died when you were gone. And now I finally got you back. Can you please let me take care of you? I want to make it up to you."

Eli can only nod in agreement.

"So much has changed in the past...three years!" Cyril beams, grabbing Eli's hands. "If you'll let me, I'll show you a whole new world!"

"Shining, shimmering, and splendid." The sass slips out of Eli's mouth before he realizes he is being a little brat again.

"Eh?" Cyril gapes.

"Nothing!" Eli gives his nanny—guardian a toothy smile. "Oh, talking about a whole new world. Is there a magical carpet in Aspenia? The type that you can fly on?"

"A magical flying carpet?"

"Is it a thing here?" Eli is excited. "I know flying brooms exist!"

Cyril muses. After a minute, he responds. "I believe I once read about the existence of a flying carpet in an old book. However, you won't find it in Aspenia but in the Dry Land continent. Also, a flying carpet is quite complicated to control. There's no saddle or safety gear for you to sit on. I think you're better off using a hot-air balloon if you want to float in the air."

"Eh, I see."

"Oh, shoot!" Cyril suddenly exclaims and startles Eli.

"What? What's up?"

"There's something extremely important I want to show you!"

"What is it—"

Cyril has already held Eli's hand and pulls him off the bed. The ravenhead quickly closes both bay windows and the curtains in their bedroom. Then he leads Eli to the wall closet and opens it.

"What are you doing?" Eli feels a little scared.

"Look carefully," Cyril says, pushing the clothes to the left side. His fingers trace on the closet wall, and when he reaches the third wooden panel, he presses on the tip of the pane. The inside wall begins to move aside, revealing a hidden space with a ladder going up.

When they get inside the hidden space, the closet wall immediately closes on its own. They climb up the ladder and enter a small attic with no windows to the outside. But it isn't dark at all up there. There are many string lights hanging all over the wooden beams and knee walls, a small bookcase, a floor mattress, two pillows, and a blanket.

"Oh my," Eli gapes, looking around excitedly.

"Eli, this is a safe room. In the future, when I'm not around, and should you ever find yourself in a dangerous situation, you must come to this room, alright?"

"Okay."

"And you should not disclose to anyone about the existence of this room. Nobody should know about this place but us."

"Okay, I won't tell anyone," Eli answers absently as he examines the light strings that seem to run on magical power—just like the ones he saw at the fair two days ago.

"Don't play hide-and-seek with Gallahan or anyone up here, alright?"

"Oh, Cyril," Eli groans, turning to his guardian. "I promise I won't bring anyone up here. This place will be our little secret safe haven!" Eli makes an **'okay'** hand gesture.

Cyril folds his hands and bows to Eli.

"What are you doing?" Eli blinks in confusion.

Cyril points at Eli's **'okay'** hand gesture.

"This means 'alright,'" Eli explains.

Cyril oohs in understanding. Eli then teaches him a few modern-world hand gestures, which Cyril immediately practices with great enthusiasm.

"Hey, Cyril...can I ask you for something?" Eli asks shyly.

"What is it, my little kit?"

"Can we bring these light strings to the bedroom? I really like them!" Eli gushes.

"Of course. I didn't know you were interested in these lights. I'll buy you a thousand of them in every color so you can hang them all over the house," Cyril announces.

"Cyril, calm down. I only need two or three strings, which we can take from here. You don't have to buy more." Eli starts to touch one of the string lights in the corner.

"Wait, don't touch that—" Cyril yells, but it's too late.

The floor beneath Eli's feet opens up, and Eli free-falls downward. "AHHHH!"

Luckily, Eli manages to grab the edge of the opening. Cyril quickly pulls him up and closes the secret door. Though Eli doesn't get any new injuries from the frightening mishap, he did have a good scare and learned a valuable lesson about not touching anything in a room that isn't supposed to exist.

After that incident, Cyril seals up that floor trap for good, and that attic finally becomes their little secret safe haven.

CHAPTER 12

CASE II - THE BLOODY BUNNY MASCOT COSTUME
– PART 1

One might have assumed that the perk of being reborn in an old-timey world while originally coming from the smartphone era is that none of this new world's obsolete technology would surprise him—or so Eli did.

He couldn't have been more wrong.

Since Eli arrived at the station, he has been rubbernecking at every train like some country bumpkin who has never seen the wonder of modern technology in his entire life.

In Eli's defense, the trains here are entirely different animals than those from his world. Aspenia's trains aren't just transportation but magnificent works of art!

Each car's design is unique and follows a specific theme. Eli has seen Phoenix, Eagle, Direwolf, and Rosette-themed trains at the terminus. The one that he and Cyril get on has a floral motif. Its body is painted in a beautiful shade of shamrock green with a shimmering gilded brim, and embossed flower carvings in bright yellow and orange run throughout the carriage's length.

"Eli, have some breakfast," Cyril tells the awed Eli. "You'll get nauseous if you keep looking at the running train for a long time."

"They are so beautiful! Too bad we don't have a camera with us." Eli looks at the mini feast on the table. There are three types of bread served with strawberry jam and fresh cheese, eggs and mushroom sausage, croquettes, grilled vegetable salad, tomato soup, tea with various pastries, and fresh fruits.

"What's a camera?" Cyril fills Eli's teacup.

"You guys have trains, but not cameras?" The current timeline in Aspenia seems similar to the Victorian period, as there is steam technology and some advanced innovations, such as gas/magic-fueled light bulbs, flushable toilets, showers, and trains. But wasn't the camera invented around this era?

Cyril shakes his head. "I've never heard of it."

Cyril then asks Eli what a camera does. After hearing Eli's explanation, he laughs and waves his hand.

"We do have something that has a similar use to 'camera' here. It's called the express portrait."

"How does express portrait work?"

"There are many Sages in Aspenia who have the gift of eidetic memory and an amazing drawing talent. They can create extremely realistic paintings. So, some of these Sages would open an express portrait gallery where the customers can come in, strike a pose, and a few days later, the picture will be delivered to their house!" Cyril explains enthusiastically.

"Hyperrealistic art?"

"Yes! That's what they call it!" Cyril exclaims. "But how do you know that term? This type of art was only popular just a few years back, and you weren't around then."

"It's common sense! I just string two correlated words together, and bam! Such a term exists!"

Cyril gives his young master a genuine look of deep admiration. "You're truly a genius, master—Eli!"

"Not at all," Eli simpers, trying to be modest.

Ten minutes later, Eli notices Cyril looks like he wants to tell him something, but isn't confident enough to do so.

"Cyril, what is it?" Eli asks, unconsciously holding his breath.

"Uh...I..." Cyril acts very fidgety, unlike his usual composed self. "As we were talking about the express portrait, I've wondered if...if..."

Cyril stops and drinks a full glass of water. Then he takes in a couple of deep breaths and says, "I wonder if you are interested in..." His voice gets very low and shaky. "...having a portrait done...with me?"

"That's it?"

Cyril nods, his big blue eyes blinking nervously.

"Dude, you scared the heck out of me. I thought you wanted to sell my kidney or something!" Eli exhales in relief. "Yeah, if you want to, let's do it when we get home."

"Thank you, Eli." Cyril's blue eyes sparkle like twinkling stars. He looks so happy that he might burst into tears.

Cyril had no qualms when he moved their beds next to each other and slept side by side with Eli *every night* since the butcher/bohemian witch incident. But now the dude has butterflies in his stomach when asking him out for some photos?

Weirdo.

After breakfast, Eli gets to see the map of Aspenia for the first time and is amazed at how massive this country is compared to the rest of the world. Eli learns that their pretty fairytale town, Glade Mallow, is in the suburb of the capital, Aegle.

"I didn't know we live right in the center of the country," Eli comments and points at the map. "So we're traveling from Glade Mallow here to Hemera Bay?"

"Yes, that's right." Cyril smiles, stroking Eli's brown locks. "Hemera Bay is a beautiful coastal town. I'm sure you'll love it there!"

"Cyril, what's the name of this place?" Eli points at a location on the map.

"That's Darya, Eli."

"Why didn't we go to Darya?" Eli asks. "It looks like a coastal region, and it is nearer to our town than Hemera Bay. Wait, Creepyville is next to Darya. What does this word mean?" He points at the symbol of trees next to Crimson Vale.

"That's the Forbidden Forest where I found you, Eli," Cyril responds, his voice sounding off. "And we don't go to Darya because that region is very unsafe and underdeveloped. I doubt there is a proper bathroom there."

Eww. Eli frowns in disgust. Cyril sees it and gives him a playful flick on his round cheek.

"I only want the best for you, Eli," Cyril fawns with twinkling eyes.

Eli grimaces at his guardian, though he finds it a bit strange to learn that Darya is an underdeveloped region. The Elgarian word 'Darya' appears in bold and considerably more prominent than all the other location names on the map, except for the capital Aegle and two other lands, Eden and Reinga.

As Eli looks carefully, connecting the three major regions, Eden, Darya, and Reinga makes a triangle with the capital, Aegle, situated right in the center.

"Hey Cyril, where did we come from before?" Eli asks.

"Here!" Cyril points at a tiny spot in the farthest place on the map. "We originally came from Melia."

"Good God! Why did we move so far away? Who came up with that decision?"

"Uh, it was you, Eli."

"Do you have any idea why I moved to the other side of the country? *Are you sure we're not wanted criminals?*" Eli whispers the last part.

"Oh, Eli, of course not. As I told you before, you had a disagreement with your relatives and decided to move to another land and start over. As for the specific cause of conflict, I do not know, since I was only a servant then, and you were quite a private person."

"I see," Eli mumbles, a little frustrated. "Oh, there's something I'd like to ask of you, Cyril."

"Consider it done, Eli!"

"Oh, okay...well, if possible, I would really like to learn Elgarian. Gallahan gave me another book to read for the trip, and I can't understand a word. Do you know if there's any Elgarian class in Glade Mallow?"

"Hmm, if you want to learn Elgarian, I can ask Haidar to tutor you at home."

"Huh? Isn't Haidar a lawyer? When did he become an Elgarian tutor?" Eli asks, confounded.

"He's not an Elgarian tutor. But I'm sure he would love to spend more time with you!"

"Well, if the tuition fee is too expensive, then I guess I can teach myself the language," Eli mutters in a disheartened voice.

"No, no, Eli, it's not about money," Cyril quickly says. He pauses for a moment to gather his thoughts before continuing. "There are other factors. I'll have to think about it more."

Eli can tell Cyril is worrying about something, so he encourages the ravenhead to talk to him about it. Cyril then goes full-blown paranoid and gives Eli a list of 7,749 reasons why he shouldn't go to school. Cyril is afraid that Eli will get kidnapped on the way home/to school, get bullied by classmates/teachers, get food poisoning from eating at the school cafeteria, etc.

Despite Cyril being hysterical and way too overprotective, Eli is genuinely touched by his guardian's deep concern for him. In his previous life, even Eli's father wouldn't give him a quarter of the attention and affection that Cyril has been showering on him.

Eli begins to sweet-talk Cyril into changing his mind. It doesn't take much time for him to persuade Cyril, since it's not like Snow White can ever deny Eli of anything—so far. After five minutes of lenient inveigling, Cyril finally caves in despite not being too keen on this idea.

"Alright," the ravenhead sighs in defeat. "But you have to promise me you'll always let me know if anyone is giving you a hard time at school."

"I will. I promise!" Eli beams in triumph. "When do schools usually start in Aspenia?"

"Usually the first day of September, I think."

"That's only a month from now! And you're also returning to work on the first day of September as well!"

"Yes, I am." Cyril is not happy about this.

"Well, well, then I suppose we have to make the most out of this last month of summer!" Eli cheers with a wide grin.

* * *

It's a four-hour train trip, and they arrive at Hemera Bay by noon. The station is packed, as this town seems to be indeed a popular vacation spot. Without wasting any more time, they take a cab to the most expensive hotel in town, but the rooms are fully booked. They check out three different locations, but the results are the same.

"My apology, sir. But I'm afraid you won't have much luck with other hotels, as it is the peak of the season. Visitors usually have to make reservations at least a month prior to their arrival. Perhaps you should try the inns instead? They might have a vacancy," advises the receptionist from the fifth hotel.

Cyril is not thrilled with that suggestion. He says he wants Eli to have the best holiday experience, and staying at a cheap inn will not do. Eli tells his guardian they come here to visit the town and enjoy the beach activities, not being inside the hotel room all day.

"We only need a place to sleep and shower. Why do you want to spend so much money on expensive lodging? It's unnecessary," Eli tells his guardian. "I'm fine with us sleeping in a tent, too. It would make a fun camping experience!"

Cyril is not on board with the camping idea, so he has no choice but to try the inn option. The friendly receptionist then turns to his co-workers for help. After twenty minutes of asking around to no avail, they finally find someone who knows about a possible vacancy.

"You should try the Golden Shore Inn. Two of my customers just checked out from there yesterday. They were also visitors like you boys," says the fruit vendor in front of the hotel.

* * *

It's a twenty-minute coach ride from the hotel to the Golden Shore Inn. Although the inn is in a rather rustic-looking neighborhood, it looks relatively new and clean. It is larger compared to other buildings in the area, which are small shops or old apartment complexes. The inn must be near the beach, as Eli can catch a whiff of the blue sea and the salty tang in the breeze.

"You two are very lucky. There is only one room left as the newlyweds checked out yesterday morning," the old inn's owner says as she takes them to their suite on the fourth floor.

"Newlyweds? Is it a single room?" Cyril asks.

"Yep. But it has one big bed!" the owner replies. "Your brother looks quite small. There will be plenty of room for you two to toss and turn."

The owner looks like she's at least in her late seventies and doesn't seem to have good eyesight. Hence, she doesn't see how deeply flushed Cyril's face is when she mentions them sharing a bed.

The suite is quite spacious and decorated with a chestnut wood floor and white walls, a large double bed, a living area, a decent-sized bathroom, and a private balcony. There isn't much of a view as there is a long row of shabby-looking apartment buildings and motels from across the street that tower over the unit.

"Let me know if you need anything," the owner says. "Have a wonderful vacation, boys!"

After the owner leaves, Cyril and Eli stare thoughtfully at the double bed. About a minute later, Cyril breaks the silence. "Eli, the bed is all yours. I'll take the couch."

Eli looks at the "couch," which is actually a tiny loveseat that would barely fit Eli, let alone a six-foot-three, broad-shouldered man. "You're kidding, right?"

"I'll draw up my legs." Even Cyril is not convinced by his own words.

"Just sleep on the bed," Eli says and begins to unpack.

"You really don't mind?" Cyril asks nervously.

"Well, it's not like we haven't been sleeping twenty feet apart back home." Eli tries to keep his voice even. He is generally an open-minded and practical person. He trusts his guardian, as Cyril has always treated him with utmost respect.

Once they have settled the sleeping arrangement, they leave for lunch right away since their last meal was breakfast and that was five hours ago on the train. They find a small restaurant just five minutes' walk from the inn and have lunch there. They can see the beach from their table as the building is built on a slope, looking straight into the ocean.

"Cyril, let's go swimming after lunch!" Eli is excited upon seeing the flock of tourists heading to the beach.

"Huh? Right now, in this blazing heat? What about your skin?"

"What's with my skin?" Eli asks, puzzled.

"Eli, you must have forgotten that your skin is sensitive to sunlight. It would be best if you don't go swimming in the afternoon when the sun is at its hottest," Cyril gently advises. "You'll get a heatstroke."

"You're kidding, right?" Eli had no skin sensitivity to sunlight in his previous life.

"I'm not! You once fainted for being out in the sun for too long...a couple of years ago," Cyril says.

"Pfft. What should we do then?" Eli asks.

"Well, we can swim early tomorrow morning. There are a lot of nice attractions in Hemera Bay besides the beach. Would you like to visit the aquarium?"

The last time Eli went to an aquarium was nine years ago. It was a school field trip, and he was around fourteen then. Since magic exists in this world, Eli supposes there would be many new and exciting things to see at the aquarium, so he says yes.

* * *

After lunch, both hop in a cab and head to the marine museum.

Hemera Bay Aquarium is a gigantic steampunk building, and it takes them close to four hours to walk through the entire place. Eli has seen at least forty new types of sea creatures (and monsters) that have yet to be discovered or even exist in his old modern world.

Near the end of the tour, they are taken by surprise when a little octopus jumps out from out of nowhere and blocks their path.

"Eh? Where did you come from?" Eli looks for the aquarium workers, but no one is around.

"He probably snuck out of that tank." Cyril points at the gigantic tank on the right. The lid of that tank is slightly opened.

"We have to get it back inside," Eli says, and the octopus hops onto his hands and nestles in them. "Oh, hey! Easy now!"

The little octopus blinks at Eli with its big, green eyes with long lashes. It looks prettier than a regular octopus with a white and lavender body. "It's so cute. What type of octopus is this?"

"He's a Pretty Green-Eyed octopus," Cyril answers as he looks at the sign on the tank. "This type of octopus is extremely rare and is said to be very smart."

"He is pretty," Eli comments as he cradles the octopus. "But how can you tell this one is a 'he'? It has long lashes and delicate features. It could be a 'she.'"

"Well, I just made a random guess because he looks a lot like you," Cyril laughs.

"You think I look like an octopus?"

Cyril realizes he just made a dumb comment. "No, no! I meant his eye color is very similar to yours since you have such a beautiful and rare shade of green eyes. But of course, there is no comparison; this little cuttlefish is cute, but compared to you, he's just so-so. You are and will always be the loveliest and most radiant person in the universe to me."

"Dude," Eli struggles not to laugh while the Pretty Green-Eyed octopus doesn't share the same amusement as Eli. He seems to understand Cyril's words as he is clearly offended for being called a so-so cuttlefish. His big eyes narrow as he shoots Cyril a dirty look. Before Cyril can utter another obsequious flattery, the small octopus inks him right in the face.

"Oh, no!" Eli jumps in shock. "Are you alright?!"

"I'm fine. Don't worry," Cyril waves his hand. Though the octopus is small, the amount of ink he sprayed is quite substantial. Cyril's entire face is now covered in unusually thick, pitch-black ink. "Oh, dear...he has quite a temper, isn't he?"

"Uh, you bad boy! Why did you spray him?" Eli scolds the little octopus, who, in turn, makes a sad face as if he's been wrongly lectured.

Their attentions shift when a string of light knocks ring out from inside the tank. The pair turn around and see a large, blue-eyed octopus gently tapping one of its arms against the glass.

"I think he's asking for the little one back," Eli comments as he observes the large octopus. It appears to have a particular liking for Eli.

I really look like an octopus? Eli thinks dolefully.

"Let's get you back home." Cyril picks up the little octopus from Eli's hands and pitches it upward into the air. Eli and the green-eyed octopus squeal simultaneously at Cyril's precipitous action. Fortunately, though he was a little rough, Cyril somehow exerted the precise force needed to toss the small octopus back to the tank without harming it. The moment the octopus touches the water, the blue-eyed octopus immediately reaches out to him and securely pulls him down to the bottom of the tank.

The aquarium tour has a *happy* ending as they successfully return the lost octopus home. However, Cyril and Eli can't wipe the black ink off with a regular handkerchief, no matter how hard they rub. The ravenhead has no choice but to leave the building in the full robber's face. It's an awful and ridiculous look, and Eli has to try his best not to laugh out loud at his guardian. As they reach the exit, the aquarium workers are thrown off by the "alarming sight" and ask them what happened. After learning about the story, the employees make a formal apology for the unfortunate incident.

"It's fine. Accidents happen. I'll wash off the ink when I get back," inked face Cyril says. But when he proceeds to leave with Eli, the aquarium workers stop them.

"Wait, sirs. Please don't go just yet," says a worker nervously.

"Why not?" inked face Cyril and Eli ask.

"Sir, you won't be able to wash off the ink of a Pretty Green-eyed octopus with regular soap. That type of octopus is known for expelling permanent ink!"

"WHAT?!" Cyril and Eli screech in horror.

"D-Don't be alarmed...yet! Our aquatic vets and researchers have been developing a specialized cleanser to deal with this particular octopus' ink!"

"And do they have the finished cleanser on hand?" Cyril's voice is deadly cold compared to his usual congenial demeanor. Eli can feel the blaze building in every syllable. However, the robber face has significantly decreased his intimidation.

"Well...uh...about that," the worker stutters.

"Go on?" Cyril grits his teeth.

"I got it! I got it!" A worker who left earlier comes back with a green bottle in his hand.

"Thank Tathagatas!" The workers shakily exhale as Cyril takes the specialized cleanser.

"Did your researchers test this product? Did it work?" Cyril asks.

There is a brief pause before the worker answers. "Good sir, the bottle you're holding is our latest and most improved version of the specialized cleanser for the Pretty Green-Eyed Octopus ink. In the last trial, the previous sample of the cleanser was able to remove ninety percent of the ink."

There is another long silence. Eli is the one to speak first. "You guys haven't tested out this new version yet, have you?"

"No," say the workers concurrently.

Cyril takes in a deep breath but shows no sign of releasing.

"But sir, there's a big chance the bottle you're holding is the final product...and if it isn't, well, fret not! Our vets are still working tirelessly on the cleanser, and we'll send it to your house as soon as we have it." The worker stops to fumble his pocket. Then he pulls out a piece of paper and gives it to Cyril. "Please accept this as a token of our apology. It's a sixty percent off coupon at the Seaside Cottontail Grill, one of the most popular restaurants in town. It's on the must-visit list of Hemera Bay. We guarantee you won't be disappointed!"

* * *

CYRIL AND ELI almost give the inn's poor owner a heart attack when they return, as she mistakes Cyril for a robber. After Eli briefly explains what happened, the elderly lady gives Cyril her deepest condolences. According to her, the chance of being sprayed by the Pretty Green-Eyed octopus is very slim; it's one in a thousand, as this particular breed is notorious for its friendliness toward humans. Cyril in no way agrees with this statement.

After twenty minutes of anxiously waiting for Cyril to finish his shower, Eli is immensely relieved to see his guardian's flawless skin again. The cleanser has worked!

Though Cyril seems to rub his skin too much, his cheeks are now flushing like an overripe peach.

"Why, hello there, stranger." Eli whistles. "What have you done to my dorky housemate?"

Cyril chuckles as he approaches Eli. He then gives the teasing Eli an affectionate flick on his nose. "You really enjoyed my little misfortune, don't you?"

"Ugh, can't believe you'd think that low of me." Eli makes a sour face, pretending to be offended at the accusation.

"Hmm." Cyril leans in very close to Eli and startles him. The ravenhead then grabs the item Eli has been hiding behind his back. It's a little potato sack with cut-outs, two holes for the eyes, and one for the nose.

"What's this then?" Cyril lifts a brow at Eli. "Did you make it while I was in the shower?"

"That was from the owner. I only drew the lashes and eyebrows." Eli points at the doodles on the mask.

"And you're not embarrassed to have dinner with a sack-head?"

"No, why would I?"

"Really?"

Eli sighs and pulls the sack back from Cyril's hands. "You really are a dork. Can't you tell there's something else inside the mask?" He starts to shake the mask until another sack falls out of it.

This new sack mask is identical to the one intended for Cyril. Eli holds up the second mask. "If the cleanser didn't work and you had to wear a potato sag for the entire trip, then I would wear the same mask as you. That way, you wouldn't be the only sackhead in town."

Cyril doesn't expect such a response from Eli. He remains speechless for a few seconds before his beautiful blue eyes start to glisten with happy tears as he throws himself at Eli and gives him a big bear hug.

"What's gotten into you now?!" Eli complains breathlessly against his guardian's firm embrace.

"Oh, my most precious Eli! It is well-nigh flagitious for someone to be so adorable and wonderful as you are. You must not be aware of the power you have over my heart. I never thought I would ever find happiness again. I thought the Tathagatas had completely forsaken me. Oh, Eli. How wrong I was. I am the luckiest man on earth. I'm blessed to have you in my life again!"

"Are you nuts?" Eli is now completely convinced that Cyril's experiencing side effects from that untested cleanser.

"Nuts?" Cyril balks a little. "Oh, yeah. I do have some with me."

"I don't think you understand—"

"You can have my *nuts* if you're hungry," Cyril says. "If you like, I'll get you more *nuts* in *different flavors* after dinner."

"Cyril," Eli looks at his guardian dead in the eye. "Don't. Say. Another *nut* word. For the rest of the night, please."

* * *

At first, Cyril hesitates about visiting the Seaside Cottontail Grill, saying the restaurant's name sounds suggestive and might not be appropriate for an underage person. Eli tells him that bikini bunnies are far from being the most *outrageous* thing he has seen in this world. After confirming with the inn's owner that the bunny grill is not an adult-themed dining spot and is just a ten-minute walk from their lodging, the two head straight to that place.

If Eli had to describe it, the Seaside Cottontail Grill reminds him of a cool hipster restaurant with wood floors, brick walls, abundant climbing plants, magic-operated string lights, and a relaxed ambiance. That explains why the grill is crawling with customers. They even have a pink bunny mascot by the entrance to welcome the customers and give out candies to children.

This setting reminds Eli of New York and makes him feel somewhat homesick for the first time since he arrived in this world. But he quickly dismisses that sensation. It's not like he can ever go back to his old life. It has almost been a month now since the day he was killed. His original body is probably lying six feet underground somewhere in a cemetery, or it has already been cremated.

"Eli, what's wrong?" Cyril's words bring Eli back to reality.

"Nothing."

"Just for a moment, you looked sad. Is something wrong? Are you feeling alright? If you're tired, we can order to-go."

"No, are you kidding? We're already at the restaurant, and I'm starving." Eli tries to speak in a snooty voice, though deep down, he feels a tinge of happiness that Cyril even noticed his brief instance of a blue mood.

There's no going back. This is his new life now, right here in Aspenia.

And Eli is ever grateful that God has given him a good home and a caring brother figure. It's more than he could ever wish for.

* * *

ELI AND CYRIL are enjoying the restaurant. The food is amazing, and their conversation is hilarious. Everything is going very well until someone crashes into a waitress and knocks them both to the floor, dragging along all the trays and the tall pile of dishes the waitress carried with them.

It happens right next to Eli and Cyril's table. Luckily, none of the broken shards or the spilled food gets on their table or clothes. But the same can't be said for the middle-aged couple at the opposite table.

"What's wrong with you? Are you blind?!" the husband exclaims. His light-colored suit is stained with brown sauce and red wine. "Do you know how much this suit costs?"

"I-I'm...s-so...sorry. I'm sorry, sir," the pink bunny mascot stutters. She is the person who bumped into the waitress. Her voice shakes like she's about to break into tears.

"Why are you running inside the restaurant?" The wife gives the mascot a disdainful glance as she helps her husband dab off the stain.

"S-Sorry, madam," the bunny girl chokes, trying to gather the broken dishes. Other waitresses also come over to help her clean up the mess.

After they finish collecting everything on the floor, the waitresses quickly leave the dining area, and the bunny girl follows right after. Suddenly, the bunny girl screams as she trips and falls back to the floor again. The broken dishes she has just gathered end up spattering more food all over her costume.

"Mommy, that pink rabbit is a klutz!" a little kid cackles. His mother hushes him.

"What's with this girl?" the middle-aged man mumbles.

This time, Cyril and Eli get up to help the clumsy girl, who is still lying floored on the ground.

"Miss, are you alright?" Cyril crouches down to offer her a hand.

"Can you stand up?" Eli asks as he brings out his hand to her.

Bunny girl takes both of their hands. But the moment the fuzzy costume touches Eli's fingers, he feels an overwhelming wave of unpleasantness so sickening it makes his skin crawl and his stomach knot in a twist. He immediately withdraws his hand from the girl; it's only then that the repulsive feeling finally disappears.

Oddly enough, Cyril reacts the same way as Eli. He also jerks back his hand from the girl as if he just touched a boiling kettle. His gorgeous face frowns in repugnance as he looks down coldly at the bunny mascot.

Because both take back their hands simultaneously, the bunny girl falls back to the floor once again. But she says nothing about why they let go of her. She quietly picks herself up and runs out of the restaurant to the curiosity and garrulous gossip of other patrons at the commotion she has caused.

"Are you alright, Eli?" Cyril asks Eli after the bunny girl is out of the room.

"Yeah," Eli nods. He wants to ask if Cyril felt the same nauseating sensation as Eli when he touched the bunny girl. But from the tense look on Cyril's face, Eli has already guessed the answer.

* * *

THEY PAY the bill without finishing their food, as they don't want to stay in that restaurant any longer. They even forget to use the 60 percent discount coupon from the aquarium's employees. After getting out of the Seaside Cottontail Grill, Cyril and Eli head to the local night market and have their post-dinner snacks at a street food stall there.

After finishing their second meal, they take a long stroll and explore the night market. It's already 10:30 in the evening, but the street is still jammed with lively tourists and the locals. Most houses in this area are still lit up. Rowdy chatting, laughter, and bargaining noises rumble throughout every corner of the market.

"This brings back the memory of the first time we visited a night market together," Cyril says as he walks side by side with Eli.

"How long ago was it?"

"Quite a long time ago. I was very young then...and you were very different from how you are now."

"Of course, I was like, what...nine-year-old then? Still a snotty kid." Eli makes a sour face. "I'm sorry if my younger self gave you a hard time. I have a feeling I was an insufferable brat back then."

This assumption is based purely on Eli's own self-evaluation. He was quite a little troublemaker during in his previous life due to the absence of adult figures in his childhood.

But the moment the words slip out of Eli's lips, he instantly regrets it. Because he knows too well how Cyril will react when he hears Eli say negative things about himself. Before Eli can open his mouth to say he takes it back, Cyril already speaks first. His response is precisely as Eli expects it to be. Cyril immediately tells Eli his speculation isn't true and that he has always been a wonderful person, along with gazillions of sappy praises, for the next fifteen minutes.

The pair watches the fireworks together and leaves the market an hour later. They are chatting on their way back to the inn until a strange sight catches Eli's attention.

There's a tall and well-built pedestrian walking fifty feet ahead of them. He's wearing a cerulean and red suit. Eli thinks he just saw the red pattern on the man's outfit moving on its own.

At first, Eli doesn't pay much attention to it as he looks at Cyril while talking to him. But now, as he's looking straight ahead at the pedestrian. It's clear that the red pattern on the man's outfit is moving in a very unusual way.

"What's that?" Eli squints his eyes to get a clear view of the red pattern. "Cyril, do you see those moving red lines on that man's coat?"

Cyril looks at the man walking from afar and then back to Eli. "Which red lines? I don't see any."

They speed up a bit but still maintain a safe distance from the pedestrian ahead. As they are close enough, Eli's heart almost pops when he finally sees what the coiling red lines on the man's coat actually are.

The red lines aren't patterns. They aren't even a part of the man's outfit.

They are *bloody human intestines* dangling from the man's shoulder!

"Eli, don't be scared. I'm here," Cyril whispers as he reaches for Eli's trembling hand. *"What do you see?"*

"Human intestines. They're wrapped around that man's shoulders," Eli murmurs. *"D-Don't you see them, Cyril? They are swaying at his every step."*

"No, I don't," Cyril whispers, his eyes fixed on the pedestrian's back. *"Let's go another way."*

Just as Cyril says that, Eli suddenly sees black hair slowly creeping up from the pedestrian's chest and moving down to his back. A white, battered female face soon appears over one of the man's shoulders. One of her eyes is gouged out. From that position, it looks as though the man is carrying her in his arms like a parent holding a toddler. However, the man's hands are by his side. He's not carrying her, yet somehow, this woman is clinging to his body, and the man doesn't realize it!

The man can't see her, and neither does Cyril.

Eli is the only person who can see her. The woman is staring at Eli with her only intact eye.

Eli doesn't want to look at her anymore but can't break off his gaze. His body doesn't listen to him. He can't even open his mouth to respond to Cyril's calling.

This is far creepier than the time Eli encountered the murderous butcher. At least then, he could look away and fight back. Now, he just stands there completely paralyzed, like a senseless scarecrow being, forced to watch the macabre sight unfolding before him by an unseen power.

Cyril forcefully turns Eli around and holds him tight to his chest.

Eli has always known his guardian is a brawny beefcake, but he's never imagined Cyril would be this crazy strong. His arms are rock-hard, like they were made from concrete. Snow White is squeezing the freaking daylight out of him!

The only positive thing about being bear-hugged to near passing out is that it snaps Eli out of his paralyzed state. Cyril keeps Eli from gasping out loud by covering his lips, signaling him to be quiet. *"Let's get back to the inn first."*

The walk home is extremely quiet as nobody utters a word to each other.

However, it isn't too nerve-wracking, as Cyril has been holding Eli's hand the entire time and smiling at him whenever he looks uneasy.

* * *

It's near midnight when the two get back to their room. They quickly wash up and get to bed. Cyril asks Eli to tell him in detail what he saw. When Eli finishes, Cyril tells him to go to bed, forget everything, and leave it all to him.

"How do you forget seeing a decapitated head dangling beside a pile of bloody human intestines?" Eli asks.

"It's not uncommon for some Sages to see strange things that regular people can't. And when that happens, it's best to ignore it and not think about it at all." Cyril speaks in a soft voice as he tucks Eli in.

"That's not very helpful, man."

"I promise I will not let anything happen to you, Eli."

Eli flinches when he sees Cyril's left hand glowing in a soft, blue halo. "Please tell me you see your left hand glowing in blue."

"Yes, I can see it's glowing," Cyril chuckles at Eli's spooked face.

Eli breathes out in relief but freaks out again when Cyril leans in very close and brings his glowing hand to Eli's face. "W-What are you doing?"

"This will help you sleep." Cyril whispers, pressing his glowing fingers against Eli's temple. He gently circles the soft skin, lulling Eli to sleep. "Sweet dreams, Eli."

But after ten minutes, Eli is still as wide awake as an owl. He nudges Cyril with his elbow. "Hey, how long does it usually take for your magic fingers to work?"

"Do you feel sleepy yet?"

"No."

"Maybe it needs a little more time. Please close your eyes. And think about happy thoughts. Good night, Eli."

"M'kay."

Fifteen minutes later, Cyril whispers Eli's name, and to his dismay, Eli responds to his call loudly and clearly. "What?"

"Are you sleepy yet?" Cyril's voice is somewhat Zen.

"No." Eli opens his eyes. Cyril stops rubbing Eli's forehead and looks at his glowing left hand in genuine confusion.

"It doesn't work. But it should work," Cyril says, still baffled.

"Not on me, I guess," Eli mumbles, and receives the strangest gaze from his guardian. "Wha-?"

"It should work," Cyril reiterates.

"It's okay, man. You're still young, and you'll have plenty of time to hone your craft."

"Young?"

"Well, you're only twenty-five. Do you think that's old?" Eli asks, and he sees a blank look on Cyril's face. "You're turning twenty-five this month, *right?*"

"Yeah, I am. That's right. I'm turning twenty-five. This month. On the same day as you. Hahaha." Cyril suddenly breaks into an awkward laugh.

"Are you having another psychotic episode?" Eli involuntarily moves a little further away from his nanny.

"I'm sorry, master...Eli."

"Psst, I'm going to sleep now. See you tomorrow."

"Good night, Eli."

"Good night."

* * *

SLEEP DOESN'T COME EASY. Every time Eli closes his eyes, he sees the bloody and mangled face of the woman over and over. When he tries to think about beautiful and innocent things, the repulsive sensation of when he touched the pink bunny mascot emerges in his mind. That thought somehow creeps him out even more than the image of the decapitated head.

He and Cyril did discuss their disgusted sensations when they touched the bunny girl. Apparently, Cyril also felt similar things, and that was why he abruptly let go, despite always being a gallant, ladies-first gentleman.

Actually...Cyril is more like an Eli-first, ladies-second gentleman.

Hopeless dork.

Eli then tries to fill his head with the thought of Cyril, hoping it would deflect him from all the unpleasant and gruesome imagery.

And it works.

He's able to sleep soundly through the rest of the night.

CHAPTER 13

CASE II - THE BLOODY BUNNY MASCOT COSTUME – PART 2

Eli didn't have any nightmares despite his unfortunate encounter with the severed head ghost the night before. He wakes up in a rather chirpy mood and reinvigorated state, which is a good thing. However, it also worries Eli and makes him question his conscience and morality.

Has he become too cold and too apathetic? People are supposed to be traumatized and have sleep problems after they see what he saw, right? Eli is sure that his old self from his previous life would lose sleep if he saw a woman's beaten-up head entangled between a pile of bloody human intestines.

Eli notices that ever since he was resurrected in this new world, aside from the gifts of occasional super-strength and super-speed, he has also inherited some kind of "nerves of steel" attribute, which has made him frighteningly unbothered and insensate to grisly and gory displays. Heck! He attempted to kill a witch on his first day here (albeit only half-successful), and then just last week, he crushed a murderous butcher's head with his bare hands. That's almost two freaking kill counts in less than a month!

That's not something Eli is proud of. If anything, he's so scared to lose his humanity. The universe has given him the chance to live again, and Eli doesn't intend to waste that precious gift by becoming a detestable killer.

The only thing he wants to do in this life is to be a good person and lives with his ditzy nanny in peace!

"Eli, how are you feeling?" Cyril's soft voice is full of concern as he puts a hand on Eli's forehead to check his temperature. "If you're tired, we should go back to our room and get you some more sleep. We can go to the beach tomorrow when you're better."

"I'm okay, Cyril, really," Eli says. They are having breakfast in the inn's dining hall. "I actually slept really well last night."

"Are you sure?"

Eli nods.

"Alright. But you have to let me know if you feel unwell and need to rest."

"Yes, sir!"

* * *

AFTER FINISHING BREAKFAST, they head to the beach. There are a couple of early swimmers there, so it isn't as crowded as yesterday. It is 8:30 AM, and the weather is nice and sunny, the perfect time for a long swim.

Another interesting thing about Aspenia is that they have pretty open-minded swimwear fashion despite their Victorian setting. The ladies wear a one-piece-mini skirt swimsuit (though Eli has spotted a few wearing a two-piece), and for the men, it's lightweight, drawstring capris.

After Eli finished changing into his swimsuit, he gleefully swaggers out of the dressing booth, excited to be wading in the cool water and basking in the soft sunlight. He finds Cyril in his swim capris, waving at him by a blue and white striped umbrella table and two white and blue deck chairs; his other hand holds a colorful cocktail.

"Dude, I was in the booth for less than a minute. How could you change and get all of these set up so fast?" Eli says in bewilderment while subtly checking out the ravenhead's flawlessly symmetrical and sculpted eight-pack. It is the first time he's seen Cyril shirtless. He can't help but wonder if it's even possible for his guardian to show any signs of physical imperfection...

just to prove that he's still a fellow mortal and not a fallen God wandering the Earth.

"Well...you can say I'm good at time management." Cyril coolly runs his fingers through his slick raven hair while flashing an alluring grin at Eli. "Here, please try it and tell me what you think." He gives Eli the cocktail glass.

Eli studies the drink and asks, "Interesting combination...what's in it?"

"Butterfly pea flowers, honeydew juice, and apple juice."

"Meh, of course," Eli pouts.

"Are you expecting me to give you alcohol?"

"I won't tell anyone. I promise," Eli whispers and winks at Cyril.

"Eli, what kind of guardian am I if I'm going to give you alcohol?" Cyril nags and gives his bratty master a disapproving look.

"The best guardian *ever!*" Eli squeals, giving the ravenhead a big thumbs-up and a wink. "Yum! This is pretty good!" He exclaims after taking a sip of the mocktail.

Cyril only sighs and rubs his forehead in despair.

ELI AND CYRIL go for a long swim. After some time, Eli gets splashed by a pretty strong rip current and loses his balance. Luckily, Cyril catches Eli's arm just in time before he trips and snatches him back from the engulfing, pulling wave.

"Ow!" Eli yelps as his face slams against his guardian's bare chest.

"That was dangerous! Are you alright?" Cyril holds Eli steady in his large arms.

"Ugh, are you made of rock?" Eli rubs his nose. Before he can say another word, they are attacked by repeated undertows. "Eek!"

"It's alright, I got you." Cyril laughs. "Don't be scared."

"You seriously laughing now, dude?!" Eli gets hit by another powerful tide.

"Well, I did tell you not to go too far, didn't I?"

Eli wants to dispute, but every time he opens his mouth, he gets hit again and again by multiple intense torrents, to the point he can't stand on his own feet. If it hadn't been for Cyril, who was holding him tight the whole time, the rip currents could very well drag him to the sea.

"Ugh, please get me back to the shore," Eli puffs, thoroughly exhausted from being assaulted by the continuous riptides.

"Alright." Cyril giggles and scoops the worn-out Eli into his arms, carrying him to the coast.

Eli lets himself rest a little in the ravenhead's arms. Then he feels something scraping against his left cheek, like he is leaning against a harsh and scabrous surface, not Cyril's smooth chest. Thinking it must have been the sand, Eli lazily splashes water on his guardian's skin, attempting to wash it off. But he freaks out when he sees countless thick scars overlapping on top of each other throughout Cyril's bare chest.

"Cyril!" Eli cries out, his hands roaming all over the scars. "What happened to you?!"

"E-Eli, what are you doing?!" Cyril jumps at the sudden touch of his young master.

"Cyril, who did this to—Eh?" Eli is shocked to find the scars on his guardian's chest are all gone.

Eli rubs his eyes and looks again. There's nothing there but smooth, pale skin.

What. The. Hell?

Eli can swear they were just there a second ago! The damn scars! He saw them clearly. They were long, gruesome cuts and deep stab marks all over Cyril's entire torso and neck, especially around the skin where his heart was.

Eli is now on full alert as he jumps out of Cyril's hold and pulls the ravenhead into the shallow water. Then, he inspects his guardian's chest to see if he can find any trace of scars or injuries.

But Cyril draws up his hands to cover his bare chest.

"What are you doing? Put your hands down." He looks up at Cyril and sees the ravenhead's face flushing in deep red. "D-Dude, are you okay?"

Cyril meekly nods and takes a step away from Eli.

What's with that reaction? Why the hell does he have that "helpless maiden being confronted by a depraved bandit who's about to defile her in just any minute now" look?!

"Cyril, what are you doing? You are scaring me," Eli says, taking a step toward his guardian, who moves a little further away from him.

"I-I am...scaring you?" Cyril stammers weakly. "Y-You were...were the one that...that—" He leaves his sentence unfinished, his face still blushing hard.

Eli has to pause for a moment to rethink what he did that triggered this damsel in distress reaction from Cyril. Then he realizes his hands might have accidentally brushed over Cyril's "nip-nips" a few times when he first saw the vision of the scars on the ravenhead's bare chest.

Oops.

Crap.

"I-I'm sorry, man. I didn't mean to...to...uhhh...make you uncomfortable. My bad. But it was an innocent mistake, man. I wasn't trying to grope you, really."

"What does 'grope' mean?"

For an instant, Eli can't come up with the right vocabulary to explain to Cyril what grope means. So, instead, he brings his hands up and makes a squeezing motion directed at the ravenhead's bare chest.

Cyril seems to finally understand as his face turns bright red again.

But Eli begins to grow impatient with his guardian's wallflower attitude. "Cyril, there's something much more important that I need to tell you right now!"

Eli then tells Cyril the entire disturbing vision he just had and asks Cyril if someone has severely hurt him before.

"Not once in the past twenty-four years."

"Are you sure?" Eli has a feeling that Cyril is not being truthful with him.

"Of course I am. I wouldn't forget if I have ever been mortally injured. I had a couple of injuries during my childhood years. Back when I was still living on the street. But none were ever serious enough to leave scars."

Eli's heart aches as he listens. The longer he lives with Cyril, the more difficult it is for him every time he learns something new about his guardian's painful past.

"Oh Eli, please don't be sad. Almost every boy fights when they are young. It's a normal part of growing up."

While Eli is glad that the awful vision didn't happen to Cyril in the past, now he's even more scared that the cursed premonition may come true in the future. His back breaks into a cold sweat, and his face blanches as he recalls the numerous scars he saw on Cyril's chest. They were all sharp and lethal injuries; each scar was from an injury that was more than enough to kill a man.

"Cyril, let's sit down for a minute. I don't feel well." Eli's breathing picks up.

Cyril immediately sweeps Eli off his feet and carries him back to shore. He sits Eli down on the deck chair and tells Eli he will get him another glass of sweet mocktail. But Eli pulls Cyril back before the ravenhead can leave. He tells Cyril he can't possibly consume anything right now and asks Cyril to sit down with him. He then talks to Cyril about his fear for Cyril's safety. Eli pleads with Cyril to be very careful and avoid making any enemies.

Cyril intently listens to him. And when he finishes, Cyril only chuckles softly.

"Thank you for worrying about me, Eli. I promise you I'll take all of your words to heart. However, I must tell you that this 'vision' you had was likely a result of overexposure to the sun rather than an actual premonition."

Eli does not agree with Cyril's statement at all. He knows what he saw, but Cyril continues.

"Eli, you have to know that *Premonition,* or *Prophecy,* the power to see the future, is not something that even an Emperor God can possess, let alone a little Sage."

"It's not?" Premonition is such a common power in so many fiction and Hollywood movies.

"No. If anyone tells you they can see the future, they are lying grifters. If they're telling the truth, then it's likely that a mystical entity is influencing them to act as a harbinger. It could be a God, a demon, a mystical animal, a witch, or even a ghost. Usually, these entities have an agenda, which most of the time isn't anything good, and they want others to fulfill it for them. After an individual has been chosen as a medium, they will start to experience visions and vivid dreams or hear strange voices that only they can hear from these mystical entities, telling them what to do or what to tell other people. Most often, the chosen harbinger would feel as if they are carrying out a holy mission or being 'gifted' the power to see a glimpse of the future. But this couldn't be further from the truth. They are just a messenger or a pawn used to do the bidding of someone who isn't human."

"Now, the reason I'm telling you this is that I want you to understand that the power of *Premonition* is not something to joke about. Though it is more or less common knowledge among Sages that Premonition is akin to a fairytale, it doesn't stop some sick and evil Sages from seeking those who they think possess this improbable power. Do you know what methods these monsters use to 'extract' the power from their victims?"

"What do they do?"

"They will devour your flesh and drink your blood while you are still alive because the flesh and blood of a dead Sage are useless. They will first force-feed you a concoction to keep you from dying or bleeding out. Then they will butcher you alive. This entire process has to be continuous, which means they will only stop when you're nothing but a skeleton."

Goosebumps form all over Eli's body as he listens. He doesn't dare to imagine that scenario.

"H-How often does this kind of crime happen in Aspenia?" Eli asks. "It must not be that common at all, right?"

Cyril shakes his head. "Since last year, the authority has convicted and executed twenty-five Sages for premeditated cannibalism."

"Twenty-five?!" Eli's face turns ashy.

"Twenty-five *known* cases. And the only reason these cases were discovered was because all twenty-five victims were free Sages from established families. Can you imagine the real number of victims who are servants or come from humble backgrounds? They are usually the primary targets for this type of crime. So far, only five cases of these victims have been brought to justice in the last forty years."

That's truly fudged up. Eli feels nauseous thinking about it. He then realizes that if Cyril didn't find him and bring him home that night, that horrific fate could very well be his.

"Eli," Cyril holds Eli's hands. "I cannot stress enough how dangerous it is out there for a young and inexperienced Sage like you. This world we live in is filled with so many evil monsters who will stop at nothing to achieve power, even if they have to resort to murder, cannibalism, or even a. I beseech you to promise that you will never discuss your Sage identity or abilities with anyone but me. And that you will also not demonstrate your power in public when you're by yourself, no matter what happens. At least not until you learn how to summon and control your Sage power properly. Can you please promise me that?"

"I-I promise," Eli stutters. Cyril's squeezing his shoulders so hard that it hurts. He has never seen Cyril being this serious with him. Cyril's expression is bleak and stern. He's definitely not joking about this.

"Good." Cyril finally loosens his iron grip. His blue eyes soften, and he pats Eli's brown locks. "You're just a regular sixteen almost seventeen-year-old human boy with no power or special abilities when you're in public, alright?"

"Okay." Eli nods obediently.

"Never mention or discuss 'premonition' to anyone. You don't have that power, do you understand?"

"Okay," Eli nods.

"You will never reveal your Sagehood to anyone?"

"Um, no, of course not," Eli shakes his head. Is it him, or is Cyril repeating himself?

"You will never show off your power in public?"

"Uh-huh, I won't."

"If you were at school and your classmates tried to bully you, what would you do?"

"I'll kick their punk asses to the moon and back!"

Cyril looks dead inside after hearing Eli's reckless response. His gorgeous face is full of disappointment that all his advice and mentoring to Eli has gone to waste.

"I'm just kidding, dude. I heard you the first time. I won't risk getting myself exposed by beating up some stupid kids," Eli cackles at his guardian, who lets out a deep, quivering sigh. "Wait, but if there is a group of bullies trying to beat me up at school and I can't retaliate, what should I do then?"

Cyril slaps his hands together. "That's the question I've been waiting for from you, Eli. The correct answer is: you run."

"Heh? That's it?"

"Yes. If someone tries to hurt you, you do not engage in a physical confrontation with them. You will run away as fast as you can and inform the adults at school about it."

...But I am an adult myself.

"Okay. Fine." Eli shrugs in agreement, though deep down, he doesn't really like this cowardly approach...

"And you will tell me about the bullies."

"And you're gonna beat them up for me?"

"No," Cyril says. "I will kill them."

"Right, of course you will." But then he sees Cyril shows no sign of humor at all, and he looks dead serious. "You don't mean that—"

"Eli," Cyril's voice is dangerously low, and his blue eyes are cold and flinty. *"Anyone who dares to harm a hair on your head, I'll send them to the next life."*

A deep chill runs through Eli's body. He can't help but shudder.

"Hahaha, got you!" Cyril bursts into a roaring laugh at Eli, who in return shoots him an overwhelmed side-eye.

"Not funny, you weirdo!" Eli nags, his face still pale with fear.

"Aww, my little, precious Eli, I'm sorry I scared you. Anyway, in the future, when I'm not around, if anyone ever gives you a hard time, you will let me know right away, alright?"

"'Kay. But what are you gonna do to them?"

Cyril is silent for a moment. Then his lips slightly curve up into a set smile. "I will talk with them and make them change their wrongdoing, of course."

Eli says nothing but shoots Cyril a highly skeptical look.

"Eli, what are you thinking? We live in a civilized society; we use words to resolve conflicts, not violence."

"I didn't say anything," Eli mumbles with a shrug. Sure it is. A civilized society where slavery is legal and cannibalism is commonplace. It seems that Emperor Haemon still has much work to tackle. While musing, Eli's peripheral vision catches something flashing on the side.

Eli turns to the left and spots a very—*very smoking hot chick* with fiery red hair and piercing blue eyes in a two-piece swimsuit. She is suggestively rubbing sunscreen on her slender neck and voluptuous bosom. Her eyes are roaming on Cyril's firm, rolling pecs, openly checking him out.

The only reason Eli can describe the redhead in such detail is because she doesn't even look at him. All her attention is on Cyril, and she appears to be going all out for him.

Eli turns to Cyril and is about to tease him. But he is downright astounded to find Cyril isn't a lick impressed or shows any sign of excitement to the redhead babe's sensual acts. He looks flat-out uncomfortable with his blue eyes squinted, and his nose slightly twitches in distaste as if he accidentally inhaled hot pepper flakes.

For a split second, Eli is very confused by Cyril's cold fish reaction. How could any man not get turned on by such a beautiful and alluring girl?! But then he suddenly recalls what Cyril told him the first time they went to the Three Bears Diner:

"I'm not really interested in women."

...Oh God, that poor girl. Eli doesn't dare to look back at the redhead bombshell anymore.

"It's getting a bit too crowded here, isn't it?" Cyril's smile is crooked as he hurriedly gathers his and Eli's beach bag. "And the sun is getting high, too. Let's get you dressed up before you get a heatstroke and pass out on me."

AFTER TAKING a shower and getting dressed, Cyril and Eli pay a visit to the Hemera Bay lighthouse, which is only a fifteen-minute walk from the beach. According to the town's manual, this place is one of their must-visit attractions because of its rich history, cultural value, and a "true," heartbreaking, captivating romance legend dating back to 350 years ago. It is said that the tragic couple now haunts this very beacon, as it was where they first met, fell in love, separated, and then passed away without ever seeing each other one last time.

A haunted romance legend at a lighthouse? Heh...some clichés are timeless across the multiverse, Eli thinks.

"For the full details, please check out our local best sellers: *The Beacon of Forsaken Love Series,* available for sale at our souvenir shop on the second floor," Cyril reads off the exhibit label at the entrance of the lighthouse and chortles lightly. "Should we buy the book? Would you like me to read it for you?"

"Dude, you really want to read 'The Lighthouse of Doomed Romance' as a bedtime story to another dude?" Eli asks wryly.

Cyril appears to be thinking really *hard* about Eli's question. Then, his eyes brighten up. "You're right, Eli! That's definitely not an appropriate book to read to you at all! Now that you remind me, I'll have to order some children's books when we return home."

"No, thank you. I'll pass. I would rather read the Constitutions of Aspenia or a history book," Eli sulks.

"Interesting...you're indeed very different," Cyril muses.

"Compared to?"

"Other kids your age, of course!" But then he catches an intense, melting glare from his young master and immediately puts on a straight face. "My bad, I meant to say sixteen-year-old young men, not kids."

* * *

THE MAIN ATTRACTION of this lighthouse is not the building itself or the tragic love legend, but the dessert cafe on the second highest floor.

The cafe is a spacious rotunda with an intricate glass dome at the center and tasteful furniture, a heavy mixture of fairytale and Rococo styles. It has golden floral wallpapers, a walnut wood parquet floor, and a large, majestic crystal chandelier. There is seating both indoors and outside on the balcony. But since the weather is quite windy, Cyril decides they should sit inside.

"I can't risk letting the wind blow you away. It took me an excruciatingly long time to find you," Cyril jokes.

About five minutes later, the waitress delivers the dessert to their table. It is by far the most beautiful thing Eli has seen this entire morning (aside from Cyril's glorious abs and the smoking redhead bombshell). This dessert is called "Little Forest," a gourmet cake made to resemble a little cottage in the woods. The house is made from chocolate with white icing; its green, mossy roof is created with green tea powder; the glass windows are made from clear sugar; there are gold flakes on the trees and the forest animals such as deer, rabbits, and little birds are made from sugar candies; they even have colorful edible flowers and a blue jelly stream.

"It's a crime to eat this masterpiece of art," Eli murmurs, wide eyes filled with awe. He has never needed a camera this much in his life; it's an utter shame not to be able to capture this magnificent dessert on film.

Even Cyril looks impressed with the cake. Upon seeing Eli's starry-eyed reaction to the dessert, he breaks into a soft chuckle and gently pats Eli's brown locks. "Let's order a couple more after you finish this one!"

"What? I can't finish this cake by myself," Eli says and hands Cyril a fork. "Let's dig in!"

"Me?"

"Of course, you. Who else? Let's try it together."

Cyril blushes and starts acting like a shy schoolgirl for a few minutes before finally sharing the cake with Eli.

Before, Snow White's cutesy little sister-next-door cosplay used to tick Eli off to no end, but now, not so much. Eli has gotten used to it. After all, every human is flawed. If Cyril can indulge Eli in being an annoying little prick 24/7, then he can certainly look past his guardian's somewhat questionable habit.

It's all about compromise, people!

As they enjoy the delicious cake, Eli brusquely puts down the fork. "Hey, that's not right."

"Hmm?" Cyril is in the middle of eating a fork full of cake. "What's not right, my dear?"

"You."

"Me?"

"You told me my vision of seeing your chest covered in numerous scars was a result of overexposure to the sun. That's not possible. I didn't have heatstroke or feel any sunlight sensitivity the entire time we were at the beach earlier!"

"A-Alright?" Cyril stutters.

"So if it wasn't a heatstroke, and according to you, that vision I had couldn't be a premonition either, then does that mean a mystical entity was influencing me?" Eli presses. "Did a God, a ghost, a witch, or a unicorn just choose me as their messenger? Why did they show me a vision of your scarred chest? Was that some sort of ultimatum? Am I supposed to carry out a mission in the near future? And if I fail, the mystical entity will hurt you?"

Eli's questions leave Cyril bereft of speech for a moment. After that, the ravenhead's face grows somber, and he reaches out his left hand to touch Eli's forehead. His blue eyes focus, and he appears to be in a flow state.

Eli sits still and lets Cyril do whatever he wants. He understands Cyril is probably working on his magic or psychic power; thus, Eli doesn't want to interrupt him. About a minute later, Cyril withdraws his hand and says, "You're fine, Eli. There's no sign of any mystical possession in you."

"I thought so, too," Eli says, nodding. "So now that my vision didn't fit all three scenarios, what's the fourth alternative? Do you have any theory?"

"I'm sure there's nothing for you to worry about, Eli," Cyril affirms with a soft smile. "I will not let anything or anyone harm you."

"Cyril, this is not about me. It's about you. I saw your chest covered with hundreds of deep scars. Aren't you at least concerned about it?" Eli inquires. He has a strong gut feeling that Cyril knows more than he has been telling him.

Cyril stays silent for a while before he responds again with his signature over-optimistic smile. "Don't worry, my little kit. I'm sure nothing's going to happen to me. I'm much stronger than I look, and I very highly doubt anyone would be able to critically injure me to that degree you saw."

"Uh-uh, nope. You're not going to do that now. I won't let you gloss over this matter. Not this time," Eli interrupts. "This is about your safety, and I know you know more than you're willing to share. I can see it in your eyes. We need to talk about this. Now."

"I'm not hiding anything." Cyril's big, blue eyes flutter as he avoids Eli's direct gaze. "Really."

Eli wishes he had a mirror to show Cyril how guilty he looks right now. Without saying another word, Eli taps his fingers on the table, waiting for Cyril to respond. But Cyril decides to play dumb all the way; a brief silence later, Eli has to be the one to speak up.

"Cyril...Are you seriously expecting me to believe that obvious lie?" Eli's voice is still calm as he's trying to suppress the impending ire rising in his throat. Cyril must think he is dumber than the village idiot if he really believes Eli will buy into that pathetic lie.

"You better start talking." He doesn't know what kind of face he's making, but it certainly intimidates Cyril.

"Um...I have a theory."

"Please, I'm all ears."

"Well. While it is impossible for a Sage to see the future, it's not impossible if the instance is of the reverse."

Eli is stumped for a few seconds. "You mean...it's possible for a Sage to see the past? Are you saying...what I saw did happen to you? But you told me you—"

"No, no, Eli. Nobody hurt me...like the way you saw. That's not what I meant. I was trying to say that perhaps...the vision you saw might belong to the previous life. Not in this life."

"So you are saying that you were possibly stabbed hundreds of times in your past life?"

"C-Could be. I mean, I'm sure nobody has stabbed me a hundred times in this life yet, so—Mm!"

"Please, don't." Eli covers the ravenhead's lips with his hand. "I don't want to hear it."

Cyril meekly nods in agreement.

"Thank God. Thank God, it was not a forewarning."

Eli doesn't elaborate, but he gives the ravenhead a long nag for his weird, riddle-filled doggerel, his habit of beating around the bush, and overall terrible communication.

As for Cyril, he does what he always does when Eli's mad: dutifully listens to the entire rant without talking back, then apologizes to Eli, and finally coaxes him back to his good mood with obsequious flatteries and bribes.

* * *

AFTER FINISHING THE CAKE, they spend another half an hour at the lighthouse before walking back to the Golden Shore Inn. On the way home, Eli unexpectedly holds Cyril's hand.

"E-Eli?" Cyril flinches at the gesture.

"There's something I want to tell you," Eli says, and they both stop in their tracks. "Cyril, are you alright? Your face is red."

"It must have been the sun," Cyril flusters and rubs his blushing cheeks, hoping to bring down the rising color on his lily-pale skin.

"Ay, it seems to me that you're the one with a sun sensitivity problem," Eli snickers and takes off his straw hat to give it to his guardian. But Cyril holds his hands to stop him.

"Aw...Eli, you're so precious. Thank you for always thinking for my sake, but I don't think your hat will fit me. I have a big head, remember?" Cyril gently puts the straw hat back on Eli's head and fixing it for him. "What is it that you want to tell me?"

Eli studies him momentarily, then speaks in a firm voice, "I will protect you."

It's clear that Cyril has never expected to hear such a statement from Eli. Subsequently, his gorgeous face fills with astonishment and inexplicable expression.

"I won't let anyone hurt you. So...don't you worry, I will always have your back no matter what." Eli awkwardly pats his guardian's back. Initially, he aimed for Cyril's shoulder, but he would have to tiptoe due to their drastic height gap.

Damn. If I only retained my twenty-three-year-old height from the previous life! Eli thinks with annoyance. Being underage and a shortie really devalues the message of protection that he's trying to convey.

"Thank you, Eli," Cyril responds with a grin. Despite the smiling, there's no trace of teasing or dismissiveness in his voice. Instead, there is a strong sense of pride and respect from man to man etched on every facet of his face.

That's how Eli knows Cyril takes his word seriously. He has been living with Cyril long enough to know his manner of speech. If Cyril regards what Eli said as childish, tough-talk nonsense, he would have fawned and made all sorts of weird faces and noises at Eli like he's talking to a baby squirrel. A brief sentence along with none of the cringy and nippily-bippily-bip babbling is usually a sign of a serious conversation from Cyril—

"Aww—my dearest, sweetest, bravest Eli, how could you be so adorable and amazing like this? You're so cute, wanting to protect me! Aww—one of these days, I might have to ask you to take responsibility for stealing my heart and melting it with bliss!" Cyril squeals and pulls Eli into a big bear hug.

"Y-You jerk! I'm being serious with you!" Eli snaps, but a terrible scream peals out from afar and disrupts their exchange.

Why does that voice sound so eerily familiar? A sense of dread rises in Eli's chest.

As they reluctantly turn their heads around to the source of the commotion, Eli's heart sinks when he spots an oversized, fluffy, pink silhouette scampering around wildly like a lunatic, toppling down everyone who stands in its way.

"Oh, for the love of God!" Eli groans when he recognizes the riotous loony. It's no other than the creepy pink bunny mascot from the Seaside Cottontail Grill!

Cyril gives no comment regarding the freakish presence of the bunny mascot. He only grabs Eli's hand and pulls him to the other side of the road, blending into a crowd away from the path of the crazy bunny.

The bunny mascot's screaming and sobbing are so earsplittingly loud and ominous that Eli's head buzzing just from listening to them.

That is not a normal scream at all.

The way she cries out seems as if she were being dipped in boiling oil. There are a couple of burly men who look like they want to hold her down, but they are too intimidated by the deafening, hair-rising holler to even attempt to stop her.

As she gets closer, Eli finally understands why she's screaming like a freaking banshee. There are bloody human entrails all over her pink mascot suit. On her neck and right shoulder hangs a battered, severed female head with disheveled black hair. The head is biting onto the bunny mascot's left breast so vehemently hard that it causes profuse bleeding.

That's the same ghost they encountered last night!

In broad daylight, Eli can see how horrifying that ghost's face is. It's evident she was brutalized over and over again before she died. Her skin is dead white, and there's blood and purple bruises covering her face. The top of her head is dented, like someone hit her skull with a bat.

"Let's get out of here," Eli whispers to Cyril. He can't stand to look at that macabre sight any longer. But the moment he speaks, the ghost suddenly stops biting on the bunny mascot and looks up right at him. She lets out a bone-chilling, hollow wail, and Eli can see there's no tongue inside her mouth, just bloodstained teeth.

Upon hearing the ghost's wail, the pink bunny mascot immediately changes her direction and plunges madly at full speed toward the crowd where Eli and Cyril stand.

CHAPTER 14

CASE II - THE BLOODY BUNNY MASCOT COSTUME – PART 3

*U*ntil now, Eli never thought a pink rabbit would be intimidating. Ever. Who the hell is afraid of a pink bunny?! If Eli had to make a guess, the number of people that are bunny-phobic (in the entire world) would probably be within the ten-finger range. He puts these individuals into two groups: ultra weirdos and ultra weirdo dipsticks.

Ah, how disgracefully awkward it is that Eli has to *painfully* admit that he belongs to the latter category he makes up: an ultra dunce, who is scared stiff of a freaking pink bunny mascot that is racing through the crowd to get to him.

To make it worse, just a minute ago, Eli declared he would protect Cyril, and now here he is, standing glued to the ground like a nitwit. There's nothing more humiliating than *this*.

The only excuse that Eli can give out to defend his dignity is that it isn't the creepy, psycho bunny mascot from Hell that he's afraid of—*but her companion, who's literally wrapped around her neck like a scarf made from human entrails.* The instant their eyes met, he could not look away or move his body at all.

He can't open his mouth. He can't even freaking blink!

The only thing he can do is stand there watching the people around him being bulldozed to the ground by the crazy bunny mascot. The ghost is ogling at him with her eye so wide open it feels like it could pop out of the socket at any given second now. Blood oozes from her mouth and deformed head, while bloody tears stream down from her only eye. Like the bunny mascot, she is also screaming at the top of her lungs, but only a hollow, airy, ominous sound comes out of those pale, bruised lips, for she lacks a tongue. Eli can even see parts of her damn brain amongst the stringy, blood-soaked hair!

When the deranged bunny mascot has plowed down the last person between her and Eli, her hand swings out to grab him. A flash of a tall silhouette appears right before Eli. Then, a precise, powerful, and beautifully executed kick lands on the bunny mascot's chest, sending her flying through the air before she crashes into the road.

Eli is freed from the hypnosis the moment bunny from Hell is down. His knees buckle, but Cyril is faster, as his arm already wraps around Eli's waist, catching him from tumbling down.

"Eli, are you alright?! Are you hurt?" Cyril lifts Eli to his feet and looks over him to check for injury.

"I-I'm fine," Eli stutters. It feels as if he just got strangled to near unconsciousness; still, he tries to act normal so that he would not worry Cyril any further. "L-Let's check...on that girl first."

A big, raucous crowd forms around the bunny girl, so takes some time for them to pass through the curious folks. Once they finally get to the scene, Eli can't help but wince at what he sees.

The ghost and her bloody intestines are gone, but bunny girl is in seriously bad shape. She is lying unconscious on the ground. Her fluffy pink costume is so dirty it looks as if someone dumped a trash can on her, or she just pulled an all-nighter party down under the sewer, or maybe both. There are several large bloodstains on her outfit, but the most severe injury seems to be on her left breast, the place where the ghost bit, as that area is drenched in blood. When they both get a little closer to her, an awful stench repels them.

"Oh...ew." Eli covers his nose with one hand. It looks like this girl has pooped inside her costume. He turns to Cyril. "Dang, Cyril, you really kicked the crap out of her!"

"She tried to attack you," Cyril responds, still holding Eli's hand. "And no, I don't think I'm the cause of her defecation. This smell isn't of fresh feces. There's also a strong odor of urine, old and new scents overlapping with each other, which, in this case, I'm certain I'm responsible for her latest urination."

"Cyril, how the—let's call an ambulance...emergency cab and take this chick to the hospital first."

Cyril agrees and summons an emergency carriage to get the girl to the nearest health clinic. A couple of sentinels who are practically police officers, arrive at the scene and take everyone's statements. Since there are many witnesses to the crazy rampage, the sentinels quickly deem bunny girl at fault and rule Cyril's kick as self-defense, so there will be no charges brought against him. He and Eli are free to go. After learning that Cyril and Eli are just visitors here, the sentinels give them a heartfelt apology for the terrible vacation experience and tell them how unusual this incident is, as Hemera Bay always prides itself on being one of the safest cities in Aspenia.

Eli is so impressed with the town's authoritative figures' overly nice and friendly attitude that he discusses it with Cyril after the sentinels have left.

"Of course, they have to be nice to the citizens. They are public servants. It's their job to serve the people," Cyril says distractedly, doing a careful check on Eli from head to toe. "Are you sure nobody stepped on you or anything? Did someone push you or hurt you during the chaos?"

"I suppose you haven't run into the cops in Creepyville yet. I'm fine, Cyril. Ugh! This is the fifth time you asked me this!" Eli groans. He swears Cyril's paranoia is growing stronger day by day!

"I know, I know, I'm sorry." Cyril gently caresses Eli's round cheeks, his soft blue eyes still full of concern and affection. "Please bear with me. I just can't stand to see you hurt even in the slightest way. I should have carried you and ran off instead of blending into the crowd. I never thought that woman would go after you."

"Right, about that bunny chick. We have to go to the clinic right now, Cyril. I have to talk to her."

"Absolutely not! You're not going anywhere near her!"

Eli then tells Cyril in detail about seeing the decapitated ghost. And just as he had predicted, Cyril didn't see the ghost at all.

No one did except for Eli.

"I think she was trying to reach out to me. She wanted to tell me something, but her tongue was missing...someone pulled it out." Eli shudders.

Cyril's expression progressively worsens as he listens to Eli's story. He stays silent for a long while before calling a cab to the clinic. Once they're sitting inside the carriage, Cyril takes Eli's hands into his and speaks to him in an earnest voice.

"Eli, next time, whenever you see something or someone unusual that isn't supposed to be there or exist in the given circumstances, you will not speak up, make any noise, or do anything that could draw these entities' attention to you. And you will never ever look at them in the eyes. This is very gravely important. Can you please promise me you will remember this?"

"Yes, I promise." Cyril's face is very grim still. "Cyril, am I getting us into trouble again?"

Cyril's a little startled when he hears that question. He immediately puts back on his cheery face and waves his hand.

"Nah, of course not. This is just a little complication. I'll take care of it." Cyril gives Eli a bright, confident smile, then pulls Eli into his arms. "Don't worry, my little kit. I promise you everything will be fine."

"Okay," Eli gives out a slight nod. "I'm sorry for always being a nuisance."

Cyril says nothing but shoots him a strange look.

"What?" Eli murmurs.

"Oh, I'm sorry, but you're quite...meek today," Cyril chuckles, an odd gleam in his eyes. "I'm not used to it."

"Oh." He has too much going in his mind right now; it's mainly about the whole vengeful ghost-bunny mascot ordeal, but the vision of Cyril's scarred chest still bothers him, and then the guilt of dragging Cyril into this bloody supernatural mess. *Again.*

"But I like it." Cyril's lips curve upward into a grin.

"Of course you like it. Unless you'd rather me be a jerk to you?" Eli mumbles. "Don't think so. You're not a masochist."

"Aw, Eli. But you have never been mean to me. You've always been an absolute angel."

"Cyril, either you have a really short-term memory, or you are actually a masochist."

"I assure you I'm neither of those things." Cyril shoots him a sly grin, and Eli rolls his eyes. "Oh, and now that you remind me, Eli, what does 'cops' mean?"

"It means police, uh, sentinels."

"Ah, I see, thank you. They were awful, weren't they?"

"Um, who were awful?"

"The sentinels from Crimson Vale. I bet they are rude compared to the nice lads here."

Eli grimaces as he recalls the horrible memory of running into the two asshole cops back then. One of them kicked him to a pulp, while the other suggested gutting him, and all because he bumped into them by accident. "Rude is a big understatement! They were absolutely ruthless and nasty!"

"I know. I already guessed," Cyril's voice drops to a cold pitch. "And you encountered them in Crimson Vale the day you woke up."

"Well, I—" It's then that Eli realizes Cyril has been inducing him into revealing the gritty details of his first day in Aspenia. Eli never shared with Cyril the full details of his story before the ravenhead found him that night. He especially cut out all those unpleasant parts, fearing his guardian would go after the people who did Eli wrong. "N-No. I didn't."

Cyril only stares at him, his eyes hard, void of emotion.

"Whew...it's a bit hot in here, isn't it?" Eli fans himself with his hand. But Cyril brazenly cups Eli's cheek and guides him back to face him. "W-What?"

Cyril looks at Eli in silence. His handsome face has grown so pale that it's only a few shades pinker compared to that ghost woman. All the usual warmth has long vanished, and only immense grief and pain remain. Then he pulls Eli into a tight embrace.

"I'm sorry," Cyril whimpers, his voice cracking. "I'm sorry I was late. I'm always late."

"You were not late. You got me out alive. Remember?" Eli says in a soft voice, stroking Cyril's back.

"Did they hurt you a lot?"

"No. They never got to me. I outran them."

Cyril lets out a broken chuckle, but it sounds like a sob. He slowly pulls back to look at Eli. His beautiful eyes are cloudy and brim with tears.

"Giant crybaby," Eli teases, swiping his guardian's tears away with his hands.

Cyril reaches for Eli's right wrist, his long fingers caressing Eli's small palm, where he eventually puts down a kiss on it.

"Never again, Eli," Cyril avows, his expressive blue eyes fixate on Eli's. "I swear to you. I won't let anyone hurt you again."

If any other guy ever told Eli such a thing, he would be creeped out, then he would politely say thank you and run for the hill. But when it comes from Cyril, somehow, those words fill Eli's heart with so much warmth and ridiculously outlandish happiness.

...Of a purely beautiful brotherhood they have, that is.

"I'll hold you to that," Eli says in the brattiest voice he can muster. "If you fail, I'm gonna move in with Wolfgang."

Eli accidentally hits a raw nerve as Cyril is visibly "shook" at the mention of Wolfgang, their dashing neighbor. The ravenhead stops his mushy crying right away.

"Oh no, no, no. Eli, you can't move in with that loser! He's a drunkard and a delusional twit. He wants to become a pirate, yet he loathes water and has chronic seasickness! He'll get you addicted to alcohol and turn you into a troublemaker. He doesn't know how to cook or clean. He can't even look after himself, let alone take care of you! If you live with him, you will be malnourished, dirty, and miserable." Though he tries to be convincing, his pupils expand, and Eli can see the blatant fear and apprehension drilling in his voice. Cyril really believes Eli's joke is true.

Oh, Cyril. How could 'thee' be so astoundingly naïve and adorable like this? Eli lets out a deep sigh inside his head as he regards Cyril with utter fondness. But instead of letting poor Cyril know he was only joking, Eli decides to be evil and messes with his klutzy guardian a bit. He puts on a pensive look and acts like he's "seriously" considering between Cyril and Captain Seven-Seas.

"Um...I'm already a troublemaker. In case you haven't noticed, we're on our way to address the trouble right now," Eli comments. "Also, Wolfgang certainly can cook! He makes a mean jambalaya every time we come to his place for dinner."

"Eli, first, you are not a troublemaker. You've always been kind and empathetic back then and now. As a Sage, it's very normal to attract unwanted paranormal energy, especially when the Sage is young and as attractive as you," Cyril avers. But his demeanor deescalates to aggravation as he continues, "And second, do you notice Wolfgang always serves mushroom jambalaya every single time we visit him?"

"Well, jambalaya is the only dish he knows how to make. The man can't fry an egg without burning it. He can't even fix a proper salad. Do you really want to eat only greasy jambalaya for the rest of your life?"

"Tempting, but probably not," Eli responds, shaking his head after a few seconds of consideration.

"Exactly, Eli. You need a guardian who is domestic, handy, reliable, sober, and, most importantly, strong. Though I'll be fair, Wolfgang does meet most of these qualifications, except for the sober and domestic part. Also, he's not as strong as I am. I'm not being arrogant; it's just an inconvenient truth," Cyril states in a matter-of-fact way. Despite the outrageously condescending statement, Cyril's face shows no hints of smugness or conceited at all.

Eli only oohs at his guardian. His head slightly cocks to the side, and his lips curl into a captivating smile. "What else?"

"I can make hundreds of different jambalaya variations for you," Cyril returns the smile with one no less alluring and indefinitely tender. His posture shifts, and he leans in a little toward his young master, narrowing the distance between them an inch closer. "And it's not just jambalaya. I can cook any cuisine in the world for you. I'll fulfill your every wish and request, no matter how great or dainty or whimsical they are. I shall never deny you anything. Should the world ever fall apart and everyone somehow turns against you, I will always stand by you and take out every last one of your enemies. No matter what you do, I'll always take your side. I will never judge you. Even if you ever commit a grave blunder, I will not let anyone condemn you. I'll bear the consequences in your place. As long as I exist on this Earth, I will not let you endure any hardship or unkindness. I will protect you and give you all the finest things in life."

"Everything that I have or will ever have is yours. Even my life is at your disposal." The ravenhead then snaps his fingers, and hundreds of orange speckles appear from thin air and rain down on the flabbergasted Eli. The glitters start to form into a sparkling red rose. The fiery petals gradually blossom and reveal a small, golden box with a pink bow at the center of the flower.

The rose and glitters only fade away when Eli picks up the box. The more he looks at it, the more it resembles an engagement ring box.

This realization makes Eli's body break into goosebumps. Even though he manages to keep his poker face, his eyebrows spasm sporadically, as if someone were jabbing him with a needle. His green eyes switch from the golden ring box to Cyril's face. After a while, he undoes the pink bow with trembling fingers. He takes in several deep breaths before opening the box.

Eli shakes with relief to find a big chestnut-sized chocolate bonbon nestled against the velvet cushion instead of a ring.

But the relief is soon sacked when Cyril tells Eli to taste the candy and that there is a "great" surprise in the filling.

"A-A surprise?" Eli splutters, a corner of his lips twitching.

Cyril then tells him he had to import the ingredients from three countries from two different continents to make this "special" chocolate, and everything is *handcrafted* by Cyril himself.

"Crafted." Eli gulps at the bigger-than-average chocolate ball in the golden ring box and then to the carriage's window.

Eli would be downright lying if he denied the thought of jumping out of the cab and running like hell hasn't crossed his mind. But after some consideration, he scraps that idea as the success rate of pulling that stunt is nil.

After some deliberate stalling, Eli ends up shrugging his shoulders and mutters "Yolo" before biting onto the bonbon.

Holy kamoley!

It's *the* best chocolate Eli has ever had in his life. The candy has a semi-sweet dark chocolate shell with lychee and vodka filling. While Eli is not too sure about the lychee, he's positive that the vodka and cacao are of top quality. Especially that vodka. It's *so* amazing. Glorious. It's like a perfect love child between Stolichnaya and Beluga. It's simply divine!

"My God, this is awesome!" Eli moans in Russian. And the best news is there's no diamond ring inside the lychee filling.

"I hope you like it."

"I love it! It's the best thing I've ever had."

"So, does that mean you'll stay?" Cyril asks, big puppy eyes blinking and lips pressing tightly.

"What?" Eli doesn't understand what Cyril's talking about.

"You won't be moving in with Wolfgang, right?" Cyril's voice cracks from nervousness.

The mind-blowingly delicious chocolate with vodka filling has Eli temporarily forget about the Wolfgang's topic for a moment. But since Cyril has brought it up again, Eli is reminded of the sheer ridiculousness of this whole shenanigan Cyril just pulled and how much of a paranoid idiot this weirdo is with the over-the-top cheesy speech, fiery red rose, and glittery ring box. But as Eli's about to open his mouth and bicker, a more important matter flashes through his mind.

"Hey Cyril, when did you make this chocolate?"

"Two days before we went on vacation," Cyril responds.

"I see...Well, I want to say thank you for making me this amazing gourmet candy. It's really incredible and wonderful of you to do that...for me. I'm really moved, man. I appreciate it," Eli thanks sincerely.

In his previous life, none of his ex-girlfriends ever gave him homemade chocolate. Heck! Not a single one of them knew how to cook. Once, Eli and his third girlfriend ended up in the ER after she attempted to make them a romantic dinner. The food poisoning was so severe it took them over a week to fully recover, and Eli lost fifteen pounds during the treatment. She broke up with him right after they got released from the hospital. Eli assumed she was embarrassed about what had happened. Nevertheless, he had never felt so relieved to get dumped in his life.

"I'm so glad you like that little treat. I'll make more bonbons for you when we're home," Cyril fawns.

"You're the best, man!" Eli chuckles and gives him a thumbs up.

They share a smile. After a brief, awkward silence, both speak at the same time.

"Hey, do you still have any of that Vodka left at home?"

"You won't move in with Wolfgang, right?"

"What?" Eli and Cyril blurt concurrently at each other.

"Cyril, do you seriously think I would leave home and live with Wolfgang?" Eli asks, his voice slightly annoyed.

Cyril looks at Eli with blinking puppy eyes, then nods in response to Eli's question, which earns him a scowl from Eli.

"S-Sorry," poor Cyril stutters, intimidated.

"Cyril, you've said a lot of...irrational things *(stupid shit)*, but this is by far the most...silly and illogical *(dumbest)* thing I have ever heard from you. Please. Tell me what makes you think I would ditch home, ditch you—my legal guardian, my only family, and move in with a neighbor?"

"Well, Eli, you have an ultimate say. If you set on moving in with any of them, Wolfgang, Mariposa, Haidar, or even Gallahan, there's nothing I can do. As long as it's your wish, I will respect it and make it happen," Cyril responds sadly, his eyes downcast.

Eli frowns in complete befuddlement as he listens to the ravenhead. Just as he's about to ask why Cyril brings Haidar's family into this move-out nonsense, Cyril continues.

"All of them care a great deal about you. Even though they are not as capable and strong as I am, they undoubtedly can take good care of you. In fact, they might be able to spend more time with you than I could," Cyril lets out a deep sigh, his brows knit together in sorrow.

But Eli doesn't share the same sentiment Cyril is feeling. If anything, he's trying his best not to snap and berate the heck out of this dum-dum. After a quick contemplation, Eli decides to be patient and uses the gentle approach instead. He reassures Cyril that he will not move into any of their neighbor's houses. He tells his guardian that while he very much treasures the friendship with their neighbors, he will always choose Cyril over anyone else. Thus, Cyril should not compete with their neighbors for Eli's affection.

Cyril is instantly elated upon hearing Eli's assurance.

"Oh, Eli. Thank you! I promise you will not regret this decision. I will be the best guardian ever for you. I'll give you the best life—"

"Okay, okay, I got it, man. Chill," Eli stops his hyperactive guardian. He knows if he doesn't intervene, Snow White will ramble nonstop for the next twenty minutes.

"Hey Cyril, what brand of Vodka did you use to make the filling?"

"It's a brand called Golden Bear," Cyril responds.

Eli has never heard of that Vodka brand. It probably only exists in this world.

"Do you have any Golden Bear left at home? Surely you can't use all of it to make just one bonbon, right?" Eli shoots Cyril an aberrantly sweet smile. And just as he expected, his klutzy guardian takes the bait, as evident by the rising colors on his pale cheeks.

"Oh, no. I used it all," Cyril answers, sounding genuine.

"You used an entire bottle to make one candy?" Eli is very skeptical.

"Well, no. I *crafted* a lot of them. There were many trials, but only one made the cut," Cyril explains.

"Cyril, you 'cook' or 'make' food. You don't 'craft' food. You use 'craft' for metal, wood, or glass. Like you craft a table or a vase. Nobody says craft a cake," Eli says.

"Ohhh, I see," Cyril exclaims. "Thank you for the lesson. It's really nostalgic. Makes me feel like a kid again."

"No problem...Wait—What? A kid again?"

"...I mean an adolescent again! It was almost...Uh, ten years ago...I was pretty much a kid when we first met...Hahaha...Time flies. Whew! Now, I'm no longer a kid!"

"Are you okay? Do you need water?" Eli puts a hand on Cyril's forehead. He's relieved that the ravenhead's temperature is normal. So Snow White isn't ill or anything; he's just being his usual batty self.

"Anyway, please don't put candy in a tiny box like that again. It's weird and can cause a serious misunderstanding that can lead to a potential heart attack," Eli remarks.

"Uh? Why?" Cyril asks, scratching his head. "Also, it doesn't look right if I put only one candy in a regular box. That box would be too big for a single candy."

Dude, that's not the point! Eli's about to refute, but the coachman informs them they have reached their destination.

"Just don't put it in a questionable box like that! Of all the boxes in the world, why would you choose a ring box to put the candy in?" Eli snaps as they get off the carriage.

"That's called a ring box?" Cyril asks, confused. "It's so small. How many rings could fit in there? That's such an unpractical design."

"That type of box is designed to fit only one ring unless you're playing big and proposing to two chicks at the same time. Dude, you seriously have never seen what a ring box looks like before?"

"Well...I don't wear rings," Cyril innocently shows Eli both of his hands. "I'm not sure what you mean by proposing to two chicks at the same time. Chickens can't wear rings."

"What the...I just can't...You're killing me, Cyril!" Eli cries in frustration while Cyril gasps out loud in terror.

"Oh no, please don't say that! How could you say such a horrible thing?! I'll never ever commit such a wicked act to you. I'd rather die a thousand times!" Cyril squeezes Eli in his iron grasp.

"Arg! It's an expression! I didn't mean it literally, you idiot!" Eli explodes, his face red. He breaks off the hug, "Either you are trolling me, or you have been extra bananas today! For God's sake, pull yourself together!"

"I will. I will. I'm sorry. Please don't be mad! Breathe. Breathe!" Cyril strokes Eli's back to calm him down.

* * *

THE MEDICAL CLINIC before them is a small building with only one floor. It's quite old, as evidenced by the water stains on the white plaster walls from the rain and humidity. The abundant green tropical plants on the exterior and the cheery yellow door and windows create a quaint and peaceful atmosphere, ideal for resting and recovery.

Upon entering the clinic, Cyril approaches the front desk nurse to ask the way to the bunny mascot's room.

"I hope she has calmed down now," Eli mutters as he and Cyril follow a doctor to the bunny mascot's room. They hear a screech from the direction they're heading.

"Or not," Eli sighs.

Once they get to the room, a strong smell of feces welcomes them. It turns out the bunny mascot is still in her dirty suit, and she is now yelling at the young nurse wearing a facemask next to her. This heated exchange ends with the pink bunny slapping the poor nurse to the floor.

"What's happened?" The doctor rushes to help the nurse up.

"I couldn't get the costume off her. I tried to cut out the part where she dirtied herself, but—"

"You did NOT try to cut off the costume! You stuck freaking scissors into my vagina, you dumb cow!" The bunny points an angry, furry finger at the nurse.

"P-Please calm down, miss," the doctor says. "What do you mean you couldn't get the costume off? There has to be an opening somewhere."

"I checked everywhere three times! There's no button or zipper anywhere on the suit," the young nurse cries. "I-It's like…like the suit is a part of her body."

Cyril and Eli exchange a look.

"You're mad! There's a zipper at the back! Help me get it off!" Bunny girl snaps and turns her back to the doctor.

The doctor begins to look for the zipper as he digs his fingers into the furry costume. A minute later, he asks the bunny mascot, "Miss, are you sure the zipper is at the back? Maybe it's on the side?"

"No. It can't be. The zipper is at the back. Right at the center back! Look again."

"There's no zipper at the back, ma'am. H-How did you get into this costume? There's not even a seam."

"Doctor, do you mind if I have a try? I think I can help," Cyril asks from the doorway.

The doctor regards Cyril from head to toe. "Of course, sir," he says, to Eli's amazement.

Cyril asks for two facemasks and a pair of gloves. He puts the first mask on Eli and then equips himself with the rest of the gears before approaching the pink bunny, introducing himself, and asking for her name.

"My name is Myra," the bunny girl responds. Her tone has notably softened. "Hey, I know you. You are the gentleman who helped me last night at the Seaside Cottontail Grill."

Very selective memory this chick has, Eli muses.

"Small world. Small town," Cyril says. "Now, Myra. I'll try to take the costume off of you. Stay still."

"Yes!" Bunny girl responds in a soft, girly voice, starkly contrasting to Cyril's deep, husky tone. Eli has a feeling she's blushing under that fluffy suit.

Cyril puts his gloved hands on each side of the bunny's face and gives it a couple of tugs, but the mask won't budge.

"T-That suit clings onto her...as if it were her skin," the young nurse mouths.

"There's no seam at the neck," Cyril mutters. "Hold on to the bedpost as firmly as you can. I'll try a different method."

"Y-Yes."

Everybody in the room holds their breath and waits for the ravenhead's next move. They all seem to have high regard and expectations for Cyril to solve this peculiar mystery and save the day, despite not knowing him. Eli guesses the reason for this phenomenon is once again because of Cyril's assertive aura that makes him appear reliable in everyone's eyes.

Cyril suddenly grabs the bunny ears and aggressively yanks them like there's no tomorrow.

"STOP! STOP! OUCH! YOU'RE RIPPING MY EARS OUT!" The bunny girl cries out in pain.

"Your ears?" Cyril lets go of the bunny ears.

"Yes! My ears really— No...h-how could it be? My ears aren't up there... They..."

The room falls into a stark silence.

Eli's eyes narrow.

"T-This is insane! I'm dreaming! This is not real! It can't be!" Myra sobs.

"What is going on?" the doctor mumbles, his face pale. The nurse behind him is terrified.

"Turn around, Myra," Cyril tells the girl.

Myra is still weeping, but she eventually does as told. Three seconds later, she screams again.

This time, Cyril pulls the pink cotton tail off the suit with all his might.

"STOP! STOP NOW, YOU PSYCHO!" Myra spits.

"You can't possibly say your tail's hurting. Humans don't have tails," Cyril says, pulling the rabbit's tail.

"NO! BUT...JUST STOP! IT HURTS! SHIT!" Myra swears. Cyril lets go of the tail, and she flops to the bed like a fuzzy cannonball.

"Where did you hurt when he pulled the tail?" asks the doctor.

Bunny girl is hesitant for a moment before answering. "My privates."

The look of puzzlement is present on everyone's face. About a minute later, Cyril breaks the silence.

"My apologies, lad. I wouldn't have pulled your member that hard had I known your true gender. A man's private is extremely important to him. Voices can be misleading, I suppose," Cyril says in a sincere tone.

"What the hell are you saying? I'm a woman, you fool!" Myra is very pissed.

"Well, to my best knowledge, it's quite impossible to pull a lady's, please excuse my language, privates, for human females generally don't have protruding genitalia. Only men do. When I pulled the tail, you said your privates hurt; that was why I assumed you were a man."

Eli can feel the heat emitting from Myra under the bunny costume as her fuzzy fists all ball up.

"When you pulled that tail, it hurts as if you just punched me in my... down there!" Myra grits her teeth.

"It was quite anatomically wrong, but alright," Cyril responds.

"What was anatomically wrong?"

"The tail is at your backside, but the pain you felt was frontal."

Confusion once again washes over everybody's face in the room, except Cyril and Myra, since she's wearing a costume.

"There is one last option we could try," Cyril says.

"What is it?" asks bunny girl warily.

"I'll cut that costume apart and get you out." Cyril holds up a pair of long, sharp scissors.

"Oh, no, no, no, no, no!" the others cry.

"S-Stay away from me!" bunny girl cries out in horror.

"I tried." Cyril shrugs. He removes the gloves, tosses them into the trash bin, and sanitizes his hands.

"W-What should we do now?" asks the young nurse.

"I believe this case is clearly out of our mortal hands," the doctor says, fixing his glasses with shaky fingers.

"Miss, maybe you should contact a monk? Or a shaman?"

"What's going to happen to me? I'm scared," Myra sobs.

"Well, miss, I'm afraid to tell you that you are going to die," Cyril speaks matter-of-factly.

"WHAT?!"

"H-How dare you—AHHHHHHH!" Myra screams upon glancing at Eli. She jumps off the bed and hides in a corner like a trapped rat that's about to be slain in the most gruesome way.

Her sudden outburst startles everybody in the room.

Eli's back suddenly feels extremely cold. But before he can look over his shoulder, Cyril calls out to him in a thunderous voice that's three times louder than the bunny chick. "ELI!"

"What?!" Eli jolts at the sudden aggressive address; Cyril has never raised his voice at him like that before. But at the same time, he can't help but shudder, as his back is getting even colder and heavier. Just like—

Just like a bag of ice leaning against him.

"Come here, Eli." Cyril beckons with his hand, blue eyes piercing on Eli's.

Myra's scream gets louder as Eli proceeds further into the room while keeping his gaze fixed on Cyril. Eli would tell her to take a chill pill and shut up if it wasn't for the inexplicable "ice pack" weighing on his back.

The "ice pack" seems to vanish when Cyril grabs Eli's wrist and pulls him to his side.

Still, Eli doesn't dare to look behind him. Cyril holding his hand makes him feel so much safer and less frightened.

"Doctor, I would like to have a few words with the lady in private," Cyril says.

"I don't want to be alone with him! He's up to no good. He wants to kill me!" Myra protests from the corner.

"Well, sir. I think this miss here is not in the right state—"

"Please, sir," Cyril interrupts the doctor; his voice is still calm, yet both his arms burst into roaring blazes, casting the room in red shadow. "Sage affair."

Eli's heart skips a beat when the unannounced fire sets off as his hand is still in Cyril's clutch. Luckily, the flame is entirely harmless to him, though he can't help but throw Cyril a subtle side-eye.

"I see. Very well, sir." The doctor gives Cyril a bow, to which the raven-head returns a nod. "I'll be in the next room if you need me."

Cyril requests that the doctor provides Myra with something to sanitize herself and cover up the poop stains. Since no one can get the costume off of her, the doctor has to give her a gigantic adult diaper and *a lot* of disinfectant spray to fend off the stink as much as possible.

When the outsiders have left, Eli has to take three seconds to wrap his head around the monumental ridiculousness of this entire bizarre situation. Two dudes are going to interrogate an oversized pink bunny in a 3XL diaper in a stinking hospital room.

A person's life can't get any wilder than this!

"Did you kill that girl?" Cyril asks.

Myra jolts upon hearing that question. "I-I don't know what you're talking about. What girl? I didn't kill anybody."

"A young lady in her early twenties with dark hair, fair skin, and a gray eye. Yes, she only has one eye left. Her other one was plucked out. Her tongue was drawn out, her face badly brutalized. Does that ring a bell with you?"

"No. How awful. That's absolutely barbaric." Myra gives a gasp so fake it's borderline insulting. "I don't know such a girl, sir. I don't have any female acquaintances with black hair."

"Didn't you just hang out with her an hour ago? She was on your neck in the form of a severed head and a mass of bloody entrails." Cyril points at bunny girl's injury on her left breast. "She even left you a 'souvenir.'"

"This...this was from a...a beaver. A beaver attacked me!"

"Like the 'beaver' behind you right now?"

"WHAT?!" Myra jumps and swirls around like a madwoman. There's no one behind her, but she can't stop trembling. "You lied to me, you—AHHHHH! YOU STAY AWAY FROM ME!" She points a finger at Eli.

Eli instinctively looks around. Thankfully, there's nothing creepy behind him.

"Woman, stop wasting my time. I'm not one with high patience, and I'm no ordinary man you can fool. I'm a Sage. I will find out what happened to that girl. I will find out what *you and your accomplice* did to her." Cyril watches as bunny girl flinches at the mention of an accomplice.

She couldn't be any more guilty.

"And I will find out today," Cyril says coldly. "Based on the severity and the gruesomeness of this case, all individuals who took part in it will receive capital punishment. Death."

Myra drops to her knees and pleads for mercy. "Oh no. Please, trust me, master. I really had nothing to do with her death. They did it. They murdered that poor, wretched girl."

They. So, there is more than one killer, Eli thinks as he recalls the man in the cerulean coat last night. The ghost also haunted him by clinging onto his body, as she did with Myra. But for some reason, the man didn't seem to see the ghost as Myra and Eli did.

"What's the name of the victim?"

"Faye, sir."

"When did she die?"

"Three days ago, sir."

"Where was she killed?"

Myra doesn't answer this question. Cyril asks her again and gets the same result. However, they find out not that she refuses to speak. She simply can't continue talking whenever she attempts to answer that question. It's as if some invisible force is strangling her.

"I...I...can't...breathe," Myra gasps, hands clasping around her throat. "Please...stop."

"Do you know the killers?"

Myra nods, weeping.

"What was your relation with Faye?"

"She used to work at the grill with me, sir."

"Aside from you, how many others participated in Faye's murder?"

She can't answer that question. Cyril begins to signal with two fingers. She gives him a nod at number four.

Cyril then asks her about the other four killers' names, descriptions, and occupations, but she cannot answer those questions. She isn't able to mention anything related to the murder of Faye or the four killers.

"Nod or shake your head. Are those killers tall?"

She nods.

"Are they well-built?"

She nods.

"Are they also Sages like I am?"

She nods and breaks down in tears. But there's not a shred of sympathy on Cyril's face.

"Are they sentinels?"

She nods.

"Do they all wear the same style of uniform?

She nods.

"Are the uniforms white with navy borders?"

She shakes her head. Eli remembers the nice sentinels they met earlier wearing the same white uniform with navy borders as Cyril described. So, Hemera Bay PD might not be the suspects in this case.

"Is *cerulean* the color of their uniforms?" The girl cries, shakily nodding in confirmation.

Cyril asks bunny girl a couple more questions. She doesn't provide any new or helpful information, except that Faye has been bugging her in her sleep in the first two days, but it quickly evolved into a lethal haunting when Cyril and Eli dined at the restaurant last night.

Heh. Eli has a strong gut feeling he's the main culprit for this sudden increase of haunting severity this evil woman has experienced.

"Please help me. What's going to happen to me?" Myra tearfully asks.

"Oh, Myra. What comes will come. You reap what you sow." Cyril walks to the door with Eli's hand in his. "You better rest while you can. Tonight is going to be a long night for you. If you can live until then, that is." Cyril waves his free hand, and the door closes on its own.

Eli hears a weeping noise that resonates through the wall.

* * *

"You must be hungry. What would you like for lunch?" Cyril asks, taking off his and Eli's masks.

"No, man. I can't eat anything right now," Eli responds sluggishly.

"How come? Are you feeling unwell?" Cyril's tone turns serious as he reaches for Eli's forehead and checks his temperature. "Are you cold?"

"A little bit." Eli looks around the clinic and sees everyone wearing light clothes and sweating, given the warm weather.

The two masks on Cyril's right hand burst into blue flame. The raven-head then discards the ashes in a trash bin.

"Just hang in there a little longer. I'll hug you when we're in the cab. You'll feel better in no time," Cyril says tenderly.

"Okay, thanks—Wait, why hug?" Eli shakes off the sudden wave of fatigue. His sleepy green eyes become alert.

"Because I can control fire, so it might help with your cold when I hold you close?"

"Ah, okay. Hey, no. Thank you. But there's no need! I feel fine now!"

Cyril raises a brow.

"I'm fine, man! I think it's the low sugar. You have any chocolate with you?" Eli blinks.

"You've had enough sweets for the day, young man. No more sweets until tomorrow."

"You said I mean the world to you." If it weren't for those healthy chubby cheeks and the expensive outfit he's wearing, Eli would look very convincing as a poor kid, as his body is already too underweight for teen boys his age.

Two years of training for a six-pack all went down the drain! Eli feels a little dead inside as he reminisces about the defined abs he used to possess.

"Oh, Eli, I'm so sorry! Please don't be sad. My heart breaks every time you're unhappy. Of course, you mean the world to me and much, much more than that! You are invaluable to me! Here are all the candies I have on me. You can eat all you want. I'll buy you more later today!" Cyril of the low willpower cries as he takes out a velvet pouch full of colorful candies from his leather crossbody bag and gives it to Eli.

"Haha—Oh...thank you, Sno—Cyril." Eli wheezes, forcing down the laughter in his throat. He takes a handful of candies and puts them in his pants pocket. *Geez, whipped!*

Eli triumphantly unwraps a piece of candy as he walks. But before he can pop it into his mouth, a surge of extreme discomfort and inexplicable coldness rips through his body.

Cyril and Eli's expressions instantly turn grim at what they see. A tall, well-built man in a tailored cerulean outfit is walking toward them.

When the man is about ten steps past them, he stops in his tracks. "Hey. Excuse me," the man calls out again. Cyril and Eli stop walking and turn around to face him.

The man and Cyril exchange sharp stares. A few seconds later, the man diverts his gaze to Eli. "Is there something on my face, little one?"

Eli only shakes his head.

"Oh? I thought there's dirt on my face since you were staring so hard you dropped your candy." He swirls up the honey candy between his two fingers. "Do you want it back?"

"Don't talk to him," Cyril says in an ominously low voice, sending chills down Eli's spine.

"Alright, relax, good fella. I meant no harm. Just being friendly." The guy changes to a friendlier tone while taking a step back.

Cyril doesn't bother to respond. He grabs Eli's hand and heads toward the clinic's front door. After about five steps, Eli's ears pick up a whooshing sound of a tiny object tearing through the air in their direction. Before he can utter "watch out," Cyril already waved the index finger of his free hand. The foreign object then shifts its route and lands straight in the trash bin fifteen feet ahead.

"I wouldn't try that again if I were you," Cyril says without looking back.

When they walk near the trashcan, Eli peeks inside and sees the honey candy lying in the center of the bin.

* * *

ONCE THEY'RE FINALLY OUTSIDE, Eli pulls Cyril to a remote area far away from the clinic, looking around to ensure no one can hear them, then whispering, *"There was blood all over him, Cyril! Blood, black hair, and human intestines! But no head, though. I think they're from Faye!"*

"I see." Cyril nods. He has to bend down to listen to Eli.

"I peeked at him before we went out. He went into evil bunny's room! He has to be one of the killers!"

"Yes, I knew that."

"So what now? Should we call the cops? Or are we gonna follow him back to his den?"

Cyril's noisy chuckle scares the daylight out of Eli, who has been trying to be secretive. Eli has to cover his guardian's mouth with his hand.

"Mmm!"

"Are you out of your mind?!"

"S-Sorry," Cyril finally lowers his voice. *"Eli, why do we have to whisper?"*

"Of course so that he wouldn't hear us! He's a Sage!"

"Oh, sweetie, I guarantee with you that phlegm is not capable of hearing us from this distance. You can talk freely."

"Man, I was nervous he could hear us," Eli exhales in relief. "What are we gonna do now?"

"We go back to the inn, of course." Cyril grabs Eli's hand and starts to walk toward the main street.

"Huh? B-But—" Eli exclaims. "Hold on! W-What about the killers? A-And the ghost?"

"Leave them to me, alright?" Cyril smiles and lifts Eli into a cab.

* * *

ELI'S BODY temperature drastically drops on the way back to the Golden Shore Inn to the point Cyril has to keep him warm by holding him to his chest during the entire drive. He also gets the second round of extreme fatigue, so he can't talk much about the case at all. Eli ends up dozing off in Cyril's arms. When he opens his eyes, he's already in bed, and Cyril is tucking him into his blanket.

"How long did I sleep?" Eli asks listlessly.

"Only twenty minutes. We just got back."

"Oh, okay," Eli croaks. Cyril helps him sit up to drink a glass of water. He then brings up a bowl of steaming soup, but Eli shakes his head.

"Is there something else you want? Let me read the menu for you!"

"Thank you, but I don't feel like eating right now."

"You shouldn't skip meals, Eli. That's not good for your health."

"I know, but I don't feel well enough to eat. I just want to sleep," Eli begs. "Please?"

Cyril puts the soup bowl away, removes his shoes, and gets in bed next to Eli.

"I'm sure you'll feel much better after a nap." Cyril gives him a sweet smile as he pulls the blanket to Eli's neck.

Eli responds with a sluggish nod.

"Sleepy Eli is the cutest," Cyril teases.

Eli only shoots him a drowsy side-eye. Cyril sees it and breaks into a giggle.

"Sleep well, Eli," Cyril says, shuffling Eli's brown locks. "I'll be right next to you."

"See ya later." Eli closes his eyes.

* * *

ELI'S SLEEPING when he feels droplets of liquid dripping on his face. But he's too tired, so he ignores them.

Probably just the rain. Eli thinks in his sleep, feeling a little annoyed that Cyril didn't put up an umbrella for him.

More raindrops fall onto his face and his lips. It tastes disgusting, just like—

What the—

Eli's eyes snap open. There's blood all over the white blanket and on his clothes. He wants to scream, but he can't open his mouth or move his body.

The wooden ceiling beam is entangled with human entrails.

Eli darts his eyes around to look for Cyril, but the ravenhead is nowhere to be found.

I'm going to die. Eli's heart thrashes. It's the patched-face butcher all over again. Only this time, he's going to be murdered for real.

Cyril.

Help me.

Please help me.

Plop.

Something heavy just falls off from the beam to the ground. Eli can hear it limping slowly toward him.

Long, stringy black hair creeps up the mattress. A bloody, disfigured face emerges at the foot of his bed.

CHAPTER 15

CASE II - THE BLOODY BUNNY MASCOT COSTUME – PART 4

he head is weeping. Blood streams from her lone left eye and hollow right socket. Her dark, delicate eyebrows knit with agony and misery; her battered lips shake at each choking sob. She cries and cries, but no matter how much she weeps, the sounds all come out either muffled or as hair-raising rattles.

And then she stops wailing. Her expression becomes twisted and fills with immense rage. Her white, blood-soaked face turns demonic, and her mouth splits open from ear to ear. The dimming, bluish tint of the room has made her appear tenfold creepier and more frightening than she already was. She then screams. Though the noises remain hollow, the inn's walls crack, all the light fixtures and glass objects in the room explode into shards, and the balcony door and windows are smashed open.

Eli has to shut his eyes to protect them from the broken glass flying amok. Faye's petrifying rampage goes on for a few minutes before it ends abruptly.

With his eyes still glued shut, Eli intensely listens to his surroundings. The room has become eerily still, and the only thing he can pick up is the sound of his heartbeat palpitating within his chest.

...Has she gone? Please. Please go away! Haunt those evil bastards and that

*stinky bunny. I'm just an innocent bystander. I have nothing to do with this. My life already sucks enough. My mom passed away when I was so young, my dad was a distant and cold-blooded jerk, the stepwitch abused me every chance she had along with her nasty children, and I was 'murdered at just twenty-three. The universe just granted me a fresh do-over, and I really, **really** want to live.*

Also, I'm trying to help you move on here!

Eli thinks he might have overshared a little too much with the ghost, but he's too terrified to be reserved. He's completely at Faye's mercy and cannot defend himself in any way. The last thing he wants is to be on the ghost's bad side.

The temperature in the room has gotten very low, yet Eli's body is covered with a thick layer of sweat. Fear and anxiety saturate him like when fire meets fuel. After several long moments of staying put, Eli dares to take a sneak peek.

Faye's head and entrails are sitting on top of the blanket on Eli's abdomen. She is staring outside the window instead of gazing at him.

What's she looking at? Eli can tilt his head a little to look in the direction Faye is ogling. He can barely see anything as the outside is so dark and filled with black, hazy fog. The most Eli can make out are the vague outlines of the apartment buildings opposite the inn.

Eli catches something through his peripheral vision and jerks his gaze back to the room. Faye is now facing him with a horrified expression, her left eye and blue lips agape. Before Eli can register what's going on, Faye's head is split in half right in the middle by a blunt, unseen force. Blood sprays like a fountain, and pieces of her brain splatter all over the white bed and on Eli's face.

"I'll be right next to you."

Cyril, you're the worst guardian in the history of the universe(s). Eli mournfully cusses in his head as Faye's blood trickles down his face and leaks into his mouth. Faye's eyeball now falls on his pillow and lies beside his left cheek.

What have I done to deserve this? Hot tears roll down on Eli's face as he clenches his eyes shut. He wants to throw up so badly, but he can't move his lips. He is more likely to die from suffocating from the revolting stench in the room before Faye can scare him to death. Just as Eli's about to give up and acquiesce to his certain doom, the whole bed shakes like it is going through a major earthquake. This unexpected convulsion results in more of Faye's bloody intestines and gooey mess pouring onto poor Eli. His heart leaps in terror when a string of Fay's innards hits him right in the face.

The shaking continues for several long minutes until Eli is close to losing consciousness. Then, a thunderous noise pierces into his ears. It's so atrociously loud it sends tremors throughout his body and makes him whimper.

When Eli realizes he can finally open his mouth, he screams at the top of his lungs. It isn't until the words hit his ears that he knows he is crying out for Cyril.

That fearsome, penetrating voice that freed him from the terrifying paralysis belongs to no other than his guardian.

And the nightmarish world begins to crumble.

* * *

If it weren't for Cyril holding him back, Eli would have jerked to the hardwood floor and hurt himself.

"Eli, it's alright. You're safe. I'm here. It was just a nightmare," Cyril says, drawing Eli to his chest and hugging him tight. Eli trembles like a wounded bird, his body dripping with sweat and his heart pounding like a drum.

Eli utters Cyril's name brokenly, then retches. Cyril has to carry him to the bathroom and help him puke out the little food he has in his stomach. The entire time, Cyril whispers soothing words to Eli's ears and strokes his small back to comfort him.

"Hush, rest," Cyril swipes Eli's lips with a clean cloth and then carries him back to bed. It takes half an hour for Eli to regain his composure. He then tells Cyril the details of his vivid nightmare. When he's at the part where the ghost's blood oozed into his mouth, he retches once again, and Cyril has to feed him a full glass of water and two candies before Eli can keep anything down.

Eli then learns that Cyril has never left this room the entire time he was asleep. Cyril tells Eli his breathing and heartbeats were steady and showed no sign of distress or anomaly. If it weren't for Eli's tears, Cyril wouldn't have known Eli was experiencing a nightmare and woke him up.

"I thought...I was a goner for real. Thanks for waking me up in time," Eli whimpers.

Cyril stares at his young master with sorrow. He pulls Eli into a tight embrace. "Don't say that. You will live a very long and happy life, Eli. I'll make sure of it no matter what."

If Eli's being honest, he doesn't share the same optimism as his guardian, considering that this new universe is significantly more dangerous and deadlier than Eli's Earth...and Eli didn't even survive that.

"Alright. But you have to be in it with me." Eli brings out his pinkie. "All the way till the end!"

"Deal!" Cyril chuckles, wrapping Eli's little finger with his.

* * *

HAVING a supportive confidant like Cyril does wonders for Eli's mental health. He is still a bit shaken from Faye's ghostly visit, but Cyril distracts him with rosy pep talks and light jokes.

"We have to help Faye move on," Eli says as he gazes at himself in the mirror. He looks like the main protagonist of an angsty, rebellious teen flick (or a blood-deprived vampire) with sunken red eyes, pale lips, and dull, ashen skin; it's freaking awful! They're getting ready to go out and grab a bite. It's not evening yet, only a little over half past four. "And we have to do it fast, or..." *Or else I'll join her soon.*

* * *

ON THEIR WAY to the Seaside Cottontail Grill, Cyril asks Eli's permission to "connect" with him in his dream lest they fail to solve the case by tonight, and Faye haunts Eli in his sleep.

"Um, sure," Eli stutters. *What a bizarre question.* "Hey, Cyril, is…eh… dream connecting common between Sages?"

"No, not at all. Even among elite Sages, Dream Telepathy is an extremely rare power. In fact, it is so rare that it used to be considered a made-up thing until the last few decades."

Eli is instantly relieved. Still, he finds it a bit comical that any unusual notion can be deemed impossible or fantastical here, considering that the people in this universe can literally walk on water, fly on a broomstick, and shoot fire at will.

Anyway, it's great that "Dream Telepathy" is not common here. It will be an absolute nightmare if anyone can invade another's dream whenever they like, and even worse, the perpetrator can even hurt or kill the victims right through their dream without leaving the bed.

"But wait, the witch from the Midsummer Fair also had that Dream Telepathy power. She sent her son after me through my dream. Does that mean she was an elite Sage as well? What's the difference between a Sage and a witch?" Eli asks.

Cyril gives Eli a quick lecture on Sage versus witch. Sages are born with a Sage core that is located at the heart or the head (but usually the heart). It is believed that their powers and unique abilities come from this core. An average Sage's life expectancy is around 280 years. However, there are a few Sages in Aspenia that are half a millennium old and still going strong.

On the other hand, witches or magic practitioners are just "somewhat" regular folks with no Sage core but interested in studying magic (or witch-craft). They have an average mortal life span.

There are many types of witches in Aspenia. Some are harmless, such as green witches, who are basically master herbalists; astro witches, who specialize in astronomy; crystal witches, palm readers, fortunetellers, etc. Then comes the real deal, the "legit" wicked witches that practice dark magic for longevity and selfish, immoral gains.

These evil witches are generally much more powerful than the others mentioned above. Their powers and abilities come from forbidden dark rituals that always require steep sacrifices that involve torturing and killing innocent people, cannibalism, and sometimes, even butchering their own family.

And right there is the biggest difference between a Sage and an evil witch: a Sage's power requires no (human) sacrifice. They can summon and use it whenever they please. In contrast, evil witches must constantly make blood offerings to maintain their powers.

"So, what happens if a Sage practices witchcraft?" Eli asks.

"Their core will be damaged and explode," Cyril responds, his face stolid. "Dark magic and Sage's power don't go together. No sane Sage would risk endangering their core by practicing witchcraft. After all, the core is their primary source of power and longevity."

"Mmm, I see," Eli mutters. "Cyril, is there a way for me to protect my dream from unauthorized dream peepers?" Eli makes a face at his last three words while Cyril openly cracks up. The ravenhead's laugh gets even more hysterical when he catches a stink-eye from his young master.

"It's a serious question!" Eli leers.

"Yes, yes, I'm sorry," Cyril wheezes, struggling to keep a straight face. "Theoretically speaking, 'unauthorized dream peepers' cannot look into your dream unless they have something personal of yours." Cyril's smile fades. "Speaking of that, back at the Midsummer fair, did you give that witch any of your belongings?"

"No," Eli falters, trying to recall his encounter with the witch.

"Did you have anything stolen? Or did you lose anything at the fair?"

"I don't think so."

"Did she touch you?"

"Yes! Yes, she did! She dabbed off my sweat with her hankie!"

"Eli." Cyril stops walking, his face turns serious. "Personal possessions, from your clothes and accessories, to your hair, blood, sweat, bodily fluids, or even nails, are key components used in witchcraft. Just a droplet of your sweat is enough for a high-level witch to go after you and turn your life upside down, which was exactly what that witch did. In the future, please never let any suspicious stranger touch you like that again. It's very, *very* dangerous. Do you understand?"

"Okay," Eli nods, frightened.

"Good." Cyril smiles and strokes Eli's brown locks. "And you will always tell me whenever you encounter a suspicious person, yes?"

"I will. I promise."

"Thank you. You're the smartest, my little kit!" Cyril laughs fondly at Eli as they resume their walk to the restaurant.

* * *

CYRIL AND ELI arrive at the Seaside Cottontail Grill at 4:50 PM. There aren't many customers inside the restaurant as dinnertime isn't until two hours later. They're promptly greeted by a waitress who remembers them from last night.

"Good evening. A table for two, please." Cyril smiles at the waitress. "Is the owner here today, miss?"

"Yes, sir. Over there, he's our main bartender." The waitress gestures at the tall, middle-aged man standing behind the bar, cleaning the countertop.

"Ah, we'd like to sit at the bar then, if that's alright?"

"Of course, sir. Um...but no drink will be served to the young master here. We do not serve alcohol to the underage in this establishment."

As Cyril and Eli approach the bar area, the owner recognizes them, too. Once they sit down, the owner introduces himself as Einar and formally apologizes for the incident last night. It turns out Einar was here when loony bunny started the chain of commotion. He meant to come over to alleviate the situation and apologize to the patrons, but by the time he was done serving his customers, Cyril and Eli had already left.

"Please order anything you like! Your meal will be on the house," declares Einar.

"Ah, thank you. That's very kind of you. But—" Cyril attempts to decline, but the owner is quite persistent. In the end, the ravenhead accepts the offer.

"Now, that's better!" Einar laughs. "What can I get for you lads? Would you like some coconut beer? It's freshly brewed!"

"That sounds nice!" Eli's eyes brighten up. He's never had coconut beer before; it sounds tasty.

"Umm, no," Cyril and Eina say concurrently, crushing Eli's heart.

"Sorry, my young lad, you can have this instead!" Einar hands Eli a tall glass of a white and yellow ombre drink with a scoop of ice cream and a red cherry on top. "This is our special pineapple-coconut mocktail! I assure you'll enjoy this way more than the ale!"

"Thank you." Eli's smile is crooked.

"I'll just have an unsweetened iced tea, please," Cyril chuckles, patting Eli's brown locks.

"Alright, folks. What would you like to order? We just got some fresh pork, and ox intestines just came in. Would you like some deep-fried intestines or organ stew?"

"I'll just have a salad, please." Eli pretends to dab his mouth with the dining napkin to hide the gag he's having when he hears the word "intestines."

"Thank you, but we are vegetarian." Cyril's voice is neutral, but his face is visibly uncomfortable. He quickly orders a couple of vegetarian dishes.

While waiting for the food, they chat with the owner. They learn Einar is a retired sailor with a knack for mixing drinks. He is down to earth, has an inviting dad vibe, and is very sociable. Thus, it doesn't take too long for Cyril to venture toward the subject he has in mind.

"Is your bunny mascot going to be here today? She fell twice yesterday and left in a rush. I hope she's doing fine," Cyril asks in a considerate tone.

Einar sighs and shakes his head. "I hope the same, my friend, but I don't think she'll be here today. Last night, the last I saw of her was when she ran out of the grill. Her shift didn't end until midnight, and she was supposed to be here three hours ago."

"Ohh," Eli and Cyril say at the same time.

"I think that bunny suit might be cursed," Einar whispers.

"Why do you say that?" Cyril asks.

"My former employee used to wear that suit. But she went missing last month. The local sentinels have been actively looking for her, but we've not received any good news yet. She was a very nice lass."

"I'm sorry to hear that."

"I hope she's doing well. Maybe she's just visiting her grandfolks. They're old and feeble, and just live by themselves, couldn't afford helpers." Einar shakes his head. "But then, if that's the case, Faye would have informed me before leaving. She's just not the type to disappear without an explanation."

"Faye. Is that the name of your former bunny mascot?" Cyril queries. When he receives confirmation from the owner, his expression remains calm and unaffected, unlike Eli's discernibly grim face.

"So, the bunny suit your current mascot's using is the same one worn by the missing Miss Faye?"

"Yes, the same exact outfit! *That's why I think it's cursed,*" Einar whispers.

Or maybe the problem doesn't lie in the suit but in the fact that the current bunny aided in the murder of the previous bunny, Eli thinks. What is the motive behind this gruesome murder? What did Faye do to Myra that made her plot her demise? What was the relationship between Myra, Faye, and the four sentinels?

"If my current bunny doesn't show up tomorrow, I'm informing the authorities," Einar says.

"That's very considerate of you," Cyril responds with a small smile. "Though your current bunny might not even be missing. She could be recuperating at some clinic in town."

Eli kicks Cyril's foot under the counter.

"Purely a speculation," Cyril adds with a straight face.

"Ay! I hope so, my friend. That's better than being missing." Einar laughs. He's truly an easygoing man.

According to Einar, Faye worked as a waitress here for a year and a half prior to her abrupt disappearance a month ago. She was a gorgeous woman, and one of the highlights of the restaurant due to her kind and bubbly personality.

"And she's a university student! How incredible is that?" Einar cries, admiration gleaming in his brown eyes.

"University!" Cyril and Eli exclaim.

"She's not even from an influential family. She works part-time here to pay for the tuition," Einar adds. "Most young lasses of the same commoner background barely finish the third grade!"

"That's very remarkable," Cyril comments. He seems genuinely impressed by Faye's academic background. "Miss Faye sounds like a well-rounded lady with good looks and intelligence. Though such notable merits are usually accompanied by inevitable envy and unwanted attention, unfortunately. I wonder if you've noticed anything unusual happened prior to her disappearance?"

"My friend, now that you put it that way, there was indeed something very odd happened!" Einar cries. "About two weeks before Faye went missing, she was set on switching to the bunny mascot from her waitress position. I was a bit reluctant as she was kind of the unofficial face of this place. When I asked her why, she told me she had had unwanted attention from a few male customers at the grill. Though she would not tell me who they were and only said they were someone not to be crossed."

"That sounds highly suspicious. Do you have any male customers in mind that fit Miss Faye's description?"

"Oh, I do. But that would be a very long list!"

"Well, from her words, these men sound dangerous. Perhaps they could be Sages? Maybe sentinel Sages?"

"Eh, I have a lot of sentinel Sage customers that are interested in Faye. The lass was very popular here," Einar says, scratching his head.

"*But*—was there a group of sentinel Sages that are notoriously more assertive and arrogant, possibly not from here but a major region neighboring to this town, like Darya, for example?"

Subtlety be damned. Eli rubs his forehead as he eats his meal.

"Uhhhhh...OH! OH! There was! There was indeed a group of sentinel Sages that exactly matched your description! They're from Darya! Cocky sods in gaudy uniforms!" Einar exclaims. "Holy Tathagatas! How could you possibly know all of this?"

"Just my observation and deduction based on what you told me," Cyril lies smoothly.

"That's amazing, my friend! You can make a...a...what do they call it? Ah! A great detective!"

"Thank you, you flatter me. I'm just an everyday man with a moderate interest in the local mystery."

"Young folks nowadays are so intelligent and sharp. You're way better than our local sentinels! You can have a promising career as a private investigator or even become a sentinel!"

"Thanks. Maybe I should consider that, and all the sentinels assigned on this case need to be immediately discharged!" Cyril laughs with the grill owner. "Anyway, have you ever talked to those Darya sentinels? Did they come back here after the disappearance of Miss Faye?"

"My friend, if you're an Aspenian, you should already hear of how snobby and uncouth major region sentinels are. Unless the Emperor himself or their superiors are in the room, they never show manners. Usually, they act like they are the Gods' incarnations on Earth. I have no contact with those people. I tried to, but they didn't bother to show the basic decency of acknowledging me when I greeted them the first time!" Einar's voice drips with contempt. "And they have not come here since Faye went missing. Do you think they have anything to do with her disappearance?"

"I don't know yet. Do you have Miss Faye's home address? I believe I can find more useful clues if I know where she lived."

"You're really going to look for her? Are you two related? You both have dark hair and attractive features."

"No, we're not related. I'm just very intrigued by your story, so I want to help find her," Cyril says in an even voice. "I want to use my free time to help someone in need."

The grill owner is touched by Cyril's noble response; he gives the raven-head Faye's address without question.

"My friend, these sentinel Sages are the authorities. They're dangerous. If they were truly involved in Faye's disappearance, only Tathagatas know what lengths they would go to, so they can weed out those who challenge them. Please be careful," Einar advises.

Cyril thanks Einar, and the man wishes them good luck while Eli finishes his meal. They leave the restaurant to head to Faye's place.

* * *

"CYRIL, WHAT'S THE PLAN?" Eli asks when they're in the carriage. Cyril has been unusually quiet and brooding ever since they left the Seaside Cottontail Grill.

"I'm sorry. What is it, Eli?" Cyril snaps out of his train of thought.

Eli repeats his question. Cyril is quiet for a good ten seconds before responding, "We're going to help Faye move on."

"I know, but how are we going to do that? What are the requirements for a ghost to move on?"

"We're dealing with a vengeful spirit. The only way for Faye to move on is to find all of her remains, or what's left of them, and give her a proper burial. Then I'll take out all the killers who took part in her murder."

"Take out as in...?" Eli makes a throat-slitting gesture.

Cyril stares at him numbly for a few seconds. "If they don't fight back. If they do, I'll roast them alive."

Eli gulps as goosebumps form all over his body.

"Cyril, I think we should let the local authorities deal with these killers instead?"

"The sentinels of this town?" Cyril lifts his eyebrow. "Faye's been missing for a month, and they still don't have a clue where she is. If I let the *authorities* handle those Daryans, you will be dealing with Faye's ghost interminably for the next few months, or maybe even for the rest of your life. Do you really want to leave your fate in the hands of these incompetent novices?"

"Point taken," Eli lets out a deep exhale. He leans his head in his hand, depressed.

"Eli, what is it? Are you feeling unwell?"

"I'm fine," Eli answers wearily, though still patting Cyril's hand to comfort him. "I just think that if Wolfgang were here with us, we wouldn't be so outnumbered like now."

"Eli, I really don't understand how you get the idea that Wolfgang is anywhere as capable and reliable as I am." Cyril crosses his arms petulantly.

"I don't know. Wolfgang seems pretty tough to me." Eli scratches his head, then starts checking out his guardian with inspecting eyes.

"Based on what?"

"He has a big collection of weapons..."

"So?"

"He told me he can use all of them. Expertly!"

"So can I. And I'm miles better than that kooky wino!"

"Dude, we don't have any weapons at home. Well, actually, the only weapons we have are the kitchen knives and some cooking tools."

"I don't need any weapons. I can protect you just fine with my own two hands!"

"Alright, I believe you, man." Eli pats Cyril's shoulder. "Team Cyril all the way!"

For some reason, instead of feeling appreciated, the ravenhead looks even more hissy-pissy.

"Eli," Cyril holds Eli's skinny shoulders.

"What?" Eli gulps, a little intimidated by Cyril's seriousness.

"I'll prove to you how capable I am. That I can protect you without the need of a weapon," Cyril declares, his teeth clenched and eyes narrowed. "And we're definitely not outnumbered, Eli. It's the other way around. You'll see."

* * *

ACCORDING to the address Einar provided, Faye's place is located in a tiny corner of a poor neighborhood where dozens of old, grimy apartment complexes line up next to each other. Unfortunately, the roads are too narrow for the carriage to get through, so Cyril and Eli have to walk to reach their destination.

Even though it's still relatively early in the evening, the alleyways are dark and dreary due to the lack of proper streetlights and few well-lit houses. The bumpy stone paths are slippery due to water leaking from the busted, rusty pipes. The air is thick with the foul odor of seafood waste, litter, and aged, moldy bricks.

The unpleasant condition of the environment promptly turns Cyril's mega-protective dada-bear mode on. The ravenhead reaches for Eli's hand and keeps him close, carefully watching Eli's every step.

Under normal circumstances, Eli would have huffed and puffed. But now, considering everything that has been happening, having someone holding his hand like this makes him feel much safer and at ease.

As they're pacing down the grubby, winding road, Eli hears the faint squeaking noise of the street rats lurking in the shadow. His body tenses up as his eyes scan the dim path ahead. His other hand that isn't held by Cyril is ready to punch away any rat that dares to jump at them. The surroundings remind Eli of the filthy slum in Crimson Vale. The contrast between these gloomy alleys and the dreamy neighborhood where Eli currently lives is night and day.

After Cyril brought him home, Eli never once imagined how his life would be if Cyril had not found him that night in the forest. He doesn't have the courage to do that.

"We're almost there, Eli. Just three more turns," Cyril interrupts Eli's thought with his ever-gentle voice.

Eli gives a small nod. Then, after a couple more steps, he mutters, "Thank you."

"Why do you say that all of a sudden?"

"No reason...I just think you're...the most amazing person I've ever met," Eli stutters, his face heating up. It's a good thing this alley is dark, or else...

"You really think so?" Cyril blinks, his face slowly turns rosy.

Eli awkwardly nods, and Cyril melts into a giant puddle.

When the pair approach the second alley to their destination, their path is barred by a large, fallen oak tree surrounded by a wet dirt mount at least three times Cyril's height. It appears that this side of the street also has a leaky water pipe problem.

"What the!" Eli stares in disbelief at the dirt mountain before them. "An earthquake?"

"It could be. But that had to happen a while ago. There is a thick layer of moss growing on this ridge."

"This is terrible. Isn't the town authority supposed to clear this up? How can people in this neighborhood commute in such horrendous conditions?"

"I agree, but citizens from the working class are often overlooked and neglected by the officials running the town. That was why I was not in the least surprised that there's been no progress made in Faye's disappearance despite it being reported a month ago. They probably never even went out and looked for her."

Poor girl. "Well, is there an alternative road we can take?"

Cyril takes out the map, and they both look at it. Faye's place is uphill, and the only road that leads there is the one in front of them, and it's blocked.

"Well, I guess it can't be helped," Eli lets out an exhale and rolls up his sleeves. But Cyril pulls him back when he attempts to touch the wet dirt.

"What are you doing?"

"Climbing over this ridge? We're still going to Faye's place, right?"

"Yes, we are."

"Well then, let's get moving." Eli turns back to the dirt mound, but Cyril gently pulls him around once again.

"Sweetie, no. You don't have to do that to get to the top. May I?" Cyril holds out his hand to Eli.

Eli gives his guardian his hand. Cyril catches him off guard when he suddenly grabs his waist and sweeps him off his feet. Eli only hears a fleet whooshing sound, and within two seconds, they are on top of the dirt mound.

"See?" Cyril beams. "Isn't this much more efficient?"

* * *

"OH, GEUD LORD, FINALLY! I ABOU' to throw her stuff out," says the middle-aged woman with a rough voice, who answers the door.

Cyril and Eli are stumped at the woman's thick accent.

"Yah her family, rite?" The woman gestures at Cyril.

"Are you talking about Faye?" Cyril asks.

"Yeh."

"No. I'm not related to Miss Faye. But I'm looking for her."

"Oh no...she owed folks' money and ran off, didn't she?"

"I don't know about that. But I'm positive she's been missing for a month."

"Faye missing?"

"I suppose no sentinels have come here and talked to you during the past month?" Cyril asks. When he hears the woman's negative confirmation, he looks irritated.

The woman introduces herself as the landlady of this apartment complex. She informs Cyril that Faye is two weeks late on her rent.

"Mister, do yah have any clue where Faye is? Do yah know if she gonna come back soon to pay the rent? I'll had to remove her stuff and lease out her room for new tenants if she is not coming back by the end of Monday."

Cyril takes out a gold coin from his wallet and gives it to the landlady.

"Tis are too much, sir. I don't have enough money to give you back the—"

"You don't have to. You can regard the extra as compensation for the late payment. Now, can you show us Faye's room, please?"

"Oh, how very generous of you, master. May the Tathagatas bless you with all the goodness in the world! Tis way, please!"

Faye's unit is a small studio with one bathroom on the third floor of the building. It kind of reminds Eli of New York. Yet despite the modest size, this place is tastefully decorated with many DIY decorations, magic-operated fairy lights, and lots and lots of books neatly categorized in a ceiling-tall bookshelf, which is also the biggest piece of furniture in the room.

A space says a lot about the person who inhabits it. By looking at this room, Eli can tell its owner was a creative and well-read young lady with high potential for a bright future.

But such a future will never happen for her.

Cyril immediately searches the room the moment the landlady leaves. He tells Eli not to touch anything, so Eli has no choice but to stand in a corner and look pretty while Cyril goes through Faye's stuff.

"Hah!" Cyril mutters.

"What is it?" Eli saunters toward his guardian's side. Cyril holds an old-looking paper.

"It's Faye's birth certificate. She shared her birthday with you."

Eli looks at the paper in Cyril's hand. Though he can't make out a single word, there are two numbers that look like the day and month of birth, and they are identical to his.

"She supposed to turn twenty in two weeks," Cyril says.

"So she was about four years younger than me."

"What?" Cyril's brows furrow.

"I mean three years older."

"This explains why she persistently clings to you despite you not being involved with her death."

"You also share my birthday too. Why did she only haunt me?"

"I strongly believe it's most likely because of your utter adorableness that thaws hearts and souls."

Eli huffs and rolls his eyes. Cyril gives him another round of affectionate chuckles before he goes back to his search.

"Hmm," Cyril murmurs after going through Faye's closet.

"What did you find?"

Cyril turns around and brings out a hanger; on it is a one-piece bodysuit with a bunny tail at the back, a choker in black glitter, a pair of fishnet stockings, and a masquerade rabbit mask.

Eli quirks a brow as he stares at the skimpy bunny costume.

"University is expensive," Cyril says.

You bet. Eli thinks as he remembers the outrageous amount of money he coughed up for his four-year degree that he barely got to use in his past life.

"Okay, so now what?" Eli asks.

"Hmm, let's pay a visit to our young lady's second workplace." Cyril returns the swimsuit to the closet.

"Eh? How do you know where she worked?"

Cyril shows Eli the inside of the masquerade rabbit mask. There are engraved Elgarian words.

"Bunny Paradise," Cyril reads.

Cyril and Eli bid the landlady goodbye and leave for "Bunny Paradise." But as they head back to the road that led them here, the landlady asks. "Why yah going that way, masters?"

"We want to get to the main street to take a cab," Cyril responds.

"Oh, blimey. Did yah climb that mound to get here? Follow me. I'll show yah another easier way to get down."

They follow the landlady to the back of the apartment building. There, a snug, dug-up staircase lit with magic-operated fairy lights trails all the way downhill.

"Faye's work," the landlady says.

"She made that trail?" Cyril asks, surprised and impressed.

"Eh, not entirely. The men also helped build it based on her design. Before Faye moved here, kids would break their arms and legs all the time, climbing up and down that mound. The town authority never bothers to fix up the street."

Cyril shakes his head in annoyance. "Why not put a ladder in the alley with the raised ridge? Isn't it easier than carving an entire path through the hill?"

"Masters, we tried to do that, but them folks down the mound wouldn't allow it. They ain't give a diddly-squat if we uphill can get downhill or not. It's our problem, not theirs. Anyway, this path ya see was made illegally without the town's permission. Please don't tell too many people, especially the authorities. We can't afford to pay the fine."

* * *

Bunny Paradise is a pink, one-story building in the dead-end of a sketchy but not rundown alley in a bustling part of the town. On the roof is a large sign with the business's name. There are drawings of two beautiful women, a blonde on the left and a brunette on the right of the signboard, both dressed in red glittery bikinis and wearing the same bunny mask Cyril found in Faye's closet.

Cyril has been moodily gazing at the strip club for a while before finally approaching it with Eli, hand in hand.

Two bouncers stop them at the entrance.

"Please turn around, sir. You can't bring children inside the club, even if they aren't free citizens. That's illegal."

Cyril is not offended. On the contrary, the broodiness on his handsome face dissipates, and the ravenhead smiles for the first time since he arrived here. He takes a handful of gold coins from his wallet and presents them to the bouncer, who just denied him entry. "I can give you more if you let us in. Both of you."

"Please, leave." The second bouncer speaks up. "Even if it's not illegal, bringing a kid to a place like this is fucked up."

Cyril lifts an eyebrow at the second bouncer's profanity. But he doesn't seem angry at all. He shifts his gaze back to the first bouncer. "I can double this amount since your friend doesn't want it."

Eli remembers Mariposa told him that one gold coin could buy one month's worth of food for a family of five. Two handfuls of gold coins must be a lot of money!

However, neither of the bouncers is impressed by Cyril's generous offer.

"Listen, you sick pervert—"

"Excuse me for interrupting," Eli disrupts the looming fight. "But I'm not forced to be here against my will. I know I look young, but I'm actually an adult."

"Sure, kid, and I'm the Emperor of the Twelve Realms, and this twit is my Empress," the second bouncer remarks.

"Screw you," the first bouncer punches his friend in the arm, and both men laugh at Eli. "Listen, kid. You and your boyfriend need to scram before we—"

"*Actually, you—listen to me,*" Cyril stands before Eli, eyeing down both bouncers.

To Eli's amazement, the two bouncers lower their hands and stand still, no longer showing any sign of aggressiveness toward the ravenhead.

"*I'm not here for the vulgar show.*" Cyril's voice is deep and airy; he sounds so different from usual. "*I'm looking for a girl named Faye. Do you two know her?*"

"No, sir. We don't know the real names of any of the girls here. They all go by their stage name: Camellia, Rose, Jasmine, Lily, or Daisy."

"*What is the name of the person in charge of these girls?*"

"Madam Cactus, sir," answer the two bouncers.

"Yikes." Eli frowns, and Cyril's lips slightly curve up at his reaction. That name sounds about right for the person managing strippers with flower aliases.

"Does she work today?" Cyril questions.

"Yes. She's here every night, sir. But she doesn't perform," the bouncers say.

"Of course, she doesn't," Cyril mutters. *"Thank you, gentlemen. I appreciate your help."*

"You're welcome, sir. We're glad we could be of assistance."

"You both seem too decent to be working at a place like this," Cyril says while filling the bouncers' hands with gold coins. *"You did the right thing, not letting us in. However, using foul language in front of a child is unbecoming. Don't do that again."*

"Yes, sir," the bouncers respond. Cyril moves his head slightly, and both bouncers turn to Eli. "Sorry, kid."

"No problem," Eli stutters awkwardly.

"You didn't see us tonight. This conversation never happened," Cyril tells the bouncers, and they meekly nod in agreement. "Eli, what are you doing?" Cyril asks in his normal voice when he sees Eli waving his hand in front of the bouncers.

"This is creepy," Eli mumbles. The bouncers show no reaction or emotion to his waving and finger snapping. They just stand there, blank faces, like two wooden statues, and they have been like that ever since Cyril told them to "shush and listen." But before Eli can make any further comments, Cyril already grabs his hand and drags him inside the strip club. "Geez, slow down!" Eli yaps. "Why are you so hurried?"

"Because I don't want you in a place like this for too long, Eli." Cyril lets out a deep sigh. "I feel so very awful for bringing you here. Believe me, I would not do this if I had any other choice."

"Gosh, you're so dramatic, Cyril. It's a strip club, not the devil's lair, big deal!"

"Eli!" Cyril gasps.

They're standing in an empty, dimly lit corridor outside the main room where the exotic dancing takes place.

"Are the two dudes outside going back to normal soon?" Eli asks.

"Don't worry, angel. They'll be fine."

"So you can really charm people, huh? Is there anything else that I should know about you, Cyril?"

"What does 'charm' mean in this case?"

"Hypnotizing people to do as they're told," Eli explains, and Cyril oohs.

"Well…I think I do possess that type of power, Eli," Cyril admits sheepishly.

"Have you ever used that power on me?"

"No! Never!" Cyril denies it right away.

Eli only shoots his guardian a cynical look.

"Eli," Cyril holds Eli's hands. "I discovered that power when you…were away."

"Oh," Eli's voice softens down. "But did you use it on me when I was back?"

"No," Cyril shakes his head, but his tone is not as firm as before.

"You sure you didn't?" Eli leans in closer to the ravenhead, like a little fox cornering the wolf, intimidating him. *"Ever?"*

"No," poor Cyril shakes his head; he looks scared.

"Alright, that's good then," Eli smiles, patting Cyril's arm. "Because if I ever find out you use that power on me without my knowledge or consent, I would be…"

Cyril's large puppy eyes are now filled with fear.

"Very mad," Eli has a soft spot for puppy eyes, especially Cyril's puppy eyes.

"Oh, my precious Eli. I swear to you I would never in a thousand years do such a thing to you without your permission!" Cyril vows in a heartfelt tone.

"Thank you," Eli smiles sweetly at his guardian. "It's not that I don't trust you, Cyril. But that power you have is too powerful! And dangerous! You could literally rob people blind and leave them with only their underpants on, and they wouldn't even know they got mugged!"

Cyril laughs so hard that he has to wheeze for air.

"Excuse me, I wasn't joking," Eli grumbles, hands on his hips.

"Right. Uh-heheheh. I'm sorry," Cyril bites his lips; his face is all red from his desperate effort to contain his laughter. He eventually fails and ends up bear-hugging Eli to his chest. "You're too precious for this world, Eli."

"You have nothing to worry about, my little kit. I'm not that powerful. I can't compel just anyone. Most of the time, my power only works on humans, not Sages, I think," Cyril laughs. "And even if I can compel Sages, I'm quite certain that my power will not affect you at all."

"Why do you say that?" Eli blinks, carefully analyzing what Cyril just said.

"Well—" Cyril is interrupted when the door behind him opens. He instinctively turns around and finds a young woman dressed in a red glittery bikini and masquerade bunny mask.

"Why, hello there, gorgeous. What are you doing out here all alone?" The lady speaks in a sultry tone as she approaches the ravenhead. "Are you lost? Would you like a private—a kid?!" she shrieks and hurriedly covers her chest with her hands when she sees Eli's head sticking out from behind Cyril's back.

Eli has to admit he is impressed with how serious and committed the people in this town are in protecting the youngsters' innocence despite the unsettling fact that child slavery seems to be legal in this nation.

"I'm afraid I'll have to pass on the offer, miss," Cyril says politely. "I have a few questions about a young lady who works here. I wonder if I can have a few minutes of your time?" Cyril hands her three gold coins.

"With pleasure. "The stripper beams as she puts the coins away in her little crossbody pouch. "How can I help you, handsome?"

"The lady I'm looking for named Faye. She's nineteen, with black hair, gray eyes, and a fair complexion. Do you know her?"

"Faye... Black hair, gray eyes...I don't think so, master. There are only three girls here with black hair, but none of them have gray eyes. Are you sure this girl is a dancer? Do you know her stage name?"

"I don't. Oh, do you have any colleague who is a university student?"

"Mmm...ahh—her! Now I know who you're talking about. Dahlia! The bookworm waitress!" the stripper exclaims, slapping her hands together. "She wore a black one-piece. She was the only girl here attending university!"

Eli's face grows ashen when he hears Faye's stage name. Dahlia. Black clothes. Gruesome mutilations. This poor girl was surrounded by all the dead omens.

"Well, master, Dahlia was not a dancer. Here, dancers wear a red two-piece while the servers wear a black one-piece."

"I see. Well, does Dahlia still work here?"

"No, master. She was actually arrested a month ago for stealing from the Sage authorities."

Cyril raises a brow. "Was she arrested here?"

"Yes, that was what I heard. I didn't work that night."

"Was your manager, Madam Cactus, here when Dahlia's arrest took place?"

"I believe she was, master."

"Thank you, miss. I really appreciate your help." Cyril gives the stripper three more gold coins.

"Thank you so much for your generosity, master! Is there anything else I can do for you? You sure you don't want a priva—never mind." The stripper stops when her eyes dart to Eli.

"Yes, there is something you can do for me. Can you call your madam here for me?" Cyril smiles at the girl as he gives her two gold coins. "One is for Lady Cactus."

"I'll be right back, handsome." The stripper chuckles and disappears into the main room.

While they wait, Eli wants to ask Cyril to continue what he was about to tell him before the stripper came in, but Eli can't, for the life of him, remember the crucial topic they were discussing. He could only vaguely recall it was related to a special charming power Cyril possesses.

"Are you feeling alright, my little kit?" Cyril asks.

"Yeah, I'm good," Eli lies badly, and Cyril looks even more concerned. "Today has been a long day."

"I know, sweetie. I'm sorry. I'll do my best to finish this case as quickly as possible. Then we'll leave this town for good."

Eli nods into Cyril's chest.

"Oh my, am I interrupting anything?" says a curvy, fairly attractive middle-aged woman dressed in a floor-length, red glittery gown as she appears by the door. Behind her is the stripper who talked to Cyril before. "Oh? A boy?" the woman drones after glancing at Eli's face.

"Madam Cactus, I presume?" Cyril lets go of Eli and moves him behind his back.

"The one and only. It's an honor to make your acquaintance, master." Madam Cactus curtseys to Cyril. "Go back to work, Anemone," she dismisses the stripper to be alone with Cyril and Eli.

Cyril gives her a slight nod and slips two gold coins into her hand, then jumps straight to the point. "I have a few questions about your former employee, Dahlia, whose real name is Faye. I believe she was arrested here a month ago for stealing from the authorities. Are you familiar with the sentinels that detained her?"

"Indeed, I do know them, master. They used to be regulars here before the arrest."

"Were these sentinels from this town or somewhere else?" Cyril asks.

"No, master. I'm quite certain they're from Darya. There were four of them. Tall, very good-looking Sages. But they were very arrogant and hard to please."

"Tell me more." Cyril suddenly cheats by using his glamor power (Eli thinks he's probably running out of money), and the madam starts to sing.

According to Madam Cactus, one of the four suspects used to be head over heels for Faye and made many attempts to court her, but she turned him down. Faye shared with her madam that these Daryans first met her at the Seaside Cottontail Grill. Then, they started stalking her from her campus to her home and, finally, the club. Apparently, Faye kept her evening job a secret, as the school would expel her if they found out she waited tables at a strip club. These Daryans knew about this but didn't seem to take advantage of it; thus, Faye was on good terms with them for a while, though their relationship was strictly on a server and customer basis. One day, the Daryan, who liked her, got drunk and forced himself on her at the club. Faye successfully fought back with the bouncers' help, and that Daryan was removed from the club by force.

To make matters worse, this Daryan was the captain of the sentinel group, and the incident was the most disgraceful thing that had ever happened to him. The fact that it was all caused by a common human girl who worked at a strip club multiplied the humiliation by a hundredfold. The Daryans then stopped stalking Faye before showing up at the club a week later after the day of the incident and accused her of stealing their money. They arrested her, and neither she nor they have been seen anywhere since then.

"My God," Eli mouths in horror.

"Do you know the names of these Darya Sages? Or where they live?" Cyril asks grimly.

"No, master."

That answer puts Cyril in an instant bad mood as his expression turns irate.

"You may go." Cyril waves his hand to dismiss the madam. But when she's about to open the door to go inside, Cyril asks her to come back. He then fills her hands with silver coins before dismissing her again for good.

He's really out of gold coins, Eli muses, then pokes his guardian.

"What is it, angel?" Cyril turns around, smiling lovingly at him.

"I'll give it to you, Cyril. You are truly the guardian of the year."

Cyril lifts a brow, waiting for Eli to elaborate.

"Bringing me to a strip club without me seeing any stripping. That takes skill."

* * *

"ARE the bouncers on break or something?" Eli looks around. The two bouncers guarding the strip club are nowhere to be found.

Did they quit their job after waking up from Cyril's glamor and seeing the huge amount of gold Cyril gave them?

"Let's go, sweetie," Cyril grabs Eli's hand, and they head to the main street.

When they approach the second alleyway, Cyril suddenly pushes Eli behind his back. From out of nowhere, two heavy objects fall from the sky to the ground fifteen feet before them in loud thuds. Sharp clanging noises sound chaotically against the stone path and the alley walls.

Eli's heart leaps when he recognizes the two mysterious, heavy objects blocking the way. They are the lacerated bodies of the two bouncers from the strip club and surrounding them are the gold coins that Cyril gave to the men.

"That's a fitting ending for insolent wretches that were ignorant of their place in this world," says an unknown male voice from above. Then, with a flash, a dark silhouette plunges from the rooftop to the pathway with a soft thump.

"And for nosy meddlers." The silhouette steps out of the shadow to reveal a tall, attractive, and muscular man with blond hair, blue eyes, and an incredibly sly and condescending face that knows no humility nor compassion. "I heard you are looking for us?"

There is blood all over that man's cerulean coat. But Eli can't tell whether it's from Faye or the poor bouncers lying on the ground.

"Where's Faye's body?" Cyril asks, his voice dull and bored.

"Let me give you a friendly advice, from Sage to Sage." The killer smiles. "Do not interfere with matters that don't concern you. You'll get burned."

"Oh! Is that so?" Cyril chuckles aloud.

"Well, in this case, I believe the right word is drowned." The killer smiles as he unsheathes a sharp, gleaming sword by his waist. "However, I personally believe drowning is such an easy and painless death. It's a blessing to be put out that way. I prefer a good old flaying and dismembering of every single body part. Starting from the bottom and working all the way up to the top."

Eli's face turns pallid as the images of Cyril's severely scarred chest spring to his mind. His eyes immediately look for an escape route, but there's no other path to the main street but the one before them.

"I see." Cyril nods. "So that's your preferred way to go down. I'll keep that in mind."

Cyril, what the hell?! Eli and the killer stare at the ravenhead.

"And they said I'm cocky," the killer snickers. "Boy, either you're astoundingly powerful, or you're just incredibly stupid. I believe it's the latter. Let me do a simple math for you. There are countless of us and only two of you. Eh—one, that mouse doesn't count."

"Countless? Not four?" Cyril asks.

"What kind of captain only has three subordinates?"

"Got it." Cyril nods, appearing to be mentally taking notes. "Any last words?"

The killer can no longer keep up with the façade. His fingers squeeze around his sword's hilt while his face twists with sadistic and murderous intention.

"Have you ever thought about what would become of that runt after we finished with you?" The killer moves his eyes to Eli. After a quick assessment, his lips form a sick smile that leaves Eli with goosebumps. "This is one lovely little runt. I'm sure he will be real popular among the slaver—"

A literal, blazing fist enclosed in roaring red fire rams straight into the killer's face, sending his entire burly body twenty feet backward through the air.

"Time's up," Cyril whispers through gritted teeth as he glides side by side with the battered, flying killer.

CHAPTER 16

CASE II - THE BLOODY BUNNY MASCOT COSTUME
– PART 5

Eli didn't notice Cyril had moved away until he found himself alone on the pathway. Everything happened too fast for his eyes to register. The next thing he knows, a blaring and painful howl resonates through the dim alley.

And the only reason Eli hasn't jumped out of his skin yet is that the spine-chilling scream isn't Cyril's but the fiendish Daryan who just threatened them.

Cyril holds the killer by his neck off the ground with just one hand and bashes his head against the brick wall with a loud crack. The killer seems to be stunned for a second before he is crudely wakened up by two powerful but non-fiery punches from the ravenhead, one on each side of his face.

Eli's mouth hurts when he sees the killer spitting out two white teeth and a small puddle of blood. He trots a little nearer to Cyril to watch the fight and is shocked to find the killer's entire left face is severely burned, especially the area around his cheek.

"Where's the girl's body?" Cyril asks.

"Ou...uh...ah," the killer garbles. And he receives another head slam into the wall.

"I can't hear you."

"You're dead meat, you son of a bitch!"

This killer must either be the most valiant scumbag in the world, or he is just extraordinarily stupid. Eli thinks it's the latter. In the next ten seconds, the killer receives three punches to the face and eight to the chest, three head slams from one wall to the opposite one, five kicks to the gut, and ends up losing four more teeth.

This is the first time Eli has seen how inhumanly strong and resilient a Sage is compared to humans. A regular man would be in a body bag after taking the first two blows from Cyril, while this killer only has his face rearranged.

"Where's the body?" Cyril asks again, his voice clear and steady, showing no sign of being out of breath or even a tiny bit of weariness.

"I...I guarantee you. You...will...die the most excruciating death...known to man," the killer pants. Then he tilts his monstrous face toward Eli, his bloodshot eyes filled with twisted malice, and laughs frenziedly. "I swear I'll shred that little rat you hold so dear to bits right in front of you, and I'll strangle you with his guts. Then I'll stab and slice you into millions of pieces with his bloody bones, you fucking bastard!"

Eli's face turns as white as a sheet from fear—not for the killer's graphic threat but rather for what would happen to Cyril after he murders that asshole.

Cyril's bangs cover his eye so Eli can't fully see his guardian's expression aside from the sight of his jaw tightly clenched together and his lips quivering with rage.

"C-Cyril," Eli fearfully calls out to his guardian, but his voice is washed out by the killer's earsplitting scream as his neck is lit on fire.

Both of Cyril's arms are now immersed in blazing red fires. He raises his left fist, aiming at the killer's head. But he suddenly stops midway and turns to Eli.

Eli hears a very faint whoosh sound through the air from behind his back. He immediately swings around and catches a glimpse of two cerulean shadows bolting toward him from the rooftop.

Eli frantically turns around to run to his guardian. But just within one step, a blazing glare flares up from behind him, and a chain of piercing screams startles him. Eli glances back and sees the two cerulean figures going after him thrash wildly on the ground, as both are on fire. And just a second later, the killer whom Cyril has been beating into a pulp, falls from the sky from out of nowhere and crashes on top of the other two.

"RUN!" cries one of the killers, and the three of them jump from the ground to the rooftops and flee.

Eli lets out a terrifying yelp when he is suddenly swept off his feet. He's about to scream for Cyril when he sees it was his guardian who just grabbed him.

"Hold tight" is the only thing Cyril tells him before he makes an anti-gravity jump onto the rooftop of a three-story building with Eli under his arm.

Hold tight to what?! That's what Eli would have asked if he isn't freaked out by the fact that he's hovering forty feet from the ground, and the person carrying him is leaping from building to building at an inhumanely fast speed like a super-mutant cheetah on steroids.

Under different circumstances, Eli would have gushed and marveled at Cyril's unbelievable stunts. But not now! Especially not in the awkward position Cyril is carrying him in; Eli feels like a stolen pig. His head is spinning from all the rapid bounces and jumps Cyril makes at various heights. Everything around him is a blur to his eyes. Eli has to clasp his hands over his lips to prevent himself from throwing up on the unaware pedestrians below.

Cyril rains fire on the killers throughout the whole chase and successfully fries two out of the three killers' hair, and lights all their asses on fire (literally). Their once impeccable cerulean uniforms now look like tattered cleaning rags. The pursuit goes on for about four minutes before the battered killers hop down to the street, blending into the busy crowd and running in a zigzag pattern.

Due to the change of escape route, both parties slow down significantly. This is a brilliant move for the killer group, as Cyril could no longer shoot fire at them freely like when he was up in the air.

Seeing Cyril's reluctance to use his power, the killers start to hurl anything they can grab on their way in the ravenhead's direction. Trays of food, baskets of merchandise, pottery, chairs, and tables. At one point, they even throw an entire food stall at him. Though Cyril easily dodges all the obstacles with little effort, several bystanders get splashed with the hot soup, and many are injured by the objects these scums blindly fling during their getaway.

Cyril's patience dwindles as the chase progresses. He starts to shove the crowds standing in his way instead of evading them like earlier. His free hand becomes engulfed in red fire once again. But just before he can aim the blaze at the killers, these fiends snatch a child from a woman's arms and throw him right at the ravenhead's blazing hand. Cyril can't catch the kid while his hand is covered in flames, but Eli manages to grab the little boy just in time.

These killers think throwing a child at Cyril would make him stop going after them. However, that cruel act only enrages Cyril even further. The ravenhead begins to run near the same rapid speed he did on the rooftop, bulldozing anyone in front of him. He even ignores Eli's pleading for him to stop, as he is determined to catch these killers at all costs.

The chase lasts for another five minutes, and when Cyril is only about twenty feet away from his targets, these heartless killers grab a deep iron pan filled with boiling oil from a fried food vendor and throw it at Eli and the child in his arms.

Eli screams and screws his eyes shut. He covers the crying little boy's face with his hands and head.

At last, Cyril has to stop.

A strong, blinding light flares up before Eli. The crowd turns rampant as people howl in pain and cry out for help.

The bubbling oil never touches Eli.

When Eli opens his eyes, there's a large, majestic fireball burning in the air. The ball lowers in accordance with Cyril's hand. Once it touches the ground, the fire dissolves, and a substantial volume of bubbling black liquid pours out all over the street. When the burned smell hits Eli's nose, he realizes the mysterious substance is the boiling oil the killers hurled at him.

The killers are long gone by now.

"Put...me...down," Eli stutters, shaking like a wounded pup. "Please."

The moment Cyril lets go of him, both Eli and the little boy flop down to the ground and throw up.

Cyril doesn't comfort Eli this time. He just stands there and stares in the direction where the killers have fled. His fists clench at his sides, and his eyes narrow with deep rage.

"Are you okay?" Eli crawls to the little boy's side to console him despite still seeing stars. The poor thing is crying his eyes out and asking for his mommy. As Eli looks closer at the child, he is horrified to discover this little boy is only a toddler!

"Hush, don't cry. I'll take you back to your mommy right now," Eli soothes the baby boy now clinging to him.

Eli wants to say a few more comforting words to the tot when Cyril unexpectedly lifts him and the boy off the ground into his arms. The raven-head then dashes in the direction they came from. After a few minutes, they spot a crying lady running toward them.

"Mommy!" the baby boy cries out to her.

After Eli safely returns the kid to his mother, he starts apologizing to her, but before he can finish the sentence, he's forty feet off the ground once again.

* * *

"Cyril!" Eli snaps at his guardian.

Cyril looks at him with moody eyes. He is carrying Eli princess-style while skipping over rooftops. At least this time, he's moving at a normal, non-vomit-triggering pace.

"That was so rude of us! Running off without a proper apology to the lady and leaving a whole mess behind."

"There was a group of sentinels twelve meters (forty feet) away behind that woman," Cyril responds indifferently, looking out at the space ahead. "I don't want to deal with them."

Cyril glances at Eli and sees the sulky look on his face. His lips slightly part, as if he wants to say something to his young master. But he ends up not doing it, and thus, the pair travels in silence.

About five minutes later, Eli speaks up first.

"You could have caught up to them if you didn't take me with you."

"What?"

"I was no help to you at all, a complete burden. You should have just dropped me off somewhere safe and continued pursuing those killers. I would have been fine on my own."

Cyril comes to a stop. He's now standing on the rooftop of a four-story building.

"I hope you don't mean what you just said," Cyril says, his beautiful eyebrows furrowed.

"Actually, I do mean it," Eli responds. He's not trying to piss Cyril off. He just says what he thinks. "Since you've been so hung up on not catching them. If you had done what I just said, you could've probably found Faye's body by now."

Cyril gazes at him for a while. "Is there any man in the world that willing to leave his heart outside from his chest unattended?"

The question stuns Eli and leaves him flustered.

"I don't think such a person exists," Cyril mutters and presumes breezing through the buildings while Eli's entire face inflames like a ripe tomato.

"Where are we going?" Eli asks after some time has passed.

"I don't know."

"What?"

"I just want to clear my mind."

Eli's brow arches. Don't people usually cool off alone?

...But then Snow White is unlike any other, so...

"I hope I don't hinder your cooling off progress."

"Quite the contrary, Eli, your presence has been a marvelous boost. My head is eminently lighter than before." Cyril looks at him again. He does seem less edgy than earlier, but his expression is still nowhere near the silly, happy-go-lucky Cyril Eli has always known.

"I'm glad." Eli blinks. Cyril's penetrating blue eyes are making him all rattled inside.

"Can you keep your eyes on the...fly zone, please?" Eli requests.

"You afraid I would drop you?"

"Believe it or not, Cyril. I have full confidence in your abilities. However, that confidence is halved when you don't pay attention to where you're going!"

"Who says I'm not focused?"

Eli lifts his chin to look at his guardian. Under the vastness of the night sky, their eyes entwine. Their irises resemble crystal gems; one pair is vivid, profound blue, and the other is expressive, unyielding green. They are so very different and yet, at the same time, they strangely complement one another. "Are you?"

Cyril's pace hastens, as does his heartbeat, but his eyes still stubbornly fixate on Eli's. It's a dangerous thing for him to do. There's no streetlight up at this height as the pale moonlight and starry stream are their only source of light to navigate through the darkness. Several moments later, the ravenhead, at last, averts his gaze to the path ahead, albeit reluctantly.

"You're right. I haven't been paying much attention to the direction." Cyril's lips are half curved. "But it was not entirely my fault. All the men in the world could relate if they were in the same situation as me."

"Oh? So it's my fault then?" Eli lifts a brow. He doesn't really get the last part, but somehow, his guts tell him he's not ready to go there with Cyril.

"Of course, it's your fault. You're incredibly distracting."

Eli's brow is a notch higher than before.

"I was not the type that trip and fall on my own. Until I met you."

Eli is ready to bicker, but then he stops when Cyril's words sink in. There is truth in it, and thus, Eli's confidence and indignation promptly deflate like a flat tire.

"I can't argue with that. I'm sorry your life went downhill after meeting me," Eli mutters. There's no sarcasm but genuine remorse in that last sentence.

"I never said that."

"I distract you. I have brought you so many troubles and headaches. I cost you money, your time, and your energy. I constantly put you in danger. Making you worry about me all the time," Eli cringes as he lists out all the negative things he has brought to Cyril so far. "Sometimes I thought if you had never found me in that forest, you wouldn't be so—"

Cyril comes to an abrupt stop. Eli jolts when he realizes they're standing on top of a very tall pine tree that is at least eighty feet high.

Cyril glares at him—for the first time ever.

Eli takes that as a cue to shut up.

The one-sided glower lasts for three intense seconds before Cyril moves on again. This time, he's jumping between trees, and after a few minutes, Cyril finally lands on the ground.

It looks like they are in a park, as their surroundings are covered with sprucely pruned trees and flower bushes. Cyril strides to a round-shaped pavilion nearby and carefully puts Eli down on the stone bench inside.

Eli stares in awe at the endless fairy lights covering the glass dome and the marble columns, admiring the beauty of the enchanting view. His attention shifts when Cyril leans down to the ground on one knee.

"Back there, did any hot oil splatter on you?" Cyril's voice is full of concern as he checks Eli's clothes for signs of burn marks or injuries.

"No. Not at all," Eli answers.

"Did anyone hurt you during the chaos?" There's visible terror in Cyril's eyes.

"No. I don't think so." Eli thinks a bit and then shakes his head. He jumps when Cyril suddenly stands up and hugs him tight. "C-Cyril?"

"I'm so sorry, Eli. Please forgive me," Cyril cries.

"F-For what?" Eli's eyes widen in confusion.

"I'm the worst guardian in the world!"

Yep. Bye-bye, edgy Cyril, and hello, Snow White. Eli rolls his eyes, gently patting his guardian's back. But before he can open his mouth to console Cyril, the ravenhead speaks first.

"Those vermin had angered me so much I completely neglected you! I didn't even check if you were injured when I ceased going after them. Then, after that, I even had the gall to mistreat you. And then frightened you! How could I? What was I thinking?! How could I do such an abhorrent thing to you? Especially after all these years, you've been through so many hardships and misery. I truly deserved to burn in the deepest pit of Avici!" Cyril's voice cracks with utter shame and sorrow.

...Eh, but aren't you like immune to fire? Eli thinks and remembers Cyril once bragged that the blaze he summons is "Inferno Fire."

"My poor Eli," Snow White laments as he pulls away to look at his young master. "Were you scared?"

"Up on that tree, I frightened you. I couldn't control my temper. I lashed out at you. You trembled in my arms," Cyril looks completely disgusted at himself.

"Oh, Cyril! I'm not a cotton ball. I don't get scared easily. And you're the least scary person in the world to me," Eli reassures his restless nanny—guardian.

"I'm so very glad to hear that, my little kit. I want you to know that you should never ever be fearful of me, for I adore you more than anything that has ever existed, even more than my life," Cyril strokes Eli's cheek and eventually gives it a loving pinch. "You're my most precious cotton ball in the entire universe!"

Eli shoots Cyril a scowl, which only makes the ravenhead chuckle even more heartily. Cyril then gives Eli a long, heartfelt apology and pledges he will make it up to him with endless promises of material gifts and sweets.

* * *

"About Faye's situation, what should we do now?" Eli asks after a short break.

"Hmm." Cyril contemplates the question. "For now, there's not really much I can do on my part."

"We're stuck?"

"Unless..."

"Unless what?"

"Can you call her out so I can talk to her?"

Eli shudders.

"Don't be scared. I'm right here with you" Cyril holds Eli's hands to comfort him. "I've tried to communicate with Faye multiple times, but she would not respond to my calls. I suppose it is due to her inexperience, having recently died, or she is just scared of all Sages since she was murdered by a group of degenerate Sages."

"But she made an exception for me and showed herself to me because we share the same birthday."

"Correct," Cyril nods, then flicks Eli's nose. "And must be because you have such an angelic face!"

Eli rolls his eyes. "Alright. Let's do it."

Cyril squeezes Eli's hand and gives him an encouraging smile.

"Um...h-how to call a spirit out?"

"Stay focused and whisper her name in your head, inviting her to come out and talk to you."

Eli follows Cyril's advice. They sit in silence, holding hands and anxiously waiting for the ghost to appear.

Twenty minutes go by, and not a single sign appears, not even a spooky shadow or a cold draft. Instead, the evening park is quiet and serene. The trees and light pink damask rose bushes rimming the pavilion are all wired with fairy lights and emanating sweet, heady perfume. The only sound heard is the calming bubbling water from a three-tier fairy fountain near where they sit.

Still, the soothing scenery fails to ease Eli's mind. The more time passes, the more visible the anxiousness on Eli's face has become. He is concentrating so hard that his eyes widen like a night owl. His gaze keeps bouncing around, fretfully looking out for any sign from Faye.

Cyril watches Eli while Eli watches out for the ghost. He thinks Eli looks just like a nervous little raccoon that's about to commit its first burglary.

"Eli," Cyril gently taps his adorable raccoon's right shoulder.

"W-What?!" Eli jolts in his seat.

"Let's go, sweetie."

"What about Faye?"

"I don't think she's in the mood for communication right now," Cyril takes out his handkerchief and dabs the running sweat on Eli's pale cheek. "Let's go get some shaved ice!"

* * *

CYRIL AND ELI find a small ice cream shop a couple of blocks from the park. Cyril buys Eli a big cone of grape-flavored shaved ice.

The chilliness of the sweet ice promptly wakes Eli up and uplifts his glum spirit. He takes two more gleeful licks of the snow cone before turning to Cyril to discuss their next plan.

But Cyril is no longer next to him.

"Cyril?" Eli calls out for his guardian while looking around, confused.

There were some people bustling about just moments ago. Now, it is only Eli standing in the empty street. The lampposts have dulled to the point Eli can barely see the path ahead. All buildings and houses on both sides of the street are closed shut, and not a single unit is lit.

"C-Cyril?" Eli lowers his voice, alarmed by now. It is so eerily quiet here that his whisper echoes back at him. The air is getting so cold Eli can see his breath coming out from his lips.

Eli turns around, and the road behind him is pitch black. He has no choice but to move along the dim path before him.

But with just a couple of steps, Eli stops dead in his tracks.

About fifteen feet away stands a shabby pink bunny mascot in a 3XL adult diaper. There are bloodstains throughout the dirty fur, especially around the mouth, neck, and eyes, as they are soaked in fresh blood. The wounds look very haphazard, like someone deliberately stabbed the mascot repeatedly in those areas with the intention of torturing her.

Myra? She's dead?! She doesn't move, only standing there and staring at Eli with her ominous hollow eyes that are dripping with blood.

Still fixing his eyes on her, Eli slowly steps backward to run. But just when his foot touches the ground, the bloodied mascot suddenly appears right before him, only a few inches apart from his face.

Eli jumps and drops the ice cone. He can even see the white bones amid the torn, bloody flesh through the hollow eyes of the bunny costume. It is an utterly gory and repugnant sight. Eli immediately wheels around to flee, but his right arm is tightly pulled back before he can make the first move. A foreign hand clasps over his mouth, muffling him from crying for help. Eli is then forcefully turned around.

Cyril?! Eli's eyes widen.

Cyril nods and puts a finger to his lips.

Eli meekly nods back in response. Only God knows how relieved Eli feels when he sees his guardian. He is so emotional that tears well up in his eyes, and his breathing becomes ragged and audible.

But Cyril quickly tightens his clasp against Eli's lips and shakes his head, implying they should not even breathe too loudly. The ravenhead then pulls Eli into his arms and gently strokes his back to calm him down.

After Eli's breathing has normalized, he warily looks around for the bloodied bunny, and it seems that she was gone when Cyril showed up. Eli then draws two bunny ears on his head and makes a throat-slit gesture and a dead face in an attempt to show Cyril what he saw, to which Cyril desperately bites back a laugh. Then, Cyril nods and gives Eli a thumbs up, gesturing to him he got it.

Cyril holds Eli's hand, and they begin their journey into the unknown.

* * *

THICK GRAY FOG draws up and quickly overcomes the feeble flame from the streetlights. Soon, Eli and Cyril are walking in near-complete darkness. But Eli is no longer afraid since Cyril is with him. Cyril transfers his heat through their handholding to keep Eli warm in the bleak weather. Occasionally, Cyril wills queeze Eli's palm to comfort him whenever they passed a totally lightless area.

They keep going like that for a long time in silence until they spot faint silhouettes wonkily slogging along a few feet ahead. When they pass a fair-haired lady, Eli glances at her. To his horror, half of the woman's right face and her lower left jaw are missing in a way that it looks like they were brutally smashed in by a metal sledgehammer. The wounds are still fresh and oozing blood all over her off-white gown.

The ghost flinches and glares at Eli as if sensing she is being watched. Her only intact eye is all white and bloodshot with no iris. Fortunately, Eli is much quicker as he manages to avert his eyes to the road ahead without getting caught.

Close call. Eli's face is pale with fear. He is startled when Cyril squeezes his hand. Eli looks up to his guardian and receives a solemn gaze along with a disapproving head shake, gesturing that what he just did (staring at the ghost) was very dangerous and he should not do that again.

Eli drops his head and repentantly nods.

They continue their endless walk through the fog. After a while, more shadows of pedestrians start to populate the hazy street, and eerie whispers emerge. There are weeping, moaning, laughing, singing, and sometimes, even screaming noises, but they are never loud. Eli can't make out what is being said since these voices all speak at the same time.

Though Eli tries to keep his eyes on the road, he notices the pedestrians surrounding them are all ghosts. They all wear a shabby white robe that looks like a burial shroud. They either have all-black sockets or eyes that only have the white part, and each of them wears one expression that remains unchanged. The creepiest is the smiling ghost with white eyes, a bloody face with bright red lipstick, and straggly black hair. She does not stop smiling sinisterly as she walks. Her entire head hangs upside down on her back as she trudges forward; it looks like someone has violently snapped her head backward, as evidenced by the protruding bone sticking out at her neck. Another has the top part of his head, starting from the nose to the crown, and his lower chin sliced off, causing the red tongue to dangle out from his throat.

Some ghosts are missing their entire head altogether. And then there is one gruesome-looking ghost that hops instead of walking since its arms, right leg, and torso are all twisted and bent, its face completely disfigured and bloody; it looks like this one was killed in a traffic accident or from falling off a cliff.

After passing through countless of these ghastly ghosts, Eli begins to foster a frightening thought that both he and Cyril are already dead. They have been ambling in this foggy purgatory for a very long time. It is not normal for a living person to appear unexplained in a place like this. Did he die, and then Cyril committed suicide to be with him? Cyril did promise he would always be with Eli no matter what.

Eli turns to his guardian. Cyril's face and lips are ashen with no hint of color. Even his vivid blue eyes appear dull, opaque, and lifeless.

Cyril is focusing on the road and probably feels Eli's gaze on him. Thus, the ravenhead turns to look at his little companion and, just by habit, gives him a bright, sweet smile as if they were strolling in a sunny flower field.

Cyril, you fool. Thick tears brim in his eyes as Eli is two seconds away from breaking down when he hears a rattling noise of metal against the stone path. Both he and Cyril look back to the road before them and spot a black hooded figure pushing an old, wooden wagon with metal wheels and a flickering oil lantern.

Eli and Cyril exchange a brief glance before speeding up, hand in hand, to catch up to that mysterious entity. As they get closer to the black hood, an unbearably foul stench that emanates from the wagon hits their noses.

The pair then walks side by side to get a clearer view of what is inside the cart. Just as they have dreaded, they find two wooden barrels of crimson flesh seeping in blood.

Eli's stomach twists into knots when he sees several strands of long raven hair scattering in between the gluey meat piles. The hair then wiggles as if it is trying to break out of the barrels.

The rotten smell gets even more fetid, to the point Eli must clasp his left hand over his mouth to stop himself from throwing up.

Faye, Eli mouths to Cyril, pointing a trembling finger in the black hood's direction.

Cyril nods and gestures with his thumb that they must keep moving forward.

However, Eli suddenly can't move his left leg. Puzzled, he looks down, and his body instantly turns to jelly. A giant, hairy black spider with eight huge, sinister eyes, red stripes, and the body of a medium-sized yoga ball is eagerly building a web ball around his left ankle!

A terrified, irrepressible shriek slips out of Eli's mouth before his brain can even register, startling both Cyril and the spider.

Cyril immediately turns to his companion and catches the distraught green face. When his eyes move down to Eli's feet, even Cyril is taken aback by the presence of the grisly behemoth, who is now baring its sharp fangs at them, ready to take a big bite at the supple pale flesh of his young master's left calf.

With no warning, a large, menacing blue fire is set off at Eli's feet, causing both him and the giant spider to jump in shock.

The fire is entirely harmless to Eli as it burns off the web ball around his left foot, freeing him from the creature's grasp. But the same cannot be said for the spider monster. The beast lets out a string of painful, hair-chilling hisses as it hops to the sidewalk and thrashes violently on the ground, trying to put out the flame in vain. After a few seconds of struggling, it dies belly up, its long, hairy legs curled up, pointing to the sky.

Eli winces in disgust upon seeing the stinky, yellow pus oozing out from the deep-fried giant spider's corpse. But before he reacts further, Cyril has already dragged him by his hand and rushed toward the path ahead.

The black hood has moved so far away from them. They can only see the man's tiny silhouette amid the thick fog! How could he travel that far when his pace was so slow? The whole spider ordeal happened just less than a minute ago!

Cyril and Eli run after the black hood. But just after a brief distance, a deeply mutilated ghost appears before their path. They would have crashed into it if it wasn't for Cyril's quick reflexes.

Cyril hides Eli behind his back. They take several steps away from the ghost, who is now standing unmoving and staring at them.

Like any of the other macabre-looking spirits in this place, the ghost before them is a horrific, pitiful mess. His chest, legs, and right arm are cut open and are still dripping blood and exposing the white bones. His face is lashed multiple times and is beyond recognizable. His eyes and internal organs are missing.

"Human." The ghost's bruised lips curve into a ghastly, crooked grin.

A roaring blue fire engulfs the ghost and burns him into ashes. Cyril hastily throws Eli over his shoulder and whispers, *"Take a deep breath."*

Cyril gives Eli exactly one second to breathe in before running at the super-mutant cheetah speed like earlier tonight. It is a major jerk move from the ravenhead, since how much of a deep breath can someone take in just a second?!

Cyril is running so fast that everything is a blur to Eli. But it seems like more ghosts are popping up in their way due to the constant blazing blue lights, sizzling noises of flesh lit on fire, and the screaming of these ghouls. The eerie talking noise is getting louder and more coherent as they are all screaming: *living souls.*

Living souls? Does that mean he and Cyril are still alive?

If Eli were here all by himself, he would have probably pissed in his pants. But since papa bear—uh, Cyril is by his side, he doesn't sweat it too much. Eli is quite certain they are gonna catch up with the shady black hood and then get out of this hellish realm in no time—

Cyril comes to a sudden stop, causing Eli's face to slam hard against the ravenhead's back.

Ouch. Eli bites back a groan and grasps his nose. He lifts his head to see what happened, and his heart drops. Surrounding the two of them is an *army* of ghosts and demons!

Eli turns his head to the front, and sure enough, this side is also packed with ghouls. They are completely trapped!

Eli does a quick assessment and estimates that there have to be at least a few hundred, if not a thousand, ghosts circling them, all aggressive. He suppresses a hard gulp and knocks on Cyril's back.

"I think it's time for us to leave this place," Eli whispers to Cyril.

"Mmm."

"Mmm" is the last thing Eli wants to hear from Cyril, especially in a dire situation like this where these vengeful ghosts literally drone "yum" and have their bibs tied and cutlery ready to carve him and Cyril like Christmas turkeys!

"Please tell me you know how to get out of here." Eli's voice cracks when he sees the ghosts' mouths are now wide open, their lower jaws stretching down to their chest.

Cyril lifts Eli off his shoulder. Then he looks at Eli in the eyes and calmly says, "I don't."

Eli can physically feel his blood freezing in his veins.

"But I promise I won't let anything happen to you."

The ghouls roar and start to race toward Cyril and Eli.

"That better be true! Because I'm going to make the most annoying ghost in existence, and you don't want to be stuck with me for eternity in this hellhole!" Eli screams against the ghosts' raucous hollers.

To his annoyance, Cyril pulls him closer. "Only you could make Hell sound so irresistibly tempting."

Lunatic! Eli's face turns red with anger.

"Trust me," Cyril breathes, pressing Eli's face to his chest.

A deafening explosion of beaming blue light and long, wailing howls blasts out. The pressure is so great it causes the earth to crack. The light is so intense that it brightens up the tenebrous road, illuminating every ghost before blowing them to ashes.

Eli dares to peek and sees a glowing circle of blue fire forming around him and Cyril. Some ghouls try to flee by running backward, but the circle acts like a giant magnet, pulling them to their inescapable demise one by one.

Over time, the sea of blue fire turns back to red again. The light becomes so unbearably bright that Eli has to screw his eyes shut. The ghosts' piercing cries fade and soon are reduced to nothingness.

CHAPTER 17

CASE II - THE BLOODY BUNNY MASCOT COSTUME – PART 6

*E*li only opens his eyes again until hearing the clip-clop sound of the horse carriages thumping on the stone road and the normal voices of people conversing around him.

"We're back," Eli whimpers, looking at his surroundings with trembling relief. They are standing on the sidewalk of a well-lit street. No more thick, gloomy fog, as the night sky is clear. Most shops and buildings are still open for business and brightly lit with colorful lights. The air smells of the fresh, salty ocean and food and sweet treats instead of the putrid stench that persisted just moments ago.

Eli glances at a shop's clock, and it is 9:10 PM. So they were in the death realm for almost two hours!

"Forgive me, Eli," Cyril murmurs, his head downcast. "I'm so useless. I keep exposing you to danger and scaring you again and again."

"I-I was not scared. Who says I was scared? Just a bunch of ghosts! I've seen worse," Eli lies.

The ravenhead is stunned by Eli's last sentence. For a moment, his blue eyes look pensive, then grief-stricken, and lastly, he just smiles gently at Eli.

"Of course not. You are the most valiant kit in the world!" Cyril teases in a chipmunk voice.

"Why, you little…" Eli scowls with his hands on his hips.

"Ay ay, don't be mad. Look." Cyril brings up his right fist. Then he counts from one to three, and a mini explosion of pink smoke and confetti pops up on his clenched hand. Then he opens his right palm, and a pink candy is sitting inside. "For you."

Eli gawks at the candy for three seconds before snapping himself out of the daze. "Hey, this is not the time for magic tricks. We have to find that black hooded dude now, or we will never be able to recover Faye's body!"

"Don't worry, sweetheart. I promise we'll catch them," Cyril states, conjuring two more candies out of thin air.

"Fine. Geez!" Eli sighs and takes the three colorful candies off Cyril's hand. He pops one in his mouth and puts away the rest in his pants pocket. That is when he realizes all the candies Cyril gave him this afternoon are gone!

"What's wrong, sweetheart?" Cyril asks upon seeing Eli's frown.

"My candies are gone!" Eli exclaims. Cyril's face instantly turns dark.

"You lost them in the Netherworld Realm?!"

"N-No, I don't think so," Eli stutters. He is scared by Cyril's sudden strong reaction. "I would have known if I dropped them there. I think I lost them when we were chasing Faye's murderers."

"Are you absolutely sure?"

"Yes," Eli confirms.

"Thank Tathagatas!" Cyril breathes out a sigh of relief. "We'd be in big trouble if you lost those candies in the Netherworld Realm."

"W-What would happen if I did?"

"Losing a personal possession in the Netherworld Realm is no different from leaving a formal invitation for the ghouls and vengeful spirits to come and possess you. They only need a single candy to do that. And you took a handful from me this afternoon."

Eli gulps, suppressing a shudder.

"Don't be scared, sweetheart. Even if you did lose the candies there, I would not let any ghost pester you. If they dare to come after you, I'll turn them all to dust." Cyril pulls Eli into a hug.

"I'm not scared," Eli grumbles but doesn't pull away. "I can't believe we lost the black hood. What now?"

"Hmm," Cyril lets go of Eli and muses. A quarter minute later, he announces, "I think we should buy a backpack carrier."

There is a moment of silence.

"A backpack carrier. What for?"

"For me to carry you on my back while I go searching for that black hood."

"Cyril...are you aware that I'm sixteen years old and *not* sixteen months old?"

"The search is going to last all night, sweetheart, and you will have to be with me the whole time. You need to rest. I will not leave you to spend the night alone at the inn. I could certainly carry you in my arms, but it's extremely implausible that I won't have to fight, so I'll need both my hands. I could also carry you on my shoulders, but that position is not ideal for you to sleep in."

"My dude, let me propose a better option," Eli snaps. "I can just pull an all-nighter. That way, you can save your money while having me act as a lookout for you, and I can also preserve my dignity. Sound good?"

"What is an all-nighter?" Cyril's brows furrow in confusion.

"Staying awake all night."

"That's absolutely out—"

"Let's go! Stop wasting our precious time! Black hood is getting further away as we speak!" Eli walks away. But within just three steps, he is pulled back and hauled over his guardian's large shoulder. "Cyril! Put me down right now!"

"I'm so sorry, sweetie. You can scream at me all you want when this is over. But now, please listen to me this one time," Cyril's voice is still gentle yet adamant.

Eli begins to protest, swinging his feet and making a scene. Unfortunately for him, Cyril's mind is truly set this time, as no amount of fuss and tantrums would sway the ravenhead's decision.

"I will not sit in a backpack! I'm a grown-ass adult! What the heck is wrong with—Cyril, turn around!" Eli stops whining and hastily turns his guardian's head in the opposite direction.

At the end of the road, right at the three-way junction, figure clad in a black hood is pushing a wagon with an oil lantern. The man is moving forward to the path before him at an even pace.

* * *

THEY FOLLOW black hood for about fifteen minutes before he finally reaches his destination—the back door of the Seaside Cottontail Grill.

Cyril and Eli exchange unsettled looks.

Black hood knocks on the door and talks to someone inside the room. A few seconds later, the grill's owner, Einar, goes outside and checks the two barrels on the cart.

"Eh? Is that you, my friends?" Einar exclaims as he sees Cyril and Eli approach. "How's your investigation going?"

"Investigation?" Black hood looks up, revealing a tanned, normal-looking middle-aged man with brown eyes.

"Oh, these good lads are helping me find my missing waitress," Einar briefly explains, and then turns to Cyril. "Do you have any clues?

"Yes, we do," Cyril responds. "We found her."

"What?! Where is she?!" Einar cries out. He looks genuinely happy. "Is she alright?"

"I fear not, Einar. She's dead. And she's right in front of you."

Einar takes several steps back from the wagon. His face turns white with terror and shock.

"Not all of her. Only some."

"What is going on?" the man in the black hood asks. He doesn't seem to understand what is happening.

"You tell me," Cyril looks at black hood. "What's inside these two barrels?"

"Veal, sir. Straight from the butcher's shop!"

"Open the lid," Cyril orders.

Once both lids are taken off, everyone looks inside the barrels and sees piles of cleaned, fresh red meat that smell just like regular raw beef.

"Cloaking spell," Cyril mumbles and waves a hand above the barrels. Immediately, the meats turn bloody and emit a disgusting odor that causes everyone except the ravenhead to flinch and back away.

"It is human flesh! What the hell, Derrick? You are in this as well?! You killed her?!" Einar grabs black hood's shoulders and shakes him like a rag doll.

"No! I swear I have nothing to do with this! I'm just a deliveryman! I'm not even allowed to go inside the butcher room!" Derrick pleads. He then turns to Cyril. "Please, sir. I'm just a man trying to feed my family. I didn't kill anyone! I'm innocent! Please believe me!"

"Calm down and be quiet." Cyril uses his glamor ability on the panicked Derrick.

After successfully having the deliveryman under his influence, Cyril turns to Einar and speaks to him in his normal voice. "May I ask you for a few favors?"

"Anything!" Einar is eager to help.

"I need a safe and secluded place to keep Faye's body. Only temporary, of course."

"You can use my equipment shed. It's right over there!" Einar points to a small, white wooden shed near the grill.

Cyril influences Derrick to move the meat barrels to the shed. Once inside the cabin, Cyril asks if Einar has finished his work shift for the day. When Einar informs them he can take a night off, Cyril asks if Einar could bring in a large table and some clean cloths. After everything is settled, Cyril charms Einar into staying inside the shed, guarding the two meat barrels with the door locked, and tells him not to answer the door unless it's him and Eli.

After that, the pair calls for a cab and travels with the hypnotized deliveryman to his workplace—the butcher shop.

Inside the cab, Cyril uses his glamor power to interrogate Derrick, and the man appears genuinely innocent. He is just a commissioned deliveryman in town who isn't even employed at the butchery. However, Derrick does offer two valuable pieces of information. The first is the butcher shop's owner acted a little "strange" earlier this evening when he handed Derrick the two "veal" barrels. The second one is this owner has a niece who works at the Seaside Cottontail Grill.

"I bet on my left toe the niece is Myra," Eli says, rubbing his hands together after hearing Derrick's testimony. "What?"

"Eli, please don't ever say things like that. You are so precious to me. And regarding your theory about Myra, it makes sense. Envy could be a possible motive."

"Yeah." Jealous, vindictive women can be inconceivably ruthless toward those they deem enemies. Eli had the misfortune of experiencing this type of cruelty firsthand with his stepmother in his previous life.

The cab comes to a stop as it reaches its destination. Cyril looks outside through the window, and his face swiftly turns dark.

"What is it?" Eli asks upon seeing Cyril's grim expression.

"The shop is open." Cyril's eyes narrow. "What kind of butcher's shop is still open at this hour?"

This butcher shop is a one-story, brown brick building located in a more remote area away from the main road. From the carriage, Cyril and Eli can see the shop's main door is not fully closed, and the light is still on.

They both have a terrible feeling about this place, and it only intensifies after they exit the cab with the still-hypnotized deliveryman. Though they are still standing outside, the thick stench of human blood is so prominent.

Cyril gives the coachman some money and tells him to wait for them to return. Then, he enters the shop with Eli and Derrick.

Except for the nauseating odor of blood, there is nothing unusual in the main lobby. But once the trio goes into the butcher room, things look straight out of an R-Rated horror movie.

A vicious massacre happened here. There is blood everywhere on the white-tiled walls and floor, the cupboards, the hanging pig heads on the hooks, and the butchering equipment, but the most substantial amount is on the long wooden counter in the middle of the room. There is a large, bloody cleaver stuck on its surface.

Eli shudders as the cleaver reminds him of the patched-face butcher incident just a week ago.

"Go back to the main room and keep it down," Cyril orders Derrick when he sees the man retching.

Eli carefully steps into the clean area and looks around. He doesn't see any meat chunks or human remains. "There is too much blood. This cannot be the work of a butcher."

"Indeed. This blood is also much fresher than the one in the barrels, so it cannot be Faye's," Cyril remarks as he studies the blood trickling from the wooden counter to the floor. Then, his ears seem to pick up something as he lifts his head. "Did you hear that?"

Eli, too, can hear it. However, the sound is very low and sounds like a... snort?

There are three other doors beside the main door to the front lobby. The first leads to a dirty bathroom, the second to a storage room, and the last to the backyard.

Cyril and Eli go through the two rooms and find no sign of any human remains before heading to the backyard.

The strange noise is a little louder in the garden. Since there is no light out here, Cyril summons a small fireball on his left hand to see things clearly. He finds a long trail of blood on the dirt path.

Cyril grabs Eli's hand, and they follow the blood trail. The longer they go, the more pungent the smell of blood becomes, to the point that Eli covers his nose with his free hand. After a few minutes, they reach a large pigpen made from stone.

"Don't look!" Cyril pushes Eli behind him.

But it is too late.

In the mud pit, a bunch of massive hogs are feasting on a pile of crudely chopped human body parts: gnawed hands, feet, legs, thighs, entrails, and pieces of torso scattered all over the pen.

Eli retches upon hearing a loud pop when a brown hog chews on the left eyeball of the half-eaten head of a man.

"Not here, sweetheart." Cyril hugs Eli and pats his back.

"I'm okay. Sorry." Eli stutters, trying to regain his composure.

"Stand behind me." Cyril then swings his left hand; a loud squeal breaks out, and every hog is on fire.

"Cyril! What are you doing?!" The fire doesn't spread as it stays on the hogs and rapidly ends their lives within a few seconds.

"We can't let them eat all the evidence, Eli," Cyril states as he lights up the two lanterns by the enclosure.

Make sense. The aroma of the roasted pigs has reduced the intense blood stench a little bit.

Cyril breaks off a branch of an oak tree near the pigsty and pokes the hogs' carcasses with it. He manages to fish out many body parts from under the mud and the dead pigs. They all belong to a male.

"Well, I guess that's the butcher," Eli comments after glancing at the neat pile of body parts Cyril arranged in the middle of the pen. From the look of it, the butcher was a chubby middle-aged man, semi-bald, and had blue eyes...eh, one *eye* now.

"Some of him," Cyril says while still poking around. "The rest is probably inside these hogs' bellies."

After some further searching, Cyril concludes there is nothing more he can find. Thus, the two of them go back to the cab. Cyril gives the deliveryman Derrick a hefty pouch of silver coins and compels the man to forget everything that happened tonight, except the part when he delivered the meat barrels to the Seaside Cottontail Grill. The ravenhead tells the coachman to take Derrick home.

"We're not coming back to the grill?" Eli asks as he watches the carriage leave.

"Oh, we are," Cyril sweeps Eli off his feet and into his arms. "I'm just faster."

Show-off.

* * *

As Cyril is jumping between the treetops, Eli begins to piece together all the clues they have so far and makes a hypothesis of what happened at the butcher shop. There is a high likelihood that the butcher is Myra's uncle. Since Myra was an accomplice, the killers brought Faye's body to the shop to be butchered and sold off as veal meat. After Derrick collected Faye's meat barrels and transported them to the grill, the butcher probably told the Daryans they could just dispose of the body by feeding it to hogs. Hearing that, the murderers then tested out the butcher's words by chopping him off into pieces and giving them to the hogs. They were amateurs, hence the messy scene in the butcher room. They know Myra is probably dead because of her bloody appearance in the Netherworld Realm. Now that her uncle is dead too, that means the only two human witnesses to those Daryans' heinous crimes are gone.

"That makes perfect sense. The meat in the barrels was sharply cut. A skilled butcher did it," Cyril adds. "Those Daryans didn't have to chop up that man. The hogs could easily break the body down themselves."

"Really?" Eli shudders. "How do you know that?"

"When I was a child, I occasionally worked for a butcher who owned a small pig farm. He was a very unpleasant individual, always threatening to feed us to the hogs if he so much found a spec of dirt after we were done scrubbing the barn. A boy who worked with me was quite tall and said he didn't believe a hog could devour a big piece of bone. The butcher proved him wrong by throwing a large bucket of cow bones into the pigpen. Turned out the butcher did not exaggerate. Pigs do eat bones. They can eat anything, including humans."

Eli only gawks at his guardian. He has no idea what kind of reaction his face displays, but it sure makes Cyril fretful upon looking at it.

"Don't be sad, sweetheart. That was a very long time ago. Nothing happened to me."

Eli smiles up at the ravenhead. "I'm glad."

"My skin is too tough for pigs anyway."

"I know. You're too hot to be pig's food. Now, next topic, please."

"Sorry," Cyril mutters.

"Cyril, what would happen if we couldn't retrieve all of Faye's body parts? What if the pigs already ate her head and bones just like they did the butcher?"

"It doesn't really matter. We should be able to find the rest of her remains when I catch those Darya murderers. They cannot escape at this point. I remember their faces."

* * *

IT ONLY TAKES Cyril ten minutes to get back to the Seaside Cottontail Grill. As soon as they get inside Einar's equipment shed, the ravenhead locks the door. He pulls out two chairs and sits Eli and the hypnotized Einar so that they are facing the corner. Cyril takes out a pair of black leather gloves from his vest and puts them on. Then he covers the large table with the clean cloth he asked Einar for earlier.

"Cyril, what are you doing?" Eli gingerly asks after sneaking a peek and seeing his guardian putting the two barrels filled with Faye's flesh next to the table.

"I want to see how much of Faye's body we have," Cyril answers. "Look away, sweetheart. I don't want you to see this."

"Okay," Eli turns back to the corner.

"I'll be done soon, and then we can go back to the inn to sleep."

"We're not searching for the killers anymore?"

"No, sweetie. It's not necessary. The sentinels will take care of the rest."

"Alright. Good luck."

Eli looks at the old cuckoo clock on the wall; it is already 11:05 PM. This morning, he and Cyril woke up at 7:30 AM to prepare to go to the beach. They have pretty much been out all day.

Today has been so insufferably long and eventful. They have gone to so many places, even to Hell (or, as Cyril fancily refers to it, "Netherworld Realm.") Damn! Eli can't wait to get back to the inn to take a long, hot shower and go to sleep. He is so exhausted that he won't react if a firecracker is lit up right next to his bed!

Einar has dozed off in his chair next to Eli's. His soft snore is contagious, making Eli feel sleepier than he already does. Eli decides to take a quick nap and closes his eyes. But just around fifteen minutes later, his left shoulder suddenly feels heavy, like something is leaning on it. Still drowsy, Eli groggily takes a quick peek with his left eye.

A head full of long black hair is resting on his shoulder!

If Eli were honest, after all the effed up gory crap he has seen today, this is weak, a minus-seven out of ten. As Eli is debating whether to ignore the head and resume his much-needed nap, the head moves and reveals a grayish-white face with blood all over it. Eli cusses inside his head before getting up from his chair and walking toward his guardian.

"Oh, what the—" Eli jolts at the bloody mess on the table.

Cyril has been assembling all the meat pieces from the two buckets into a complete body. So far, he has nailed down most of the torso, legs, arms, and all of Faye's organs.

"She bothered you again?" Cyril asks without looking at Eli. In his hand is a piece of meat that is still dripping with blood.

"Yes," Eli admits, staring at the fragmented corpse and the bloody fillet in the ravenhead's hand. He is unsure whether he should be impressed or terrified of his guardian's spectacular talent at reconstructing human body parts. "Cyril, please don't. She was the victim of a gruesome murder. She needs our help," Eli pleads when he sees Cyril squeeze the meat piece.

Though he still looks pissed, Cyril unclenches his fingers and puts the meat down on the stomach position. Eli moves closer to look inside the barrels, and there are only a few pieces of meat left.

Less than five minutes later, Cyril finally places the last piece of flesh on the body.

"Ugh." Eli grimaces at the bloody corpse on the table.

The corpse is now only missing the head, hands, feet, genitals, and skin.

"Einar, wake up," Cyril shakes the grill's owner. "I need some letter papers, an envelope, ink and pen, sealing wax, and some red or blue ink, too, if you have it."

The compelled Einar leaves the shed for a few minutes and then returns with all the items Cyril has requested.

Cyril then composes a letter. Though he is hurried, his writing is crisp and beautiful. He doesn't sign his name at the end when he's done. Instead, he tucks his left hand behind his back and takes out an intricately engraved silver dagger with a scabbard underneath his vest. He twists the pommel a few times to remove it from the handle. Inside the pommel are three engraved coins.

Eli watches in fascination as Cyril attaches the four-star medallion to the top of the dagger handle, making a stamped seal out of it. The ravenhead then dips the seal into the red ink and stamps it at the end of the letter. He repeats the process with the second medallion, which has the crest of a phoenix surrounded by fire. Then he puts the letter into the envelope, summons a small flame with his left hand to melt the wax stick, then pours the thick crimson liquid onto the envelope's closure. Finally, he seals the letter by stamping the consolidating wax with the last medallion that has an engraving of an eight-petal lotus.

Cyril speaks to Einar with his glamor power: "Take a cab and go straight to the central sentinel hall. Present this envelope with the back side up so they can see the seal. The sentinels will take you home afterward."

After that, the three of them leave the shed. Cyril puts a spell around the cabin to keep the stench of Faye's corpse from leaking outside, which could attract attention. Then they part as Einar travels to the sentinel station, while Cyril and Eli return to their lodging.

* * *

"You sure we don't have to find the rest of Faye's remains?" Eli asks languidly when they are walking back to the Golden Shore Inn. "What if the town sentinels still refuse to take this case seriously? Or what if they purposely let the killers escape?"

"If they cover for each other, all of them will receive the same punishment as those Daryans."

"Okay."

"Don't worry, Eli. I guarantee you that scenario will not happen."

"*Ayko.*"

"Pardon?!"

"Heh? Ugh, I meant, okay!" Eli jolts awake. He believes he just zoned out while walking. "What did I just say?"

"Nothing, sweetheart." Cyril smiles fondly at Eli, trying hard to suppress a laugh. "You are tired. Let me carry you back."

"No thanks. I can walk. It's embarrassing," Eli mumbles woozily. Only ten percent of his brain is working. The rest has blissfully shut down.

"What's embarrassing, sweetheart?" Cyril now speaks in his gentlest voice, like an adult talking to a child.

"I'm...not a kid," Eli slurs. "I'm an adult. I...I just got...de-evolved...back into a snotty brat... What're you doing? Put me down."

Cyril has swept Eli off his feet into his arms. "Hush. Sleep."

Eli shrugs and snoozes. A few seconds later, he wakes up and slurs, "I have to shower first. I stink."

"No, you don't."

"I do. You're so unhygienic."

"Alright. I'll wake you up as soon as we get back so you can shower before bed." Cyril chuckles fondly.

* * *

"I'm so glad you two are back safe and sound!" the inn's owner cries, waking Eli up. "I was so worried since you boys were the only guests that were still outside. Everyone else all got back to the inn by 9:30!"

"Did something happen?" Cyril asks as Eli hops down from his arms.

"Oh yes! Horrible, horrible things!" the old lady cries. "A gruesome massacre occurred today at a clinic in town in the afternoon. Everyone, from doctors to nurses to patients, were all killed! And then there was another horrific murder of two doormen near a gentlemen's club tonight! There was also a commotion at the night market earlier this evening that injured many people. They suspected it was a vigilante justice, but those murderers managed to escape. According to the witnesses at the market, those criminals threw a pan of boiling oil at a baby, forcing the brave vigilantes to stop to save the child! Unbelievable! How cruel could one be? Here, you can read more about the details in the newspaper."

Cyril and Eli take the paper, thank the lady, and quickly retreat to their room. Once they are inside, Cyril reads the newspaper out loud:

"At 4:13 PM today at the Sunflower Clinic, an unidentified female patient dressed in a pink bunny mascot outfit was found brutally murdered. She was stabbed fourteen times in the eyes and twenty times in the mouth, and her throat was punctured ten times with a very sharp blade. The doctors, nurses, and the rest of the patients were stabbed in the chest or had their throats slit. The total number of victims is forty-five. According to the local sentinels, the clinic was bathed in blood by the time they arrived at the scene."

"Wow...So in the course of just three days, those deranged bastards have killed at least forty-nine people," Eli slurs, tiredly scuffing his hair to keep himself awake. "Cyril, I really think we need to pack up our shit and immigrate to another country ASAP if you still want your dream of playing jigsaw puzzles with me at eighty to have a chance of happening. I can already tell you the probability of us surviving past forty in this country is as high as the chance of those four murderous scumbags getting to heaven."

Cyril gapes at Eli. "Sweetheart! Language!"

"Well, sorry, but there is no polite vocabulary for those who murdered almost fifty people."

"I know Aspenia might look less than ideal to you, but I guarantee with you this country is the safest place on Earth at the moment, and many people would kill to come here. There is an eleven-year-old world war going on as we speak, and a third of Earth's population has been wiped out in the past decade."

What the fudge? Eli forces his eyes open, frowning. "What was the cause of conflict?"

"All the nations with the strongest Sages as rulers claim to be direct descendants from the Gods, and they claim it is their birthright that everything on Earth belongs to them."

"This is a very interesting topic. Let's discuss it more when we get home. Now, I have to shower and go to bed, or else I might pass out on the floor." Eli gets up from the loveseat and walks to the bathroom.

"Do you want me to help you bathe?"

"No thanks. I'm not four." Eli grimaces.

"Alright, call me if you need anything! I'll be right outside."

* * *

ELI QUICKLY BRUSHES his teeth before getting into the bathtub to take a hot shower. The wonderful sensation of clean, steamy water rolling off his body after a long, stressful day makes him feel like he is in heaven. Eli takes time to wash his hair and rubs the soap on every inch of his skin. Within a day, he went to so many filthy places and saw too much bloodshed, corpses, and dead people. The last thing he wants to smell before bed is blood lingering on his body.

When Eli finally feels clean and refreshed, he opens his eyes to turn off the shower. To his horror, he finds the bathtub floor underneath his feet flooding with red water. He looks up at the showerhead and finds the liquid is running clear. Then, his ears pick up a small sob amidst the steady rhythm of the falling drips. He looks down again and sees the blood flow coming from behind him.

Eli spins around faster than he should have. The bloody sight before him turns his body cold despite the constant spray of hot water raining over his bare skin.

Faye is standing before him with nearly all her body intact for the first time, albeit the entire body is flayed except for her head. Her hands, feet, and eyes are missing. There is a large gap in the middle of her face, like it was split with an ax. Her arms are bending up toward her face, just like the gesture of a person crying.

Help me.

Please help me.

I'm begging you.

Her lips were moving, though no sound was coming out. Yet Eli could hear every word clearly.

This is the first time Faye has spoken to him. It is a young and soft female voice laced with lament and tears.

The pleading resonates again and again in Eli's head. The steamy mist rapidly invades the small bathroom, drowning out the oxygen in the air. Eli already loses consciousness before his body collapses against the bathtub wall.

* * *

ELI KNOWS he is dreaming as soon as he finds himself standing in a dark and dusty stone corridor with no window. He doesn't know what to do until he hears a muffled scream in the distance. Thinking he is seeing Faye's memory before her demise, Eli follows the noise, which leads him to a wooden door with iron bars.

A dungeon? Eli speculates and peeks inside through the bars. He sees nothing but an empty cell, yet he is certain the crying noise comes from behind this door. Eli presses his right ear against the wood. Somebody is beating the living crap out of another person.

"Please stop. Please! It's hurt! I'm sorry," the victim sobs.

...Is that Faye? Eli listens intently.

"You miserable wretch! How dare you run away? Do you have a death wish?" shouts a man as the sounds of a whip tear through the air. A heart-breaking scream breaks out each time the lash lands on its target.

Hitting a defenseless girl, what a cowardly piece of shit! Eli fumes, raising one leg up to kick down the door. But before his foot hits the wood, the door suddenly opens, making Eli crash onto the stone floor.

Fudge. Eli groans as his eyes temporarily see stars.

"Greeting, Your Grace." The guard's tone swiftly turns from vicious to reverent.

Your Grace? Eli turns his head around.

Behind him stands a fairly tall and muscular man dressing in an immaculate dark green velvet equestrian suit adorned with many precious jewelry embellishments. Despite the generous number of accessories, the man's outfit is not tacky; it gives off an extremely regal and imposing aura, evoking intimidation. Similar to the guard, the man's face is completely blurred, though Eli can see he has a fair complexion. His shiny brown hair is done in the pulled-back formal style.

Eli feels an intense dislike for this noble stranger at first sight. Something about this dude just…pisses Eli off. It's probably the douchey way he is standing in between the door arch like he is too cool to be here. Everything about this guy screams "I'm a pompous asshole."

"This runt tried to run away, Your Grace. We caught him wandering in the forest not far from here," says the guard with the bloody whip. He wears the same cerulean uniform as the murderers Cyril and Eli have been chasing all night.

He? Eli is confused. He looks at the victim cowering in the corner, hiding her face between the walls. She is stripped naked; her back is marred with countless overlapping red welts that still dripping blood; her chestnut brown hair is short and choppy, like it was cut in a rush.

"Master," the victim whimpers, slowly turning around to face her abusers. Her voice is parched and faint, like she has been deprived of food and water for an extensive period. She is so thin her breasts are non-existent. Her body is literally just skin and bone.

Wait a minute. Eli begins to realize something is not right about this person. He moves closer to take a careful look at the victim and is horrified to learn this person is not Faye!

It's him!

"Master…Please forgive me," Ilya whimpers as he slowly crawls toward the noble. "I learned…my lesson…I…I will…never dare to…leave home again."

Ilya abruptly stops to puke out a small puddle of blood, startling Eli. Not just his back, Ilya's entire body is abused from head to toe. Even his blurred face is covered with bloody injuries, purple bruises, and dirt. He doesn't look like he can last through another hour in his current state without immediate medical attention.

"I'm…hurt…" Ilya sobs. "I…I'm dying…Please…help me…"

To Eli's utter disbelief, the noble dude orders the guard to bring in a doctor.

"Can you stand up?" the noble asks Ilya.

"No…master," Ilya weeps, and the noble huffs in irritation.

When the doctor gets to the cell, the first thing the noble asks him is "Can these wounds be treated without leaving scars?"

The old doctor walks toward Ilya and roughly turns him around to inspect his injuries. He pays no heed to the poor boy's painful sobs as he grabs Ilya directly on his open wounds, causing him to thrash and scream. After a minute or two of this callous examination, Ilya looks like he is taking his last breath. The doctor says to the noble, "I'm afraid most of these scars are going to be permanent, Your Grace. His ankles are showing signs of severe infection. He won't be able to walk again unless getting treated with the Crimson Powder or by the Grace of the Tathagatas."

"Crimson Powder?" the noble scoffs. "Not even my dying mother could ever get to use that thing."

"He's damaged beyond repair, Your Grace," the doctor says.

The noble turns around and kicks the guard that tortured Ilya right in the chest.

An excruciating howl and a string of crunchy, bone-cracking noises break out and echo throughout the cell. The guard crashes to the stone floor, his mouth full of blood.

This noble has to be a Sage, Eli thinks.

"Damn you, worthless wretch!" the noble Sage rages as he stomps on the guard's body over and over. "How dare you damage my asset like this, you miserable human cur! He was supposed to be a gift! A goddamned GIFT! Damn you! O' Tathagatas, please forgive me for speaking profanity," the noble Sage prays, folding his hands together. "Such language is vulgar and beneath of me...But I can't help it. This filthy cur has ruined everything. He ruined my plan. You ruined my fucking plan! Die! Die! Die!" He crushes both of the guard's hands with his foot.

Eli shudders as he looks away from the violent assault. He suspects most of the guard's bones are broken by now.

Meanwhile, Ilya has retreated to the corner, shaking, with his legs pulled up to hide his naked lower body. He looks extremely terrified as he watches the noble Sage brutally assault the guard who abused him.

"Your Grace, please refrain from getting too angry. Like humans, negative emotion isn't good for Sages," the doctor advises.

"I know that. But LOOK!" The noble Sage points at Ilya, making him flinch and tremble even more. "Look at him! He's disabled now! That cur crippled him! He is a scarred, worthless cripple!"

"...Master," Ilya sobs.

"Silence! Who allowed you to open that filthy mouth?!" the noble Sage shouts.

Ilya clasps his hands over his mouth, desperately trying to keep quiet. But his little body still trembles at every breath.

"Guards!" the noble Sage shouts. A few seconds later, four men dressed in cerulean outfits come to the cell and bow to him. "Get this worthless cur out of my sight and bring me back his head!"

The death-sentenced guard screams and begs for his life, but he only receives another brutal kick to his face from the noble Sage. As he is being dragged out of the dungeon to be executed, the noble Sage orders for him to be brought back.

"Why did you cut off his hair?" the noble Sage asks the guard while pointing at Ilya in the corner.

"N-No, I never touched his hair, Your Grace! When I found him in the market, his hair already looked like that!" the guard cries.

The noble Sage turns his head at Ilya, and both Eli and Ilya flinch in fear.

"Who did it?" the noble Sage asks Ilya, no longer shouting. But this only makes him more frightening, just like an impending tsunami.

Ilya is too scared to answer. He just hyperventilates in the corner, his scrawny, abused body shaking like a leaf.

"WHO CUT OFF YOUR GODDAMNED HAIR?!" the Sage roars, and everybody in the room, even the invisible Eli, jumps out of their skin.

"I...I," Ilya can't answer the noble's question but breaks into a pitiful sob.

"Did you cut your hair?"

"Yes."

The entire time Eli has been here, there has not been a single moment he has not seen Ilya trembling or crying.

"Why did you do that? Your hair was so long and beautiful. How could you cut it?"

"I ...I—" Ilya splutters, but the noble Sage cuts him off.

"Was it that you thought you could blend into the crowd and success-fully escape if your hair was short? DID YOU REALLY THINK YOU

COULD RUN FROM ME?! YOU ARE MY PROPERTY! I COULD RECOGNIZE YOU EVEN IF YOU TURN TO ASH!" The crazed noble Sage stomps toward Ilya.

"Yo, chill the hell out!" Eli throws himself in front of Ilya. But the noble Sage passes through him, and Ilya's heartbreaking scream reverberates through the cell.

"Crap!" Eli panics as he helplessly watches the noble Sage grab Ilya by his hair, drag him out of his hiding corner, and violently throw him to the floor in the middle of the dungeon.

The noble Sage then slaps Ilya so hard that his head swings back to the stone floor with a bang.

"NO!" Eli screams in shock and horror as he sees Ilya, his counterpart, jerk on the ground, no longer able to cry as blood pools out from the position of his nose, mouth, and the right side of his face.

"Get up, slave! I'm not done with you yet!" The crazy noble Sage grabs Ilya by his small neck to face him. The rough strangling causes the boy, who is already bleeding too much, to choke and spit out blood at the noble Sage, enraging him even further.

"How dare you!" the noble Sage gasps, looking at Ilya's blood on his expensive suit. He swings out his hand to slap Ilya but stops midway.

"No...more," Ilya whimpers, his voice so faint that it's barely audible.

His plea is unheeded. Instead, the noble Sage throws him back to the floor and summons the bloody whip with which the guard beat Ilya to fly over to his hand. Then, he starts to whip the living soul out of Ilya.

Eli can't watch this anymore.

He wants to get out of this room. He wants to wake up from this nightmare. But his body just sits glued to the floor, unable to move.

His heart lurches every time he hears the whip hitting his counterpart's already broken skin again and again. Ilya is sobbing out for so many things. He sobs for mercy from the cruel noble Sage, to no avail. He sobs about how hurt he is. He sobs for the Gods to save him. He sobs for his papa to save him. He sobs out many unfamiliar names that Eli has never heard before. And then he sobs for someone to come save him.

He never sobs for Cyril.

Not once.

Eli has never wanted to hug a person so much as he does now. His poor counterpart of this world, the *real Ilya* that Cyril has been looking for, looks so frail and helpless. He has never seen such a pitiful, miserable person as the boy before him. Eli wants to pull Ilya into a hug and comfort him. He wants to tell Ilya he doesn't have to be so terrified because he will come home soon. Someday. Soon, Cyril will find him and save him.

Cyril will take him home.

Eli wants to tell his counterpart all of those things. But his hands go through Ilya's body. He can't touch him.

Eventually, Ilya finally stops crying and moving for good.

But the whipping doesn't stop. Even after little Ilya no longer moves.

Eli watches as the noble Sage keeps on flogging Ilya's lifeless body again and again, cursing, kicking, stomping, and spitting at it.

Then something happens. The blurriness on Ilya's face starts to dissolve.

Eli sees his own face slowly appear on Ilya's. As the facial details finally set in, the sight is too gruesome for him to look at.

Half of Ilya's face that touches the stone floor drowns in blood, while the other half is swollen with black and purple bruises. His lips are torn, and his nose is broken.

He is dead.

Ilya of this world is dead. Eli is seeing his counterpart's demise with his own eyes.

Eli gasps in horror when he sees Ilya jolt. But it isn't that he moved. It's just the body bouncing every time the noble Sage whips at it.

Eli breaks down into a mournful sob. The last time he wept uncontrollably like this was when his mother passed away when he was five.

* * *

"Eli, wake up, please. I'm begging you," cries a broken voice. "Please wake up."

Eli feels someone shaking his shoulders. It takes a while for Eli to finally open his eyes and realize the loud, sobbing voice belongs to no other but himself.

And the other is Cyril.

"Sweetheart, don't cry. I'm here." Cyril's eyes are red and teary. "You're safe. I won't let anyone hurt you ever again."

Eli says nothing but cries his heart out, causing Cyril to weep along with him. And just like two little toddlers on their first day at preschool, they hug each other and sob together.

Something seriously wrong is happening here.

Eli doesn't want to cry, at least not like a blubbering mess like this. His heart and mind are collected, but tears just keep flowing out from his eyes.

Simply put, Eli can control his thoughts, but not his body or emotions. It feels as if somebody coexisting within him is using his body to cry, and Eli cannot stop that entity from doing it.

"No! No! Get away from me!" Eli screams, startling Cyril, who is embracing him.

"Sweetheart, calm down. It's me, Cyril," Cyril begs, but Eli pushes him away.

Actually, Eli didn't push the ravenhead away. It was his hands that did it on their own without his approval.

"What is happening to me?!" Eli screams, holding his head and panicking. He wants to ask Cyril to help him, but his mouth won't speak out those words. Instead, he keeps sobbing over and over for mercy and for Papa to save him.

Oh God.

OH, GOD! IT IS ILYA!

It is Ilya who is saying these things. Ilya is alive inside Eli's body right now, and he is trying to take back his body from Eli!

"AHHHHH! Cyril, please save me! Please! Please! I don't want to die!" Now it is Eli that sobs out loud as he crashes into Cyril's chest, his skinny arms wrapping around the ravenhead tightly like a drowning man hanging onto a buoy.

"Eli, my little sweetheart, you are not going to die! Do you hear me?!" Cyril embraces the trembling Eli. His clench is so tight it leaves red marks on the Eli's pale skin. "You will live a long and happy life. You must because I won't allow anything otherwise. I swear to you, Eli, this time, as long as the last shred of my soul still lingers on this earth, I will protect you."

"This time…I won't let you down." Cyril's voice cracks, tears streaming down from his blue eyes. "Please give me one more chance."

A lone tear trails down Eli's cheek. His heart finally stops racing, and his trembling arms fall to his side.

"Eli?" Cyril's teary face turns white with fear.

"I can't breathe," Eli whimpers.

Cyril immediately loosens his iron grip around his young master's frail body. As soon as he does, Eli gasps for air.

"Oh, sweetheart, I'm so sorry," Cyril apologizes, gently stroking Eli's bare back and chest to help him breathe.

"I'm okay," Eli stutters after his breathing finally stabilizes and he can regain control of his body again. "Cyril."

"Yes, I'm here." His tears have dried up, but the frightened look on his gorgeous face remains.

They stare at each other for a few brief seconds before falling into each other's arms once again. They stay like that for a long time and only let go when their hearts beat with the same rhythm.

Eli slowly looks at his surroundings before glancing down at himself. He freezes when he sees he is wearing *nothing.*

"Cyril, what the hell?! Why am I naked?!" Eli yells and looks around for any clothes to cover himself, but he sees none. He has to pull the blanket over his body to shield himself from Cyril's eyes.

Cyril jumps at the screech and hurriedly finds clothes for Eli to wear. His face fills with fear once again. "Uh…I…It—"

"Did you just stare at me while I was out and naked for the last." Eli stops to look at the wall clock; it's exactly one o'clock in the morning. "Forty-five minutes?! Cyril! What the—"

"No, no, no. I did not! I-I can explain!" Cyril panics as he hands Eli his pajamas. "Uh…I…when I found you in the shower, you were naked and unconscious."

"Well, no shit, I was naked in the shower! Who the hell wears clothes while showering?! But that's not the point! The point is, after you found me, why didn't you put something on for me while I was out cold in the last forty-five minutes?! What did you do that entire time?!" Eli berates while putting on his pajamas under the blanket.

"No, no, I-I did not look at you without clothes f-for forty-five minutes! I-I was looking into your dream."

"You what—oh," Eli groans, closing his eyes. He rubs his temples to calm himself down. For a moment, he completely forgot about Cyril's dream-peeping superpower and the magical nature of this world he resides in.

"Eli." Cyril's puppy blue eyes brim with fear and concern.

"What?"

"Are you...alright?"

There is a brief pause as Eli truly takes time to think about Cyril's question by evaluating his current physical and mental state. He concludes that aside from his cognitive capacity approaching negative ten, he doesn't feel hurt anywhere on his body, nor does he have any severe headaches right now. "I'm fine."

"Good," Cyril looks relieved.

"Can we just...go to bed? Please?" Eli exhales. He feels so exhausted. His brain is so muddled that it's practically a mass of tofu.

"Yes, let's sleep," Cyril agrees. But before he can put his other leg under the blanket, Eli screeches. "W-What is it, sweetie? Are you hurt?!"

"No, I'm not. Cyril, we can't sleep! I haven't told you what happened in the shower! Faye showed up behind me in her full body, uh, nearly full body, except for her hands and feet and...and her skin was missing. She was covered in blood, and she—"

Eli suddenly goes quiet.

"Sweetheart, what—"

"She's behind you," Eli whispers, his face as white as a sheet.

Cyril wheels around and shields Eli with his large body. Before him, by the tall, open window, a petite, scarlet female silhouette with long black hair and missing hands and feet, is standing with her back facing him.

"Do you see her?" Eli whispers as he creeps closer to his guardian.

"Yes, I do," Cyril murmurs back and slowly gets off the bed with Eli behind him.

Faye remains still at her spot by the window. Then, slowly, she brings her right handless arm up and points at something through the glass.

Cyril and Eli venture near Faye to look out the window. On the opposite block from their room, there is a row of cheap, claustrophobic apartment buildings. Following the direction Faye is pointing, they spot a unit that stands out amidst the myriad of similarly built rooms.

The reason for that unit's uniqueness is that it has blood splattered all over its shabby white walls. Its window is wide open, and the inside of the apartment, from floors to walls to furniture, is covered in blood, just like the exterior.

Faye disappears, and the blood on the suspicious unit also vanishes, with its window now closed and curtained. It looks no different from the rest of the other apartments in the long row of tall buildings. That unit is on the same level as Cyril and Eli's room, directly facing each other.

"Let's go." Cyril grabs Eli by his waist.

"W-What are you doing? Let me change my clothes first!" Eli nags, wiggling in Cyril's arms.

"Why change? You're not going to do anything, sweetheart," Cyril says as he looks at Eli in his short white summer pajamas.

"At least let me put on my shoes!"

As soon as Eli finishes tightening his bootlaces, Cyril carries him princess-style and leaps out of their balcony, making a long jump to the suspicious unit on the other side of the street.

Within seconds, Cyril flawlessly lands on their targeted apartment. Cyril makes a dramatic entrance by blowing the door off with a single kick. The force exerted is so great it sends the poor wooden door airborne right into the opposite wall, making it shatter and creating a large crack in the wall that spreads throughout the room.

"Jesus!" Eli flinches at the deafening racket caused by just a kick.

"What the hell?!" screams a male voice. A tall and well-built man wrapped in bandages bursts into the living room.

An acquaintance, after all: the bandaged man is one of the two murderers who attempted to snatch Eli back in the alleyway earlier this evening. When he sees Cyril, his face twists in sheer horror, and he gasps. "How—"

The bandaged murderer can't finish his sentence as Cyril lands a kick straight to his face, breaking his nose and sending him flying back to the bedroom that he just came out from.

Eli gulps as he sees the murderer smash into his bed, collapse it, and lie motionless between the broken bed frame and torn mattress with his legs up against the wall in a V-pose.

"Roland, what the hell are you—" says another male voice from a room opposite the knocked-out murderer's bedroom. A man in his twenties, also covered in bandages, sticks his head out to the living room to see what the commotion is about. When he sees Cyril, his eyes widen in terror as he immediately slams his door closed.

One simply does not slam *the door* on Cyril.

Ever.

After the second murderer slams the door shut and hides inside his room, that poor door stays closed for two seconds before an immense force blows it off. The door flies into the second murderer and slams him into the wall with a loud bang. A harmonic string of bone-cracking rhythm peals out along with a painful grunt as the murderer collapses to the floor on top of the shattered wood shards with his nose broken and his forehead bleeding. Not yet dead, only out cold.

Eli shudders after glancing at the two murderers lying in their ruined bedrooms. He can't believe they are so easily defeated by just a single kick from a man roughly the same size as them, while also carrying a young man in his arms, no less.

"You alright, sweetheart?" Cyril smiles upon catching Eli staring at him.

Eli says nothing but gives his guardian two big thumbs up.

"Two more, and we're done."

When the other two murderers don't show up in the living room, Cyril begins to kick down the remaining three doors in the apartment. The first two rooms are a bathroom and a bedroom, both empty. The last bedroom, however, is occupied. In the bed, a man wrapped in bloody bandages is moaning in pain. His face is so severely burned that the skin has peeled off, uncovering the raw flesh filled with horrifying blisters.

That miserable bedridden man is the first killer that Cyril and Eli encountered back in the alleyway. He is the cocky one that murdered the two bouncers in cold blood.

"How…" the killer croaks, terror and rage shining in his bloodshot eyes.

"Where is the last one?" Cyril asks.

"You…will…pay." The killer grits his teeth. "My…Lord…will…"

"Pay dearly," Cyril swings up his right hand, and a force yanks the killer out of bed, drags him across the room, and then forces him to kneel before the ravenhead.

"All of you will pay." Cyril stares down at the shaking killer at his feet like he was some kind of vermin.

"Who…are…you?" The rage in the killer's eyes is gone; only pure terror remains.

Cyril waves his hand, and the killer is tossed through the air back to his bed, which he crashes through. The killer ends up lying unconscious on top of the ruined mattress.

Cyril and Eli then search the killers' apartment and find a wooden box in the kitchen cabinet. Inside, it stores a blood-soaked black one-piece swimsuit with a bunny tail at the back, a lock of long black hair, thirty-two bloody teeth, and an entire set of Faye's flayed skin.

They further search and find a hidden room behind the closet in the missing killer's bedroom. Multiple torture devices, a dog cage, adult toys, and chains, all covered in blood, are stored in this secret chamber. It must be where these animals kept Faye before they murdered her.

Eli only manages a quick glimpse inside the horror room before Cyril promptly shuts off the closet. The ravenhead doesn't want him to see too much of it.

When they return to the living room, they hear thunderous footsteps on the creaky wood stairs from the units below. A moment later, the footsteps end before the killers' apartment, and a series of loud knocks hammer on the main door.

Cyril waves a hand, and the door swings open. A group of ten armed men in white uniforms with navy borders burst in, pointing their swords at them. "Halt! You are in the presence of the Hemera Bay Justice in His Majesty's Service! Surrender your weapons now and hold your hands up where we can see them!"

Eli holds his hands up. Cyril lifts a brow at the justice squad's order.

"Get out of my way!" A blond man of forty in an elaborate uniform pushes through the sentinels to get inside the apartment. He seems to be the chief of the justice squad as the sentinels immediately stand aside behind him. He looks up and down at Cyril. "Are you the Fire Sage that sent me the letter?"

"Yes," Cyril says.

"Prove it."

Cyril's arms burst into two colossal columns of roaring blazes, painting the entire apartment in red. Everyone feels the heat except for Cyril and Eli.

"Holy Tathagatas!" the sentinels cry out.

"I am the leader of the Hemera Bay Justice in His Majesty's order, Captain Alwin Eisenhardt. May I ask what happened here, sir?"

Cyril tells Captain Alwin what happened, and the sentinels go through the apartment to collect the evidence and detain the three killers. After the criminals are escorted out of the unit, Cyril asks the captain if he has found the last murderer.

"Indeed, we did, sir. He was captured thirty minutes ago when he showed up at the butcher shop with a bag of the girl's remains. Just as you said in the letter, he came back to check if the pigs had taken care of the butcher's body and was planning to dispose of the rest of the body the same way."

The captain then thanks Cyril and Eli for their assistance in arresting these dangerous killers and offers them a ride home.

"Thank you, captain, but that won't be necessary. We're staying very close to here," Cyril says.

"Oh? Where, sir?"

Cyril points at their room in the building on the other side of the street.

"You got some humor, lad." Captain Alwin chuckles. But when he sees the blank look on Cyril's face, he stops laughing and turns to Eli. "He's not kidding?"

Eli shakes his head.

"You live next door to these murderers?!" Captain Alwin cries.

"We don't live there. It's a rental. We're on vacation," Cyril says, a hint of impatience in his voice. "Are we done here? It's 1:30 in the morning."

The captain apologizes, and everyone makes room for Cyril and Eli to leave the apartment. Eli pats off Cyril's hand when he sees the ravenhead attempting to reach for his waist.

"We are using the stairs," Eli says firmly.

"But why? Our room—" Cyril stops protesting after catching the melting glare from his young master. "We are using the stairs! Let's go."

* * *

THE FIRST THING Eli does after returning to his room is wash his face, brush his teeth, and immediately retreat to bed. He falls asleep as soon as his head touches the pillow. He is too exhausted to say good night to his nan— guardian.

Eli gets to sleep for an hour before waking up again due to thirst. As he opens his eyes, he finds Cyril not in bed but sitting alone in a chair by the window, looking at the killers' apartment unit, his back facing Eli.

"Cyril, what are you doing?" Eli yawns, approaching his guardian, who is holding his head with both hands, trembling. "Are you alright?"

Cyril doesn't respond or even turn around to look at him.

"Cyril, what happened? Are you hurt?" Eli rushes to his guardian's side. He is taken by surprise when Cyril suddenly grabs his hands and pulls him into a tight embrace. "C-Cyril!"

"Forgive me," Cyril whimpers, his voice thick and hoarse. *"Please forgive me."*

Cyril's skin is hot and clammy. His heart is thrashing wildly against his firm chest.

"Cyril, please don't cry," Eli whispers, tightening his arms around his guardian's quivering body. "I'm here. I don't know what to do when you cry.

328

I...I can't help but feel guilty when you cry in front of me," Eli stutters clumsily. "If you keep crying like this, you will make me into a crybaby. A-And when I go to school, I will cry at every little thing, and my classmates will bully me for sure."

Eli hears Cyril's choking laugh amidst the sobbing. "Hey, I'm being serious!"

"I'm listening, sweetheart," Cyril responds, still sniveling, but not as much as before.

Eli tries to pull away to look at his guardian's face, but Cyril refuses to let him move.

"Please let me hold you for a little longer," Cyril pleads, wiping away his tears.

"Fine," Eli sighs. "Don't mind me if I doze off on you."

"Never," Cyril whispers, squeezing Eli even tighter. *"I wouldn't mind if you stayed in my arms forever."*

"...And you mean that in a literal or figurative way?"

"Both."

"So you're fine with carrying me while doing number two?" Eli scrunches his nose in disgust.

"...What does 'doing number two' mean?"

"Pooping," Eli replies.

A long pause starts before Cyril finally speaks in his normal voice. "I think I meant it figuratively."

"What a relief!" Eli sasses one last time before passing out in his guardian's arms.

* * *

CYRIL CARRIES Eli back to bed and puts him down on the mattress. Then he goes to the closet and takes out a clean pajama shirt. He returns to bed to undo the shirt Eli is wearing and puts the new one on him. When he's done, he pulls the blanket up and tucks Eli in.

After that, Cyril walks to the bathroom with Eli's old pajama shirt in his hand. He turns on the sink and starts washing away the bloodstains on the white fabric. In the mirror, the reflection of Cyril's face is smeared with dry blood, especially around the corner of his eyes and cheeks. The ravenhead occasionally glances at himself in the mirror while wringing out the shirt.

When he has successfully gotten rid of all the bloodstains on his young master's pajamas, Cyril hangs the shirt in the bathroom to dry and then hops into the shower.

After he's all cleaned up, he goes back to bed and sees Eli's dry lips. The ravenhead bites back a self-reprimand and leaves to bring back a tall glass of water. He gently guides Eli to rest on his chest and brings the water to his mouth.

Eli frowns and makes a small fuss in his sleep, but eventually empties the glass.

Cyril sighs and puts the glass down at his end table. Then he lies down next to Eli.

Cyril doesn't sleep. He looks at the face of his beloved for a long time.

Through the sheer curtain from his window, Cyril can see the unit in the opposite building across the street is brightly lit and filled with sentinels going in and out. They are searching every single nook and cranny of that filthy apartment and leaving no evidence behind.

"My poor sweetheart," Cyril whispers as tears well up in his eyes once again. His trembling hand carefully reaches for Eli's brown hair as he gently strokes the soft locks in his palm. All the rage and vengeance in his heart simply vanish every time he looks at that little face.

Eli will never know how much his guardian cried that night.

CHAPTER 18

THE TWO FEET

yril and Eli's schedule the next day after the murderers were caught is just as hectic as the previous day. Cyril's initial decision is to return to Glade Mallow first thing in the morning after he has graciously spent a very generous sum of money for Faye's funeral and paid for the fee to move her furniture back to her grandparents' house. However, Eli tells his guardian he wants to attend the poor girl's funeral and help pack up her belongings, especially her books, since Eli feels they might mean a lot to her.

Cyril remains silent for a while before asking Eli why he wants to do that.

"Because she shared the same birthday as me. That day is approaching, and yet only one of us can age," Eli responds.

"That's it?"

"Of course that's it. What other reason do you think I have?!"

Like a scolded puppy, Cyril apologizes and tells Eli he will do anything he wants him to.

* * *

"She wanted to become a mathematician," Cyril says as he flips through the pages of Faye's old assignment. "Very bright girl. She got full marks on advanced calculus and geometry. Calculus and geometry are types of math."

"Yeah, I know. They are hard." Eli sighs sadly. He is sitting on the floor by Faye's bookcase and organizing her books to put them in the moving trunks. "She could have discovered the Maxwell's Equations and changed the world. But thanks to those bastards, we've receded back to a quarter of a century into the future."

"You know calculus and geometry?" Cyril puts down the papers.

"Uh-huh," Eli mumbles absentmindedly as he still focuses on arranging the books.

"How could you possibly know about those subjects?"

Eli stops what he's doing and turns around to his guardian. "Wasn't I supposed to be a 'child prodigy,' according to you?"

"So you forgot how to read and write in Elgarian, but remember the algebraic formulas?"

Eli thinks for a bit and then answers with an uncertain nod. "Yeah...I think so."

Cyril appears pensive. A moment later, he speaks again. "Did you remember?"

"Remember what?" Eli lifts a brow.

"Us."

There is a pause before Eli answers. "No. I don't. I'm sorry."

"What are you apologizing for, sweetheart?" Cyril's brows narrow in perplexity as he starts to approach Eli.

"I'm sorry if I have disappointed you," Eli breathes, his hands unwittingly clenching up. "...I."

Cyril now kneels down, facing Eli, and gives him his full attention.

"...I might never return to be the Ilya you knew," Eli mutters, evading his guardian's eyes. He is too scared to see Cyril's reaction. "...The Ilya that you knew," Eli stops to take a deep breath and gathers all of his courage. "...Might be gone forever."

As soon as the words leave his mouth, Eli immediately regrets them.

Eli flinches when he sees Cyril swing out a hand. His body involuntarily backs away and hits the bookcase behind him.

Eli's frightened jolt throws Cyril off. The ravenhead puts down his hand and stares at Eli in mute surprise and bewilderment. Then his expression softens, and he slowly scoots closer to his young master.

"Eli," Cyril says in his most gentle voice. "Sweetheart. I used to think that the most blessed day of my life was when we first met many years ago. But now, that thinking no longer holds true because the most blessed day of my life till now was the day I found you again."

Eli blinks "Really?"

"Yes. I am serious. In fact, I was never more serious than I am now. I don't live for the past, Eli. The past you are as relevant as my old self back then. Both no longer exist beyond my memories. You, the person I'm seeing with my own eyes right now, are the only one that matters the most to me."

The worry and anxiety on Eli's face vanish as he listens. However, the relief only lasts for a moment before he thinks of something, and his expression becomes wary. "If the past is not important to you, why did you ask me if I remembered it?"

"I asked because I was worried you would become traumatized had you recalled our past along with all the memories of the time you were gone," Cyril's face hardens, but his expression promptly turns to anguish. He pauses for a bit before continuing. "The truth is, Eli, I don't want you to ever remember anything about the past at all. It was nothing but pain and misery and arrant failure on my part. I was young and incompetent. I failed to protect you, and as a result, you were taken away from me. I truly thought I had lost you forever."

"Cyril..." Eli's heart twists when he sees his guardian's blue eyes redden.

Cyril smiles and strokes Eli's soft cheek. "With all the Tathagatas as my witnesses, the only thing I have ever wanted in my entire existence is to protect and give you a fulfilling life. I want you to stay carefree and have only the happiest memories of the future. Can't we just put behind our painful past and start over again?"

"I would really like that."

The ravenhead's grin widens to his ears and his face overflows with elation. He leans in and gives Eli a giddy bear hug.

"Let me help you with the books," Cyril proposes, and the two start to sort out Faye's books together.

A few minutes later, a faint female voice rings out behind them. "Masters."

Cyril and Eli freeze, but before they can turn around, the voice speaks again. "Please stay where you are. I...I am not presentable for you to look at. I'm sorry to show up again like this. I know you don't want to see me ever again after all the trouble I have caused you. But I want to express my deepest gratitude for your help, masters. You caught the killers and found my body." She breaks down and weeps.

"We're not mad at you, Faye," Eli says as he stares at the bookcase. The temperature in the room has dropped significantly despite the intense summer heat outside.

"I'm so sorry. I didn't mean to scare you. Y-You were the only person who could see me. And you were staying so close to them. I only wanted to tell you what happened. But I couldn't speak. They mutilated my body beyond recognition. I was so desperate. I-I swear I never meant to frighten you like that."

"I'm not...that scared," Eli lies. But his delivery is so bad he might as well shut up, as he can feel Cyril glancing at him with his brow lifted.

Even Faye is not convinced by Eli's statement. "You are very kind, master. You have helped me so much, and I could never repay your kindness. If there is a next life for me, I gladly vow to be in servitude to you both."

"That will not be necessary," Eli and Cyril say together.

Amidst the silent weeping, they hear Faye chuckle faintly. "I'm forever indebted to your unbounded kindness. Since you have helped me so much, may I shamelessly beg you one last favor, masters?"

"What is it?" Cyril asks.

"Please don't inform my grandparents I have gone. Both are senile. The only thing they remember is the memory of when I got accepted to university, and that was years ago. If they learn what happened to me, they will not be able to live on," Faye sobs bitterly. "Please tell them I have found a job abroad. On the top of the bookcase to the left, you will find a small box behind the row of yellow books. That's all the money I saved. It's not much, but enough for them to get by in a year or two."

"Faye, don't worry about money. Those killers will have their assets forfeited, and all the funds will be sent to your family and the victims' they have slain. I promise your grandparents will be taken a good care for the rest of their lives," Cyril says in a firm voice. "As for the killers, I will make sure they get the penalty they deserve."

Faye tearfully thanks them again and tells them they can donate all her books to the local library since she can't use them anymore.

"Except for the three books at the bottom shelf on the far right." Faye's voice drops suddenly.

Cyril picks up one of the books, and Eli tilts his head to look at it. This book has a blue cover and features an illustration of a couple in sheer clothing sensually embracing each other under the moonlight.

Cyril gasps and flips the book to hide it from Eli, but in doing so, exposes the illustration of the couple from the front cover now canoodling while wearing their birthday suits on the back cover.

"They are not mine. The librarian down the street lent them to me," Faye explains mortifyingly and then disappears for good.

* * *

AFTER CYRIL and Eli finish packing all of Faye's books into the moving trunks, the ravenhead instructs the movers to deliver them to the nearest library and take care of the rest of the girl's furniture. He even thoughtfully wraps up the three racy novels in a handkerchief and asks for them to be returned to the librarian...down the street.

Despite Captain Alwin's request for them to show up at the sentinels' central hall in the morning to give testimony against the murderers, Cyril decides not to go. Instead, he sends out another triple-stamped letter to the captain. After that, the two go out for lunch and then return to the inn to change into black attire, which only Cyril has since he didn't buy any black clothing for Eli. Eli ends up wearing the darkest outfit he has: a navy sailor suit with knee-length shorts and a matching beret. The pair then leaves for the Hemera Bay cemetery to attend Faye's funeral.

The unfortunate news of Faye's passing travels fast. The cemetery is nearly packed with a motley of people, from young to old, bidding a final farewell to the poor girl. There are Einar and the entire Seaside Cottontail Grill's staff, along with some of the restaurant patrons, Faye's classmates and professors, her landlady and neighbors, her male suitors, and even her strip club coworkers and ex-boss, Madam Cactus, are attending the interment (without revealing Faye's part-time job). Faye was indeed very popular, just as Einar said.

It is an emotional afternoon. After the ceremony is over, Einar thanks Cyril and Eli for everything they did for Faye and says it is an honor to assist them with the murder case.

Cyril smiles and thanks Einar for his help. He gives Einar a paper with some cursive writing, telling the man he can reach out to Cyril should he run into any trouble in the future. Then, Cyril and Eli say goodbye to the kind man and leave the cemetery. A carriage packed with their suitcases from the inn has already waited by the gate to take them straight to the train station.

Cyril was not kidding when he said he wanted to get Eli out of Hemera Bay as soon as possible!

* * *

ELI IS glum during the train home, and this concerns Cyril. The ravenhead starts to make small jokes, hoping to brighten his spirit. By the fifth time Cyril attempts to juggle twelve balls simultaneously, Eli finally has enough and elbows the ravenhead hard in his ripped chest.

"Can you please stop doing that before I throw up all over the cabin?" Eli nags with an annoyed pale face due to all the nauseating circus tricks his idiot nanny has been performing.

"Oh no! How are you feeling now?!" Cyril cries out.

"Terrible! Urg!" Eli clasps his hands over his mouth. "Why did you pack a dozen balls to a vacation?! What's the purpose of them?!"

"Oh...I didn't pack them, sweetheart. I just made them up," Cyril simpers silly grins as he hands Eli a cup of tea. Then, he quickly gathers the juggling balls scattered on the floor.

"Oh, I see," Eli blinks as he drinks the tea. But by the second sip, he finds an absurdity in Cyril's answer.

"W-What did you mean you just made them?" Eli asks in shock.

Cyril appears clueless, which is typical of him, so Eli clarifies. "The balls, Cyril. You said you didn't pack them with you, so where did you get them from?"

Cyril now finally gets it and gasps in utter astonishment. His hands let go of the balls, but they all disappear into thin air before any of them hit the ground.

"What the actual—" Eli jolts, staring in disbelief at the empty floor.

There is a moment of silence, then Cyril speaks up. "I wanted to cheer you up...I thought about the balls, and they...appeared on the table."

"Cyril, all the times you have been conjuring candies out of thin air for me, did you possess them, or did you just think about them and make them appear?"

"I had those candies. These balls, I didn't," Cyril responds pensively.

"So this is the first time this has ever happened? You conjuring things to appear from nowhere?" Eli asks.

"I think so," Cyril seems to think hard about something, and then suddenly, he slaps his hands together. "Ah! Last night! The colorful papers!"

"Colorful papers? What?" Eli is confused.

"Last night, I didn't have any colorful paper scraps, but they appeared along with the candies!" Cyril cries, overwhelmed with excitement.

Eli thinks, and a few seconds later, he finally understands what Cyril is saying. Last night, after they escaped the ghost armies from the Netherworld Realm, Cyril gave him three pink candies he pulled out from a puff of pink smoke and confetti.

"Those colorful paper scraps are called confetti," Eli says. "You have never bought any confetti before?"

"No, I didn't know what they were called until you just told me," Cyril discloses.

"Cyril, are you telling me you can...make things you don't have to appear

from thin air?" Eli whispers so that the conversation is only audible between the two of them.

Cyril stares at Eli in silence; eventually, he falters, "I-I'm not really sure... But I think...Yes?"

"This is so sick, dude!" Eli cries, no longer able to contain his excitement. However, Cyril recoils with a visibly hurt expression on his face. "No! Sick here means awesome, great, Cyril!" Eli sighs.

"Ah! Like lit, right?" silly Cyril is happy again.

"Yes! You are really amazing, Cyril!" Eli genuinely compliments, and Cyril blushes.

"I think we should keep it down, just to be safe," Eli cautiously lowers his voice.

"Good thinking!" Cyril giggles. "However, you don't have to worry too much about that, sweetheart. I'm quite certain the two cabins beside us are empty."

Nonetheless, the two still lean in closer to each other to discuss their spectacular discovery.

Cyril begins to test his newfound ability by summoning a white beret identical to the one Eli lost last night during their thrilling chase after the Darya murderers.

"Cyril, this is unbelievable!" Eli exclaims as he looks at the hat in awe.

Cyril then conjures a little puppy with white fur and a light brown spot on his left eye.

"Oh my goodness, Cyril! He's so cute!" Eli's eyes are starry as he is wholly smitten by the pup's adorableness.

Cyril smiles as he watches Eli melt in bliss when the little pup licks his cheek and makes a cute bark at him.

"I love animals," Eli gushes while cuddling the puppy. Now that he looks closer at this little cutie, he resembles the dog face icon on Eli's smartphone from his past life...Quite a lovely coincidence?

"I see," Cyril chuckles.

"Isn't he the cutest thing ever?" Eli swoons and the pup makes happy barks.

"He is quite cute, but you are and always will be the cutest thing in my eyes," Cyril fawns.

"You learned nothing from the Pretty Green-Eyed Octopus incident, didn't you?" Eli gently reminds Cyril while desperately trying to maintain a straight face; the little pup, on the other hand, makes a soft growl and gives Cyril side eyes.

"I'm just stating the fact," Cyril laughs fondly. Then, he conjures up a small cracker and brings it to the puppy. "Am I right?"

The puppy finishes the cracker and licks Cyril's fingers as an act of accepting the truce.

Next, Cyril waves his fingers, and a gigantic bouquet of red roses appears from a puff of glittery golden smoke. Then he hands Eli the flowers.

"Oh…Thank you," Eli is a little caught off guard by the gallant gesture as he awkwardly takes the massive bouquet. Cyril is thoughtful by making the roses thornless. Each flower is perfect and in its full bloom.

"It's my pleasure," Cyril smiles charmingly.

"They are beautiful," Eli comments. He wonders what the meaning of twenty-nine roses is.

"They are not even a fraction as beautiful as you are," Cyril laughs.

Eli almost falls off the chair upon hearing that corny compliment. But before Eli can say anything, a distinct snicker breaks out.

But...weren't the two cabins beside them vacant?

Eli opens his mouth, but Cyril gestures to him to quiet.

Cyril's solemn face scares Eli. The ravenhead signals Eli to stay put in silence, then he gets up from his seat, goes outside, and closes the door.

Cyril approaches the cabin on the left and knocks on its door. After a few seconds pass without any response, the ravenhead opens the door to find an empty room. Then he does the same thing to the right cabin and gets the same result: both spaces are unoccupied.

However, these findings don't ease Cyril's mind at all. His expression becomes even more serious. Without moving from his spot, Cyril listens through every single noise and conversation from every compartment of the moving train, from the locomotive to the last car, searching for any anomalies. He never lets his and Eli's cabin out of his sight the entire time.

Cyril finds nothing out of the ordinary or any sign of a supernatural presence. Eventually, he goes back to his cabin.

Cyril finds Eli lying half-face down on the leather bench, his eyes closed, and one arm hanging off the edge of the seat. The rose bouquet lies scattered on the floor along with his navy beret and the motionless puppy.

Cyril stands frozen in the doorway. Then his legs stumble to the ground, and his shaking hands reach for his beloved's face. "Eli?" Cyril calls his name. No response. Eli's skin and lips are still pink, but he is not breathing. Cyril grabs Eli's wrist to check for a pulse. There is none.

"No...Eli...no," Cyril's voice breaks. Disbelief, confusion, and terror shroud his blue eyes.

"W-Wake up. Please," Cyril stutters, grabbing Eli's cheek. "No...not again...please..."

That is when his eyes catch the sight of two pairs of barefoot male feet under the table on the opposite bench. Cyril immediately looks up and sees no one in front of him. Right at that moment, his vision suddenly turns dark, and his ears ring as indomitable drowsiness floods over him to the point he can't stay sitting up.

Cyril grits his teeth. With one arm holding Eli tightly, the other shakily summons a fire, but not even a spark appears. All the veins are popping on his arms, neck, and forehead. His eyes become bloodshot as he tries to fight off the lassitude. But it only makes him even more drained. Blood starts to trickle from his nose and lips.

Cyril resists the sleeping spell for another two minutes before he is finally defeated.

The ravenhead slips into unconsciousness with Eli in his arms.

The weather outside is still bright and windy. The mid-afternoon sun rays cast their sparkling orange shades onto the train windowsill, where they bounce a steady rhythm like a soft summer waltz.

* * *

"CYRIL! CYRIL, WAKE UP!" Eli cries, wriggling to break away from his guardian's iron grip.

It takes a little more time till the ravenhead wakes up. And as soon as he does, his right arm swings out and bursts with a ferocious, scorching blaze.

"S-Sir, calm down!" two conductors jump back in horror. They reacted fast; both narrowly escaped getting burned.

"Cyril, stop!" Even Eli, who is usually immune to Cyril's fire, feels the heat this time.

Eli shivers when Cyril looks at him. He has seen Cyril mad before, but this is the first time he sees Cyril's enraged face up close in broad daylight.

All Eli can say is he hopes he is not the reason for the face Cyril is making. To describe the ravenhead's expression as frightening is an understatement.

But Cyril instantly mellows after looking at Eli; thus, the menacing fire on his right arm soon dissipates.

"You're alive." Cyril's lips tremble. The deadly rage on his face is gone, and in its place are astonishment and fright. "You are still alive!"

Cyril then hugs Eli so tight that he gasps for air.

The poor conductors breathe out in relief that the "fiery" passenger has finally calmed down, and the situation is under control. They inform Cyril that the train arrived at the station forty-five minutes ago. Eli and Cyril are the only passengers left.

Cyril's eyes sweep around the cabin; there's no sight of the rose bouquet, the white hat, or the puppy. When he asks the conductors, the two men seem surprised and tell him they didn't see any of the things Cyril mentioned when they first got inside Cyril and Eli's room.

* * *

THE CARRIAGE TRIP home is eventful. The moment Cyril and Eli get inside the cab, the ravenhead does a full health check on Eli: listening to his heartbeat and pulse, checking for any injury, then searching for signs of hex or curse. When Cyril finally confirms Eli is healthy and not under any curse, he hugs Eli and has a breakdown, babbling about what happened and how he thought he had lost Eli forever. Again.

Eli rubs Cyril's large back and consoles him. Under a different circumstance, he would have deemed Cyril's excessive behaviors overprotective and neurotic. However, this time, Eli thinks Cyril's panic is valid. He tells Cyril that a few seconds after Cyril went out to check for the mysterious chuckling noise, an immense surge of sleepiness took over him and he passed out.

Eli also confirms with Cyril the existence of the roses, the white hat, and the puppy, so unless they were both asleep and shared the same dream the entire trip, somebody drugged them (somehow) and took away all the stuff that Cyril conjured up.

But whoever did that to them did not touch their money or belongings.

Cyril tells Eli about seeing the two supernatural, shoeless male feet under the table on the train before Cyril was attacked by a powerful sleeping spell.

"Spooky," Eli shudders. "Cyril, how are you feeling now? Are you hurt anywhere?"

Poor Cyril looks two years older than when he got on the train in the afternoon. He is *that* traumatized by what happened.

"I'm fine, sweetheart. Don't worry. It's just minor bleeding." Cyril smiles, rubbing his nose and lips.

"You were injured?!" Eli exclaims and gazes at his guardian from head to toe. He doesn't see any blood and wounds on Cyril. "Where is it? Where are you hurt?"

Cyril is stumped by Eli's puzzled expression. Then he takes out his multi-purpose silver dagger from his blazer and looks at his reflection on the gleaming blade. There is no trace of blood anywhere on his gorgeous face.

"What?" Cyril's brows knit together. He was sure that not just his nose and lips were bleeding; many blood vessels inside his body busted as well during his resistance to the sleeping spell.

"Cyril, are you alright?" Eli falters. Cyril is making that scary face again.

Despite his somber façade, the ravenhead still gives Eli a small pat on the head and smiles at him. Then, his eyes switch back to the empty space before him, and he begins to focus. Cyril snaps his fingers, making a pop.

Eli holds his breath and waits.

Nothing happens.

Cyril snaps his fingers six more times, and just like before, nothing happens. The ravenhead then puts two hands up like he is waiting to catch something that is about to drop off from the sky. He remains in that completely concentrated state.

Still, nothing happens.

Eli was expecting some magical revelations. Instead, he gets to witness the comical transition of his guardian's expressions from utter seriousness to wide-eyed puppyish confusion.

Personally, Eli likes the last expression the most, of course.

"Um...Cyril, have you considered that maybe everything that happened on that train was just...a dream?" Eli says after some hesitation.

Cyril appears unconvinced and a little flustered. He looks like he wants to disagree with Eli's point, but he doesn't know how to refute it.

"I mean, it's not the first time we shared the same vivid dream with each other, right?" Eli says.

"That was a nightmare."

After all, the ability to create things from thin air is far-fetched, even by the Sage standards. From what Eli has learned from Cyril about Sages so far, while they seem magical and physically stronger than humans, they aren't Gods. They still have to work to earn money and make ends meet.

"Welp, cheer up, Cyril! We are both alive and well and not...cursed. That's the most important thing, isn't it?" Eli grins, trying to lift his guardian's spirit. "I suppose we both shared the same nightmare is because of all the dreadful events we went through yesterday had finally caught up to us. I can't wait to get home and take a long shower. I miss home!"

* * *

ELI'S HEART leaps with happiness when he spots their fairytale cottage behind the birch grove. It is a little past 6:30 PM; the sun hasn't fully set yet, and the house is basking in the golden stream of lights.

"We're home! Home sweet home!" Eli exclaims cheerily after they get inside the house, while Cyril only lets out a big, worn-out sigh.

"I'm so sorry, my little kit," Cyril says. "This vacation was a complete disaster. I'm a failure of a guardian."

Not again. Eli sighs and makes a face. But he quickly puts on a patient look and turns to his fragile guardian. "No. It was not a disaster at all, Cyril. We solved a murder case. We brought justice to an innocent girl and helped put away a very dangerous group of serial killers. If anything, I would say this vaca—trip was very...meaningful and...good! And you are not a failure! You are a wonderful man and an amazing nan—guardian!" He gives his guardian an encouraging pat on the arm.

Eli's liveliness and positivity finally ease Cyril's mind. The ravenhead looks at him softly and says, "Thank you, my dearest. You're such an angel, always be so kind and forgiving to my glaring incompetence."

Eli scowls at Cyril, putting his hands on his hips. *Did my encouraging words mean zip to you?!*

"Ay, don't be angry, my sweet. I got you." Cyril giggles and affectionately pinches Eli's cheek. "I just want to say I promise I'll try my best to be worthy of your gracious praise."

* * *

AFTER BRINGING THE LUGGAGE UPSTAIRS, Eli suggests Cyril to shower first as he wants to unpack and rest a bit. Cyril agrees and heads to the bathroom, leaving Eli alone in their bedroom.

Eli hops into his bed right after he finishes unpacking and putting away his suitcase.

"Home's the best," Eli moans blissfully, burying his face in his fluffy silk pillow.

Cyril has spoiled him so much that Eli's becoming a snobby brat. That's bad!

As Eli rolls around in bed reflecting, he unwittingly notices the top left corner of the fittest sheet is hiked up halfway.

That's odd. Eli thinks and reaches out a hand to tuck in the sheet. While Eli does not have OCD tendencies (like Cyril), he is not a slob. After his legs were healed, Eli has always been making his own bed, and he's sure that he *always* tucks the fitted sheet underneath the mattress properly.

A few seconds later, a thought flashes through Eli's mind; he immediately sits up from his bed and lifts the top of the mattress up.

DESPITE THE SILLY, goofy appearance he puts up for Eli, the whole "nightmare" ordeal on the train this afternoon still deeply bothers Cyril. He is not entirely convinced that this incident was "just a dream." For once, Cyril knows he did not fall asleep at any time prior to encountering the sleeping spell. Second, there was no foul play in the food or drink he and Eli consumed on the train, which could lead to unconsciousness and hallucination. Third, Cyril was injured during the silent resistance to the spell. And fourth, he was certain his beloved did stop breathing in his arms.

Cyril clenches his fists as he recalls that horrific memory. The thought still sends chills down his spine; that is to say, Cyril is not in any way faint of heart.

But then, if all of that were real, how could his sweetheart still be alive right now?

The two pairs of barefoot male feet, those entities, also healed Cyril's wounds and wiped off the blood on his face. What kinds of enemies do that?

Whatever they are, Cyril is sure they can't be Sages and certainly are not mere humans. No. He's dealing with something much more powerful than that.

...Could it be—

Cyril's musing is interrupted as the bathroom door suddenly slams open, along with a scream of his name.

"Eli—" Cyril yanks open the shower curtain.

"Someone was in the house when we were away!" Eli cries out. "And they were on my bed!"

* * *

"You were right. Indeed, someone was here when we weren't home," Cyril concludes after a minute of standing in silence with his eyes closed.

"He was on your bed," Cyril mutters ominously.

"H-How can you tell it was a man?" Eli asks.

"It doesn't smell like a woman." Cyril turns to Eli. "How did you detect an intruder was here?"

"Well, I don't really know how I did it...I just felt a strong presence of a stranger in our bedroom."

Eli knew someone was here because the yellowing envelope addressed to Ilya, which Eli hid under the left corner of his mattress, was gone. He is sure it was still there before he went on vacation with Cyril.

"Could the intruder be one of the kidnappers that abducted me years ago?" Eli asks.

"No, it wasn't them."

"How can you be so sure?"

"It's the scent," Cyril answers, and Eli lifts a brow. "It wasn't the same as those who took you...years ago."

The mention of the kidnappers aggravates Cyril's temper. His face turns ominous and ruthless.

"Alright, I guess I'll have to be extra hygienic from now on since you have such a spectacular sense of smell. I don't want to be a stinky, smelly housemate."

"You don't have to, sweetheart. You always smell like the sweetest flower in the world to me, no matter what," Cyril chuckles.

Before Eli can respond, he is interrupted by a string of knocks at the front door downstairs. Cyril and Eli get down to answer the door. It turns out to be all four of their neighbor friends.

"We saw the light, so we decided to check out," Wolfgang says. "Why did you come back so soon? Did something happen during the trip?"

Cyril says nothing but lets out an exasperated huff. He jerks his head, beckoning the neighbors to come inside.

"Why are you in a towel in front of...Eli?" Haidar gives Cyril a disapproving look.

After hearing Eli's distressed call, Cyril jumped out of the shower and didn't even have time to put on his clothes or a robe. He only has a towel around his waist.

Cyril shrugs. "Did any of you come to my house when I was away?"

The question baffles the neighbors, and they all say no.

Cyril then briefly tells them about the home invasion, the homicide case during his vacation, and the nightmare incident on the train.

"I will fill you in during dinner. Now, go get me some ingredients for hot pot," Cyril tells his utterly flabbergasted neighbors. "And a new mattress as well."

ELI'S SHOWER took fifteen minutes. When he gets out, he finds his bed already made with a new mattress, and dinner is ready. When he asks Cyril if one of their neighbors has given them a spare mattress, Cyril tells him Wolfgang just bought it brand new at a shop in town.

The town is twenty minutes from the house, traveling one way by carriage. None of their neighbors have horses, so unless Wolfgang possesses a jet pack or has access to a destination portal, it takes supreme speed and strength to carry a new mattress from town to here in such a brief time. This confirms Eli's hunch about Wolfgang's Sage identity.

Not just Wolfgang—Eli has always suspected all his neighbors are Sages. Except for Gallahan, since he is still a child, all his neighbors are good-looking, have athletic builds, and possess a composed and capable aura similar to Cyril's.

The hot pot dinner is scrumptious, with abundant side dishes and fresh vegetables. Yet, aside from Eli, no one seems to have an appetite for such a feast, as they all focus on Cyril's story.

Cyril is very thorough and honest, sparing no details. After he finishes his story, the neighbors turn to Eli and console him, asking him if he's feeling well and so on.

"I'm fine! Didn't get a single scratch. Please don't worry," Eli beams. He knows the caring and affection his neighbor friends have for him is genuine, and it makes him very moved and ever grateful for their constant support. "Cyril was a real hero. He has always protected me and looked after me so well."

However, his neighbors don't share Eli's sentiment regarding Cyril's nanny efficiency. They turn to the ravenhead and nag him to pieces.

Cyril doesn't argue back as he takes in the heavy criticism, which is a little surprising to Eli. Cyril, as courteous and gentle as he appears to be, is quite unreceptive about being reproached by anyone unless it comes from Eli.

Eli can't bear to see his guardian under fire. It's not fair. Thus, he must convince his neighbors how wonderful of a guardian Cyril is and how Eli always feels safe and happy under Cyril's care. He also emphasizes that what happened during the trip was partly his fault, as he was staring at things he shouldn't look at.

Deep down, Eli knows he is an extremely unlucky person. His presence often brings bad luck to people close to him, even in his previous life.

Cyril is probably the only person who still stands by him after all the horrific trouble he has caused so far.

"Eli, none of this was your fault! How could you think like that?!" Cyril and his neighbors exclaim.

"It was entirely this clodhopper's fault. I specifically told him not to take you to the beach, and he kept persisting in bringing you there!" Gallahan says. "And you were attacked and injured by two despicable fiends just last week!"

"That incident was his fault as well! If he didn't leave you roaming alone at the fair unprotected, you wouldn't have run into that vile witch!" Mariposa snaps.

"In less than a month, he has repeatedly caused you many injuries, both directly and indirectly! The first time he dropped you on the floor and the second time at the serpent vivarium, I reluctantly wrote them off as freak accidents. Then came the midsummer witch affair, and now this whole vengeful ghost, reckless mass murderers' pursuit, and taking you to the Netherworld Realm!?" Haidar loses his last shred of cool. "Cyril, what in the world were you thinking?!"

"Not even at my worst drunk would I ever consider involving Eli in a *human* serial killer hunt, much less they are a group of deranged Sage killers," Wolfgang grits his teeth. He looks like he's refraining from punching Cyril. "Why did you act alone? The afternoon after you encountered one of those killers at the clinic, you should have called us. You should have called ME! I would have been there in just a few hours and helped you catch them. Or look after Eli."

Suddenly, Eli feels like a child in a heated custody battle between Cyril and their neighbors. He didn't expect everyone to react so strongly, especially Haidar, as he has always been the most mature and collected among the group.

Eli feels it's a bit harsh and unfair that his neighbors are being so critical of Cyril. As amazing and tough as Cyril is, he's still not a God. How could everyone expect him to be invincible all the time? Also, Eli thinks Cyril did a marvelous job solving the complex murder case of Faye and capturing all the killers on his own in just a day. That was insane now that Eli thinks about it; the entire Hemera Bay PD oversaw this case for a month, and they didn't get anywhere.

Eli respectfully tells everyone what is on his mind. He first thanks them for their concerns and then emphasizes that without Cyril, he would not be able to sit here in one piece and get to know all these wonderful people.

"Cyril can be a bit clumsy at times, but that's true of any of us. I am truly grateful he is my guardian," Eli says and looks at Cyril. "I already told you this last night, but I will say it again. You are the most amazing person I have ever met, Cyril. I can't possibly think of having anyone other than you as my guardian. Thank you for always looking after me and protecting me."

The atmosphere in the room suddenly splits into two distinct spheres. On Cyril's side, the air of triumph, bliss, and complacency heightens, while on the neighbors', it is the complete opposite. Though it's not like there is intense animosity or any extreme feelings. The neighbors all carry a complicated and resentful look, and these negative emotions aren't directed at Eli but the ravenhead.

...Eli never dreams that there are people, aside from klutzy Cyril, would want to adopt him this much.

Bruh.

"I am truly and eternally grateful you think that highly of me. Thank you, sweetheart." Cyril grins softly at Eli and pats his brown locks. Then he turns to their neighbors and makes the smuggest face, adding fuel to the fire.

Cyril, you little—

The neighbors' mouths already hung open when they heard Cyril address Eli as "sweetheart." Then, when they see Cyril's punch-able expression, they get real hissy-pissy.

"Hey, shouldn't we talk about the intruder?" Eli asks. "There seemed to be no sight of breaking in. Did you happen to leave a spare key under the flowerpot by the door or something?"

"No, Eli. Who would leave a spare key out of their house? That's no different than inviting the burglars in," Cyril wrinkles his nose. "But don't worry, my dear. I'll make sure no one can break into our house ever again. Even in the astral world. And when I catch that intruder, I'll break...I will not let him off easily."

Eli thinks he saw his neighbors' expressions change again, but it's very brief.

"Oh, and I'm thinking of sending Eli to school," Cyril announces.

"What the actual—are you insane?!" the neighbors exclaim angrily.

Crap, here we go again.

CHAPTER 19

THE BALLAD OF SCARLET

The next morning, Cyril has their house locks changed. Then, he spends the following days making it up to Eli after the nightmarish vacation. Aside from all the gifts like new clothes, flowers, and sweets, Cyril takes Eli to a picnic at the most beautiful lake in Glade Mallow, to visit museums, scenic landscapes, and parks, fine-dining at fancy vegan restaurants, and hosting lavish al fresco luncheons with their neighbor friends.

Cyril also takes Eli to a gallery to have their express portrait done. A Sage artist looks at him and Cyril from head to toe for three seconds and then shows them an album with empty background paintings. Cyril chooses the backdrop he likes and pays the money. The Sage artist informs him the portrait will be sent to their residence in seven to ten days.

"Wait, that's it?" Eli is shocked. It hasn't even been two minutes since he entered this store. "You don't need us to pose or do anything?"

The Sage artist laughs and explains to Eli posing for a painting is a very dated human practice. Sage portrait artists don't need their clients to sit still for hours as they can accurately visualize the customers' pose and movement with just a quick glance.

Eli is mad-impressed. This whole process is faster than taking passport photos at CVS.

* * *

ONE MORNING, Eli is woken by a fluffy surprise; a white and brown Pomeranian puppy with a teddy bear cut is ogling him with its big eyes!

Eli lets out an ecstatic squeal and springs up from his bed so fast he doesn't even notice the gigantic fresh rose bouquet on the nightstand.

The little Pom hops into his laps and makes cute introductory barks. Eli spends the next minute oohing and aahing at the puppy.

"I'm glad you both are getting along so well." Cyril smiles, leaning against the bedroom door.

"Cyril, when did you get him? He's sooo adorable!" Eli buries his left face into the pup's fluffy fur. "You didn't conjure him out from the air, did you?"

After the day of the train incident, Cyril tried to conjure things many times but never succeeded. It was as if the whole scenario on that train was truly just a shared dream between him and Eli.

"I adopted her two days ago and kept her at Wolfgang's place till now. So, you don't have to worry about her disappearing later on." Cyril laughs and approaches his bed next to Eli's.

"Her?" Eli flips the Pom around, which is indeed a "she."

"Happy birthday, my dearest Eli!" Cyril suddenly pops a confetti cannon, startling Eli and the pup.

"Aw, thank you, Cyril. She is so very adorable. This is the best gift you have ever given me!" Eli chuckles at his guardian while the Pom pup paws at the raining confetti.

Cyril beams dotingly at him. However, shortly after, Eli has a second thought.

"Well, maybe that's not entirely true," Eli mumbles, looking at the Pom pup in his arms.

Cyril's eyebrows rise at Eli's statement. Eli's cheeks turn pink.

"Yes?" Cyril gently tugs Eli's sleeve hem, urging him to finish what he has wanted to say. He also gives Eli a bonus irresistible puppy eyes glance.

"You...are the best gift...to me," Eli tries to say with a straight face, but the stuttering and rosy cheeks give him away. "I-I'm gonna go change." Eli puts the puppy into Cyril's hands and scurries to the bathroom, fleeing the scene.

The Pom barks at Cyril, who then snuggles her to his chest.

"Your young master is adorable, isn't he?" Cyril blushes, grinning at the pup.

* * *

AFTER ELI HAS breakfast with Cyril, Wolfgang and Gallahan come over to ask him to spend time with them in town. Eli hesitates as he and Cyril plan to prepare for their birthday party together. However, the ravenhead seems on board with the outing idea. He tells Eli that Haidar and Mariposa have already volunteered to help with the cooking and decoration.

"Today is your birthday. You can't do anything but have fun!" Cyril strokes Eli's brown locks. Then he turns to Wolfgang and Gallahan, and his expression swiftly turns neutral. "I entrust him to you. Don't let him out of your sight even just a moment."

"I will look after him with my life," Wolfgang responds solemnly.

"If anything happens to Eli, even just a scratch, I will not forgive you. I'm serious," Cyril says.

"Huh! Look who's talking?!" Wolfgang's handsome face darkens. "That should be my line, you ninny! How many times did you get master in bandages again this past month?"

"Hey, guys, chill! I'm just going to town. You two act like I'm leaving for a pilgrimage overseas." Eli throws incredulous glances at both immature men before him.

"Eli, don't bother. These two have always been over-the-top. It runs in their blood, and you can't change it," Gallahan says, holding Eli's hand and giving him the sweetest smile. "I will protect you."

"Aw, thank you very much." Eli kneels down to give Gallahan a big hug, which makes the boy extremely happy.

Gallahan shoots Cyril and Wolfgang the smuggest gaze over Eli's shoulder and mouths, *Jealous?*

To Eli's disbelief, the ravenhead and Captain Seven Seas get genuinely pissed at an eight-year-old boy's taunt.

"You brat!" Cyril barks.

"I'm gonna kick your—" Wolfgang glares at Gallahan.

"Eli, they are bullying me!" Gallahan hides behind Eli's back.

"Dude! Dude! Are you two freaking kidding me right now?" Eli snaps and glares at both men. "You two should stay home and work it out with each other. I know the road to town. I'll go out with just Gallahan!"

"No. I'm sorry!" Cyril and Wolfgang cry out simultaneously.

In the end, Wolfgang still accompanies Eli and Gallahan to town while Cyril stays home to cook with Haidar and Mariposa.

* * *

WOLFGANG TAKES Eli and Gallahan to a popular local winery up on a sprawling green hill, where Wolfgang spends two hours giving an expert critique on each glass of wine and beer he has been sampling while the boys are nibbling on dry, salted pretzels and grape juice unenthusiastically. By the time Wolfgang is about to deliver his thirty-sixth speech on a magnificent twenty-five-year-old Pinot Noir, Gallahan mercilessly kicks him in his shin.

"Hey! Today is Eli's birthday, NOT your birthday! Are you intended to make us cart your drunk bum home or what?!" Gallahan berates as he kicks Wolfgang's legs repeatedly.

"Well, since it's my seventeenth birthday, maybe I can have a sip of the low alcohol—" Eli insinuates, but both Wolfgang and Gallahan promptly turn him down with a firm "No!"

* * *

THEIR NEXT STOP is a theater in downtown Glade Mallow. Eli is pretty excited, as Cyril has not taken him to see a play before. According to the hand-drawn posters, four plays are currently showing.

"Mmm, definitely not *The Beacon of Forsaken Love Part Eight*," Gallahan comments, looking at the first poster featuring two black silhouettes embracing each other in front of a lighthouse in the sunset.

Is it me, or did the title of the play sound really familiar? Eli scratches his head.

"Dangerous Liaison." Wolfgang grimaces at the second poster of an aristocratic woman surrounded by two gorgeous men possessively holding each of her hands.

"I think we should see this play: *The Bizarre Adventures of Dalmatian Bunny and Albino Raccoon,"* Wolfgang says, pointing at the third poster, which shows two titled furry animals gleefully skipping and holding hands in a forest.

Eli and Gallahan concurrently shoot Wolfgang intense side-eyes.

"What? It's kid-appropriate!" Wolfgang states.

"You need to get your head checked. Pronto!" Gallahan snaps, shaking his little head as he points at the poster. "That's the most disturbing thing I've seen this week!"

"Hey guys, what about this play? What does it say?" Eli points at the fourth poster that features a mysterious silhouette of a person wearing a golden crown circled by twelve heraldic flags.

"Oh," Wolfgang and Gallahan mutter.

"That's *The Ballad of Scarlet,"* Gallahan answers. "It's about the history of Aspenia and the Emperor."

"Emperor Haemon? Our current ruler?" Eli gasps.

"Yes, that's right," Gallahan responds with a small smile.

"Can we watch this play?" Eli asks, his green eyes gleaming with excitement. He has been wanting to learn about the history of the country he lives in and its well-regarded ruler, but he hasn't had the opportunity until now.

"Oh, is the play not suitable for young children?" Eli asks when he sees a sudden lack of reaction from his friends.

"No, it's not. It's for all ages." Gallahan shakes his little head. "Would you like to watch this play?"

"I do. Or do you guys want to see something else?"

"Nah. I just realized I need to catch up with history. Let's watch *The*

Ballad of Scarlet." Wolfgang laughs and proceeds to buy the tickets to attend the play.

* * *

THEY ENTER twenty minutes early before the show starts. The auditorium is packed with people, mainly ladies dressed to the nines, as they are giggling and gushing about the male lead who plays Emperor Haemon and going on about how handsome and impressive he is. From what Eli can overhear from the ladies, Aster Glendrome, the lead actor, resembles the real Aspenian Ruler so much that they wouldn't be able to distinguish them if both men were to be in the same room.

Spot on casting, I guess, Eli thinks. The girls' gossiping has piqued his full interest in the upcoming show.

"I heard Aster is a fire Sage. Isn't it amazing? I think this play is going to be marvelous!" says the young lady in pink in front of Eli.

"The impresario of this theater must have spent quite a fortune on this play and the troupe," the young lady in blue comments. "I wonder why Mister Glendrome wants to become an actor? He could easily find employment as a fire Sage in His Majesty's Service."

"Passion for art, I suppose," the young lady in green giggles to her friends. "And I'm not complaining. Aster is so dreamy!"

"He is!" the pink and blue young ladies swoon.

"Is the Emperor a fire Sage?" Eli asks Wolfgang.

"The Emperor is special," Wolfgang responds. "He can control all the elements, not just fire."

Wolfgang then tells Eli about the Sage Ranking System in Aspenia. Even among the Sages, the ability to control Earth, Water, Air, and Fire is quite rare. Thus, any Sage certified to possess the power regarding the Four Great Elements is automatically grouped in the High Rank—Three Stars, also known as Class A, followed by Class B (Mid Rank—Two Stars), then the last one is Class C (Low Rank—One Star).

The highest Aspenia Sage Rank is Class S (Top rank—Four Stars). Sages in this group can control the Four Great Elements at will. And yet, most Class S Sages usually only control one major element. Emperor Haemon is the only Sage in known history who can control all Four Great Elements at the highest scale.

"Woah," Eli is very impressed. "So, Emperor Haemon is way stronger than an S-class Sage, right? What is his rank, then? Quadruple S?"

Wolfgang and Gallahan break into a hearty laugh.

"The Emperor is above all the ranks, Eli," Gallahan chuckles. "He is acknowledged to be the strongest and most powerful Sage in the world."

"Wow!" Eli exclaims.

"Yes, he is that powerful." Wolfgang and Gallahan nod. "He keeps Aspenia at peace despite an eleven-year-old World War happening right now out there. Nobody dares to invade us, as they are all scared of Emperor Haemon."

Eli then asks if a regular human with no Sage power is considered Class D —Zero Star. Wolfgang chuckles and shakes his head, then tells him that the Aspenia Sage Ranking System only has four official classes. There are many Sages out there who don't belong to any of these classes, as their powers are too mundane or impractical (basically useless). As for regular people with no superpowers (good old humans), if there were a category for them, it would probably be called Class F.

Cyril once told Eli that his superpower is his adorableness (whatever that means!). If Cyril wasn't bluffing and Eli had to rank himself, he would probably fall into Class E (Extremely Useless Sage).

Eli remembers Cyril possesses three intricate medallions that he used as stamping tools to communicate with the sentinel chief during their vacation in Hemera Bay. One of them has a four-star engraving; he wonders if that means Cyril might be a Class S Sage?

Then, the theater announcers inform the audience the show is about to start. The auditorium's lights dim down, and the red curtains begin to rise.

A SHOWMAN in a black tuxedo walks to the center of the stage and bows to the audience. "Ladies and gentlemen, I, Iago Finnerty, on behalf of the Victory Theater and the troupe, would like to express our warmest gratitude and appreciation to you for attending our show today. To our returning audiences, thank you so much for your continuous support. And for the first-time audiences, thank you for choosing Victory Theater. We promise to give you an enjoyable and memorable time. With today's play, I guarantee your experience won't stop at just remarkable. It will be epic. Oh, I'm very sure of that. For this play is a homage to our beloved ruler, the fairest and most benevolent, the Impossible, King among Kings, his Imperial Majesty, Emperor Haemon the Magnificent!"

"Long live His Majesty! Long live the Emperor!" The whole arena roars up as everyone claps and cheers in excitement.

* * *

The Ballad of Scarlet - Act One

PERFORMERS IN DAZZLING and colorful costumes divide the stage into twelve groups. Each holds up a banner that seems to be a regional flag. Eli can only recognize the Darya one based on the tacky cerulean color and the golden seahorse mural.

"Long ago, in the olden days, we were of twelve realms," the troupe sings in unity.

"Eden—Scions of Light and Hegemony," sings the group with a golden eagle on a white flag.

"Darya—From the waves we rose," sings the group with the golden seahorse on a cerulean flag.

"Reinga – Justice and honor reign," sings the group with a golden three-headed wolf on a deep purple flag.

"Mitra – Let there be eternal light," sings the group with a golden sun on an orange flag.

"Candra – Guidance through the darkness," sings the group with a silver moon on a navy flag.

"Karmara – Bones of Mother Earth," sings the group with a golden axe and a silver sword on a brown flag.

"Terra – Pulse of Mother Earth," sings the group with a golden female head with a crown made from green leaves on a brown flag.

"Vesta – Eternal beacon of light," sings the group with a golden fire phoenix on a red flag.

"Nada – Peace and compassion," sings the group with a golden sheep on a sky-blue flag.

"Coro – Silent protectors of the realms," sings the group with a golden spiral emblem on a white flag. The performers wear white outfits with hoods.

"Glenora – Reflection of truth," sings the group with a silver cluster of rhombuses on a lavender flag. The performers dressed in winter attire with fur trims.

"Maska – Evergreen and ever surviving," sings the group with a golden tree on a green flag.

"Our story takes place in the Astasamaya Period, or so it's called the Sunset Era. Though we were safe from foreign forces, life was hardly great. There were injustices and deep ignorance in every realm. Every man for himself. The morality was at an all-time low," sings a female performer in peasant clothes. "The humans were treated like dirt. The orphaned children were sold into slavery, and the elders were left to death by their own flesh and blood in the woods, but all the tragedies outside could never reach the inner castle walls, where the Lords and Ladies lived their finest life."

"Dissidents were growing in number, but we all ended up on the chopping block!" sings a male performer in a peasant costume. "The humans could never stand a chance against the chosen race."

"Until one blessed day, a fire broke out at an evil place in Coro at the death of the night, and the then greedy and depraved ruler had perished in the angry blaze!" the singers throw flowers and confetti all over the stage.

"It was a blessed day indeed! For the successor was a kind and fair Sage. His name was Diamond Heart."

"Saint Diamond Heart!" the female's choir sings in harmony. "His serene beauty was like the silver moon. His heart of diamond was akin to the golden sun."

"Unlike the rest of the Lords, he cared for the weak and feeble human. He opened the gate and welcomed the poor to his realm."

"For the first time ever, the people were given land to grow and farm. The poor children were allowed to go to school just like those from rich homes. No elders were left in the woods. No more women or orphans were captured and sold. The guards no longer dared to beat or kill us. Slavery was abolished in the land of the Wind. Life was magnificent under Saint Diamond Heart's reign."

"Saint Diamond Heart was the heavenly prince in the people's hearts. The stories of his compassionate deeds traveled through the twelve realms to beyond the Seven Seas."

"The other rulers were green with envy and red with anger at the Lord's beauty and benevolent reputation."

"How dare you let those lowly serfs sit beside our precious kin? Allow them to learn how to read and write?" sing three young men in noble clothes with the symbols of Eden, Mitra, and Candra as they lead a group of troops toward the Coro flag. "We will overthrow you and bring the right order back to Coro!"

The music stops, and a fighting scene happens. But it only lasts a few minutes before the nobles are lifted from the ground by an invisible force.

An actor dressed in an elegant white hooded outfit gracefully appears at the center of the stage. Unlike the other soldier performers, he holds no weapon. Yet, as he moves his hands through the air, his floating enemies start to slam into each other repeatedly before they are brought to their knees on the ground.

"They got a real Air Sage to play the Grand Duke? That's incredible!" The audience gasps. Everyone starts to clap and cheer boisterously at the actor in white's appearance.

That character must be Lord Diamond Heart, Eli muses. He thought the character Diamond Heart was Emperor Haemon, but he wasn't.

Eli takes a quick peek at Wolfgang and Gallahan and notices these two don't share the same enthusiasm as the rest of the audience. They both carry a similar strange, unreadable expression on their faces. But it isn't boredom, though, as they seem to pay their full attention to the play.

"Coro, how dare you treat us like this?! Do you know what family we come from?! You can't choose those weak, mortal serfs over us. You are out of your mind! You have betrayed our kind!" The nobles sing while writhing on the stage.

Lord Diamond Heart punches the noble, and fake blood splatters all over the ground.

"Huh? I thought you would bleed gold or silver," Lord Diamond Heart speaks in a dulcet voice as he looks at the red "blood" on his right fist.

"All of you fail to 'teach me a lesson' with that puny Sage 'Power' you're so proud of," Diamond Heart sneers at the word 'power' as he stares down at the nobles under his feet. "What exactly is the difference between you and the...mortal human serfs, again? Ah, talk about mortal, you give me the implication that you are not mortal," he unsheathes his sword.

"C-Coro, what are you doing?!" The defeated nobles sing fearfully, staring at the sharp, gleaming sword that seems real and not a prop.

"I," Lord Diamond Heart raises his voice. Though it wasn't loud, and only a word was spoken. Yet, the intensity is so great that Eli could see a visible ring of air movement radiating from the actor's lips throughout the hall, muffing any other noises and rendering everyone in absolute silence.

"Lion's Roar." Eli hears Gallahan on his right mutter the phrase. The poker-face expression from earlier is gone as Gallahan seems intrigued by the actor's deliverance of the line.

"Want to test the legitimacy of that Divinity conception you've espoused," Diamond Heart swings up his sword, aiming at the noble's head.

"Lord Coro, please stop," pleads a new male character in a white robe with the Eden symbol. He kneels at Diamond Heart's feet and holds his hands up to cover for the defeated nobles. "Please calm down."

"Who are you?" Lord Diamond Heart asks in an intimidating voice as he stares down at the new character.

"I am an advisor of the Supreme Leader of Eden, your Lordship," the adviser sings and bows down. "I'm here to deliver my Supreme Lord's message of sincere apology to you, Lord Coro. My Supreme Lord wasn't aware that our young Lord had arbitrarily marched to your realm of his own volition. It was an unacceptable and brazen behavior on our young Lord's part. The Eden, Mitra, and Candra councils will take full responsibility for the young Lords' mishap."

"Marching an army of 35,000 fully armored troops to Coro's sovereign territory is hardly a mishap," Diamond Heart states.

"With my utmost respect, your Lordship, it is a mishap. The young Lords are misguided children who didn't know any better. If they did, they wouldn't have thoughtlessly marched to your land. Any mature Sage knows they can't stand a chance against you," the advisor actor sings. "Though you and the young Lords are similar in age, they are not on the same rank as you, your Lordship. You are the Ruler of Coro. They are the coddled children of your ruling peers."

"Stop groveling to him, you old fool! We're not in the wrong! He's a traitor to his kind!" the three young nobles sing, glaring at Diamond Heart.

The music stops. The advisor sighs. He turns around and smacks the young lords of Mitra and Candra with just one whack, but it is enough to send them flying to the side of the stage.

"The adults are talking, young Lords," the advisor shoots the noble brats a warning smile. Then he turns back to Diamond Heart. "I know unwarranted invasion of another sovereign territory is punishable by death. My Supreme Lord Eden and the other two Lords agree they will take full responsibility for this incident. If your Lordship could look past the young Lords' misguided offense, the Lords of Eden, Mitra, and Candra will compensate Coro with three million gold coins."

"Three million!" Everyone on the stage, except the advisor and Lord Coro, cries out.

"I believe this approach is the best for everyone, your Lordship! The other Lords can have their unruly children back while you can use this new fortune to continue your noble philanthropy work, providing for the poor. All the Lords know how dwindling Coro's treasury has become after your Lordship's decided to...be the savior to the mortal humans."

There's a hint of derision in the last two words.

Diamond Heart narrows his eyes. But the Eden advisor is unfazed as his lips form an insincere smile.

"So, what do you say, your Lordsh—"

"Six million."

Every performer gasps in shock, even the Eden advisor, as he can no longer retain his fake diplomatic grin. "P-Pardon? I must have misheard—"

"Six. Million. Gold. Coins!" Diamond Heart swings out his hand, and an unseen force lifts three young nobles from the ground and pulls them toward his side.

"L-Lord Coro, you—" The Eden advisor is flabbergasted while the nobles scream for help. "You're being very unreasonable and avaricious, Lord Coro! Three million gold coins—"

"Is just the compensation for this insolent invasion into my realm," Diamond Heart looks at the nobles hovering helplessly above him. "The other three million is the fee to get these losers back in one piece."

"Lord Coro, if you harm them, you will make enemies not just with Eden, Mitra, and Candra but also with the other two major clans, Darya and Reinga!"

"Ah, I'm sure Darya and Reinga will fund a war to retrieve these felons who violated the Alliance Peace Order first," Diamond Heart sits down with crossed legs on a silver throne. "If Eden, Mitra, and Candra refuse my request. No problem. Their sons will spend the rest of their life in Coro. They will work and be useful to society, probably for the first time ever."

"No!" The three nobles cry out in horror. "Save us! Let our Lord parents know! Just gave him what he asked!"

"B-But six million gold is too much!" The Eden advisor cries.

"Bring me two million, and I'll give one of them back," Diamond Heart shoots the advisor a sly smile. "The other Lords can save up for the gold while their sons stay here."

The music starts again, and the play progresses to the next scene, where the Eden advisor goes home and relays Diamond Heart's demand to the other Lords.

"Two million for each son?! Is he a Lord or a robber?! What a greedy little scoundrel!" The Lords of Mitra and Candra sing angrily.

At the center of the stage is a regal-looking man with blond hair sitting on an eagle-shaped golden throne. He wears a magnificent outfit with a crown on his head. Unlike the other two Lords, the man only chuckles and says nothing.

"My Supreme Lord," the Eden adviser bows to the man on the throne.

"Bring two million gold coins to Coro and get my son back," The regal man orders.

"Eden?! How could you easily accept that insolent brat's ridiculous demand without any negotiation?!" The Lords of Mitra and Candra cry out in disbelief.

"Uncalled-for invasion to an Alliance's realm is punishable by public execution," Lord of Eden says calmly. "Our sons are in the wrong. No one will support us. We would be the villains if we were to launch an attack on Coro. When that happens, not just the minor houses, even Reinga and Darya will jump in and form an alliance with Coro. It will be a golden opportunity for them to undermine my influence as the chief Lord Supreme. I would be fine, but you two will be in deep trouble. Do as you will."

The following sequence shows the three spoiled nobles being released back to their families. The brats receive a serious beating from their angry fathers, while for the young lord Eden, the punishment is carried out by his father's advisor instead.

"Victory to Coro! Victory to Lord Diamond Heart!" The soldiers and citizens of Coro sing and celebrate the successful deal. They throw confetti and flowers at their beloved leader.

"Lord Diamond Heart didn't use the large fortune for himself. The kind Lord built houses for the poor and the lonely elders, food banks, schools for both humans and Sages, public libraries, hospitals, and temples. Many of these buildings have survived the wars and become historic landmarks in Coro," says a hidden female narrator as the actors perform a construction scene of said facilities. Building cutouts emerge, and the people of Coro rejoice at the development of their realm.

On the left side of the stage, the three bratty nobles, now in black and blue, glare in Diamond Heart's direction. Their fists clench as they sing in unison, "We'll never forget this humiliation! You better be careful, Diamond Heart! We'll destroy you at the first opportunity!"

"One day, I'll cut out your heart," the young Eden Lord says sinisterly. "We shall see if it's really made of Diamond. Just you wait."

* * *

The Ballad of Scarlet - Act Two

"CORO ENJOYED its period of peace until one fateful, storming night, a bright light akin to the sun suddenly appeared and lit up the sky of the twelve realms. The rain stopped, dead plants were revived, and fruits and crops ripened before their time. All types of flowers blossomed as their sweet scent spread throughout the continent. This strange phenomenon lasted thirty minutes before the blinding light started to fade and let the night resume its cycle," says the hidden female narrator.

The peasant and the ruler actors react surprised and alarmed by the event.

The next scene shows the Lords investigating this phenomenon. Lord Diamond Heart is seen coming to a religious temple setting to greet a new character in a yellow hooded robe. He bows down with his hands folded to this person, who returns a similar courtesy.

"Dear Master, I've spent the last ten days in deep meditation, hoping to find the cause of that peculiar light, but I didn't have any luck. I wonder if you have any idea of what happened that night and if it were an omen or a sign of blessing," Diamond Heart inquires respectfully.

"Diamond Heart, I cannot tell you anything regarding that incident, for the consequences would be world-shattering," the female monk says.

"W-World shattering? Are you sure, dear Master?" Diamond Heart exclaims.

"This is not an exaggeration, Diamond Heart. Not only this planet but our entire universe will be destroyed if anyone discloses what happened that night until the right time comes. The only thing I can share with you is the future will be magnificent."

"That's...good then," Diamond Heart nods. "I hope we can be a part of that wonderful future."

The entire theater suddenly groans and startles Eli. Everyone is shaking their head and sighing deeply. Even Wolfgang and Gallahan look visibly upset.

...These spoilers. Eli props his cheek on his hand, annoyed. Just when he's become so invested in this badass character, and now, he probably won't survive. Also, isn't this play about Emperor Haemon? When will he show up?

"Just like Her Holiness Nirbhaya said, the investigation for strange bright light was soon abandoned as none of the Lords could find anything no matter how much they tried," says the female narrator. "A few years have passed, and people started to forget about the peculiar incident. Little did they know the first in the series of significant events that will change the fate of the world is about to take place."

The following scene shows a group of children not older than ten, five boys and one girl, in tattered clothes, doing chores at a nice house. They focus on their work until a fat, richly dressed middle-aged man enters the room. He bumps into the blond boy carrying a bucket of water, causing the poor kid to fall face-first to the floor.

"Scrawny!" the four children yell as they rush to the blond boy, who now has a red bruise on his chin.

"How dirty, you clumsy oaf!" The rich man knocks the blond boy's head hard, causing him to wince. "Clean it up now, or you'll know the taste of my new whip!"

"Scrawny, no," the children hold the blond boy's clenched fists and shake their heads.

As the children begin to clean up the water, the rich man circles behind the little brunette girl. It isn't clear what he does, but it seems he nudges her skirt with his foot, causing the child to yelp aloud.

"Stop it! Stop touching me that way!" the girl cries.

"Grace, what happened?" The boys ask.

"Big deal! You should be flattered I show any interest in you, wench!" the rich pervert scoffs and mimics a spitting motion at the children.

"I have had enough of you!" Scrawny throws the rag down and stands up, facing the rich pervert.

"Did you just raise your voice at me?!" the rich pervert looks down at Scrawny, who only stands to his abdomen. "What are you going to do, you filthy slav—"

Before he could finish his insult, Scrawny had already landed a punch on the rich pervert's fat belly, knocking him to the floor. The man is dazed for a few seconds. Then he quickly gets up and punches Scrawny's face, sending him flying all the way to the side of the stage.

"I'll skin you alive, you filthy, wretched slave!" the rich pervert yells as he strides toward the blond kid and drags him by his collar back to the center stage. In the next three minutes, he then beats the living out of Scrawny with a whip.

"That beating's not real, right?" Eli whispers to Wolfgang as he starts to be concerned when he sees red welts forming on Scrawny's child actor's body.

"Don't worry, Eli. It's just acting and special effects," Wolfgang whispers back.

Eli breathes out in relief. Though the child actor's sobs and screams are too realistic and heartbreaking, they cause a stir in the theater. The audience is very upset at the cruelty of the rich man. As for Eli, he's beyond disturbed. This scene hits him too close to home. It reminds him of the horror little Ilya was subjected to.

"STOP!" Scrawny suddenly screams, and the entire stage is lit on real fire.

Everyone is startled and alarmed when they feel the actual heat from the flame. The audience starts to cheer and clap enthusiastically.

What the hell are you all clapping at?! Eli is confused and appalled. Aside from the blond kid Scrawny, all the actors on that stage, including the children, are screaming for help!

How is this play appropriate for all ages?!

And then, on the left side of the stage, Lord Diamond Heart is strolling toward the center with a bag of fruits.

"Fire! Fire!" actors in civilian clothes scream and run around.

"Oh, no!" Lord Diamond Heart flinches at the fire and runs toward it while others try to get away.

Building props start to collapse due to the flame. Diamond Heart tries to save as many people as he can.

"Anyone here?!" Diamond Heart yells as he runs around the flaming ruins to find survivors.

Scrawny is sitting on a high platform surrounded by fake fire with his knees drawn to his chest. He looks up when he hears Diamond Heart's voice. Eventually, they see each other.

Diamond Heart struggles to climb the fiery stairs to get to the boy. Scrawny only stares at him with an expressionless face. His face and body are full of bruises.

Diamond Heart falls several times but doesn't give up on saving the child.

"Hand!" Diamond Heart screams. "Give me your hand!"

The child stares at Diamond Heart for a few seconds before crying out loud.

Diamond Heart grunts as he finally gets to the tall platform and holds the kid to his chest. "I got you."

"Please save me," Scrawny weeps. "Please take me away from here!"

The next scene shows Diamond Heart bringing the battered Scrawny back to Coro and personally nurses the child back to health.

"What's your name, little one?" Diamond Heart asks the boy, who is now in bed. Scrawny's head and body are wrapped in bandages as he resembles a little mummy.

"They call me Scrawny," mummy Scrawny says.

"You poor thing," Diamond Heart sighs as he brings a spoon of porridge to Scrawny's lips. "You have to eat so you can be healthy again."

"Do I have to leave when I recover?" the poor kid asks. "If that's the case, I don't want to be healthy ever again."

"No. You're not going anywhere. The castle of Coro is your home from now on."

"R-Really?!" Scrawny rejoices.

"Of course!" Diamond Heart playfully flicks mummy Scrawny's little nose. Two of them laugh together. "I'll call you Cygni from now on."

"What does Cygni mean?" mummy Scrawny asks.

"The swan," Diamond Heart smiles. "Though in your case, you're still just a little cygnet."

Scrawny blinks. Diamond Heart explains, "Cygnet means baby swan."

"I love the name," mummy Scrawny smiles and hugs Diamond Heart. "Thank you for everything."

"Aww," the audience coos. Some young ladies cry happy tears. Eli looks at his two friends, and of course, unlike the rest of the majority, they look really bored.

Diamond Heart leaves the stage, and little Cygni stares at the theater ceiling from his bed. His blanket slowly moves like it is being pulled to the other side of the bed. Cygni's confused and turns over to look. A child in a white hooded costume suddenly pops his head up, making the little mummy jump. "Ah!"

"Shhhhh!" the child in the white hood shushes Cygni, putting a finger on his lips.

"Who are you?" Cygni whispers.

"The name is Procyon," Procyon grins as he introduces himself. "How old are you?"

"I don't know...Maybe six?" Cygni stutters.

"I'm nine," Procyon says with his little nose up. "You'll have to call me big brother."

"Yes, big brother," Cygni meekly nods.

"Here's a gift to our acquaintance," Procyon hands Cygni a small sachet.

"What is this, big brother?" Cygni opens the sachet and takes a sniff. "Ooh, it smells yummy!"

"It's chocolate," Procyon grins.

"Cho...What?"

"Chocolate. Candy," Procyon clarifies, and Cygni finally gets it. "It's the best sweet in the world!"

"C-Can I eat it?" mummy Cygni drools.

"Of course! But not at night, or all your teeth will fall out!" Procyon says, and Cygni gasps in horror. "That's what master said—"

"Hellooo? Can I come out now?" says a mysterious child's voice.

"Oh! I totally forgot about him!" Procyon yelps. Another boy in a white hooded costume pops up from under the bed.

"Idiot, why didn't you come out? I had a long conversation with Cygni," Procyon chides, crossing his arms.

"But you said I can only show myself when you give me the signal!" the new child argues. Then he turns to Cygni and gives him a wide, toothy smile. "Hi!"

"H-Hello," Cygni stutters.

"I'm Sadr. I'm eight years old. So that means I'm two years older than you. So, you will have to call me big brother," Sadr grins.

"I will, big brother!" Cygni gives Sadr a sunny smile.

"I am the big brother!" Procyon complains.

"Eh, don't mind him. Here's a gift from your big brother to you, little brother," Sadr hands little Cygni a brown teddy bear.

"I love it. Thank you so much, big brother!" mummy Cygni hugs the teddy bear.

The cheery music starts, and the next scene shows Cygni getting used to his new life in Coro. He now wears the same white hooded uniform as the other Sages at Coro Castle. No matter what activity he engages in, he's inseparable from the teddy bear Sadr gave him.

"Life has turned for the better for the baby swan. He finally has a loving family and a true home in Coro, the blessed land of the Wind," the performers in colorful costumes sing and dance merrily. "Everybody loves him for his adorable face and gentle demeanor."

Three kid bullies throw multiple balls at little Cygni's head and make a face at him, "Bleh. Bleh. Milksop! Milksop! Little pansy still playing with dolls!"

"Almost everybody loves him," the female choir sings.

"Stop it, you little brats!" a Coro teen Sage throws a yoga-sized ball at the three kid bullies and knocks them to the ground.

"Altair!" little Cygni runs toward the teen and hugs him.

"Cygni, you have to fight them back!" Altair tells Cygni.

"But...I don't want to hurt them," little Cygni stutters.

"Then they'll continue hurting you, silly," Procyon says as he and Sadr approach Cygni and Altair.

"But the last time I resisted, a really big fire happened, and a lot of people were burned," little Cygni says as he clutches his teddy bear tighter to his chest. "Master Diamond Heart was burned while trying to save me too. I-I don't want to use my power anymore."

"Little brother, you just need to not make a big fire, then it will be fine," Sadr pats Cygni's shoulder. "I will need you to make a small fire for me later so I can roast my marshmallows. Nobody at this castle allows me to be anywhere near the matches."

"Sadr, that's not gonna happen," Altair shakes his head disapprovingly. "You almost burned down the castle the last time we left you unattended in the kitchen! No matches for you until you turn fourteen!"

"Humph!" Sadr pouts, crossing his little arms together.

"Sadr, you can give me your marshmallows since I'm not forbidden to make fire," Procyon licks his lips. "I promise I'll eat them all and not waste a piece."

"I might be young, but I wasn't born yesterday!" Sadr makes a face at Procyon. "Nobody's taking my marshmallow stash!"

"I'll be taking those marshmallows," Diamond Heart says as he appears onstage. Behind him is two Sages, one male and one female.

"Master!" Altair, Procyon, Sadr, and Cygni stand in line and bow to Diamond Heart.

"No sweets allowed after dark," Diamond Heart brings out a hand. Sadr grunts softly and reluctantly gives his master the bag of marshmallows.

"My, this is a lot of marshmallows. Do you want to stay up all night in the infirmary like last time?" Diamond Heart lifts a brow after he looks inside the bag.

Sadr bites his lips and shakes his head.

"Alright, go do your homework. Altair will help you. Then after that, you'll finish your homework too, Altair," Diamond Heart waves at the kids.

"Yes, master," Altair, Procyon, and Sadr say unenthusiastically as they leave the stage.

"Vega, Rasalas, you two bathe Cygni," Diamond Heart orders the two Sages behind him.

"Yes, master," Rasalas and Vega give Diamond Heart a small bow. After he leaves, they smile and bring out their arms to little Cygni.

"Brother! Sister!" little Cygni comes over to hug the two Sages, who embrace him back.

"Oh no! You were hit again?" Vega cries after touching Cygni's hooded head, and Cygni nods. "That's terrible! Those naughty kids!"

"I'll have a talk with them tomorrow," Rasalas sighs as he takes Cygni's hand. "You'll have to learn to defend yourself soon, sport."

The next scene shows Lord Diamond Heart sitting on his silver throne, surrounded by many Coro Sages in white hooded costumes.

"Good luck, brother!" Rasalas, Vega, and Altair squeeze little Cygni's shoulders. Vega takes Cygni's teddy bear. "I'll hold it for you, little one."

"Show them what you got!" Procyon cheers as he and Sadr hold a banner with colorful Elgarian words.

"Marshmallow! Marshmallow!" Sadr cheers, and the entire theater, including Wolfgang and Gallahan, laughs, which surprises Eli a bit.

"Boo! Boo!" the three little bullies from earlier sputter and give Cygni a thumbs down.

Little Cygni lets out a big sigh. He straightens his back and walks towards Diamond Heart and the adult Coro Sage, giving them a bow. Then he turns toward the audience and opens his arms wide. A real and massive blaze flares up, and everybody jerks back to their seats.

"Fire Sage!" a Coro Sage declares, and all the Sages on the stage applaud.

Suddenly, all three little bullies are lifted up from the ground and fly into a circle in the air, according to Cygni's hand movement. "Help! Help!"

"A-An air Sage?!" the Coro Sages gasp. "We have a Hybrid!"

Cygni lowers his hand. The blaze ceases, and the three bullies are gently lifted down to the ground. Then, a massive vortex of water appears and circles every actor. Flower props then blossom and quickly spawn all over the stage.

The audience claps and cheers fervently. "Long live His Majesty!"

"He could control earth and water, too?!" the Coro Sages cry out. Lord Diamond Heart stands up from his silver throne.

"My Lord, this is the first time in the known history of the world that there is a quadbrid Sage! The Tathagatas truly bless our realm!" the Coro Sages rejoice.

"Come here, Cygni," Diamond Heart smiles and opens his arms to Cygni, who joyously skips over to him. Diamond Heart picks up the child and hugs him. "You're incredible!"

"Oh, little one, I'm so proud of you!" Vega runs over to join the hug and return Cygni's teddy bear.

"Yes, Brother! Woohoo!" Rasalas, Altair, Procyon, and Sadr cheer.

"Master, everyone is very happy," little Cygni says.

"I and all the people of Coro rejoice for you, my little swan, the next ruler of this land," Diamond Heart says gleefully.

"Ah! What will happen to you then?!" little Cygni freaks out and hugs Diamond Heart tighter. "Please don't leave me! You have to live with me forever!"

The actors chuckle at Cygni's innocent remark, but the audience turns quiet.

"No one can live forever, my little swan," Diamond Heart smiles softly at Cygni. "Everything in the universe is by nature impermanent."

"No!" little Cygni sobs. "No! I won't allow that. You will live with me forever. I-I'll protect you!"

"Well, that's my responsibility, but thank you," Diamond Heart giggles as he strokes Cygni's back to comfort him.

"I promise I'll protect you," little Cygni mumbles.

When the red curtains close to prepare for the next act, the audience groans and becomes very emotional. The young ladies in the front seat of Eli sniff and moan. "Lord Diamond Heart."

Eli is so annoyed at these audience spoilers. He crosses his arms in resentment.

"Are you doing alright, Eli?" Gallahan chuckles.

Eli smiles at the boy and shrugs. "Are you enjoying the play, buddy?"

"So far, it's better than my expectation," Gallahan responds. "I want to see the rest of it."

"How about you, Wolfgang?" Eli asks Captain Seven-Seas.

"Let me give you my full critique after the play is finished," Wolfgang muses, hand on chin. He seems really into the show.

"Oh dang," Gallahan groans while Eli giggles.

"Shut up, kid," Wolfgang grumbles.

Eli is glad both of his friends aren't bored with the play he chose.

* * *

The Ballad of Scarlet - Act Three

THE THIRD ACT opens with a lively dancing and singing sequence of Cygni's great childhood in Coro and how his reputation has spread to all twelve realms. The noble and civilian actresses swoon over how handsome and strong Cygni is, while the male actors act either jealous or indifferent.

A tall and extremely gorgeous new actor with blond hair in a Coro Sage costume struts toward the center of the stage, where Diamond Heart sits on his silver throne reading a book. He hasn't spoken a word yet, but the audience already claps and cheers excitedly.

"Oh, here he is! Aster~" the three young ladies gush.

According to the young ladies from the front seats, Aster Glendrome looks exactly like Emperor Haemon. If what they said is true, Emperor Haemon must have been a real eye candy when he was young. Eli thinks as he observes Aster.

"Good afternoon, master," Cygni shows his pearly white teeth to Lord Diamond Heart.

"You are late!" Diamond Heart says. "By three hours!"

"I'm terribly sorry, master. I was helping an elderly lady home after she tripped and hurt her ankle in the forest," Cygni explains, and Diamond Heart looks concerned. "Don't worry, master. I had a healer check her up before I left. She will be fine."

"Here's my assignment," Cygni hands his master a paper scroll. "Just as I promised you to take my study seriously, I stayed up all night to do the research for this homework."

"...Mmm," Diamond Heart's eyebrows rise as he reads through Cygni's scroll. "Indeed, you did spend a lot of thought on your chemistry assignment."

Cygni chuckles confidently. His handsome face is full of contentment.

"...But Cygni."

"Yes, master?"

"I didn't ask for this. You're supposed to give me twenty-five pages on advanced biology," Diamond Heart shoots Cygni an incredulous look.

"...What?" Cygni's wide smile freezes. "No...You're mistaken, master... It's chemistry."

"I'm mistaken?!" Diamond Heart raises his voice as he stands up from his throne and shows Cygni other paper scrolls on the small table beside his seat. "Look! Advanced biology!"

"Nooo!" Cygni screams agonizingly, and everybody in the theater cracks up.

Eli doesn't know how historically accurate this play is, as Emperor Haemon's character seriously reminds him of a certain gorgeous airhead he knows.

"Hush up, you idiot!" Diamond Heart smacks Cygni's head with his chemistry scroll. "How can you rule Coro with that inattentive mindset?! Don't you know to be a good ruler, just strength isn't enough! You must use your head as well! Before you commit to spending all night writing a twenty-five-page assignment, you must ensure you're doing the correct subject first!"

"I-I'm sorry," Cygni weeps, and the audience is rolling with laughter.

"Go back to your room and get some sleep," Diamond Heart sighs and waves his hands. "Give me the correct assignment in three days."

"I...will...Thank...you...master," Cygni sniffs and trudges away in complete devastation. After a few steps, two adult male Coro Sages swagger in from the left side stage while another Coro Sage approaches Diamond Heart from the right side.

"Afternoon, brother~" the new characters wave at Cygni. "Why's the long face? Who took your teddy bear?"

The two actors and the audience roar with laughter at that line.

Cygni explains to Procyon and Sadr what happened. Instead of consoling him, they laugh hysterically.

"Jerks," Cygni sobs.

"My Lord, you must stop providing provision to those peasants in Reinga!" the new Coro actor raises his voice at Diamond Heart. "That realm isn't our ally. Lord Reinga doesn't even like you! Why would you continue helping his subjects?!"

"The subjects you mentioned are the starving people in Reinga," Diamond Heart reasons. "Lord Reinga and I may have our differences, but the poor civilians aren't a part of it. There's been a long drought in Reinga. If I don't send them food, Lord Reinga will let them die. Besides, we have so much surplus of food that can feed the entire realm of Coro for the next five years."

"So? Those people aren't Coro citizens," the Coro Sage says, and Diamond Heart is shocked at that selfish statement. "My Lord, you have to put Coro first before others."

"Listen to me carefully," Diamond Heart's tone turns serious, and the Coro Sage instantly drops his tough attitude. "All lives are precious and deserve to live. It doesn't matter if they are citizens of Reinga, or Karmara, or some other country on this planet, or in any universe out there, or whether it's a Sage or a human or an animal. If I can help save an endangered life, I will do it."

Eli can feel his hair rising on his arms as he listens to Diamond Heart actor's intensely captivating voice. The actor receives a long ovation for his powerful delivery.

"As you say, my Lord," the Coro Sage bows to Diamond Heart. "However, please remember your loyal subject's words: your heart might be of diamond, but others might not understand or even appreciate your kindness. They might not help you or even shed a tear if you ever, may Tathagatas forbid, be in dire straits. Good day, my Lord."

The Coro Sage rudely smooths his robe and turns away to leave. The audience boos at him.

"I don't care if nobody acknowledges my deeds. I'll help them anyway," Diamond Heart mumbles to himself and exits the stage to the right.

"How dare that buffoon be so insolent to master like that?!" Procyon exclaims angrily as the three brothers have been eavesdropping on the entire disrespectful exchange on the left side of the stage.

"We have to teach him a lesson!" Sadr announces. Both brothers then look at Cygni.

Cygni says nothing, but his lips curve into a wide, mischievous smile. Procyon and Sadr respond with an equally impish grin.

"Bwahahaha~" Cygni, Procyon, and Sadr laugh evilly as they exit the stage.

In the next sequence, the rude Coro Sage leisurely strolls in a garden setting. But when he approaches a spot in the middle of the stage, he can no longer move.

"Huh?" The Coro Sage tries to lift his feet, but it's useless. He then leans down a little to inspect the ground. Suddenly, a tomato hits his face, causing him to lose balance and fall on all fours. Now, he is completely immobilized. It seems like the ground has been applied with a layer of superglue.

The theater's lights move to another area near the ceiling where Cygni, Procyon, and Sadr stand with their hands on their foreheads. Beside them is a large sac of tomatoes.

"He's down!" Sadr says. Then, all three brothers mercilessly rain tomatoes on the stuck Sage.

"Help! Ouch! Help! Ouch! Somebody!" the Coro Sage cries out as his face and white outfit are dyed red from the tomatoes. The entire theater shakes with laughter.

Fortunately, Diamond Heart, Rasalas, and another male Sage walk in and see what happens. They immediately rush to help the poor Sage, but each receives a tomato right on the face. The three stagger and end up stepping into the superglue area.

"Master!" Rasalas and the male Sage cry out. But they can't move their feet. "T-These are rotten tomatoes!"

Lord Diamond Heart winces in disgust as he swipes the tomato off his face. He wants to move away, but his feet are glued to the ground.

"Hey, I think that clown got reinforcement!" Procyon says.

"Anyone that helps him deserves to eat snail slime," Cygni says as he pitches four tomatoes simultaneously, and they all land on his targets' faces. "Those who disrespect master must be punished!"

"Agreed!" Procyon and Sadr cheer.

Diamond Heart finally manages to get out by jumping out barefoot to the safe ground. He then runs up toward the direction where the three delinquents are. However, during his first high jump, a bucket of yellow slime pours on top of his head and causes him to fall to the ground. He then receives another bucket of bird feathers.

"Yes!" Cygni, Procyon, and Sadr are excited and still unaware they are about to be in deep trouble. They continuously pelt rotten tomatoes at their beloved master's face.

"AHHHH! YOU. ARE. DONE!" Diamond Heart screams.

Cygni, Procyon, and Sadr immediately stop celebrating upon hearing the scream. They look at each other with confused, wide doe eyes.

"...That voice...sounds...awfully familiar," Procyon stammers fearfully. All three brothers lean down to take a closer look at their victim.

"Ahhh! Master!" the three brothers jump and panic. "Oh no! Oh no! Oh no!"

Cygni immediately throws away the rotten tomato sack to the backstage and whistles an awful tune. Sadr poses with a hand on his forehead like he's musing about something deep. Procyon pretends to check his nails.

"Oh, master!" the three brothers act surprised when the tattered Diamond Heart finally gets up to the high spot. "What a surpri—Ouch! Ouch! Ouch! Master, I'm sorry!"

The audience is in stitches at this point.

"No way this actually happened in real history, right?" Eli asks Wolfgang and Gallahan during the transition to the next scene.

"Unfortunately, Eli, this whole segment is very historically accurate," Wolfgang says. "It's called the *Foul Tomatoes Incident,* when the young Emperor Haemon and his two clan brothers accidentally ganged up on their master just like we saw."

"Wow," Eli chuckles in disbelief and amusement.

"Isn't that right, Gallahan?" Wolfgang asks.

"...Yeah, he's right," Gallahan stutters. "Though there are a few inaccuracies. For example, the slime was green, not yellow...That's what I read in the history book."

* * *

The Ballad of Scarlet - Act Four

THE RED CURTAINS REOPEN, and the scene shows many Coro Sages and a group of monks on the stage. Surrounding them are horse carriage props and trunks.

"Master, do I really have to go on this quest?" Cygni speaks to Diamond Heart. "I want to accompany you to the capital."

"Of course, you must do that quest. Don't you want to claim the sacred Phoenix Bow?" Diamond Heart asks.

"But I already have my diamond sword," Cygni says as he unsheathes a beautiful sword made from crystal. "Why would I need another weapon?"

"Because that bow belongs to you, Cygni," the female monk Nirbhaya says. "Nobody can lift it but you."

"Master Nirbhaya, can I go claim the Phoenix Bow after the Century Feast?" Cygni asks.

"I'm afraid not, sweet child," Nirbhaya smiles, shaking her head. "You must claim this bow within three days. Trust me, Cygni, that Phoenix Bow will change the history of the world."

Cygni says in defeat. "I will go take the bow and join you in the capital then."

"Don't be silly. I'll only stay there for three days. I'll see all of you at Coro," Diamond Heart says. He chuckles softly upon seeing Cygni's sad face. "I'll bring back a souvenir for you, alright?"

"I'm not a child anymore," Cygni pouts. "But please do that. Thank you!"

"Yes, now go," Diamond Heart laughs and waves at Cygni and his siblings. "Be safe, children."

Cygni, Rasalas, Vega, Altair, Procyon, and Sadr bow to their masters and leave the stage. But after a few steps, Cygni runs back to hug Diamond Heart.

"Please, be careful, master," Cygni says.

"Cygni, I'm attending to a party, not a war," Diamond Heart sighs, patting Cygni's back.

"Don't worry, Cygni. We'll protect your master," the six Coro Sages around Diamond Heart say. "We'll see you kids in a few days!"

"Goodbye, uncles," Cygni sighs. Before he can say anything else, his brothers have already dragged him away.

"Take care of your little brother!" Diamond Heart calls out.

"We will. Have a great trip, master, uncles," Altair and Procyon wave.

"B-Be careful!" Cygni calls out to Diamond Heart before he is shoved off the stage. Diamond Heart and the six Coro Sages turn to the monks and give them a deep bow. "We'll be off too, Masters. Please take care."

The monks only nod at them. Nirbhaya grabs Diamond Heart's hand before he turns to leave.

"Yes, Master?"

"Remember what I taught you," Nirbhaya says. "No matter how wrong or unfair things are, you must do the right things. Do you understand?"

"I will always do that, Master," Diamond Heart smiles brightly at her. "Goodbye! I'll see you in a few days!"

The monks look at Diamond Heart and his retinue until they're off the stage.

"Nirbhaya, let's go," a male monk says. "We don't have much time left. We must leave to the border now."

Eli is startled when the entire theater suddenly groans and moans at that line. Everyone looks very emotional, and some ladies even use their hankies to dab off their tears.

The next scene shows Cygni and his siblings rushing to the stage. Cygni now carries a beautiful bow on his back.

"I can't believe it took us eleven days to get out of that hell pit!" Cygni complains, agitated. "We have to go back to Coro now! I want to see our master!"

"Relax, Cygni, we just got out of hell. Literally," Procyon pants.

"Master probably waits for us at home," Vega says.

"I can't wait to tell master about our adventure," Altair says excitedly.

"Yeah, yeah, just hurry up," Cygni says.

The group approaches a town setting where many civilians gather to discuss something.

"I can't believe Lord of Coro is that cruel," a villager says.

"How scary. And we thought he was different from the rest of the Lords," another villager says. "Turn out he is even worse than them!"

"Hey, what are you saying?!" Cygni shouts at the crowd. "How dare you—"

"Please excuse my little brother," Rasalas pushes Cygni behind his back. "Can you folks share with us what you are discussing?"

"Oh my! You lads don't know what's been going on the last couple of days?" the villagers ask.

"No, what happened?" Rasalas inquires.

"Lord Diamond Heart of Coro is undergoing the *ten-day interrogation* in the capital," the villagers disclose.

"What?!" Rasalas and his siblings gasp in shock and terror. "Why?!"

"He tried to poison all the Lords at the Century Feast, and he was the one who murdered the previous Lord Coro, his own master," a male villager says.

"They found out he has two twin sons with the Lady of Nada," a female villager says. "He raised his two sons in court with him. They were also captured along with their father."

"Did you know he was a slave? Lady Nada was his mistress," a villager gossips. "The former Lord Coro knew about this. That was why Diamond Heart killed him to protect his lover and sons."

"Aside from murdering his master, he also massacred his clan brothers and their families. What a wicked Sage!"

"Hold your tongue, you lying, evil peasants!" Cygni screams, his two arms covered with red fire. "How dare you slander my master with such outrageous and vile lies?! I shall burn all of you to ashes!"

The villagers scream and run away to hide.

"Cygni, don't!" the siblings hold their little brother back. "Don't fight with them!"

"Let go of me!" Cygni shakes off his siblings' hands and points at the villagers. "You fool! Lord Diamond Heart helps everybody in all twelve realms, not just his people! The food you eat is from Coro. Your Lords wouldn't care if all of you starved to death from the long drought! Lord Diamond Heart is a virtuous and pure-hearted Sage who has not executed anyone during his seventy-two years of reign. Coro no longer had any natural disasters the moment he became ruler. He abolished slavery in Coro and let the children of the poor go to school. He always shares his resources with all of you ingrates, even though his advisors berate him for helping the outsiders! How could a kind and wonderful Sage like him ever do any of the evil things you said?!"

"We have to head to the capital now," Cygni turns around to leave with his siblings.

"Master," Vega weeps. "How could he agree to that barbaric torture?! No Sage can last after six days...H-How many days has he been in there?"

"Almost nine days!" Rasalas panics.

The actors leave the stage. The lights shut off to prepare for the next scene.

"I think we should leave," Wolfgang says.

"I agree," Gallahan approves.

"Wait, what? Why?" Eli is confused.

"I think the next part is going to be quite violent and traumatizing," Wolfgang explains.

Eli hesitates. He really wants to watch the next part, but Gallahan grabs his hand and looks at him with pleading eyes.

"Please, Eli, I'll get nightmares," Gallahan begs.

"Oh no! Let's go then," Eli gasps. But the red curtains open, and a terrifying scene displays before their eyes.

On the center of the stage, Diamond Heart's hands and feet are chained on a wooden post. He no longer wears his elegant Coro outfit but a bloody rag. His copper hair is seen for the first time, and it looks like it was roughly chopped off in a rush. His entire body, from head to toe, is dyed with scarlet.

"Oh, Holy Tathagatas!" the audience gasps in horror at how realistic and gruesome that scene is.

"What in the?!" Eli immediately covers Gallahan's eyes with his hand.

Gallahan didn't exaggerate. Even Eli can get nightmares from this scene!

"Master?" only Cygni appears on the stage. He freezes upon seeing Diamond Heart's corpse.

Cygni staggers toward the corpse. He stares at it for a while before hurriedly and clumsily unchaining it from the stake.

"Master, please wake up," Cygni talks to the bloody corpse in his trembling arms. "I-I don't like this. Y-You are scaring me."

"Please talk to me," Cygni bursts into tears as he looks around in complete loss and despair. He desperately wipes off the blood on Diamond Heart's face, but it won't come off. "Please wake up...I'm begging you...I...I do whatever you want me to do...Anything...Just please..."

"Don't leave me," Cygni sobs out loud, cradling the bloody corpse to his chest.

The audience weeps along with him. Eli flinches when he feels hot tears rolling down his cheeks and on his hand as Gallahan is also crying.

Gallahan leaves his seat to sit on Eli's lap and hugs him, burying his face into Eli's chest.

"It's okay, the play's going to end soon," Eli whispers to the boy while gently stroking his back to calm him.

Cygni's siblings eventually appear on the stage. They pant, complaining that Cygni ran too fast for them to catch up, but the group soon recognizes the bloody corpse in their little brother's arms. They rush to him, and everyone cries together.

"Uncles?" Rasalas murmurs as he looks at the dark area behind Cygni. The entire stage is lit up, and the severed heads of the six Coro Sages from the beginning of Act Four are displayed on a platform.

"Uncles!" Vega, Altair, Procyon, and Sadr scream.

Cygni slowly turns around and stares at the bloody heads for a while until a group of soldiers in Reinga uniform gather on the stage.

"What the hell do you think you're doing?" The soldiers point their swords at Cygni and his siblings. "Surrender your weapons now and put that sinner's corpse back on the stake. Burial is forbidden for these wicked criminals. The crows will take care of their filthy carcasses."

The audience screams and curses at the guards.

A massive real blaze appears and spreads throughout the entire stage, setting all the soldiers on fire.

Cygni quietly stands up with Diamond Heart's bloody corpse in his arms. Rasalas holds the two heads of their uncles while the rest carry one head each. Together, they slowly disappear into the roaring fire while the soldiers scream and run amok in vain.

The following sequence shows Cygni and his siblings arriving at Coro Castle, which is filled with Eden soldiers dressed in white armor with a golden eagle on their breastplate.

However, the Eden soldiers aren't hostile to Cygni and his siblings. They split into two lines to make way for Lord Eden and some Coro Sages, who freeze when they see Diamond Heart's bloody corpse in Cygni's arms.

"Lord Diamond Heart!" the Coro Sages rush to Cygni and sob their hearts out.

"Lord of Eden, why are you and your army here?" Rasalas asks in a faint voice.

"Coro was attacked by Darya, Reinga, Karmara, Mitra, and Candra when Diamond Heart was held in the capital," Lord Eden explains. "Fortunately, it wasn't the Lords who led the invasion but their useless sons. I managed to kill the young Lords of Reinga, Mitra, and Candra. The sons of Darya and Karmara ditched their troops and escaped. I was able to defend Coro from the invasion, and there were no troops lost on your side."

"No troops lost? What do you mean?" Rasalas asks.

"Coro troops didn't participate in the battle. It was only my army against the rest at the border of Coro," Lord Eden says.

"That doesn't make sense. Why didn't Coro soldiers aid you?" Rasalas is flabbergasted as he turns to the Coro Sages. "Why didn't any of you help Lord Eden defend our realm against the invaders? What were you doing when the battle took place?!"

"They couldn't help even if they wanted to," Lord Eden says.

"Why?" Altair speaks up.

"I think it's better if I show you," Lord Eden waves his hand, and his soldiers stand aside to reveal seventeen corpses in bloody white cloth on the ground.

Cygni strides toward the row of corpses and pulls off the bloodiest shroud.

"Master Nirbhaya!" Vega and Procyon scream.

Rasalas, Altair, and Sadr pull off the rest of the bloody shrouds, and all the victims are the monks.

Lord Eden explains that the seventeen monks arrived at the border of Coro the night before the invaders came and used their power to put up a magical shield, preventing the enemies from entering Coro's soil. When the Coro army reached the border, the monks asked them to not interfere, or there would be massive bloodshed in Coro.

"Then how did they die? They had a protective barrier!" Altair asks.

"By the time I arrived, the Saint monks had been bleeding badly from trying to keep up the protective shield," Lord Eden discloses. "When the battle broke out, the Saints were very weak and were eventually killed by the enemies' arrows or getting their cores exploded."

"She didn't die from the core explosion," Cygni croaks. "These are arrow marks."

"Master Nirbhaya was killed by multiple arrows," a Coro Sage sobs.

"How many arrows?" Cygni asks, his eyes and voice lifeless.

"A hundred...and eight," the Coro Sage weeps.

"Master Nirbhaya!" Vega, Procyon, and Sadr sob, burying their faces at the monk's corpse.

Rasalas and Altair drop to their knees and break into tears.

Cygni suddenly bursts into a wild and eerie laugh, startling everyone.

"C-Cygni," even his siblings are concerned for him. "Brother."

Cygni's crazy laugh stops, and the entire stage is consumed in real flame, so immense that even the audience at the furthest seats can feel the heat.

"C-Cygni, stop!" The siblings scream at their little brother. All the other actors must stay close to the siblings to avoid the angry blaze.

"Master...You spent your whole life helping others and being kind to your rivals who thought you were naive...You believed love and forgiveness could change the world," Cygni talks to Diamond Heart's bloody corpse. "And this is what you received."

"Slanders by those ingrate peasants that you helped and tortured to death by your peers," Cygni chokes up. "I'll never forgive them."

"If all those realms want to play with fire. Then fire is what they shall get," Cygni laughs maniacally, but tears stream down his eyes. "If they want a war, they shall get one! I'll burn all of those who harmed you to ashes!"

"And I will bring happiness and prosperity to this continent," Cygni smiles gently at his master's corpse. "I promise you."

The announcer informs the audience that the Ballad of Scarlet is over and thanks them for attending the show.

"We would be honored to see you again for the premiere of the Ballad of Scarlet Part Two on September 13. Victory Theater wishes you a very merry day! Long live his Imperial Majesty, Emperor Haemon the Magnificent!"

CHAPTER 20

HAPPY BIRTHDAY, ELI!

"Gallahan, I'm so sorry for bringing you to this play!" Eli says after they get out of the Victory Theater.

"Why are you sorry?!" Gallahan and Wolfgang cry out.

"Because that show was too violent and very inappropriate for children. I'll explain to your mom and dad when we get back."

Wolfgang and Gallahan gawk at Eli as if he were a talking squirrel.

"Eli, I am the one who told you that play was for all ages." Gallahan holds Eli's hands. "I had a really good time. It was a good show. And besides, you were comforting me during the violent scene. I didn't see anything scary at all!"

Wolfgang scoffs at Gallahan, who sticks out his tongue at him.

Eli laughs in relief and playfully pinches Gallahan's round cheek. "I'm glad, buddy. I'll compensate you with the cookies I made when we're home!"

"You cook?!" Gallahan and Wolfgang appear shocked at this discovery.

"Yeah. There are some for you, too." Eli grins at Wolfgang.

Wolfgang and Gallahan thank Eli and say they are thrilled about the cookies. Wolfgang then leaves to find a carriage, as they have been waiting for the last five minutes without a cab passing by.

Eli waits on the sidewalk outside the theater with Gallahan. As he is watching the street, his eyes catch an illustration of a newspaper behind the glass window of a bookstore in the opposite lane. He walks Gallahan there for a closer look at the picture, which depicts a witch on a guillotine about to be executed.

"Gallahan, can you tell me what this newspaper is about, please?" Eli requests as he stares at the drawing. The witch is a thin, elderly woman with menacing eyes and a long, hooked nose with a wart.

"An evil witch responsible for killing many people and consuming their corpses was captured by the authorities when she was out searching for her missing broomstick."

"Missing broomstick?"

"Yeah. 'During the interrogation, the witch revealed her latest victim stole her broomstick and fly away with it,'" Gallahan reads.

"When and where did this event take place? Did they say in the newspaper?" Eli asks.

"'This incident happened about a month ago on the blood moon night in the Forbidden Forest's section in Crimson Vale,'" Gallahan reads. "She was executed yesterday."

"Do they know the witch's number of victims?" Karma is very real. He is certain this witch is the same one that nabbed him on his first day in this world.

"Oh yes, she murdered at least 260 people. Mostly youths under eighteen," Gallahan says, and Eli shudders.

"'Due to the witch's confession, authorities were able to crack down on an illegal slave trading ring in Crimson Vale.'" Gallahan frowns. "'This witch sometimes sold the youths she caught to these illicit slave markets. They were then sold into underground brothels all over the nation.'"

"That was so sick and evil." Eli feels nauseated, his stomach churns at the thought of how close he came to being another one of her victims—had it not been for Cyril.

"There's a good ending, though. The authorities were able to return most of the victims to their homes and compensated them with money and medicine. Those without families were brought to public housing where they would be taken care of and assisted until they can start over again." Gallahan smiles as he reads the paper.

"That's so wonderful!"

Wolfgang comes back with a cab. The three of them leave downtown Glade Mallow and return home, where a double birthday party awaits them.

* * *

THE THREE CHAT about *The Ballad of Scarlet* when they're inside the carriage. According to Wolfgang and Gallahan, the play is fairly accurate to the actual history. The only creative parts are probably the characters' past, since civilians can't know the authentic personal details of the Aspenian elites.

"Yes, that makes sense. Which character do you like best?" Eli grins at his two friends.

"Lord Diamond Heart," Wolfgang and Gallahan answer simultaneously.

"I see." Eli chuckles.

"How about you, Eli? Who is your favorite character?" Gallahan asks.

"Same as you, buddy. Lord Diamond Heart."

"May I ask why you like him?" Wolfgang asks with a charming smile.

"He abolished slavery. A ruler who believes in equality between humans and helps everybody without discrimination is an excellent ruler in my eyes. Sadly, slavery still exists in this nation even though the Emperor was brought up by Lord Diamond Heart." Eli lets out a soft sigh. "It's a real pity."

Gallahan squeezes Eli's hand and gives him puppy eyes.

"My dear Eli, if it'd make you feel any better, slave trading in Aspenia is strictly illegal. Thus, slave markets aren't allowed in this nation. Over the last century, His Majesty has gone to great lengths to protect the slave population. Those who inflict torture, mistreatment, or public humiliation on their wageless servants are heavily prosecuted, especially if they are nobility," Wolfgang informs Eli with a tender smile.

Eli's eyebrows lift as he mulls over the information. "So, if the Emperor banned slave trading, that means he doesn't want new slaves in the country?"

"That's right."

"Okay. The Emperor also forbids the abuse of the 'wageless servants,' which probably means he's somewhat aware that slaves are also human beings like free citizens. They shouldn't be subjected to ill-treatment, so what keeps him from abolishing slavery nationwide?"

"What do you think is the reason that keeps His Majesty from emancipating the slaves?" Wolfgang asks with an ambiguous smile.

From what Eli has gathered so far, Emperor Haemon seems to be genuinely adored by the Aspenian people. Aspenia is an absolute monarchy; it would be suicidal for the theater company to slander their Emperor's past. Hence, if Emperor Haemon used to be a slave and was then rescued and brought up by Lord Diamond Heart, a benevolent Sage who freed the slaves, there's no way the Emperor would be pro-slavery. This is evident by the way he bans slave trading, limits the slave population to a fixed number, and passes laws to protect them from inordinate abuse from their owners. And yet, despite all of that effort, he refuses to end slavery nationwide.

"Punishment?" Eli says. "And political reasons?"

"You are smart!" Wolfgang and Gallahan exclaim.

Eli grins at his friends. "Did I guess it right? Does the Emperor keep slavery alive because he wants to punish the slave population?"

Wolfgang nods keenly.

"Did he punish them because they were related to the death of Lord Diamond Heart, his uncles, and the monks? And they probably also opposed him during the war to unite the twelve realms into one nation?" Eli asks.

"You're absolutely correct, Eli," Wolfgang responds. "It is a political punishment. In this country, criminals are usually fined, imprisoned, or executed, but never made into slaves. The entire slave population in Aspenia consists of former nobles and traitors who plotted against the Emperor and his family. When His Majesty first became Emperor, he wanted to abolish slavery nationwide, just like how Lord Diamond Heart did in Coro, but those iniquitous Sage nobles viewed his decision as a sign of weakness and rebelled against him. They even sold out our nation to foreign enemies, leading to a seventeen-year of foreign invasion on Aspenia's soil, spilling the blood of countless innocents."

Damn. Eli is aghast.

"And there are many more horrendous things they did, but it would take me days to list them all out," Wolfgang states. "These traitors were known to treat their slaves like dispensable livestock when they were in power. The Emperor simply returned the favor, but even then, His Majesty is still merciful and forbids the killing and inhuman torture of those former noble slaves."

"How long has the Emperor been ruling this nation?" Eli asks. If he remembers correctly, Cyril once told him Emperor Haemon has been in power for almost 200 years.

"Nearly two hundred years, but only counting from the peaceful era," Gallahan answers. "Prior to that, there were twenty years of constant wars on this continent."

"Two centuries...the Emperor must be very old now," Eli muses, but his friends chuckle. "What?"

"Two hundred years old is considered young for a Sage, Eli," Wolfgang laughs.

"But I thought sages lived to be nearly three hundred years old?" Eli remembers back to the conversation he had with Cyril about sages and superpowers.

"There are many Sages in Aspenia that are over five hundred years old and still kicking," Gallahan reveals. "A Grand Sage's lifespan is immeasurable, and His Majesty is definitely one."

"Are you guys saying he's immortal?" Eli's eyes widen.

"We're not sure," Wolfgang says. "However, most grand Sages in history lived for so long they got bored. After nearly a thousand years living on Earth, they either let themselves get killed or simply disappeared into forgotten history."

Eli sits in silence, lost and overwhelmed, as he absorbs all the new knowledge. He glances out the window and sees verdant grass with abundant colorful wildflowers edging along both sides of the unpaved country road. This planet is very different from the Earth he came from. It's beautiful and magical, but also dangerous and brutal. It's like an enchanting fairytale doused in a macabre glaze.

"I'm with you, Eli." Gallahan gives Eli a squeeze on his hand. "I'll be your best friend for life."

"As will I." Wolfgang smiles brightly. "I will protect you. If Cyril ever acts up, I'm more than ready to take his place! You're never alone, Eli."

Eli has lived alone most of his life since he was eight years old. While he doesn't think of himself as highly spiritual, his intuition is not so bad, and right now, Eli believes his friends' words.

"Thank you." Eli's voice quivers. He is deeply touched by the love his friends have for him. "I'm grateful for you guys. Truly."

* * *

WHEN THE THREE GET HOME, they see new fairy lights winding around the front gate and the porch railings. After opening the main door, they are welcomed with three blasts of confetti cannons.

"Happy Birthday, dearest Eli!" Cyril, Haidar, and Mariposa cheer.

"Woof woof!" The little Pom pup also welcomes them home.

The house is decked with teddy bears, colorful flowers and balloons, multicolor banners, ribbons, and magic-operated fairy lights.

"Oh my!" Wolfgang and Gallahan gawk at the heavily decorated background.

"Woah." Eli's jaw drops. Though the decor looks like it's intended for a kid's birthday, Eli is still very touched. It must have taken them hours to put up all of these decorations.

"I-I love it so much. Thank you, everybody," Eli utters, profoundly grateful.

Cyril beams and opens his arms. Eli comes in to give his guardian a tight hug.

"Thank you, Cyril," Eli says softly.

Cyril pulls away to gaze at Eli, who can see his own reflection in those crystal blue eyes. Eyes that only ever look at him with tenderness and adoration.

"It's I who has to say thank you." Cyril squeezes Eli's round cheek. "You're the meaning of my life, Eli."

And thus, Eli and Cyril's birthday party officially begins!

There is a big birthday cake with white frosting and berries and many colorful vegetarian dishes that look extremely appetizing.

"I hope you had a great time in town. Where did you go?" Cyril asks when everyone sits down to eat in the dining room.

Eli tells Cyril, Haidar, and Mariposa about his visit to the winery, and these three, along with Gallahan, glare at Wolfgang. Eli quickly mentions the play to get Wolfgang out of the hot water.

"That sounds nice. Did you enjoy the play?" Cyril asks, smiling.

"I like it very much. It's very interesting...and educational," Eli stutters.

"Educational?" Cyril chuckles, brows rising. "What's the name of that play you saw?"

"...It's called *The Ballad of Scarlet.*"

Cyril, Haidar, and Mariposa look perplexed upon hearing the play's name.

"That didn't sound very child-friendly," Haidar comments, and Eli flinches.

"What was that play about?" Mariposa asks Eli.

"Marie, I'm so sorry—"

"It was about the Emperor's past when he was in Coro," Wolfgang cuts in, and the room quickly turns uncomfortably quiet.

"Which part?" Cyril asks.

"When Emperor Haemon carried Lord Diamond Heart back to Coro Castle," Wolfgang answers.

Cyril's eyebrows furrow as he appears to be thinking hard. "What?"

"Lord Diamond Heart's corpse, I mean."

"What?!" Haidar and Mariposa cry out, and then they turn to Eli.

"Haidar, Marie, I'm so sorry for choosing that play and watching it with Gallahan," Eli apologizes to his friends.

Haidar and Mariposa look y stunned. Mariposa snaps out of it and speaks to Eli in a motherly tone. "No, no, Eli. We're not blaming you in any way. We're worried for you because that part of history is notorious for violence, and you are prone to having nightmares. A-Are you alright, sweetie?"

"Aw, I'm fine, Marie," Eli grins sweetly at his Mariposa. "I covered Gallahan's eyes during the...loud scenes...I hope he won't have any bad dreams... later on."

"Trust me, Eli. He won't," Haidar snickers.

"My mom and dad are cold. I think we should move out and live together, Eli," Gallahan suggests.

Cyril gapes, his blue eyes widening in shock and fury. Eli elbows his guardian hard in the chest and shoots him a disbelieving glance.

"Buddy, that's not true. Your parents are sweet—"

Three taps at the front door interrupt their conversation. Except for Eli, a look of puzzlement flashes on every face at the dinner table. It's safe to assume that no one expects additional company.

Cyril is about to get up to answer the door, but Haidar stops him and says he will do it. Haidar leaves the dining room for about twenty seconds and returns with two guests.

"Dante?" Eli and Cyril shout.

* * *

DANTE, Cyril's drop-dead gorgeous friend whose unparalleled beauty is rival only to the ravenhead himself. He's also the unwilling co-owner of Cyril's successful and profitable woodshop, or so Snow White has claimed.

"Good evening," Dante scans the dining room. When he sees Eli, his lips curve up into a jolly smile.

"Happy Birthday, Eli!" Dante beams at Eli, and so does the stranger behind him. Just like the first time he and Eli met at Three Bears Diner, Dante dresses in a high-collared black suit and matching leather gloves despite the summer weather.

"Happy birthday," the stranger says to Eli. He's a middle-aged man with a kind face and a very intriguing fashion sense that prompts everyone's attention. He wears an intricately distressed, avant-garde beige hooded robe with a large sac of the same color on his back.

The man reminds Eli of a young Santa Claus, if he ever snuck out of the

North Pole and spent a full decade in 1960s America, living van life in a happy hippie commune. Ten out of ten.

"Thank you, Dante. Sir." Eli smiles and gives small nods to both men. He's a bit taken aback by Dante's affable disposition to him since Dante didn't talk much in their first meeting. Though Eli is elated that a good friend of Cyril has warmed up to him.

"Dante, who's this gentleman?" Cyril asks Dante, gesturing at the stranger behind him.

"This is my new friend. He's a very talented express portrait artist I caught when I was on my way to your house." Dante giggles.

"No, not caught. Mister Dante and I ran into each other, and he invited me to this lovely party," the express portrait artist explains, and everyone breathes out in relief. "Good evening, everybody. My name is Claus. I'm a wandering merchant, a Fengshui master, and a spiritualist who can do instant realistic paintings."

Except for Eli, who is ecstatic the moment he hears the name Claus, everyone else at the table is dumbstruck at the new guest's peculiar introduction. It takes Cyril a few seconds to recollect himself and give the guests a bright and cordial smile.

"Please to make your acquaintance. My name is Cyril. Welcome to our humble house party," Cyril speaks cordially to Claus. Wolfgang and Gallahan give Dante and Claus their seats so the guests can be close to the master of the house.

"Thank you very much, gentlemen," Dante and Claus tell Wolfgang and Gallahan and receive courteous nods from them.

Cyril then introduces all the people in the room to Claus. It seems like all the neighbors are already acquainted with Dante. Mariposa sets a new plate for Claus but not Dante.

"Please help yourself. I apologize for the lack of meat since we all are vegetarians," Cyril explains to Claus, smiling.

"Ah, that's wonderful! I'm a vegetarian, too," Claus laughs merrily.

"Dante, would you like to eat something?" Eli asks, seeing Dante's empty dining spot.

"Thank you, Eli. I'm alright," Dante responds with an alluring smile. "You're such a sweet and caring person."

Eli is once again taken aback by Dante's compliment. Those seductive feline blue-gray eyes fixate on him.

"T-Thank you." Eli blushes and chuckles awkwardly. At the same time, Cyril, who is sitting beside him, raises an eyebrow at his gorgeous friend.

"Are you alright, Dante?" Cyril asks frostily. The polite smile has long gone from his handsome face.

Dante turns to Cyril, and the two briefly stare at each other before Dante shrugs and shakes his head. "No. I'm not. I'm intoxicated."

"I found Mister Dante passed out in a bush in the forest, completely drunk," Claus explains after finishing a forkful of food. "I helped him sober up a little, and he told me he had to go to his friend's young master's birthday party. Please be aware that he's not completely sober."

The aloofness swiftly drops from the ravenhead's face as he becomes concerned for Dante.

"Do you want to lie down?" Cyril asks Dante.

"No, thank you. I wouldn't want to miss Eli's birthday party," Dante says, turning to Eli and giving him a cheery smile.

Eli lightens up the mood. "Ah, heh heh. It's Cyril's birthday as well."

Dante and Claus seem equally surprised when they hear this, as both turn to look at Cyril.

"Well, I don't know my real day of birth. Eli let me celebrate my birthday on the same day as his," Cyril explains to Dante. "I didn't celebrate mine in the past...couple of years."

Eli squeezes Cyril's hand, and this makes the ravenhead very happy.

"But from now on, I'll celebrate our birthday every year." Cyril smiles at Eli, who returns a wide grin.

"Aww," Mariposa and Haidar coo. Wolfgang and Gallahan give a thumbs up.

"Well, I only prepared a present for Eli," Dante says, then he stands up and opens his arms wide. "Come here, Cyril."

The room turns quiet once again as all eyes are on Dante. Based on the shocked expression of Cyril and the neighbors' faces, Eli guesses Dante's gesture isn't what he would usually do when sober.

"…W-What?" Cyril blinks up at his good friend, flabbergasted.

"Stand up and hug him." Eli elbows his guardian.

"Oh!" Cyril clumsily gets up, but before he can do anything, Dante has already pulled Cyril into his chest and hugged him tightly.

It's a long and intimate hug. Cyril stiffly pats Dante's back. But after a long time, Dante still doesn't let go of the ravenhead.

"Dante," Cyril clears his throat as he tries to pull away, but Dante doesn't let him.

"Cyril," Dante mutters.

"What?"

"Give me a real hug, and I might consider taking care of your little shop until February next year."

They're like magic words. Cyril hugs Dante so hard like his life depends on it. It's almost half as passionate as when he embraces Eli.

"Ah, there you go." Dante chuckles, holding Cyril tighter. After a minute or so, he finally releases the ravenhead.

"Are you really going to take care of our business until February?" Cyril asks.

"Of course not," Dante responds with a warm smile. He gives Cyril a friendly pat on the shoulder.

The neighbors burst into soft giggles, but quickly make a straight face when Cyril glowers at them.

* * *

"What a marvelous dinner," Claus exclaims after finishing his plate. "Thank you so much for all of this amazing food."

"You're so welcome. I'm glad you enjoy it." Cyril smiles at Claus.

"Mister Cyril, I have to say your house has very good Fengshui," Claus comments. "You have an eye for decorating. It's very cozy and inviting."

"Thank you very much," Cyril laughs.

"However, I think there's one item that can elevate your lovely home a notch higher."

"Oh? What are you suggesting?" Cyril's still smiling, but his eyes are guarded.

"A musical instrument," Claus says. "Like a harp, for example."

"Why a harp?" Cyril blinks. "And not a violin or piano?"

"You're seriously comparing a violin to a harp?" Dante's handsome face twists like he just bit a lemon.

"Hey! Violin is great!" Haidar shouts. Eli guesses Haidar plays that instrument.

"It can be, but the harp is superior to all," Dante asserts. "I love listening to harp. It's a shame none of you know how to play it."

"This is the first time you told me this," Cyril tells Dante with a raised brow. "Do you play the harp?"

"Yes." Dante shrugs. But then he hiccups and shakes his head. "No."

"So, yes or no?" Wolfgang inquires.

"No, I don't. But my wife does." Dante hiccups and Cyril's eyes widen. "No. I meant my mother."

Eli, Cyril, and their neighbor friends shoot Dante wary stares.

"My mother used to play harp. She learned it from my father." Dante hiccups. "Harp music brings me peace."

"Mister Dante kept talking about harp after I found him in the bush; he wouldn't stop talking about it our entire way here," Claus adds, and Cyril sighs.

"We'll go see a harp concerto someday, alright?" Cyril pats Dante's shoulder.

Dante holds Cyril's hand and brings it to his heart. "Thank you."

"Don't mention it. You're my brother," Cyril says firmly, but slowly withdraws his hand.

"But I'd rather listen to someone I know play it for me," Dante slurs. "Like Eli."

"You want me to play harp for you?" Eli can't suppress a laugh. He feels somewhat guilty for preferring drunk Dante to his sober version.

"Yeah, that would be nice!" Dante guffaws.

"Alright, let's have you lie down in the living room," Cyril stands up, as do Wolfgang and Haidar.

"Eh!" Dante yelps as Wolfgang and Haidar gently grab his shoulders and haul him to the living room. "Eli's birthday!"

"We'll have the cake in the living room." Cyril sighs. "You will not miss out on anything."

* * *

Everyone pops their confetti cannons after Eli blows out the seventeen candles on the cake.

"This is so delicious!" Eli exclaims after taking a bite. It's a fluffy chocolate sponge cake with a berry filling.

"Cyril spent a lot of time perfecting this recipe," Mariposa tells Eli.

"Cyril, it's amazing!" Eli looks at his guardian affectionately.

"Aww, sweetie." Cyril caresses Eli's soft cheek. "Anything for you."

After dessert, everyone gives Eli presents. In Aspenia, it's a custom to open the gifts at the party. Each neighbor gives Eli more than one present. Aside from a lot of cookies and various types of candies, Eli receives a hand-made quilt blanket from Mariposa, Elgarian alphabet books from Haidar, three beautiful winter coats from Wolfgang, and high-end school supplies from Gallahan.

As for Cyril, he gives Eli an expensive school bag made from brown leather, a new pair of boots, three thick scarves and three silk scarves, children's storybooks, several knit beanies in different colors, and a lunch box.

"Ah, it's my turn now," Dante slurs from the couch and waves at Claus, who then takes out a present box from his sac and hands it to Dante.

"This is for you, Eli. Happy birthday." Dante gives Eli the present.

"Aw, thank you very much!" Eli grins and accepts the gift with two hands. He unwraps the present and finds an exquisite gold pocket watch inside.

"Wow!" the neighbors exclaim. Haidar says, "That's a vintage model! They don't make this style anymore!"

"You lot have good eyes. It is pre-owned but in a pristine condition." Dante smirks. "The shell is made from pure gold."

"This present is too valuable, Dante. I can't—" Eli utters, but Dante interrupts him.

"Eli, it's nothing. Cyril is...my family, so that makes you family as well," Dante says in a sincere tone.

"Thank you, Dante." Eli's voice slightly quivers. He is touched that Dante thinks so highly of him.

"Well, if you really want to thank me, you should learn to play the harp," Dante says and receives multiple eye-rolls from Cyril and the neighbors.

"Mister Claus, do you still have the thing that made my friend slightly sober earlier?" Cyril asks Claus as Dante is now napping on the couch.

"Oh no, Mister Cyril, Mister Dante refused to eat or drink anything I gave him, so I could only give him a body massage on the side road," Claus says. "And it worked like a charm!"

The living room falls into silence until Claus breaks it with a cheery voice: "Okay, it's my turn to give the young master a birthday present!"

"Happy birthday!" Claus pulls a small pouch from his beige sac and gives it to Eli.

It's a gold chain to go with the pocket watch Dante just gave Eli.

"Oh, Claus. This looks expensive. We couldn't possibly take it from you," Cyril says when he looks at the chain and recognizes its value.

"Ah, please accept it. I had that chain for a long time and didn't know what to do with it. When I ran into Mister Dante today and discussed his gift for the young master, I instantly knew the chain would finally be of use," Claus explains, laughing. "Besides, I had a spectacular meal tonight and met many wonderful young folks like you lot. I can't give you nothing for your kindness and generosity!"

Eli and Cyril eventually accept the gold chain and thank Claus.

"I apologize for not having a good present for you, Mister Cyril," Claus says.

"Don't worry about that. Your presence is a gift to me. We all enjoyed your company very much, Claus. And please, you can call me Cyril." Cyril smiles courteously.

"You're such a wonderful young man!" Claus then looks at Eli and the neighbors. "You all are very good people. May you all be blessed by the endless lights of the Tathagatas!"

Everyone smiles and thanks Claus for his kind praise.

"Well, Cyril. Though I don't have a gift for you, I suppose I can give you a free palm reading. Would you show me your hands?" Claus asks.

"Sure." Cyril chuckles as he shows Claus both of his palms.

Claus carefully observes Cyril's palms for half a minute. Then he fumbles in his sac and pulls out a thick book.

"Palm reading for beginners?" Cyril blinks as he reads the book's title.

"Well, I've never seen palms like yours before!" Claus remarks as he flips through the book. Then, he appears to find the section he is looking for and reads it. When he finishes, he slowly looks at Cyril and smirks.

"What do you see?" Cyril asks.

"A lot of things," Claus says mysteriously. "You are way different from others I've read for."

"Oh? So, what are your predictions?"

Claus stands up and approaches an armchair in the furthest corner. He waves at Cyril. "Come here, please."

Cyril complies and comes to sit near Claus, who takes out a stack of tarot-like cards and quickly flips through it. Then Claus gets a card from the deck and hands it to the ravenhead.

"Hmm," Cyril looks at the card in his hand and then flips it down on his thigh. "What does this card mean?"

"It means exactly what you're seeing," Claus says, giving Cyril another card.

Cyril looks at the second card and then puts it on top of the first one.

"This was you." Claus hands Cyril the third card, which makes the ravenhead's expression visibly darken.

"This is the current you." Claus hands Cyril the fourth card, and Cyril seems to relax a little.

"And this is how you were able to be the current you." Claus hands Cyril two cards, and this time, Cyril appears amazed and impressed.

"That's all," Claus says.

"Wait, that's it?!" Cyril exclaims.

"Yeah. You want something else? Maybe this?" Claus takes a wrench from his sac.

"No. I meant, aren't fortune tellers supposed to give out future predictions?"

"Mister Cyril, I'm a legit spiritualist, not a con artist. How can I possibly know about the future? Now, while I can't give you an exact future prediction; but based on the lines of your palms, I can give you an overall view of your life. However, this will be subject to change if you ever stop being kind and compassionate like you are now."

"Of course not," Cyril says. "Please give me an overview."

"Alright," Claus takes out his palm reading book and reads it. Then he takes back the cards in Cyril's hands and only leaves one behind. Claus looks through his deck and gives Cyril another card.

Cyril looks at the two cards in his hands, and his face brightens up. "Does this mean..."

"Yes." Claus nods.

Cyril is so exhilarated that he turns to Eli and gives him a wide and ecstatic smile.

"You got a good reading?" Eli grins at how innocent Cyril looks when he's happy.

"It's excellent, Eli!" Cyril chirps, and Eli cheers for him with a fist pump.

"Congratulations! Now, all that is left is for you to continue doing good deeds and reap the excellent rewards!" Claus pats Cyril's shoulder.

"I will definitely do that. Thank you for the reading, Claus." Cyril smiles and returns the cards to Claus.

"Wah, hold on." Claus grasps Cyril's hands and stares at it. Then he opens his palm reading book again and quickly skims through it. His expression becomes confused the more he reads.

"Please don't tell me you gave me a wrong reading!" Cyril cries out.

"Never! I have a ninety-nine percent accuracy rate," Claus is defensive. "The one percent depends on the client's free will."

"Okay, then what is it? What did you see? What does that book say?"

"There's no change to your life overview. However, to get to that excellent outcome, you must do this." Claus gives Cyril another card.

"Oh," Cyril mumbles.

"That's very crucial, Cyril." Claus taps the card on Cyril's hands.

"I understand."

"And soon." Claus gives Cyril another card.

"What?!" Cyril yelps and shakes his head. But Claus gestures for Cyril to lean in and whispers something in his ear. "Okay... But still—"

"No, but Cyril." Claus firmly shakes his head. He gives Cyril two other cards. Then, he whispers something to the ravenhead that causes him to hang his head down in defeat.

"It's all up to you, Cyril. Like I said, every being has free will, and no higher being can force someone to do anything against their will," Claus says. "Anyway, do you agree with what I told you?"

"I do." Cyril nods.

Eli is curious. Cyril seems to take this reading seriously.

"Then perk up! Your excellent outcomes await you!" Claus beams and pats Cyril's shoulder. Then he turns back to Eli and the gang. "Alright, lady and gentlemen, please gather around the young master. I'll do an express portrait of everybody on this very special evening!"

Cyril walks back to the sofa and shakes Dante awake for the group painting.

"Morning yet?" Dante mumbles sleepily.

"Wake up, boozer. We're doing a portrait together," Cyril says as he sits between Eli and Dante.

Claus looks at the group. Then he pulls a blank parchment from his sac. "Can I use the table in your dining room? I will be done with the painting in twenty minutes."

"Only twenty minutes?!" Cyril and the neighbors are shocked.

"Sorry, it takes longer than usual since there are eight people in the painting, including myself." Claus grins. "Or do you want me out of the picture?"

"No, of course not," Eli and Cyril say simultaneously.

"Perfect! I'll see you lot in twenty minutes!" Claus laughs and then goes to the dining room to work on his express portrait.

*　*　*

In the meantime, the gang plays a strategy board game in the living room. Though it is Dante's first time playing, he quickly owns everyone, including Haidar and Eli, who usually dominate this game.

"Genius move!" The gang is mad impressed as they stare at the game map.

"Aha!" Dante gloats and basks in the awe.

"I finished the painting!" Claus announces as he walks into the room and hands Cyril his twenty-minute express portrait.

Cyril thanks Claus and unrolls the parchment to reveal a beautiful, semi-realistic painting of everybody in colors.

"This is incredible!" Eli exclaims, marveling in delight. The group gives Claus incessant praise.

Haidar even suggests Claus open an express art shop, which Claus laughs off and says express painting is just a hobby of his. Then he looks at the clock, and it is 7:45 PM. Claus stands up and tells everyone he has to leave now, or he will be late for his train.

Cyril insists on helping Claus find a carriage and has Wolfgang leave the house to do that. During the wait, Cyril asks where Claus is heading, and the man responds he's going to Coro.

"Do you have family there?" Cyril asks.

"Nah, it's just me, by myself." Claus sighs, shaking his head.

"I heard Coro has the best blueberry pies and grape cider in the summer. They usually give out great discounts to tourists."

"Eh? I believe Coro is known for its seasonal peach cobblers and cherry tea in summer. Are you mixing it up with Maska, my friend?" Claus rubs his chin. "Anyway, I'm not there for sightseeing."

"Are you visiting a friend?"

"I'm going to see a Holy Master. He's quite famous in Coro."

"Fascinating. May I ask what's the name of this Holy Master?"

"His Holiness Arata. Have you heard of him?"

"I have. And I think most native Aspenians know about him. But I also heard Master Arata has been retreated in isolation for centuries and hasn't given any public sermons since then."

"Yes, that's true. But he does give out private sermons for those he allows inside the Emerald Tower," Claus states, then pats Cyril's shoulder. "Well, Cyril, I think my cab is here. Thank you for your great hospitality, my friend."

Dante dozes off on the sofa again, so only Eli, Cyril, and the neighbors see Claus off.

"Have a safe trip," Cyril tells Claus.

"Thank you. Perhaps you could use a vacation to Coro soon. Bring your young master with you," Claus smiles and waves at the gang. "Good night! Goodbye everyone!"

* * *

THE BIRTHDAY PARTY lasts another hour before it finally ends with everyone putting away the leftovers and helping with the dishes. Dante is out cold on the couch in the living room, with the Pom pup snoring beside him. Eli puts a blanket over Dante and the dog.

Eli also sneaks two bags of cookies he made to Wolfgang and Gallahan, just as he promised them earlier. When their neighbor friends have left, Eli and Cyril sort out the birthday presents and put them away accordingly. There were six guests at the party, and yet Eli received fifty-two gifts, including the Pom pup, and not counting the sweet treats.

That's certainly more presents than Eli had ever had in his entire past life in America.

This new universe really loves him more than the previous one.

"May I see the pocket watch Dante give you, sweetie?" Cyril asks Eli.

Eli hands Cyril the watch and receives a pat on the head. "Thank you, angel!" Cyril smiles affectionately.

Once Eli goes upstairs, Cyril inspects the pocket watch and the gold chain. A minute later, Eli comes down and sees his guardian sitting on the bay window seat in the front hall, still examining that watch.

"Cyril, is there something wrong with it?" Eli whispers as Dante is sleeping in the living room.

"There's nothing wrong with it." Cyril's still staring at the watch. "It's just...this watch looks strangely familiar to me. But I don't have any memory of ever seeing or possessing it."

"Do you want to keep it for a while?" Eli asks Cyril.

"No. You keep this watch, sweetheart. You'll need it to tell the time when you attend school in three weeks. If I need to look at it, I'll just borrow it from you," Cyril says as he turns to Eli. "What are you holding behind your back?"

"Well..." Eli sheepishly approaches his guardian and hands him a small present box with a red bow on top. "Happy birthday, Cyril!"

Cyril is completely taken off guard by Eli's gesture. He happily receives the present and opens it. The present is wrapped in a lace handkerchief and there is a handmade birthday card written in Elgarian. It reads:

Cyril, you are the best guardian one could ever ask for. Thank you for bringing me home and putting up with my annoying attitude. I'm truly grateful for

everything you've done for my sake, and I want you to know I will always have your back, no matter what!
– Eli

Tears well in the corner of the ravenhead's eyes as he reads the card. His handsome face turns a pinkish hue.

"Oh my God, please don't tell me I butchered the grammar," Eli gasps in mortification. He wrote that message himself without help from anyone, and it took him a week to piece the sentences together.

"No, no. Your grammar is perfect, sweetheart. Come here," Cyril says, opening his arms and hugging Eli.

"Ay, you're so emotional, man." Eli lets out a sigh of relief as he pats Cyril's broad back.

It takes the ravenhead a couple of minutes to compose himself. When Cyril does, he unwraps the lace handkerchief. Inside is a handful of cookies in a teddy bear shape with white chocolate for the muzzle and regular chocolate for the eyes and nose.

"Oh! They are so adorable!" Cyril gasps as he picks up a cookie. "Did you make them?"

"Yes, I did!" Eli grins. "Mariposa and Haidar let me use their kitchen yesterday."

"Ahh, I see!"

"Try it!" Eli smiles eagerly.

"But you made them yourself for me. I don't have the heart to eat them!" Cyril gives Eli heart eyes.

"Cyril, just eat them. I need the feedback now!" Eli rolls his eyes. "I'll make more for you."

Cyril takes a bite and seriously evaluates the taste. Then he gives Eli a bright smile. "It's absolutely delicious! I've never had a cookie like this before! It's crispy and chewy at the same time. What did you put in there?"

"Oatmeal!"

"I've never heard about putting oatmeal in a cookie before!" Cyril takes the third bite. "I never knew you could cook so well!"

"I'm glad you like it." Eli chuckles and then sighs softly. "Sorry, Cyril. You gave me so many wonderful presents, and this is the only thing I can give you. I promise I'll get a job soon and get you a better present next year!"

"Eli, what are you saying?!" Cyril almost chokes on the cookie. "You have to stay in school for the next six years, at the very least!"

"Six years!" Eli shrieks in panic. "Why?! I only need to learn how to write Elgarian! I—"

I already finished college. That's what Eli wanted to say. He even worked for nine months before getting killed. Totally missed that annual bonus!

Cyril then spends the next five minutes explaining to Eli that children aged six to eighteen must attend schools in Aspenia. After that, most people from the middle class and above tend to pursue higher education at universities. Those who don't are generally looked down on by their peers of the same social class.

"Ugh. But I want to find a job and help you out," Eli groans. But Cyril shoots Eli a firm look, indicating he won't hear otherwise.

"Okay, okay. Geez. I'll get that university diploma and make you proud," Eli grumbles.

"Yes, please do that. Thank you." Cyril chuckles and strokes Eli's brown locks. He then reveals they have enough money to live very lavishly without lifting a finger for the next 1,200 years—at least.

"What?!" Eli jumps. "You're bluffing, dude!"

"I'm not, Eli. Why would I lie about that? I can show you our bank papers right now if you want."

"You're really serious?" Eli blinks, and Cyril gives him a firm nod.

Since their fairytale cottage is humble in size, Eli always thought they came from a very middle-class background. But turns out they are secret millionaires!

"Wow, I couldn't really tell," Eli mumbles. Now it makes sense that Cyril could easily pay off the damage to the Peridot Arboretum for the anaconda incident and gave the bouncers in Hemera Bay piles of gold coins like it was nothing.

"Do you want to move to a manor? We can do it right tomorrow morning," Cyril says in a serious tone.

"No! I don't like big houses! I love our cottage! It's so cozy and plenty spacious for two of us."

"Aww, I think so too." Cyril beams and gives Eli an affectionate flick on the nose. "Besides, we designed this house together. It had a lot of sentimental value to me."

"Say no more. We'll live here until our teeth fall off or till this house gets swept up by a tornado, whichever comes first," Eli quips. Cyril laughs so hard Eli has to pat his back to help him breathe.

* * *

"I'm sorry you had to see that outrageous play at the theater. I promise we'll see better ones in the future," Cyril says when he tucks Eli in bed.

Eli tells Cyril he really enjoyed the show and learned a great deal about Aspenia and its ruler.

"I'm glad you had a good time, sweetheart," Cyril chuckles. "Who's your favorite character in that play?"

Eli responds Lord Diamond Heart. Cyril smiles and says he also loves that character very much. When Cyril asks his opinion about the Emperor, Eli only shrugs and makes a so-so face. Cyril asks why, and Eli shares with the ravenhead the same opinion he gave Wolfgang earlier in the cab.

"I understand the Emperor's reasons for punishing the former Sage nobles, but as long as slavery still exists, there will always be illegal human trafficking and mistreatment to the enslaved population in the nation no matter how many policies he makes to protect them," Eli says.

"I completely agree with your assessment, sweetheart. But we never know. Slavery could be abolished in the near future."

"I very much hope so." Eli sinks into the mattress. All of this talk about slavery reminds him of the witch execution article Gallahan read for him this afternoon.

If Cyril never found him that night, Eli's fate must have been similar to the poor victims in the news. He would either be sold into those underground rings or eaten by sick cannibals or monsters like the flying werewolf.

Those morbid thoughts make him tremble in his blanket, and Cyril sees that. The ravenhead immediately asks if Eli is okay.

"I just want to tell you again that I'm very grateful to you," Eli says softly. "You saved me, Cyril."

Eli's words leave Cyril stunned. After a moment, his beautiful blue eyes turn red once again.

"You saved me, Eli," Cyril whispers back. "More than you could ever know."

CHAPTER 21

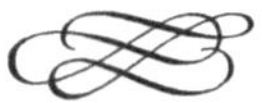

THE WATCHERS

That night, Eli has a very interesting dream. He sees himself in a place where he's 99.9 percent certain is Heaven, for the ground is made of colorful pastel clouds. Grand and magnificent castles are made from multicolored marble, gold, and abundant precious jewelry. Surrounding these palaces is an exquisite garden that holds a plethora of flowers and trees that are all blossoming in their prime.

Eli is checking out his surroundings in absolute delight; his ears catch the most ethereally beautiful music he has possibly ever heard. So, like a bewitched man, Eli follows the enchanting melody and stumbles upon a pavilion made entirely from crystal, where a Goddess is playing a golden pedal harp inside.

Unlike his previous dreams, where the faces of the characters are mostly blank, this one isn't. Eli's breath is taken away the moment he lays his eyes on the Goddess' face. She looks about eighteen years old and has waist-length, silky hair akin to golden sun rays. Her round almond eyes are a mixture of shimmering green and yellow gemstones. Her skin is as radiant as the pale moon with a pink tint underneath. She is literally the most gorgeous girl Eli has ever seen. Everything about her is flawless...except for the gems-glutted gown and ornate tiara she is wearing, they seem excessive for her slender frame.

Eli doesn't know much about fashion, especially women's clothing, but the outfit the Goddess is wearing is hands down the most magnificent (and complicated) design Eli has ever seen. It's a flowy Greek-style gown with many layers of shimmering white, green, and yellow silk chiffon. Literally, everything related to women's fashion is on that dress: glitter, lace, flower appliques, embroidery, gold, silver, feathers, and a gazillion sparkly rhinestones. The belt is made from gold, emeralds, and white pearls and has multiple dangling chains. Her necklace, bracelets, earrings, and tiara are as glamorous and complex as the gown. Somehow, all these extremely sparkly clothes and accessories don't look tacky on the Goddess at all, as she looks absolutely majestic in them.

Eli's eyes and ears have been blessed with heaven's finest. He makes a victorious double fist pump and sits down on a golden bench near the pavilion to listen to the Goddess' magical music. Eli enjoys the marvelous harp symphony for the next three minutes before a dulcet male voice interrupts it.

"Here you are, darling. I've been looking all over for you," says a tall man who appears before the Goddess, his back facing Eli.

The Goddess stops playing the harp and rushes toward the man to give him a hug. Then she says something entirely unintelligible to Eli and plants quick pecks all over his face.

It looks like they are a couple, which makes the man a celestial being as well. Since no one here seems to notice Eli, he decides to walk around the pavilion to see the face of the God

But the God's face is all blank. Based on the perfect build, glowing pale skin, and long, elf-like braided blond hair, Eli has a feeling this God must be just as stunning as his sweetheart.

The couple is having an incoherent conversation, and the Goddess suddenly refers to the God as her husband. Then, the exchange becomes audible again, where Eli hears the God say, "I would love to, darling."

The Gods walk to the crystal pavilion and sit down. The Goddess resumes playing the harp while her husband enjoys the performance. Together, they make a perfect picture of marital bliss.

However, there's one thing that makes Eli chuckle. It is how contrasting this couple is in terms of style. The God looks dressed down compared to his snazzy wife. He wears a simple, elegant white Greek-style outfit with very sparse gold accessories, while she is literally rocking an entire jewelry shop on her petite body.

"My love, your music is akin to a miracle lifting the heavy boulder weighing on my psyche. I feel like I'm in Heaven whenever I listen to your harp," the blank-faced God says seductively to his wife.

"But we are in Heaven," the Goddess remarks.

"It only feels like Heaven when I'm with you."

The Goddess laughs at her husband's smooth pickup line, and they go in for a quick kiss. But his long hair gets caught up in her elaborate tiara, and they end up getting stuck together.

"I'm sorry, darling. Don't move," the God says as he tries to untangle his hair.

After struggling for a while to no avail, the God has to remove the tiara from his wife's pretty head along with a few strands of her golden hair.

"I bet your little neck doesn't hurt anymore now since this torture device is off," the God says humorously, and Eli entirely agrees with his assessment regarding that extravagant headpiece.

"My hair! Nooo!" the Goddess screeches in despair when she sees her hair on the tiara.

"Oh, darling. I would love you forever even if you are bald," the blank-faced God laughs, and his wife gasps in horror. "I'm just kidding. I assure you your pretty head is still chock-full of hair."

Their following exchange is a blur to Eli again, but it seems that the Goddess is nagging her husband. Then, they make up as he pulls her in for a quick kiss.

"Darling, you know I'd do anything to ensure that happy smile forever stays on your beautiful face. But we are living in a turbulent time with *long blank.* And those *blank* hate me. They can't win against me, so they will target my greatest weakness—you. Darling, how would you be able to fly away and escape them if you wore such heavy dresses?" the God gently tells his wife.

It is as if the speech is being censored for Eli. He can't hear any of the identifying details in their conversation. It's just pauses with no sound, nevertheless, Eli is intrigued by what he is observing.

"It's not heavy," the Goddess says, and her husband shifts his posture. Eli can feel the God is giving her a "seriously, woman?" look, and that offends her. "My clothes are nowhere as heavy as your armor, and you fly around just fine!"

"My armor is my scales! They are a part of my natural body!" the God exclaims.

"Are you implying I'm vain?" The Goddess glares at her husband, and he flinches.

"No, darling, that wasn't what I meant. I just said it wasn't a fair comparison at all."

"*Blank* you know I'm a *blank,* so I was born fashionable, alright? In fact, ever since we tied the knot, I've been ridiculed by many female *blank* for being severely underdressed. I feel like a plucked bird whenever I visit my homeland," the Goddess reveals.

"How dare they make fun of you! Those *blank* are out of their mind. If this is severely undressed, then what does that make me?!"

"You don't want to know." The Goddess shakes her head.

"Tell me!"

"Broke and tattered," the Goddess stutters and the God gasps.

"Beggar," she finishes, and he is pissed.

"Those ridiculous birds! Don't listen to them, darling. You have to trust me, your husband, when I tell you that you are perfect without all of these... convoluted things," the God snaps. Their conversation becomes a blur to Eli afterward. Nonetheless, it seems like the God goes on a long rant regarding the Goddess' peers from her homeland.

The Goddess goes back to playing the golden harp. The enchanting music swiftly soothes her husband's anger. The God wraps his arms around her and says something to her, to which she responds with a soft smile, "I love you, too, *blank.*"

Aww. Eli is so happy for the couple. Then, he suddenly hears a dog barking, which makes him slightly confused but glad that there are dogs in Heaven. However, the sound becomes louder and eventually pulls Eli out of his dream and jolts him awake.

* * *

THE CULPRIT that wakes Eli up is none other than the little Pomeranian puppy Cyril got for him. She eagerly licks Eli's cheek like it is a pot of honey.

"I'm up. I'm up," Eli groans as he lifts the pup away from his face.

"Woof woof!"

"Good morning to you too, baby." Eli sits up and gives the dog a kiss.

It's 7:30 AM, and Cyril's bed next to his is already neatly made. Eli can hear noise from the kitchen downstairs; Cyril must be preparing breakfast.

Eli quickly makes his bed and goes to the bathroom to wash up. He feels terrible for constantly waking up late and not helping Cyril in the morning. It must be because his new body is still growing. Teenagers usually need to sleep more hours than adults.

As Eli changes his clothes, he thinks about his latest dream. Ever since he reincarnated in this new world, Eli tends to have very vivid dreams (and nightmares). Eli wonders if they hold any significance, since this world operates on a magical standard compared to his old, boring planet.

After Dante and Claus showed up at the party last night, the harp subject was mentioned many times, to the point it made its way into Eli's dream. Is it a sign that this new universe is pressing him to learn the harp?

Or is there another supernatural force with an ulterior motive at play?

Ugh. Why was it not a piano? Eli grumps. He can play the piano. The harp is a feminine instrument. Even in his dream, the gorgeous Goddess played the harp, not her husband.

Eli walks to the desk and opens the drawer to get a paper and a pen. He starts to write down the music notes the best he can as he hums the Goddess' harp melody. Then he walks downstairs to meet Cyril, who is setting the table in the kitchen.

After exchanging their usual morning greeting, Eli peeks into the living room and finds Dante still zonked out on the sofa. Whatever booze Dante had before he arrived last night was some serious stuff.

During breakfast, Eli asks Cyril if Cyril is in any way allergic to harp music.

"Of course not. The harp creates one of the most beautiful sounds in the world. I doubt there is anyone out there who can't stand harp music," Cyril responds with a crooked smile. "Why did you ask me that?"

"Well, I have to make sure. I don't want you to lose your mind or have your Sage core explode due to a wrong harp tune."

In his past life, one of Eli's exes was Chinese. They used to watch a few historical fantasy Asian dramas where some characters used musical instruments as their primary weapons and killed people with their lethal tunes.

The way Cyril and the Sages here can fly around like Spider-man reminds Eli of those fantastical dramas. He can't help but wonder if killing music exists in Aspenia. Eli then shares this concept with Cyril, and the ravenhead is amused. Fortunately, Cyril confirms it isn't a thing here.

"Well, if lethal music were real, wouldn't the player die or go insane first since they are the closest to the instrument?" Cyril theorizes, laughing.

"You're right. Anyway, I'm glad there are no killing tunes here. You're already way off your rocker. I can't let you get any nuttier than that."

Cyril is stumped for a few seconds at Eli's slang and starts to mull over the meaning. But he soon gets it, and his beautiful blue eyes widen. "Oh, you!"

Eli pulls down his lower eyelid and sticks his tongue out at Cyril.

The ravenhead chuckles and pinches Eli's cheek. Then, he remembers their initial topic and asks Eli why he is suddenly interested in learning the harp.

"Um...I don't know. It just feels like the universe is dropping strong hints about me learning the harp," Eli falters.

"Eli, I highly doubt Dante and his new friend's drunk idea is a hint from the universe. You absolutely don't have to do anything you don't want to," Cyril affirms. "That said, if you want to learn the harp, I wholeheartedly support you."

"Thank you."

"Sweetheart, there's no need for thanks between you and me. I'll do anything to make you happy."

Eli melts. But his face suddenly drops as he realizes he heard Cyril's last phrase very recently.

Then Eli remembers in his dream, the blank-faced God said something similar to his wife.

"Darling, you know I'd do anything to ensure that happy smile forever stays on your beautiful face."

Eli gasps as he cautiously regards Cyril, who only stares back at him with big puppy eyes, holding his breath, anxious and concerned.

"Are you alright, sweetheart?" Cyril is worried

"Cyril."

"Yes, sweetie, what's wrong?"

"You don't...happen to have...scales, do you?" Eli asks tentatively.

The worried look on Cyril's face vanishes and is replaced with utter stupefaction.

"Um...I do, actually," Cyril answers, and Eli jolts in his seat. "But only one. There," Cyril points at the kitchen scale on the kitchen counter. Eli bursts into a hysterical laugh.

"No, dude," Eli wheezes. His stomach hurts from laughing too hard. "I meant...scales like...fish scales?"

"What?" Now it's Cyril's turn to guffaw. "No, of course not!"

"And for the record, have I ever told you that I...Uh...descended from a magical bird lineage?" Eli is aware of how absurd the question is, but he has to ask it once and for all.

"Eli, just a month ago, your legs were in casts from falling off a flying broomstick."

"Okay...So, you're not...a magical fish, and I'm...not a magical bird," Eli mumbles.

"Who's off the rocker now?" Cyril correctly uses Eli's slang, and they both crack up together.

Sometimes, a dream may be just a dream.

* * *

"Should we prepare something for Dante to eat when he wakes up? He hasn't had anything for over twelve hours," Eli asks Cyril when they are cleaning up the table after breakfast.

"Dante has never eaten anything for as long as I've known him," Cyril reveals. "That fella can easily survive a century of famine, quite literally."

"You're joking!" Eli exclaims.

"Not at all, Eli. Dante is very special." Cyril laughs. "He doesn't need to eat. If he ever consumes regular food, it would be very bad for him."

Eli has a hard time believing that. Fortunately, there is a noise coming from the living room, and it seems that Dante is finally awake.

Cyril and Eli come to greet Dante. He still looks dazed and doesn't seem to be fully sober yet.

"Cyril, when did I get here?" Dante croaks, holding his head.

Cyril and Eli exchange glances before Cyril informs his friend about his visit to their birthday party last night.

Dante's gorgeous face grows ashen as he listens to the ravenhead.

"Dante, do you remember meeting and befriending a wandering merchant named Claus, who is also a psychic, a Feng Shui master, and an express portrait artist yesterday?" Cyril asks. "He said he found you wasted in a bush on the side road and gave you a body massage to sober you up. Does that ring a bell with you?"

"Cyril, are you out of your..." Dante snaps but trails off mid-sentence when he sees the group portrait Claus did yesterday hanging on the living room's wall.

"W-Was that the man?" Dante points at the cheerful Claus in the painting with a horrified look on his flawless face.

"Indeed. That was the gentleman who gave you the full body massage," Cyril confirms. Dante gasps out loud in dismay and mortification.

"Hey, take it easy. You're fine. Do you remember what you did before you visited us yesterday?"

Dante tells them the last thing he remembers is drinking with a close family acquaintance two days ago! Either Dante has the tolerance of a hamster, or that giggle juice must have been brewed by Dionysus himself.

"Did you and your acquaintance consume human beverages?" Cyril asks.

"No."

"Good. Can you still be able to use your power?"

A scorching blue fire suddenly flares up and covers Dante's right arm. The little Pom pup jumps and hides her face in Eli's lap.

So, Dante is a fire Sage, just like Cyril, Eli notes.

"My apologies, little dog. And Ilya." Dante turns to the puppy and Eli.

"No worries." Eli smiles and nods at the gorgeous man. "Call me Eli like you did last evening."

"I'll be right back." Cyril runs upstairs.

"Eli, I apologize for my bad manners yesterday evening. I must have ruined your party," Dante tells Eli.

"No, you were great, Dante. The party was a blast—wonderful because of you and Claus. We all had a fantastic time," Eli assures Dante. He isn't lying. Dante and Claus' presence made the party extra memorable and entertaining. Eli then gives Dante a summary of their fun group activities last evening.

"I'm glad," Dante breathes out in relief.

"Would you like some hot tea or a plate of food?"

"I'm alright, Eli. Thank you.".

"You haven't eaten anything since yesterday evening, and it's been over twelve hours. Are you not hungry at all?"

"No. I...don't really need to eat. My body doesn't tolerate human food."

Cyril didn't exaggerate at all. Dante's so buff it's insane that he doesn't need food to maintain that impressive physique. Eli is tempted to ask Dante how he's lived all these years, but the footsteps on the stairs cut in. A few seconds later, Cyril returns to the living room.

"Do you recognize this item?" Cyril holds up the gold pocket watch Dante gave Eli yesterday.

Dante takes the watch and regards it carefully. "I don't know. Maybe. I'm not sure. What is this?"

Cyril tells Dante the watch is Dante's birthday gift to Eli.

"Do you remember where you got that pocket watch?" Cyril asks Dante. "Did you buy it from your new friend, Claus?"

"No...I think...I took it from a...trunk...somewhere. After I got drunk...I went to a room and took this from a trunk."

Cyril and Eli exchange disturbed glances. Cyril then asks, "That room is at your house, right?"

"No," Dante concludes and proceeds to freak out along with Cyril and Eli.

"You return this item to your family acquaintance this instant!" Cyril cries out as Dante hurries to leave.

But once Dante reaches the kitchen, he stops. A few seconds later, he returns to the living room.

"No. Hang on." Dante sits down in an armchair. "I remember now. I didn't steal this watch. My acquaintance was with me when I took it from a trunk at his place."

"Are you absolutely certain?" Cyril presses.

"Yes, I am," Dante confirms after some contemplation. "Hmm, this object is man-made," he comments as he inspects the watch.

"Can you please check the watch and its chain for me?" Cyril requests.

"Solid gold. Well-made. Has a lot of positive energy. I think it's safe to use." Dante hands it back to Eli.

After they are certain the pocket watch was not stolen, everyone starts to sit back and relax.

"Dante, did your mother use to play harp?" Cyril asks.

"How did you know about that?!" Dante is stunned.

"You told us last night. You also said that she was taught by your father."

"I'll never drink again." Dante exhales. "What else did I say last night?"

"You insisted Eli learn the harp and play it for you," Cyril says, and Dante's alluring feline eyes widen.

Dante then profusely apologizes to Eli, who blithely laughs it off.

Eli's first impression of Dante was that he possessed a regal and unapproachable princely aura. But now that Eli looks at Dante's sincere repentant face, he kinda resembles a big Ojos Azules cat with pure black fur and stunning eyes.

"Do you also play the harp, Dante?" Eli grins.

"No, I don't." Dante's expression saddens. "My father thinks harp is for the ladies."

"But he plays harp, doesn't he?" Cyril asks with a raised brow.

"He's different. He can do anything," Dante says with a proud smile, but his expression gradually saddens.

"Are you alright?" Eli asks.

"I haven't seen him in a very, very long time," Dante says with a forlorn smile.

"Can't you visit him?" Cyril asks.

Dante only shakes his head. Cyril and Eli feel so bad for him and promise to bring him to a harp concerto at the theater soon.

"Thanks, gents." Dante chuckles brightly.

* * *

AFTER DANTE LEAVES, Cyril and Eli finish cleaning up the kitchen and then go to the backyard to tend their new vegetable garden.

The seeds were recently planted the day after they got back from their (horrifying) vacation. Cyril extended the backyard for more space to grow vegetables. Only then did Eli learn that they actually owned a large piece of land but built a humble-sized cottage for better upkeep and sustainability. Still, Eli and Cyril don't plan to be farmers anytime soon, so they keep their vegetable garden small enough for two people.

Since it is already August, they missed out on planting pumpkins. So far, they have planted both regular and cherry tomatoes, carrots, lettuce, cabbage, radish, zucchini, kale, spinach, broccoli, turnip, eggplant, green beans, mini cabbage, garlic, onions, and potatoes.

The herb garden is smaller and next to the vegetable garden with its own fences. Most of the culinary herbs are grown here.

Eli is excited because all the seeds have sprouted, and the plants seem to grow stronger and faster than the regular ones he remembers from his previous life. At this rate, he can harvest the radish and spinach next week.

"Cyril, either our soil is super fertile, or you got a serious green thumb!"

"I actually learned gardening from you, Eli." Cyril laughs.

"What?!"

"Yes. You were a master farmer. All the plants you grew always yield twice the produce compared to others!"

"That's so cool! I hope I can continue my green thumb streak going forward."

"I know you can do it, sweetheart!" Cyril beams and gently fixes Eli's straw hat. "Don't eat the cabbages!" Cyril shrieks and startles both Eli and the Pom pup, who is about to sneak a bite at the cabbage's sprout.

Eli could have sworn the pup gave Cyril a mean glare before strutting toward Eli with her nose up. She makes a cute bark at Eli and licks his hands after he picks her up.

"Aww, are you still hungry, baby?" Eli coos at the pup.

"No way! She already had two full bowls of steamed vegetables before you woke up!" Cyril cries out.

"What?! That much?!"

The Pom pup seems to understand their conversation. She starts to make a sad face and growls weakly at Eli, begging for food.

Cyril and Eli bring her back to the kitchen and give her a small carrot, but the pup ignores it. She glances at the cabbage on the kitchen counter and barks instead. Cyril has to steam a few cabbage leaves for her, and she finishes them in just a few seconds.

"Woof woof!" the Pom pup barks happily at Cyril.

"You're welcome, little cabbage." Cyril chuckles and pets her.

"Hey, that's a good name for her!" Eli exclaims, clapping his hands. "Cabbage, come here, baby."

The pup responds to the name and runs to Eli.

* * *

CYRIL AND ELI go mushroom picking after they've finished watering their vegetable garden. Cabbage also comes with them. During their walk to the forest, Cyril asks if Eli wants to go to town with him today to pick up a harp.

"Right now?" Eli asks

"I thought you wanted to take harp lessons?"

"Um...I wonder if it's expensive to learn the harp."

"Don't worry, sweetheart. Dante will pay for your harp lessons, since he was the one who suggested it," Cyril says, and they laugh together.

"Claus also suggested we get a harp to increase our Fengshui energy," Eli recalls. "It's kind of odd that Fengshui is a thing in Aspenia."

"Sweetheart, Fengshui is universal."

Fengshui is a Chinese word from the Earth Eli originally came from. This new planet is also called Earth, but there is no country called "China" here, and yet the word Fengshui exists. This is a paradox, just like how Eli can communicate in English, and everyone here thinks he speaks Elgarian.

"Talking about Fengshui and Claus. He gave you a palm reading last night. What did he tell you?" Eli asks.

"Oh, I got a really good reading! The cards said we will live happily ever after!"

"That's great. But I thought you told me you don't believe in psychic and premonition?"

"Sweetie, he didn't give me any future premonition, only life advice."

"He didn't? But isn't palm reading a form of future predictions?"

"Not really. Palm reading, astrology, and similar things generally give an overview of a person's life. It doesn't predict a fixed future. This means one's life outcome can be drastically changed for the better or worse based on the way he acts and leads his life," Cyril explains. "For example, if I act up and commit bad deeds, I likely won't have a long and happy life with you."

"Mmm, I see. Gotcha." Eli nods and then laughs at Cyril's straightforward example.

* * *

CYRIL AND ELI'S foraging trip is a huge success. Not only do they find an abundance of mushrooms, but they also discover a huge wild strawberry bush. It is close to noon when they get home, and just an hour later, they sit down and have homemade lunch in their beautiful backyard garden. Most of the dishes they make are from the fresh ingredients they just gathered in the woods: herbed mushroom rice, roasted tomato soup, and green bean salad.

Since the weather is warmer than usual, they decide to stay home for the day and get the harp another time. Eli helps Cyril bake a wild strawberry pie, which they later have with iced pink lemonade on the front porch. It is a wonderful way to spend the summer afternoon.

While Eli is not an introvert, he's also not overly sociable. Yet, when he's with Cyril, the topics never run out. They can talk about all kinds of things and never get bored. After an hour of chatting, Eli's eyelids grow heavy, and he dozes off. When he wakes up, he finds himself resting on Cyril's shoulder but is too lazy to move his head away.

"Cyril, tell me the truth. How do you manage to stay so ripped? Do you secretly work out at night after I go to bed or something?" Eli asks, half teasing, half serious, and Cyril erupts in laughter.

They chat for a few minutes until Eli spots a young lady in white leisurely ambling past their cottage. She stops and takes a sniff at the big sunflower by their gate. Then, it seems that she senses Eli watching her and lifts her face to look at him. A soft smile forms on her lips as she slowly raises a hand to wave at Eli.

"Hello," Eli smiles, waving back.

"Eli, what are you doing?" Cyril asks.

"Saying hi to the lady."

"What lady?"

"There." Eli points at the gate, but she's gone. "Uh? She was just there, smelling our sunflowers," Eli explains, but balks when he sees the grim expression on Cyril's face. "You didn't see her?"

"How did she look like?"

"Young. Brown hair done in a bun. She wore a long white dress. And she has really white skin." Eli slowly realizes he didn't see her face clearly even though she was just a few feet away from him. She looked a little blurry, like when you look at someone through foggy specs. *I just saw a ghost, didn't I?* Eli whispers.

There is a brief silence before Cyril breaks it up by smiling at Eli and mercilessly rubbing his round cheeks. "It's getting cold out here. Let's go inside!"

Eli agrees with no further words. He turns his head around and suddenly screams.

"What's wrong? Are you hurt?!" Cyril panics.

"Someone is inside our house!" Eli cries out.

* * *

THEY IMMEDIATELY DO a thorough house check from top to bottom but find no intruder. When Cyril asks Eli if it was the same lady he saw earlier outside, Eli shakes his head.

"It was a man," Eli tells Cyril. "He also wore white clothes but with a hood. He was staring at us through the front door's side window. Mmm…I think I recognize the outfit he was wearing."

"You do?!"

"Yes. Let me think," Eli starts to rack his brain. A moment later, he gasps with wide eyes. "Oh my God!"

"Yes?! What is it?!"

"I think I saw Lord Diamond Heart," Eli cries out.

"What?" Cyril drawls. His face looks like a pricked balloon.

"I know it sounds crazy. But the ghost was wearing a very similar outfit to Lord Diamond Heart!" Eli says and is slightly embarrassed by Cyril's unenthusiastic reaction.

"It's not possible, Eli," Cyril states and sits down on the bay window seat near the front door. "Impossible."

"How are you so sure?" Eli's eyes round up as he sits down next to Cyril.

"Because Lord Diamond Heart of Coro passed away 215 years ago. He must have moved on and reincarnated already."

Eli slightly recoils upon hearing the word "reincarnated" from Cyril's mouth. "You believe in reincarnation?"

"Sweetheart, I don't believe. I know it is real. Didn't you tell me about my past life?"

"What?! When did I do that?!"

"When we were swimming on a beach in Hemera Bay. You told me you saw my chest full of fatal wounds. Remember?"

If there is anything that can instantly spoil Eli's mood, it is the mention of that cursed vision Eli had the misfortune to see that day.

"Aww, sweetheart, don't be sad." Cyril pulls Eli to his chest and hugs him tight. "We are alive and well now. That's the most important thing. Let the past be bygones."

"You think what I saw was your past life?" Eli mutters weakly.

"Of course, sweetheart. What else could it be?"

Eli looks at his guardian with worried eyes. Cyril sees that and comforts Eli by snuggling him even tighter, but Eli doesn't mind.

"Don't you worry, my little precious kit. I promise I will be kind, be strong, and live a long, long, loooooong life with you!" Cyril giggles with over-the-top schoolgirl energy.

"Here goes that chorus again."

"I will protect you from everything as long as I live," Cyril says, and Eli repeats at the same time.

"You're so cheesy." Eli flicks his tongue out at Cyril.

"I don't really like cheese," Cyril admits after some contemplation.

Eli sighs. As usual, the joke flies over Snow White's pretty head again.

All jokes aside, not a day goes by that Eli ever forgets how grateful he is for a second chance to live and meet Cyril. This new world, while magical, is filled with vile crimes and downright insanity. But Cyril has tried so hard to shield him from all of those bleak aspects and give him a beautiful fairytale life.

Eli is so lucky.

He can only wish there won't be any more spooky ordeals from now on, and they can live a long and happy life together just like those cards predicted. Claus looked kind and gentle like Santa Claus. He wouldn't lie, would he?

Outside in the forest, an all-black silhouette stands behind a large oak tree and stares into Cyril and Eli's little storybook cottage, closely watching Eli's every move. This entity arrives after the last ray of sunlight has gone and will stand there all night until dawn.

In the same forest, a few hundred feet away from the black silhouette, two pairs of unmoving, barefoot male feet also point toward the little cottage.

To be continued.

Acknowledgements

This book began on June 5, 2020, and reached its final chapter on December 31, 2023. It was written through moments of peace, storms of doubt, and long stretches of quiet perseverance. For three and a half years, it lived in my heart before it arrived in yours.

To my mother, thank you for being my light, my strength, and my sanctuary. Your immense support and unwavering presence made this dream possible.

To Shelby, my best friend forever, thank you for walking beside me since the beginning. Your constant belief in this story, your feedback, your edits, and your heart carried me through every version. You've been with me through every iteration, and this book wouldn't exist without you.

To my artist, Chaosringen, and the talented team who contributed to this project, thank you for bringing Eli and Cyril to life with such care. Your art became the windows to their souls.

To my editor, Lauren, thank you for respecting my vision. Your gentle polish helped this story shine while keeping its voice intact.

To Amanda, you rock.

To Eli and Cyril, you ROCK!

And to you, dear reader.

Thank you for holding this book in your hands.

Thank you for entering this world with an open heart.

Whether you laughed, cried, or paused to reflect, I'm grateful you were here. May something in these pages stay with you long after the last one turns.

With love and clarity,

Eina Mai

About The Author

Eina Mai is the writer, creative director, and founder of Emaho Publishing LLC, an independent studio dedicated to meaningful, high-quality fiction. With a formal background in technical fashion design, she approaches every story like a couture project: crafted with care, layered with intention, and tailored for the soul.

When she's not polishing prose or reviewing art, she chills with tea, dreams of a more compassionate world, supports charitable causes, and quietly studies cosmic truths.

Through her work, she hopes to share a message of love, peace, and equality for all beings: sentient and otherwise. She believes that love transcends lifetimes and that fiction holds the power to plant real seeds of change.

P/S:

Want more? To watch the animated book trailer, art gallery, and explore behind-the-scenes content, visit my website: einamai.com

The desktop version has custom cusor!

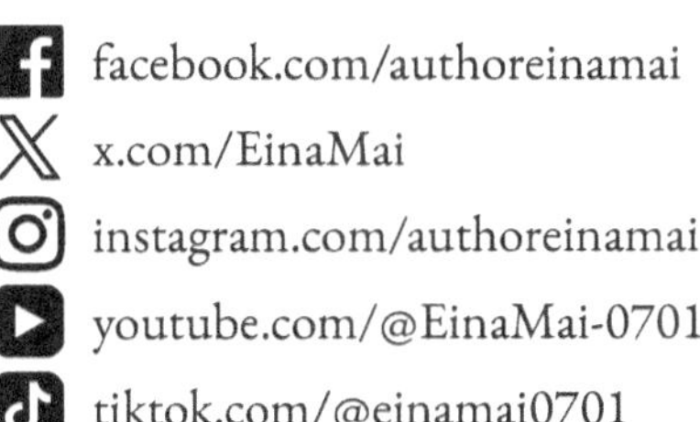